UNTIL THE CROWS DELIGHT

UNTIL THE CROWS DELIGHT

VOLUME IV OF THE GIFTBORN CHRONICLES

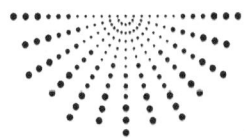

DREW BAILEY

FALSTAFF
BOOKS
WWW.FALSTAFFBOOKS.COM

For my brothers and sisters, blood and found. For without you, this tale of found family would have never come to pass.

DRAMATIS PERSONAE

HOUSE LANIER

Aiden Ashborough/Prince Desmond Lanier/Hrathgon, the eldest son of King Whitman II and Queen Larissa Lanier, the true heir to the Throne of Lancastle, twenty-three cycles old/one of the last surviving dracari

Princess Marsea Lanier, the eldest daughter, twenty

Broenwjar, Marsea's wolf familiar

Prince Rembrandt Lanier/Yvemathira, the youngest son, eighteen/Queen of the Dracari

Larissa Lanier, Queen of Lancastle (deceased)

Whitman Lanier II, the last and former King of Lancastle, died during the coup of the Midnight Men at the age of fifty

Magwyn Lanier/Emyria, Empress of Courowne, Whitman's sister, Aunt to Desmond, Marsea, and Remy/one of the last surviving dracari

HOUSE HARVER

Raelan Harver, General and High Commander of the Lancastle Royalguard Regiment, Larissa Lanier's husband

Pion Harver, Raelan's son, twenty-two, a magus loyal to Ravenholme

Julia Harver, the daughter of Raelan and Queen Larissa, half-sister of Pion, Desmond, Marsea, and Remy, nine

FURTHER PLAYERS

Rhymona Curie/Morgandrel Tully, an ashaeydir battle-magus with a violent past

Edgar Alewine, a scout, former Kingswatch soldier, and friend to Marsea

Priscilla "Poppy" Pelvenyn, a chronicler and friend to Marsea

Stella Ashborough, Aiden's step-mother (deceased), a storied magus, and former archivist to Lancastle Library

Vincent Ashborough, Aiden's step-father, a winemaker

Autumn Ashborough/Tetherow, Aiden's younger step-sister, fifteen/a demonic entity that can split its essence, possess sentient beings, and control the nether

Caitlyn Ellsbury, Aiden's former girlfriend, a magus whose family is loyal to Ravenholme

Dysenia Luiryn, an ashaeydir assassin, Morgandrel's aunt

Imogen Thirsby, Lirae Mother of the Lancastle Abbey

Lita Drufellyn, a mythical magus shrouded in mystery

THE MAIDENS' REJECTS

Hilda 'Giantsbane' Veranski, an Innkeeper's assistant in Maidstone, Marsea's former dance instructor, and a retired Royalguard soldier of some renown

Clive Veranski, Hilda's father, Innkeeper of The Overlook Lodge in Maidstone

Asher Veranski, Hilda's nephew, one of Maidstone's protectors

Gareth, a former soldier, one of Maidstone's protectors

Daisy, Gareth's daughter, one of Maidstone's protectors

Rufus, a magus, one of Maidstone's protectors

WHAT HAS COME BEFORE

AIDEN: Trapped in his own body by the demon Tetherow, Aiden begins to experience flashbacks and memories of a y'deman magus named Malthus Tetherow. Aiden learns that Malthus was born cambion. Malthus, in an attempt to rid himself of the demon half, studied magic and the darks arts growing increasingly more powerful. But as he became stronger, so too did his demon essence. Eventually, the demon begins to win, usurping more and more control of Malthus. Desperate, Malthus and his partner Ankaira attempt a soul-splitting spell, which works, but leaves Malthus badly injured as the demon essence possesses Ankaira.

Days later, after finding Ankaira butchered, Malthus's apprentice Elsymir Beldroth confronts the broken Malthus, and blaming him for Ankaira's murder, slays his master in combat.

In the present, Aiden is dealt a mortal strike to the neck, weakening Tetherow's possession over him and allowing him to briefly resurface. Battling for control, he and Tetherow manage to fend off cultists, only to find that one of them is possessed by a dracari soul named Hrathgon. The skirmish leaves Aiden in such a pitiful state that Tetherow abandons his possession.

During his absence, Tetherow performed a familiar ritual, bonding Aiden with Lenore, Emperor Drezhal's pet crow. Weak and near death's door, Aiden unwittingly vargs into Lenore and searches the palace halls for survivors. He finds Remy, Rhymona, Julia, and Goss. With Yvemathira's aid, Remy opens a link to The Spellbind and heals Aiden's wounds.

MAGWYN: Magwyn recalls a prophecy from her youth that was spoken to her brother, Prince Whit Lanier, by a scullery maid named Selwyn Shawley.

Before she can give it much thought, her nephew, Aiden, now possessed by the demon Tetherow attacks the palace with dark magic and the powers of the nether, slaughtering everything in his path, Emperor Drezhal included. Magwyn narrowly escapes the throne room and survives the blighted chaos beyond only with the aid of her dracari passenger, Emyria.

Eventually, Magwyn stumbles upon Ledgermaine in the lower halls of Courowne palace, where they defeat a gnaudrylax and search for Rhonyn, who was being kept in the dungeons. Rhonyn is missing, but they find evidence of a portal and decide to venture through it, arriving in a cabin outside the township of Marrovard. Ledgermaine reveals secrets about his past with Whit and Stella during the cycles Magwyn was away in Courowne, describing Whit's fall into madness and obsession with soul-splitting, and the results of his continued dark-dabbling.

Magwyn and Ledgermaine arrive at Marrovard to find the entire township under a mind-control spell. They come across Solindiel Alyfain who explains that cultists have overtaken the town. They capture a cultist patrol, including Caitlyn Ellsbury and Calem Reid, and interrogate them, learning about a ritual that is to take place involving human sacrifice and possession. They arrive as the sacrifice begins and all hell unfolds. Many are killed during the battle, including Rhonyn, Ledgermaine, and Solindiel.

In completing the five-soul sacrifice, Pion Harver successfully opens a gateway from the void allowing Tetherow to take possession of Autumn Ashborough. Magwyn, once again, narrowly avoids death, but is now alone, far from home, and on the run.

MARSEA: Marsea and Broenwjar manage to escape Yongrin and the blood witch, holing up in a cemetery for the night.

Beset by nightmares, Marsea awakens the following morning in a mausoleum and begins to read from the grimoire *Dusk*. Until she hears someone singing in the forest nearby. She chases after the voice and finds a traveling troupe, convincing them to take on her services as a sellsword as she heads south. During her time with the troupe, she grows close with Edgar Alewine and Poppy Pelvenyn.

As they travel south into wildkin territory, Yongrin, having survived the blood witch, catches up to Marsea and attacks the troupe, killing a number of them, and sending Marsea and Edgar fleeing as wildkin savages surround them. They race toward a tower, fighting through wildkin and ghouls alike to reach it. But Yongrin remains close and with Poppy held hostage forces Marsea into a duel or risk her friend's murder.

Marsea wins her duel with Yongrin, but the blood witch returns and begins tearing Yongrin's dying body to shreds, a floating pool forming from the mage's blood loss. Marsea realizes this is actually a portal, and the haxanblade, drawn to it, pulls her through.

Alongside Rhymona, Marsea arrives inside a realm called The Bloodbind where the pair discover they are part of a time loop curse. They can only visit The Bloodbind during dusk and as dusk ends, they are pulled back to their proper realm. Marsea, Rhymona, Edgar, Poppy, and Broenwjar venture out to Marrovard, a nearby town, believing there is a ward in the university's library that will lead them back to Lancastle where they can also retrieve *The Kingstome*. They find the ward and also Magwyn, pushing through to Lancastle.

Back home, Marsea and Magwyn open a rift into The Spellbind and speak with King Whit. Marsea learns that she is with child.

RHYMONA: Courowne is overrun by ghouls and nether creatures. Rhymona, Remy, Julia, and Ledgermaine fight their way toward the palace in a desperate attempt to end the threat. Rhymona recalls Stella Ashborough's warning of a blood curse between her and Marsea. She, Remy, and Julia flee into the palace and find a repository and an Oathsworn magus named Victor Goss. They battle further into the palace, eventually arriving at the library.

In the library, Rhymona argues with Aiden when she finds Val's sword in his possession, but Val is nowhere in sight. Aiden admits that Val is dead, a victim of Tetherow. Before they can properly resolve their conflicted emotions, the nether attacks and forces them down into a passageway that leads beneath the library and deep underground below the city of Courowne.

A sense of timelessness has overtaken the group as they make their way through the dark and treacherous labyrinth. It is within these depths that the witch god from Rhymona's dreams appears, conjuring a blood mirror. Rhymona realizes it is a portal and steps through it, arriving beside Marsea and Broenwjar in a strange new realm.

Here they meet a variant of Stella who explains that they are in a place called The Bloodbind and are just the latest versions of themselves to pass through. It turns out they are stuck in time loop curse. Stella explains that the blood wraith is a past version of Rhymona. And the Selwyn Shawley that warned Whit Lanier and Magwyn of the prophecy was a past version of Marsea. The two of them, along with Lita Drufellyn and Stella are stuck in the curse. It is insinuated that a possible method to lift the curse and save their world may be to conjure a godsgate, which can be done by reading passages from the four grimoires of *Dawn*, *Noon*, *Dusk*, and *Haunt*.

After retrieving *Dusk* and *Haunt*, Rhymona, Marsea, and Magwyn go through a portal in lower Lancastle that will take them to Courowne where they will attempt to find Remy, Desmond/Aiden, Julia, and the other grimoires.

REMY: After Rhymona disappears through the blood portal, Remy with Julia and an unconscious Aiden come upon a great cavern. They discover it is the lair of a nether-infected dragon named Hrathgon. Hrathgon, finding Yvemathira bound to Remy, convinces them to help him move what remains of his soul into Aiden. In return, he will lead them out of the temple labyrinth. Although reluctant, Remy agrees. Aiden is once again possessed, this time by Hrathgon. They flee the labyrinth as Hrathgon's dracari form, riddled with nether plague, returns to life and races the underground passages after them. They manage to avoid the dracari drylax, hiding beneath the ocean's surface as it passes them by, out into the night, and back toward the palace. As they swim away from the cavern and gain a view of Courowne, they find another gargantuan mass in the middle of the city destroying everything in its path.

CHAPTER ONE

I WAS DAMAGED before I cried my first breath. Despised before mine eyes found first light. Written off before being cleansed of my hemorrhaging mother's spewing lifeblood.

Twisted up, choking in our umbilical cord connection, it was the first, last, and only instance I shared a living moment with the woman that bore me. And to the present, that moment has defined every ill-starred second of my life.

Welcome one, welcome all, to the grand sprawling shitshow that is yours truly, Pion Hells-damned Harver.

THE OTHERS NAMED IT A DEMON, but Pion knew better. Tetherow may have once counted its cards amongst the infernal legion, some many ages ago, but its power and reach had long since surpassed that of a mere demon. No, to Pion's knowledge, though modest as it endured, there wasn't a word yet fashioned for what his master had become. And how, exactly, it had managed to forge a familiar bond with an entity as vast and formidable as the nether was a question he doubted even the gods held a proper answer for.

Pondering thusly, it certainly made for a curious affair, didn't it? Why a man would choose to aid a creature as ghastly and dangerous as Tetherow; and, sadly, his answer might come off as a bit of a disappointment, considering. It most assuredly would have to him, were he the audience for the account. It was precisely the sort of maudlin tripe he scoffed at in stories of the like. For at its roots, his oath to Tetherow came about because of love. Or, rather, the lack thereof. And, no, it wasn't that Mummy didn't love him enough. If only that were the circumstance. For the truth was that Mummy never had the chance to love him at all, giving her life to bear him, and in the cycles to follow, no one else offered even the smallest form of affection to make up for it.

Quite the opposite, in fact.

Before he could form words or even the smallest shape of an opinion, his presence became viewed as vexing and burdensome to all, including his own bloodkin, and he was treated as a leper and a noxious drain amongst the courtly catch. Ostracized simply because his appearance failed to match the expectations of the patronizing nobility.

After a time, as one might expect, the endless days of cold shoulders and condescension made of him a rather bitter, cross, and mistrustful fellow.

And then one day, some seven cycles back, Tetherow came to call, a side effect of a fledgling warlock's ill-conceived dabbles into dark magic, and altered the course of Pion's life-long pity parade, offering him a chance at love and acceptance. A way to fill some portion of the emptiness. A method to end his seclusion and foster some measure of meaning in his life. And what's more, the creature vowed to repair his crooked form and broken vanities to boot.

Then it showed him his mother. Rather, a version of her. One without him. Where he was the missing piece in her life. And it explained the truth about time and reality and its many layers. And it made a pair of promises to him for his undying allegiance. All he needed do was remain loyal and obedient for as long as it took Tetherow to bring about the end of the Giftborn Age.

Simple enough, right?

If only…

Quints would pass before he acquiesced.

As one might imagine, the invitation was a great deal for a lad of fifteen cycles to consider, especially given the litany of hearthfire haunters spun up to caution against making such darkly deals with

2

devilish creatures. So, he gave it an honest deliberation. Tossed through a slew of sleepless nights. Sent up a few thousand unanswered prayers. But regardless the shape of his rationale, and in spite of his fight for the contrary, he kept arriving at the same place. For when it all came down to it, what more did he actually have to lose in this life? He was reviled by nearly all for merely existing.

What was the old watchword the ancient talebearers used to natter on about regarding The Vael's forsaken?

Those who've never had the taste of love from a silver spoon, learn to lap it off the sharpest of blades.

And, thereafter, the *well* followed. The 'what-if' delusion. The fool's charade. The one that refused to be ignored. The one that haunted his heart through every beat and breath, no matter the state of his conscience. The other side of the coin, as it were. To the nine fucks with Lady Luck and her bastard stones.

For a man with nothing left to lose had but one path left him, be he bold enough to bear it.

For a man with nothing left to lose and a mind for sport, had all the world before him, and, thusly, every bit of it to gain.

OH, but those days seemed an age ago at length and he was nearly at the other end now, for better or worse, the horrors of the ritual chamber leaving him a mad, shaken mess, forcing him to question just how far he was willing to let this lunacy press on for.

Was it worth killing a world to chance some bastard version of his mother would muster half a care for a grotesque? Was it worth it to simply run about like all the other lads? To wield a sword like a proper soldier? To never have to rely on another soul ever again? To never have to endure another gaze of pity. Was it worth his life for a nothing feeling?

Pion shook the doubts from his head.

A bit late for regret now, old boy.

He massaged around the warlock's well cut inside his left hand as he gazed into the study chamber's depths, the scent of ward magic still lingering within, all firewood and spoiled eggs. He knew precisely where the portal led despite not knowing its name. It would open inside

3

Lancastle Library and Marsea's quaint little shrine to her father. *Though mayhaps the greater question here was not the where, but rather the how.* He scratched at the dark stubble on his chin. *As in, how exactly did Empress Magwyn know about it?*

Something wrapped around his ankles and he glanced down at his tabby familiar, Ripley, only recently returned to him after cycles in the Southlands playing spy to the Ashboroughs at his master's behest. Grandpa, they'd come to name him, thinking themselves clever, never once realizing his truth, the pompous halfwits.

"Runt," a voice called from behind as it approached, clapping a dainty hand atop his shoulder.

At her touch, a wave of pain shot through the entire right side of his deformed body, his eyes taking on water in consequence.

"Lord," Pion returned, mouth bowing in a rictus of anguish, tension rising up his gnarled spine to his uneven shoulders. He didn't dare behold his new master's form, that of Autumn Rose Ashborough. Truthfully, it rather perturbed him that he now took orders from a doe-eyed girl barely past her budding, as though the drunkard buffoon Desmond Lanier hadn't proven insult enough all these cycles.

"Your friend will pull through her collection of injuries," Tetherow spoke through the girl.

Caitlyn. He nodded.

"She is quite spirited, that one. I can see why you favor her."

Yes, yes, Pion the Lovefool, ever the soft touch for a dashing smile and a pair of easy eyes.

Though, all things honest, Caitlyn was about the only one of the Kanton crowd that feigned a shadow's breath of decency toward him during his stretches varging into Grandpa, and all of this before she even came to know his true identity, not that the like mattered much given how most folk reacted to his apparent off-putting company, judging his book for the cover despite the tender tale within.

For Pion, it was enough just to experience even the smallest sliver of affection most days, even if it wasn't real, even if it was had in the form of a fat, indolent, little furball that had long since worn out the greater half of his nine lives. But to be given so kindly by another giftborn of a similar age and predilection that was well-read and unusually empathetic to the less fortunate, how in vaelnation could he not become utterly smitten?

He scowled at his revolting romantic nature, recalling Caitlyn's reaction to finding out the truth, only a few short days ago, as though he'd ruined her favorite pastime. She displayed more embarrassment than anger, all told, but it had undoubtedly changed her perception of him, and not for the better. Though, truly, all things square, what else was new?

"We are done with Marrovard." Tetherow's hand slid away and clutched at the amethyst pendant hanging from Autumn's neck. "A coach has been arranged outside. You are to join Dysenia in Lancastle at once. She has already taken most of our remaining contingent with her."

"You're not coming with us?" An eyebrow arched.

"I will travel north," Tetherow said flatly. "There is another matter I must attend to."

Though it came from a different owner, Pion recognized Tetherow's tone, both dignified and hostile. From horrors past, he knew better than to question why.

"There's a nest in Wyrmswold Hollow that will take you back."

"Why Lancastle?" Pion brushed long strands of hanging hair behind an ear.

"Oh, you haven't heard?" The girl sneered. "It yet stands. The Laniers, despite their ignorance, have proven a mite more resilient than Ravenholme could have ever anticipated. A minor inconvenience, but we can't have the riffraff believing they've actually accomplished something, now can we?"

Though it was fleeting, Pion thought on the riffraff, namely his father and sister. He couldn't help but wonder if they were yet amongst the survivors. Though, he reckoned the Lanier siblings would sooner see the old man six feet under had they any choice in the matter. Julia, on the other hand, was another story. Julia was a half-blood, after all. The wrong half, according to the Commonwealth, but a half nonetheless, and from what he knew, Seasea loved no other more than her darling baby sister.

"I will gather my effects," he said as he started away from his master.

"There is one more thing, Pion," Tetherow said.

The warlock stopped, the end of his cane digging into the stones at his feet. His innards bubbled at the pregnant pause.

"I haven't forgotten my promise to you," the girl murmured.

Pion glanced back at Autumn Rose, taking her in properly for the first time since the ritual chamber massacre. Her hair now showed more gray

5

than red, her irises flaring a wintry nightmare against the whites of her eyes, and her sea of freckles screamed like specks of bloodshed across the youthful plain of her alabaster skin.

"Shelly Manson," she said. "Once this is all finished and I have the haxanblade, I will splice you into The Bloodbind's curse, and we will carve your mother from whatever timeline you wish. But you must not lose focus before then. As with the dracari before it, the age of the gift-born must find its gallows."

It's testing you. Feeling you out. Assessing your loyalty. It can sense your fear. Your reluctance. Your indecision. Stay in control.

"Worry not, milord," Pion answered, pretending at courage, envisioning himself as his father, as he'd always done when a situation called for a mite more mettle than he truly possessed. "I've never been more resolute."

"And I'm encouraged to hear it." The curve upon her mouth was pure poison. "As for your deformities," she held up *Dawn* and...*Noon*, otherwise known as *Flesh*, the carnomancer's tome. "We raze Lancastle and I will see the ritual through myself. Savvy?"

"Savvy," the warlock echoed. He had to give the creature credit. It certainly knew how to pull at his shriveled little heartstrings when the time called for it. Though, Pion reckoned, if he were going to be played as the fiddle, he may as well act a most fetching bow.

"May your luck stones prosper, apprentice," Tetherow added.

"And yours to the flourish," Pion returned as he started away, one shoulder stooped, cane tapping toward the study table where he'd left his cloak and travel sack, Ripley padding along quietly beside him.

As he turned the aisle's corner for the common area, he found Caitlyn Ellsbury waiting in the lantern light beside his belongings, freshly mended.

For a lass who just lost both of her parents, she was keeping herself together with surprising poise. And that wasn't even taking into account her scrap with the Lanier rebels. Pion didn't know whether to be impressed, terrified, or enamored. Though he supposed, all affairs considered, there was room yet for all three.

"It's strange seeing you and Grandpa together," she greeted.

At least she didn't say creepy. He held her honey-colored eyes. "I'm sorry I couldn't save them. I wish I could have done more."

"They knew the risks," she answered icily, and suddenly Pion became exceedingly aware of the wand twisting between her fingers, midnight black stem culminating in a grip of scored antler. It belonged to her Magister father, Florian Ellsbury, one of the best-known spellslingers walking the moon. Well, formerly walking the moon. But for the ashaeydir's wretchrot, which saw an awful end to all that. To both Florian and his buxom bride, Lady Lydia.

"If there is anything—" he began.

"You can stop feeling sorry for me and let me join you in Lancastle," she interrupted. "No use mewling about bygones."

You confound me yet again, Caitlyn Ellsbury, he thought, not expecting such a callous response.

Ripley leapt atop the seat of a chair, barely making it, and made a second jump to the tabletop beside Caitlyn, nudging his head against her wrist.

"I'd be glad for the company, milady," the warlock found himself saying. And where Caitlyn Ellsbury was concerned, he damned well meant it.

"I'm pleased to hear it," Caitlyn ruffled the striped fur atop Ripley's noggin, "because you really didn't have much of a choice." She scootched off the table's end and met his hunched height, holstering her father's wand.

Remarkably, amidst the hum of herbs and elixirs, he could still smell a hint of yesterday's wash on her, apple cinnamon sweet, straight from the baker's cooling shelf, as she whisked her long, black hair forward against the front side of her right shoulder.

"You just promise me one thing, Pion," she said. "It's the only thing I will ask from here on out."

And here comes the death wish proclamation.

"If we come upon Magwyn Lanier, she's mine to sort as I see fit."

Commendable, if not predictable. "You are aware she is housing a dracari's essence, I presume?"

"But of course."

"Do you mean to kill her?" he asked.

"I don't know what I mean to do with her. And I don't know how I'll react inside her company. But I do know if she's still amongst the living, then we have unfinished words that need tending."

7

The warlock could practically taste the anger in her words. Burning across her bones. Shrieking beneath her skin. Straining the air between them. Something had shifted inside of her. Oh, yes, something indeed. Something beyond the loss of her parents and a few beauty points. Something beyond his reason and remedy. This was not the same girl that had come through the headmaster's portal from Perciya only a few days ago. Not even close.

All the same, Pion swallowed, knowing damned well he could never actually preserve such a promise, especially not with the demoness Dysenia Luiryn lurking about. "Hand to heart, she's yours," he said anyway, sweeping a fist up to his chest with gentlemanly aplomb, presenting his best stab at sincerity.

After everything, what was one more disappointed soul, after all?

CHAPTER TWO

As SWORN, a carriage awaited them on the cobble just outside the Marrovard Archives, a dreary face staring down at them from the coachman's box. The gods only knew where Tetherow conjured it up from. Though it likely belonged to one of the local high lords, or mayhaps the university headmaster himself. It wasn't quite as ornate and handsome as the carriages he'd become accustomed to from the Lanier's collection, but it certainly outclassed walking or riding horseback.

Pion labored clumsily up the creaky wooden footsteps, pulling a cloth from his vestments once he was inside, and began to daub at his forehead.

Ripley joined him, kneading a place of comfort at the warlock's side, and Caitlyn sat atop the bench across from them. The coach jerked forward before the door could close, bumping up and down the cobblestones behind the sound of clopping hooves. At least the seats were padded and set well with fabric.

Once settled outside of town, he pulled a flask from his travel sack and took a nip. The last of his absinthium. "Bit of flavor?" he asked in the sway of lantern light, not wanting to appear rude.

"I've had my fill of tonics for a long while," Caitlyn answered, tracing fingers down the line of the bright white scar tissue that ranged the curve of her bronze skin from nose to ear.

The warlock's mind slipped back to that morning when they found her barely conscious in an alley just shy of the university grounds. Given her state, it was a wonder she was able to stand half a day later, much less find fitness for travel. Yet, here she was.

"Does it hurt?" he asked.

"Mercifully, no. It just feels strange. Unnatural." Her eyes found his. "Ugly."

"Trust, it will take a mite more than all that to ruin a beauty such as yours, milady," Pion replied. "That is if you don't mind my saying."

Scant comfort had from the resident grotesque, no doubt, though the words were no less true. Pion would never dream of admitting it to the girl, but he rather thought the mark added a certain essence to her comeliness.

"For a creature that claims to hate magic as much as Tetherow does, it certainly knows its way around the gift's properties," Caitlyn said. Shadows flickered upon her face in the firelight. "All told, it could have been considerably worse."

"What exactly happened?"

"Calem and I were ambushed by Empress Magwyn, a rogue, and a swordsman. We were interrogated about the ritual." She inched up straight in the seat and crossed her legs. "I gave them nothing. Then Tabbie Reid showed up and all manner of the nine broke loose. Believe it or not, Magwyn actually saved me as the building caught flame. And she could have just left me."

Caitlyn gazed out the window, back into the forest gloom. "They pressed me more outside, and I diverted until the townsfolk arrived. I remember screaming as the townsfolk tore past me in pursuit of the rebel party, squirming in the chair, wriggling, trying to free my hands, then I felt the chair teeter and tip backward in the rush. My heart leapt from my chest as my breath caught and my feet rose overhead, then everything went black." She glanced back at him. "The next thing I knew, it was morning and I was lying in a puddle of my own blood and filth, coughing up smelling salts and feeling like I'd just caught the ass-end of a back-alley mugging."

And there was that illustrious Southland charm.

"Come to find, my misfortune may have actually become my salvation with all the goings-on in the ritual chamber." She rubbed at the back of her head where it cracked against the cobblestone. "I've heard we lost half to the wretchrot."

"To the number," Pion said. "Sixteen of us remain. Not including those unlikely to pull through their injuries and ailments."

The ritual chamber survivors managed to save a few spellbrothers that endured blade wounds in the skirmish, but none that suffered the wretchrot's poison. Even the nether refused to take in that luckless lot, Florian and Lydia Ellsbury among them. Pion couldn't help but ponder if Caitlyn saw what remained of them, the missing chunks of flesh and bone from their faces and necks, the pools of thick yellow and pink liquid left in place of their melted skin. He shook the thought from his mind.

"What else did our Master tell you?" he inquired.

"Nothing of import," Cailtyn answered. "It mentioned Lancastle and that the survivors would be raiding her walks within the day. Which is why I followed it, assuming it would lead me to either you or the ashaey-dir. And now here we are."

Orphaned, scarred, and left for the crows in a single night, if that's not enough to prepare you for the last great war then whatever was? Pion's lips thinned to a hard line. *If nothing else, it certainly made running toward the arms of death a mite easier to swallow.*

"Have you ever been to Lancastle?" the warlock asked.

"Gods, no. Marrovard is the nearest I've come to any of the highland kingdoms."

"There was a time I might have said you were in for a treat, but honestly, I haven't the faintest inkling what repair she's in. Not that I much care these days. I'd rather hoped I'd seen the last of her, to have it true."

"I know well the sentiment. I'd begun to feel the same way about Kanton in recent days. I'd even made plans to abscond, but then all this madness started happening."

A wantaway, was it? Scandals aplenty with this one.

"Not that it's any of my business, but when I was varged into Ripley, I overheard you and Desmond..."

"Ugh," she groaned. "Pion, prithee, one last promise. No more talk of *him*, yeah?"

"I'll do my best," he replied.

The request wasn't so much a surprise as was the way she expressed it.

Not that he was any sort of expert on such affectations, but there was undoubtedly a deep pain behind the words. A pain not unlike his understanding of love.

Though he had no right to it, Pion became cross at the realization. And it took everything within him to stay his tongue in regards to Desmond the Dullard. Caitlyn, no doubt, held her own host of issues, but Desmond Lanier was a tosspot, a libertine, and a selfish wastrel far beneath the worth of a kindly, clever lass such as she. The brooding warlock wondered if she knew about Desmond's bedding other women whilst they were courting.

All that's going on right now, and this is what you worry about? His wits returned. *Tighten up, you bloody simp.*

"I presume the nest in Wyrmswold will place us in one of the kingdom's lower hamlets," Pion said. "In an old tanner shop. Assuming it's not been torn to the ground already. If Dysenia is still there, we will likely strategize. If not, we will travel the back alleys of Darrowyn's Rut to an escape passage that will take us inside the castle. I believe another one of the eldritch bindings is stashed inside the library, and I mean to uncover it."

"Sounds like a needle in a haystack."

"If my instincts are correct, it should be within a secret alcove. The princess thought she'd kept it hidden, but the walls have eyes as they say. And I've seen her with it before. It's an eyesore like the rest and should be easy to spot." He cleared his throat. "Of course, this is all hypothetical. For all we know, the entire citadel is already in shambles."

"My folks largely kept me in the dark about Ravenholme," Caitlyn began. "And they certainly didn't prepare me for what all's gone on this past quintweek with Tetherow, the nether, and ending the Giftborn Age. Pion, *I'm* giftborn. My parents were giftborn. Help me understand. Why would they choose to end their own kind? Why would *you* choose this?"

"You misconstrue, milady. Ending the Giftborn Age is not about *killing* all giftborn. That would never work. It's about thinning the herd. About reform. About assimilation."

"Assimilation?"

"The nether has always been here. Beneath the surface of things. Under the earth and the sea. Within the air you breathe. Inside the meat you wear around your soul. Behind every whispered prayer and every conjured spell, be it a healer's chant or a sorcerer's hex. Taking as much from us as we from it. Hence its namesake.

"It is bound to the gift, and, thusly, to us. Born of antipathy. And, for centuries, our society has misinterpreted its purpose, simply because it doesn't suit our fancies. Naming it chaos. When in truth the gift is chaos, scattered and wild, where the nether is as one. The nether is its control. The mouth devouring its unruly tail.

"The cycle has been written and played out countless times before, most notably to our annals on Ashira, and it's the same every time. The gift is found and nurtured. As it grows and begins to spiral, so too does the nether, until an eventual breaking point, and thereafter the inversion begins. We are now at the precipice of that inversion, which commenced at the splitting of The Pale. So, you see, the end of the Giftborn Age was always inevitable. It was only a matter of when, not if. The nether will not be stopped. It cannot be stopped. Not by anything on this moon. Sure, it can be slowed, but even that is being generous."

He let out a heavy breath as Caitlyn stared at him owl-eyed. The gods only knew just how far out of her depths this girl had fallen. By her lovely haunters, he'd wager about as far as he had, if not further. But there was always a certain measure of madness in control, wasn't there?

"Somehow, Tetherow has found a way to control the entity," he continued. "Or rather, somehow, they are working as one. Only instead of the nether running roughshod across the moon as it did Ashira, its destruction is now kept to a concentrated order. It will make an example of the High Houses in the hopes that the lesser lot will see the punishment for rebellion and adhere to their new god's ascendency."

Preach on, Brother Pion. He of no true alliance. He of no true religious claim. The godless heathen.

"Eventually, the elements will counter the nether's imbalance, returning the world to the other side of the cycle, a fresh serpent of fate swallowing itself anew. Such is every measure as inescapable as the nether's coming reign. But, trust, we'll all be long gone before then."

"What is it?" Caitlyn inquired. "Tetherow, I mean?"

"*It* was a demon, once. One of the ancient fold. That was how it began. But it's something else now. And as far as our world is concerned, it's the lesser of two evils. The High Houses will fall, Caitlyn. One by one. It has been written. And so it shall pass."

"And what happens once they've fallen?"

"Would that I could name it. Truthfully, at this point, I have no expectations. You see what I am. How I am. As you might imagine, I was not treated well in the prior version of our society. And though I am not proud to admit it, there was a time I almost took my life because of it. Because of others. As such, for your present company, almost anything different from what was is an improvement. Everything that's happened since the nether's arrival has been a boon in my life. I have purpose now. Meaning. I have a tiny scrap of importance. And no offense, but I'm sitting here talking to you. A cycle ago, if you saw someone like me, would you have sacrificed even the smallest moment of your day for a chat?"

Caitlyn swallowed, a mask of shame taking shape, and her gaze lowered.

"I thought as much. And, prize well, dear Caitlyn, I take no affront." A smirk settled. "Because that was the old world. And no matter what horrors may come, it can never go back."

I can never go back.

CHAPTER THREE

Dark fluids splashed across her frontage the moment she passed through the portal, flecking her cheeks and glasses in black and red, as Broenwjar burst from one clicking shape to the next like a battering ram, then out onto the cobble, just barely fitting through the chamber's skinny doorway.

"Oh, you want to fuck, bitch? Let's fuck," Rhymona rasped from some rest just outside, chased by a defiant clicking sound and a clash of steel.

Once.

Twice.

"Rhymona," Marsea howled.

"And a thick arse cock for the young lord," the magus crowed. "Oh, and fuck me, he's an all-time gusher at that."

The princess unsheathed Blind Widow as she dashed across the room, leaping ghoul parts and the maidens only knew what else, out into the starlit chaos of Courowne where screams, smoke, and flames rose from every direction and a giant incomprehensible mass the size of a blooming castle lorded over all, bellowing mightily across the stolen horizon.

The stars keep us, Marsea thought, words utterly beyond her.

"Looking awfully foolish with a sword sticking out of your face, good sir," Rhymona mocked, watching her ghastly opponent stagger about aimlessly, blood spurting out unnaturally from the blade lodged through his eye socket.

Marsea's nose scrunched up at the remarkably hideous ghoul, clad in the finely cut attire of high Vinteyaman fashion.

"Viscount Fuckwit here actually thought he could take me," Rhymona scoffed as the fiend began to spasm. "You believe that shit?"

Viscount Fuckwit clicked crossly at her as though in retort.

"What's that?" Rhymona played the part, cupping a hand behind her ear, pretending at banter. "Oh, but of course," she indulged, casually gripping the mae'chii's hilt. "Allow me," and she tore the blade free from the blighter's face, slinging gore and brain matter from its silver length, the ghoul slumping to the stones, joining the half dozen carved-up corpses surrounding her.

Not a quint past such a scene would have sent Marsea squeamish into the nearest bucket, but now she barely batted an eye at it. She thought about Julia then, and how she'd tried to shield her from Raelan's violent pageantry only but a few short days ago, failing miserably, and about Remy and all the horrors he'd likely encountered on his way home from The King's Wall. And Desmond. Murdered. Resurrected. Possessed. All the luck of a beggar's bastard…

Oh, but the times were something else now, weren't they? Stars alive, *she* was something else now.

They all were.

She sucked in a deep breath to steel her nerves, and a bright white tether of magic rippled through the crowd up ahead, burning from one body to the next, dropping the last of its undead chain in a smoldering heap.

In the dreary haze of flame and fog, the figures were like shadow folk, nigh impossible to discern if they were blighted or not until it was much too late.

"Wand magic, and quite powerful," Rhymona said, frost clouds forming at her words as the princess took to her side.

"And what's with the weather?" Marsea asked, a chill befalling her.

Every footstep felt different, shifting from patches of extreme cold to a midsummer swelter, one stride to the next.

"The laws of nature are going to shit," the magus answered. "I've felt the change before, back in the palace walks. Some bastard reaction between the elements and the nether's bingeing."

Broenwjar stampeded down the cobblestones behind them, snapping at the crawling blighted, chomping through spriteling snatchers fool enough to show themselves.

Another tide of magic lit the avenue and one of the nether beast's grotesque appendages rose up high.

"Find cover!" Magwyn called as the massive tentacle came swinging down, slamming across the township ahead, crushing everything underneath, buildings, blighted, spellslinger and all.

"Oh, shit," Marsea spluttered, bracing for impact, trailing Rhymona off the main cobble and crashing hard against a shop wall, curling into a ball as the ground shook and a violent wind tore down through the pathway past them.

But the maidens knew, the smell alone was enough to take one off their feet.

"Everyone all right?" Marsea called out into the settling miasma.

"Up to our tits in fuckwits and nether piss? Never better," Rhymona said, shaking dust and dirt from her snow-colored mane.

"There's a honey," the princess let loose one of her best-liked Rhymona-isms as they stared up in unison at the colossal creature.

"Veradon's sake, look at this fat cunt," the magus carped. "You think a godsgate's going to swallow a turd that thick?"

"I suppose we're going to find out," Marsea returned for lack of anything better.

"A bridge for the morrow, yeah," Rhymona said. "Right now, we need to be anywhere else before Big Bertha decides to play the cobblestone drums again."

Squinting into the spreading fog, Marsea inspected the surrounding passageways, each one more daunting than the last. "Which way to the palace?"

"Assuming there's anything left of it," her aunt said as she joined them, panic written on her face.

"Look up," the magus said. "See that big arse tower of smoke over yonder?"

It was quite impossible to miss, even within the nether beast's murky trail.

"That's us." Rhymona darted across the street and into a foggy back alley. "And we should probably keep any magic use at a minimum until we're out of Big Bertha's reach."

"Agreed."

"Blades and fades only. Nothing unnecessary."

They crept on cautiously through the fireflies and back-alley gloom until they approached an intersection about midway down, shouting and clicking coming from the left, where Marsea discovered a ghoul stabbing down at a cowering couple, the man defending the woman from the blighter's strikes with the shambles of a buckler that appeared more decoration than proper defense armament.

Dammit all. Marsea held but for a moment. *You can't just leave them.*

A curse on her breath, she abandoned Rhymona's hunt, rearing Blind Widow high overhead and slicing it down at the ghoul from behind. It wasn't her finest touch all told, but it proved more than enough to put the frenzied fiend off its assault.

The creature rounded on her, as she ripped the sword from its feast of skull, its nose missing, jaw hanging slack to one side, widened by a long incision from lips to ear, and a pair of spritelings squirmed out from the steaming wounds, one through the stretched mouth, the other through the split in the crown leaking netherblood viscous as a wandering slug.

The ghoul dropped like a sack of grain, its cleaver clattering to the cobble, and the man with the buckler wilted back into the woman's arms, having taken quite a few nasty cuts on his face and neck.

"Chuffing hells, Marsea. What part of nothing unnecessary did you not follow?" Rhymona scolded from beyond her shoulder. "We haven't the time for knights and knaves, yeah."

Frowning, Marsea met the whimpering woman's eyes, nodded her condolences, and turned back to join her swordsisters.

Can't save them all, girl.

Only a man. A slab of meat, Other comforted in her own queer manner.

Broenwjar offered a disapproving glare.

I had to, B. Just this once.

She grazed her bad hand through his fur as she passed. *I had it under control.* He let out a low growl to match Rhymona's frustration. *Never again then, I promise. Sheesh.* The maidens know, Old Boy could be as controlling as Vaustian. Though she supposed he had a decent claim to the complaint, what with his life being tied to hers and all.

Corpses crowded the side street labyrinth, growing in number the further inward they progressed, leaving scarce enough space to advance in places. Marsea hacked and slashed at anything that moved, the ravenous haxanblade seething a soft pink mist from the fresh glut of savagery, as they met another avenue and a raucous party of battling survivors.

"At least there's some manner of resistance left," Rhymona said as they approached.

"Captain Grueta," Magwyn shouted at the group.

A dark-haired behemoth of a man whirled around to face them, his once golden surcoat caked in enough gore to sicken even the hardest of butchers.

"Empress," he grunted, eyes given to a certain madness.

"We mean to push for the palace," her aunt said. "What's worse, the yards or the wood?"

"Haven't seen either in hours. But there is no more palace to speak of." He glanced down briefly at Broenwjar. "Strange bit of company you're keeping, Majesty. You don't mind my saying."

"I could say the same of whatever this is," she motioned to the wall of warring soldiers.

A few amongst the grim-faced lot still donned their coats of gold, but most appeared like characters of a far less savory sort, undoubtedly throwing in for the thrill of the kill over any true claim to honor or brotherhood.

"May your luck stones prosper, milady," Captain Grueta said before turning back into the fray, splitting the wall between two shieldmaidens, and promptly caving a ghoul's face in with his spiked club.

"Real peach, that one," Rhymona quipped.

"Can you blame him?" Magwyn replied.

"We took the woods last time and it was a clusterfuck," Rhymona said. "At least the yards will grant us a better—"

A shriek like nothing Marsea had ever hearkened before cut through the nightfall from the direction of the sea, followed by a brilliant azure glow.

"What the fuck now?" Rhymona grumbled.

"Dracari," Magwyn answered as the creature slithered into view against the heavens, its long, winding silhouette painted black as nightmare against Y'dema's emerald radiance, Eldn flame spewing from its many maws, showering the docks and outer hamlets in conflagration as it soared toward the palace courtyards.

"I'm sorry, did you just say dracari?"

"It would appear the nether found one of us," Magwyn said, her eyes burning azure.

"Grand." Rhymona rolled her eyes. "Clusterfuck Woods it is then." She started away and Marsea followed, Broenwjar at her side, Magwyn just behind, as they picked their way through the mayhem of ghouls and goldcoats until the cobblestones ended and the forest began.

They weren't amongst the trees long before they came upon a clearing strewn with writhing bodies in the hundreds, shouts and cries ranging the grisly expanse; the hollered names, curses, and prayers nearly drowned out by the unceasing clicking sound of the turning blight.

"Maidens' breath," Marsea uttered.

"It's a fucking blight hatchery," the magus hissed.

Drylax creatures patrolled the hellscape silencing the damned and dying one by one, their ichorous forms shifting from thick to thin with each burst of movement, goblins and spritelings swarming and infesting anyone that dared to escape their wretched fate.

Beyond the field of horrors lay the crumbling remains of Palace Courowne. Marsea had heard countless tales of its unmatched magnificence from all walks over the cycles, but now the Jewel of the South appeared little more than a pile of overgrown glass shards swept into a pit of cinders.

"I daresay, the good Captain wasn't taking the piss, was he?" Rhymona said as the trio sank back into the shadows of the forest's edge.

"I hope your plan wasn't to cross this field," Marsea said before blowing a loose strand of hair out of her face.

"Obviously, I wasn't aware of all this."

"Good gravy." Marsea paced deeper into the forest.

This is bloody impossible. Think, Marsea. There must be something you're missing here. There must be another way.

She cocked her head back to Rhymona. "You said they were underground, yes?"

"They were. Though, prize well, the temple had a most unusual structure. Like no temple I'd ever heard of. There were odd markings and scripts memorializing celestial beings and noting a wreckage from the sky. There's no telling how long it's been here."

"Is it possible it could have protected them from the palace collapsing?"

"I reckon. Luck stones willing."

"And what are the chances it would have only had the one entrance? Isn't that unusual for a temple, city, or whatever the heck it once was?"

"Your guess is as good as mine, Marsea, but we were down there a while, hours, mayhaps a day, and we never found a second, so..."

A rough cawing sound from above grabbed Marsea's attention, and she found in the branches the ugliest bird she'd ever beheld. Her nose wrinkled up in disgust. *It's even taking the wildlife*, she thought, her heart breaking.

"Speak of the devil and he shall come to call," Rhymona said, a lopsided smirk pulling at her lips as she held out her hand toward the abomination.

"What are you doing?" Marsea asked, a brow raising in confusion.

"Of all the massacres on all the moon," her mad friend answered.

The crow eased off the branch and landed awkwardly on the edge of Rhymona's fingers.

"I think they are most certainly still alive," the magus said, angling the unsightly fiend at her. "Marsea, meet Desmond."

CHAPTER FOUR

Oʜ, how he yearned for the days of yestercycle. When his worst days saw him crawl inside a bottle for a sad little wank and his best ended in a perfumed bed and an equally forgettable orgasm.

YOU HAVE AN ODD MIND, PRINCELING.

And I bet you say that to all the lads, Aiden returned as he, Hrathgon, and Lenore soared over the palace rubble and out over the field of corpses. He found the dracari's experience with flying somehow translated to his own understanding of aviary workings and progressed him from a novice to a master in the blink of an eye.

After escaping the sunken temple, the brothers Lanier and youngest sister Julia swam back to shore, emerging a fair distance away from the pit of cinders that formerly housed the docks and market. Spent, the trio found camp in a thicket at the forest's edge, where Remy and Thira coerced Aiden and his new soul companion to gain a better lay of Courowne before they made their way back into the city. You know, because living for half a second in relative safety was just too bloody much to ask for these days.

A BAD EGG, IS IT?

'Fraid so, though I'm the fun, cheeky sort of bad egg you'll come to find.

IS THAT A FACT?

Oi, this shit is on you, old bean, whatever becomes us. You wanted in as I recall. I might suggest next time you have half a care what you wish for.

DULY NOTED.

Lenore's head twitched from side to side scanning the landscape as they circled back over a trampled hedge maze to a corpse-covered clearing. Aiden still hadn't completely adjusted to his familiar's black-and-white vision, but he didn't need a clear view to understand what horrors lay in the fields below.

All of this devastation. He glanced over to the gigantic mass of moving flesh making its way through the kingdom and rattled off a series of curses in crow's tongue. Though, mercifully, the dracari drylax was nowhere to be found…

LISTEN, the dragon bade.

What is it?

DO YOU NOT HEAR IT?

I'm hearing quite a lot of things, H. Can you be more specific?

QUIET YOUR MIND A MOMENT AND YOU WILL HAVE IT, Hrathgon said, slight irritation in his tone.

Aiden closed his eyes, stopped flapping his wings, Lenore gliding straight, as he severed himself from the muddled cries below and concentrated on the wind blowing through his feathers, chilling Lenore's frail frame beneath. A few seconds later he had something, faint as it was. A soft pulse, like heartbeats in the quiet of night, head sunk into the pillow's depths.

EMYRIA.

His eyes opened.

SHE IS NEARBY. IN THE WOODS.

They dove for the tree line and flew across the forest's edge until they found movement within. The first few sightings appeared to be blighters. Though one was a stray survivor moving swiftly, clutching a bow and wearing a bloodstained goldcoat tabard.

THERE.

Aiden could feel the second dracari aura now pounding hard as a war drum as they wove through the branches just under the canopy of treetops, narrowly navigating the shifting spaces between, and before he knew it, they'd reached the thunderous source. It belonged to one of the three women below.

Gods' breath. And wouldn't you know it? He actually recognized all three. Each one holding a different piece of his paltry past.

Rhymona. Magwyn. And a face he couldn't forget had he been murdered and gravedanced a dozen times over. Marsea. Somehow, he missed her more within her presence. She appeared both scholar and swordswoman. How peculiar it was to find the three of them all together.

And here I was thinking the fates had left us all to go fuck ourselves.

Without even realizing it he began cawing ferociously, alighting a branch just above them, and Rhymona stared up at him.

"Of all the massacres on all the moons," she said, beckoning him to her outstretched arm like a practiced falconer.

"What are you doing?" Marsea asked.

Aiden swooped down and landed on Rhymona's hand, Lenore's claws clutching tight to her fingers.

"I think they are most certainly still alive," the magus said, bringing him face to face with his sister. "Marsea, meet Desmond."

"Desmond?" Marsea nudged up her odd-shaped old nan glasses.

Oh, but the look on his sister's face almost made all of the bullshit worth it. The dying, the cycles of deceit, the possession, the dying again...

"Are you after the loon?" she quibbled.

"Says the girl with her own familiar," Rhymona returned.

"What?" Marsea said.

Own familiar? Aiden's attention fell on the dire wolf prowling toward the group from the forest drear, fresh blood oozing from its snout, as it came to heel at Marsea's side.

Wait a tick? Marsea has a big ass wolf and I get the moon's ugliest branch goblin? How is that fucking fair? No offense, Lenny.

AND WHAT AM I? CHOPPED GIZZARD?

Do rein it in, Mister Sensitive. I haven't exactly had the chance to properly process what you...what we...are yet.

AS THE THREE women hewed a path through the clusters of broken fingernails and gnashing teeth, Aiden discovered Marsea and Rhymona had apparently forged some measure of a friendship at some point, close enough that they spoke like kin, and weren't afraid to bust the other's bollocks if one of them slipped in form or said something daft.

A sort of relief found him at their bond. A sense of hope. Mayhaps it meant he'd get on better with Marsea than he had with Remy thus far. Though, looking back on it objectively, it was anyone's guess just how many of his conversations were actually had with Remy and how many belonged to Yvemathira.

Even at a decent pace, it still took them the better part of the nightfall to traverse the blight-infested forest for the shore, where in the pink glow of dawn's first light, they found scorched sands flecked in silver and black as the nether's bowels.

Remy leaned against a boulder, hand shielding his eyes from the morning sun, peering out at them as they approached.

Once clear of the tree line, the archivist drifted out into the salty breeze, skimming just above the ocean's surface before twirling upward high above the others, carving through the wind like a skinner's knife.

Pure poetry, he thought. *The gift at its finest.*

At a certain altitude, the air began to gust, making it tougher to scale, and he leveled his ascension, sailing smoothly. *Breathtaking.* Amid all the hate and horrors Tetherow brought him, somehow, amazingly, this bit of beauty made its way through.

The fates and their fucking wretched sense of humor.

A little further down the beach from Remy, Julia sat next to his stuffed husk of a body dozing by the remains of a campfire. He came in gently, landing atop a length of driftwood and let out a woeful little caw at the sight of his natural form. The gods know, in the daylight he was nearly as pale as his winged companion and twice as hideous.

All right, H. Do your thing.

But before he could even complete the thought he was waking inside his own body, and rolling onto his backside, aches and chills spanning from the space of his missing tooth down to the spasms ranging the arches of his calloused feet.

"Fuuuuuuck," he groaned, staring up into the heavens as the sun joined the sister moons' watch.

Gods' wounds, put me back, he couldn't help but think.

What did it say about the state of him that he would almost rather go on as a flying rat than wear his own body?

"Marsea!" Remy ran up to his sister and wrapped her in a warm embrace, their cares for one another immediately apparent.

The fresh excitement roused Julia, and Aiden sat up, watching the youngest kick up sand down the shore before joining the others in a big hug. The archivist couldn't take his eyes off of them. His family. His blood. After all these cycles. He wanted like fire to smile, to rush over to them and share in their joy, to pretend at some measure of happiness, but his body wouldn't cooperate, his lips bending opposite as a wet heat formed behind his orbs. It was just enough that he could find his feet at all.

"Aunt Maggie, aren't you a sight for sore eyes," Remy said as he pulled away from his sisters.

"And you, Remy," Magwyn returned, the hint of a smile forming around her large front teeth. "All of you." She fixed on Aiden.

"Is that really you, Des?" Marsea asked as the entire group turned toward him.

Shit, this is fucking awkward.

IT WOULD APPEAR WE SHARE AN AVERSION FOR ATTENTION, WE OF THE BLACK SHEEP FOIL.

His vision drifted to the ocean. *So neglected, yet so necessary…*

Suddenly he could feel her advancing, his sister, catching her at the edge of his periphery, though he refused to take her in.

"All this time, Desmond. Can you not even look at me?" Marsea questioned, stopping just short of him, the top of her head barely meeting his shoulders.

"Sorry," he answered, as he took her in properly. "Reckon you caught me on an off day."

Not enough liquid amnesia.

"That's one way of putting it." Her lip quirked up.

"It's good to see you, Marsea." The words felt appropriate enough. Like something distant family would say after a lifetime apart.

"And it's good to be seen," she answered, giving him a once-over. "You have no idea how often I've dreamt of you. How often I've wished I could see you again, praying to the star maidens to bring you back, never believing it possible. And yet here you stand. An actual living, breathing person." Her eyes fell on the tattoo burned into his forearm. "And we've got a brand in common, haven't we?"

He glanced down at the wretched stain of scar tissue screaming a thousand obscenities against the milky-white plane of his ocean-washed skin.

"Don't lose that arm by the way," she said, "or you'll lose your friend there. First rule of familiars, never bind on a limb. Or so I'm told."

An odd fucking thing to say considering the rest of me, but full marks for the counsel.

The dire wolf padded up and halted at her side as Lenore took her place atop the archivist's good shoulder.

"Would that my former haunter gave half a toss about this old fuck-wit," Aiden returned.

"And you've a black tongue for it, I see. A Lanier to the letter."

IT WOULD SEEM SISTER DEAR IS A BIT OF AN OVER-ACHIEVER.

Is that your expert opinion or are we just digging a little too close to home now?

AND HERE I THOUGHT WE OUTCASTS MIGHT STAND HALF A CHANCE TO GET ON.

"The stars know, I wish we had more time to swap tales, but alas we've other matters," Marsea said. "Namely our other sister. Autumn."

The fuck? Gut meet fist. Other sister? Marsea knows about Tam?

He cleared his throat, playing at some measure of competence. "It has her, doesn't it?"

"I'm sorry, Des." Aunt Magwyn approached. "We tried to halt the ritual, but…"

"We'll get her back, yeah," Rhymona finished from behind the group, inspecting her silver-toothed husband. She still refused to meet Aiden's eyes, but her mere acknowledgment was more than enough to sate his expectations.

"First order of business," Marsea started, retrieving a tome from her satchel. "The grimoires. We've managed two of the four." She offered it to Remy. "I believe this one calls to you."

"So, it does." Wearing a chafed expression, Remy took up the wretch by its chain bindings.

"The other two lie with the enemy," Marsea said. "*Dawn* and *Noon*. Together, the four of them can be used to summon a godsgate, which is likely our best shot at banishing the nether."

As a whole, the group all stared back toward the woods where the beast's destruction could be heard from a lengthy distance beyond.

A GODSGATE IS NOT WHAT YOU LOT THINK IT IS. ITS SUMMONING WILL BE INCREDIBLY DANGEROUS AND THAT MUCH MORE VOLATILE. THEY ARE AS UNPREDICTABLE AS BIND CASTING AND DARK-DABBLING AND THEY REQUIRE THE UTMOST CARE AND PRECISION. ONE WRONG WORD, ONE ERRANT INFLECTION, COULD SEND THE ENTIRE SPELL INTO UTTER CHAOS.

Worse than what Tetherow's done us? Worse than the nether?

POSSIBLY.

Whatever the risks, at this point, it has to be worth the attempt, right? We cannot simply stand by and let that fel monstrosity seize our world.

"Exorcise Tetherow, gain the other grimoires, and summon a godsgate, got it," Aiden said. "But how the hells do you propose we expel the demon from Tam? I literally had to kill myself to drive it out." The scar on his shoulder itched at the telling.

"We destroy *The N'therN'rycka*," Marsea replied. "I know, easier said than done, but it's the best plan we've managed thus far."

MAY I? Aiden felt Hrathgon scratching for release.

By all means. The archivist receded, allowing the dracari to have his say.

"...Tetherow's codex lies within The Scar..." the dragon stated.

"You know this for certain, brother?" Magwyn asked, eyes glowing azure.

"...Who do you think put it there? And why do you think the demon targets Chandii hosts and those of the old blood?..."

"Because they are the only ones that can survive the fumes," Remy said, Yvemathira making her presence known.

"...Precisely..."

"We'll have to split up," Marsea said. "I can accompany Des to The Scar to find the codex. Being godsblood, there's a high probability we can both withstand its desolation."

"I suppose that stands to reason," Remy said.

"For the present, Rhymona and I have decided it's probably best we are not in the same place together given our link to the time loops."

"I...uh...the uh what now?" Remy asked, clearly back in control.

"Long story short, we're connected by some curse to a pocket dimension named The Bloodbind. We know the curse is linked to myself, Rhymona, Stella, and the Wyrmstower Witch. It's believed that if all of us die within a loop, it will reset the world…"

"Meaning we'll have to do this shit all over again," Rhymona appended, sliding the hatchet inside the belt at her waist.

"Or some variation within," Marsea finished.

"Not that I'm altogether opposed given how smashing well this one's going to the present," the magus snarked.

"At best it buys us time, if one of us bites it," Marsea added. "At least in theory."

"Right, buys us time," Remy groused. "Any other barmy bullshit you want to clue us all into since you've been away?"

"I think that'll do for now." Marsea placed a hand against Remy's shoulder and, for the first time, Aiden noticed she was missing a few lengths from it. "We're all alive," she continued. "That's what matters. And for a small moment, we all get to be together." Her attention returned to Aiden. "I don't know Autumn. But I'd like to. She is one of us, after all. A Lanier. And I promise you, I will do everything in my power to rescue her from Tetherow."

A Lanier? "How do you mean she is a Lanier?"

"I mean it like Stella and Father, they…"

"Oh, please do not tell us what I think you're about to," Remy said, disappointment dripping from every word.

So much for that'll do.

"She's Whit's bastard, isn't she?" Aiden resolved.

"I only just found this out myself a few hours ago," Marsea said. "We visited Father in The Spellbind and he confirmed as much."

"So, is it true then?" Remy asked. "Father's prophecy?"

"To a certain degree, I suppose. Though it's become clouded and altered by each time loop. There's no telling what actually remains of it."

"And how many loops are we talking here?"

"Would that I could name it," Marsea answered. "At least six or seven. Bygones to bygones. The only detail we have with any consistency is the grimoires. That they are somehow tied to our bloodline and that they can potentially be used to vanquish the nether. Which makes expelling Tetherow from Autumn imperative. And not *just* because she is our sister. But because without her we may not be able to complete the gods-gate ritual."

"Do you reckon Tetherow knows about this?" Remy questioned, trailing fingers nervously through his hair.

"I don't think it does," Aiden said, sifting back through what memories remained of the demon. "At least not fully. I think it knows the grimoires have value, but lacks the requisite minutiae, as it were."

"What if it just kills her?" the youngest brother asked. "Do you think it would if it knew?"

"I think it's running short on options," Aiden answered. "And I wouldn't put anything past the wretch."

"But Autumn was his game all along," Magwyn argued. "At least from what I know of it. She is the nether's chosen. The bastard born of summer's blood and winter's kiss."

Aiden recalled reading about such a figure from *The N'therN'rycka's* pages. Calem, in particular, was quite dismissive of the telling.

"Descending from both the Chandii and one of the eldest lines of the godsblood makes her rather special, I would say," Magwyn kept on. "That, and I've seen her...their power firsthand. It was able to summon the nether at will, and it smothered a cast of Eldn flame like it was a breath over a candle. I doubt the demon would relinquish such power unless it was absolutely necessary."

"I hate to say it, but I prefer Aunt Maggie's reasoning here," Marsea said. "All the same, we can't let what-ifs stand in our way. We can only control so much. But what little we *can* control, we must make count for all the stars." She backed up to take Aiden's side and faced the rest of the group. "For now, it would seem the nether hasn't sensed the ward nest, isn't interested, or, for whatever reason, cannot use them as we can, which gives us some time to prepare. We should return to Lancastle forthwith, assess the damages, then Des and I will portal north to retrieve *The N'therN'rycka.*"

"While the rest of us rally the guard and fortify the citadel," Rhymona added. "At least as much as can be had. I can only assume that is where the nether beast is headed next, given its present course."

"What do you reckon we have?" Aiden inquired. "A day? Mayhaps two?"

"Two feels generous," Rhymona said. "Either way, that is where The

Spellbind currently resides, and we'll likely need all the juice we can get to conjure a godsgate."

"What about the other grimoires?" Remy asked.

"I have a feeling they will find their way to us," Aunt Magwyn answered. "Tetherow aims to end the Giftborn Age, which means it will be hunting the other grimoires, *our* grimoires, and in doing so, all of us."

CHAPTER FIVE

THEY FOUGHT AS ONE. Taut as a clenched fist. As though they'd done so a thousand times before. Each member an essential extremity bound to the next, a blade's span apart, carving a black and red tide across the ghoul-ridden forest back to Courowne's corpse-strewn cobble.

Alley to avenue and back to alley, they kept a tight line, one bloodbath to the next, collecting a stray here and there, up to a half dozen by the time they reached the street containing the ward house, where considering the dreadful state of the other nearby dwellings, it was something beyond remarkable that the rickety old cottage somehow still clung to its walls.

Remy chased the fire in his veins, pushing down the corkscrew terror squeezing at his heart, as he reached the cottage first.

We're going to make it.

GUTTING THE SHADOWS. BLADE WHAT SPARES MAY COME.

On it.

Clicking from within sent his fever spiraling, as Thira whispered a Chandiian curse into the moving obscurities, and multiple shapes altered from solid to liquid in an instant, painting the walls with their insides, the remains of their bodies thumping to the floor.

One. Two. Three. Four.

Remy thrust his watchman's blade into the screeching maw of the nearest ghoul, the Eldn-hot steel melting bone and brain matter slick as a warm knife through butter, spilling a thick, black goo across the hardwood in cuts and chunks.

Such was his madness that he barely felt the exchange as the gift-blessed blade passed through the whole of the fiend's skull and out the other side.

Clear, he thought as Thira surged to the surface, the ward's name crackling off their tongue before he even reached the far wall, where he compressed his hand to the shimmering sigil.

"Wards open!" he shouted through the din of clicking sounds and buzz of corpse flies, his voice cracking. "Move your asses!"

They had mere seconds before they were overrun by a city's worth of undead.

Marsea, Rhymona, and a pair of goldcoats defended the ward house entrance from outside as the survivors followed Magwyn and Julia into the portal one by one.

"Keep moving," Remy ordered. "Don't stop. Don't look back."

Once they were all through, his attentions returned to the last of the lot outside the cottage.

"Final call!" he yelled as Marsea darted across the span of the open doorway, that terrible blade of hers radiating all manner of crimson nightmare, a trail of airborne blood chasing her every movement. A goldcoat appeared in the entryway window a blink later, wrestling a ghoul to the ground, as a couple more survivors trickled into the cottage. Remy watched as the goldcoat scrambled back to his feet in time to get mauled by a second larger ghoul, taking him out of the doorway's open view.

"That's the last of them," Desmond said as he and Lenore disappeared into the portal.

Rhymona backstepped into the cottage next and a blighter rushed in after her, clipping itself against the doorjamb, sending it tumbling violently to the floor. As it made to rise back to its feet, the battle-magus lunged at it, piercing it between a pair of ribs with her mae'chii to keep it at bay before bringing Fucker down into its crown, retracting both blades, smooth as a switchblade's spring, and shifting her momentum back toward the ward.

As the magus passed through to Lancastle, Marsea and Beldroth's wolf raced through the cottage doorway, a river of floating blood and ghouls pouring in after her.

Remy dropped his sword through the ward and snatched a fresh egg of Eldn flame from the gift's hoard.

"*Thas'kon ech vira dhu leckt!*" he growled, hurling the azure curse across the room before twisting back into the portal after Marsea's shadow.

He landed on his ass on the other side as half a blighter's arm passed through after him, severing at the elbow upon the ward's collapse, slapping down onto the stones between his legs, its ruinous red fingers still twitching with reanimated life.

He kicked away from it as screams defiled his eardrums.

New frying pan, new fire, he thought for what felt like the thousandth time in the past quintweek. *A fucking freezing cold fire.*

Remy retrieved his watchman's blade, pushed up to his feet, and shifted toward the latest series of cries and shrieks, which could be seen in the snowfall just outside the freshly missing outer wall of the shop.

A ring of corpses surrounded a rather nasty-looking phaedrylax that had impaled one of the Royalguard with its massive nether appendage while its human remains drove a knife into a second screaming soldier again and again and again. And in the middle of all this horror, a girl scarce older than Julia, knelt before the skewered bluecoat, crying out to her father as his body gushed the last of its lifeblood and convulsed unnaturally.

A second portal rippled to life somewhere off to his left, and Marsea tugged at his arm. He turned toward the white-gold ward glow and found Rhymona had called this one forth. By its placement, he knew it would take them back into the guest quarters of the citadel.

Desmond, Julia, and one of the survivors lifted up their mother's body and carried it through the undulating puddle.

"Remy?" His name filtered through in the guise of Marsea's voice. "Come on, we have to go. There's nothing more to be done here."

The girl.

The phaedrylax shifted its malevolent gaze inside the shop at them, its smile stained in scarlet, as though it knew what it was doing, as though it took immeasurable joy in it.

Just enough of the abomination's human half remained for Remy to recognize his face from back when about the castle walls, though he couldn't quite place the name. At Remy's glower, the phaedrylax's smile opened wider, showing a row of broken teeth, before his lips curled up further unveiling a second series of long jagged fangs.

The watchman jerked away from his sister's pulling, raising a crackling sphere of azure in his palm, and took a step toward the netherspawn, the memory of the father and daughter from Brymshire flashing through his mind.

Not this one.

Not this time.

"Remy!" Marsea howled. "Don't be a bloody fool. There's too much yet to be done and there's too many out there."

"Oi, I'm fresh out of fucks to give, you two," Rhymona spat, "and I'm through this ward in five seconds flat, so get your arses through it or you can go fuck along your merry."

"Remy, leave it," Marsea pleaded. "We all need you. I need you."

I said fuck off! His words came back for the haunt.

No more running.

The phaedrylax squared its shoulders at Remy, daring him to make a move, grinding its nether appendage slowly inside the writhing bluecoat's gut, adding insult to injury. Impossibly, the girl wailed louder at her father's miserable bellowing, cold clouds masking her lament.

YOU CANNOT SAVE HER, REMY, Thira contended. *IT WILL NOT LET YOU.*

Like hells.

IT IS ONLY TOYING WITH YOU. IT CAN TASTE YOUR FEAR. YOUR SHAME.

"I have to try."

And as the watchman crunched a step forward, the appendage tore free of the bluecoat's stomach, viscera in tow, and fastly slithered around the crying girl, constricting about the span of her body as it took her up into the air and crushed her to a silent pulp before her disemboweled father's body could hit the ground.

"You fucking bastard!" Remy flung the egg of Eldn fire at the grinning wretch, watching it catch upon the human part and begin to boil the skin.

Burning, trudging forward, the fiend maintained its devilish grin, until the flame ate away the skin from its face and reached the growth of nether protruding from its shoulder and backside.

"Remy, we have to go." Marsea's voice again.

And the watchman turned back with his sister into the guest chamber portal as the creature commenced its death shrieks, its nether flesh bubbling up and bursting into wet clouds of ash and obsidian.

"STARS ALIVE, Remy what in vaelnation was all that?" Marsea berated him the moment they were through.

"You wouldn't understand," he murmured, sending his scowl astray of the group.

"Really? That's what you're going with?"

"Stay the lecture, Marsea," Remy said. "I was being a fool. Let's just leave it at that, yeah? It won't happen again."

"It had better not. We can't afford to...*I* don't want to lose you again." She turned to the others as the Courowne survivors stole into the castle corridors. "Any of you."

I MUST REST FOR A TURN, Thira said.

Do as you must.

Remy found their mother laid out upon the bed, Julia covering her face with fabric taken from one of the pillows.

Exhaustion stole upon him in Yvemathira's absence.

"Marsea?" A voice rose from the hallway outside.

"Poppy?" Marsea replied.

A figure appeared inside the torchlight a moment later and Remy locked eyes on the instrument clutched firmly in both of her hands, reared back and ready.

"Good gravy, is that a ruddy frying pan you're wielding?" Marsea asked, speaking the words straight from Remy's head.

"What?" Poppy lowered the cast-iron killer, a sheepish expression creeping across her cherubic countenance. "I was in the scullery when all of this started. It seemed a right decent choice considering." By the look of the thing, it appeared she'd cracked a few noggins with it in the place of eggs and rather freshly.

"I'd have gone with the butcher's blade myself," a second voice said as its owner poured inside the chamber behind Poppy and stopped cold as he met Remy's gaze.

"Edgar," the name stumbled clumsily out of the watchman's mouth as though half-soused. Hardly a word at all, really.

His mere appearance drank the air from Remy's lungs and sent a tingle throughout his loins as their nights spent patrolling The King's Wall came rushing back over him. Their long walks and talks, which naturally lead to dalliance. The cold, which inevitably forced them near to touching. The inviting gaze in Edgar's eyes that wouldn't seem to let him go, despite his reticence.

It's a lark, he'd thought at first. A cruel jape. He'd seduce me and play me for the fool. The same old song and dance that always found him, even amongst the dogs and drear of the Kingswatch. Still, he indulged, the fool he was. But Edgar Alewine surprised him. Bending in with purpose. His lips tasting of liquor and mint leaves. His—

"Oh, that's right." Marsea purred. "You two know each other from The King's Wall, don't you?" And then her lip quirked up slightly and she made that annoying Marsea face that always seemed to find a fashion whenever she uncovered something most unexpected.

"You could say that." Remy brushed off the thundering of his heart.

"What all started exactly?" Aunt Magwyn asked, mercifully saving him from Marsea's prying.

Though, knowing his sister and her eerie ability to read him like an open book, he suspected she already knew something scandalous passed between him and the good Captain Alewine.

A tale for another time, mayhaps.

"The madwoman and her masked marauders," Frying Pan Girl answered.

"They appeared as though from thin air," Edgar added. "Only a few of us made it out of the dining hall unscathed. Most of the others are holed up a few quarters down."

"It's not safe here," Rhymona said. "Dysenia knows about this portal. Hells, it was likely her which crafted the damned thing. And she likely knows more about these walks than most."

"They left a while back," Edgar asserted. "The councilman said they were after something in the upper halls."

"Or someone," Magwyn ventured, "namely Raelan Harver. Don't forget, Pion is a Ravenholme loyalist. I expect he was one of the marauders with Dysenia's group."

"Pion?" Julia questioned from their mother's bedside. "He wouldn't."

"Darling, your brother cannot be trusted," Magwyn came quick to the cut.

"It's true," Marsea appended.

"The bastard tricked me," Desmond said. "And helped the demon complete its possession. He's lost himself to Tetherow's artifices."

"I'm afraid they're right, Jules." The youngest's scowl fell on Remy last. "Pion has gone too far. I know he is your blood, but he is the enemy and must be treated as such."

"I understand," she mumbled.

"Hey," Remy halved the space between them. "I would never ask this of you if I didn't believe in its importance."

"I know."

"Promise me, Jules. Promise all of us. If you find yourself in Pion's company, promise you won't hear his pleas for your aid. He is a vile snake with only his own ambitions at heart."

"I promise," she managed through a furrowed brow and an even deeper frown before taking in the rest of the group. "Do you all mean to harm him?"

"Only if he forces it from me," Marsea said, sheathing her haxanblade horror.

"I'll do everything not to," Remy followed. "But if he endangers others..."

"Then he will deserve it," the girl finished in typical Harver form. "Fair is fair."

"Speaking of others," Rhymona said, "we need to be gathering—"

"They are gathered," a voice rasped from the doorway, belonging to that of Wils Gilcrest.

"Wils," Magwyn gasped.

Gilcrest's sudden attendance was as much of a shock as anyone's, Remy reckoned, especially given his age and long-standing bouts with poor health, but it was good to see a familiar face that hadn't yet become twisted by the nether's plague.

He turned to Marsea as Magwyn wrapped Gilcrest in a gentle hug and found a mask of dread sprawled across her face. *That's odd.* Gilcrest looked like hammered shit to be sure, but certainly not enough to produce an expression like the one his sister presently wore.

The watchman pulled Marsea aside. "What's wrong?" he whispered.

Her eyes glistened with guilt. "Sir Wils and I...we had an episode before all this began."

"What sort of episode?"

"Cas had him chained in the cellars. Ravenholme believed he was withholding information regarding Ledgermaine's whereabouts."

"Gods' wounds, Marsea, what did you bloody do?"

"I might have given him the bum leg there."

"You *might* have?"

"Lower your voice, please. I had to, all right. I was still..."

"You know what, no," Remy said. "I'm not doing this with you. Not again. This is your burden to bear, Marsea, whatever it is. I have enough of my own already."

"You pulled me over here to ask, didn't you?"

"And that's because you looked as though you'd soiled your trousers at the appearance of a dodgy old geezer with a bad hobble, I thought he might be possessed or..."

"Fine," Marsea interjected, rolling her eyes. "Care to explain you and Edgar then?"

Remy swallowed, briefly glancing at his swordbrother, careful not to seize his attention entirely.

"Hester's heart, I knew it," Marsea uttered. "You fancy him, don't you?"

"Fancied, fucked, forgot," Remy said before he started back toward the group. "Do catch up."

"Fucked!" she breathed, lighting up like a candle.

"You lower your voice, yeah."

"Remy!" she answered in a whispered yell. Though Marsea would never admit to it, she loved gossip as much as the next incurable busybody, in particular when it involved his, shall we say, intimate affairs.

"We survive all this I'll dish along the details," he promised. "Hells, I'll sing it from the King's balcony with bells on." *The fool you are.*

"Oh, you better believe we're surviving all this now, Rembrandt Lanier. Maidens to morrows."

"Maidens to morrows," he returned. "I like the confidence." And despite the times, the first true smile in a wolf's age passed between them.

CHAPTER SIX

DESPITE HIS GHASTLY APPEARANCE, the Empress couldn't suppress her delight at the sight of him, pulling Sir Wils in close, a wave of ginger root and cellar dank washing over her at their embrace.

"I can't believe it's you," Magwyn whispered into the stench of his soiled cloak, her emotions welling, as though no time at all had passed since they'd last beheld one another.

It went without saying really, but her heart still sang his name, high as the hallowed heavens, and low as the uncharted sea.

She could still envision the scene perfectly before her, though it was now a quarter century to the rot. Sir Wils, at her brother's side, eyes downcast yet determined, lips thinned in obedient frustration, and she inside a carriage bound for Courowne sobbing uncontrollably. His hardened gaze flicked up to meet hers one last time as the carriage passed, an eternity in an instant, a lifetime's worth of love languishing within. Enough to let her know he was hers regardless of the turn; and at that moment, she knew unerringly that she would forever remain his. No matter her House name or titles. No matter what bed she lay in and what bedfellow found her side.

Go figure, it would take the bloody end of the world for the fates to allow their reunion.

"And you remain an absolute spectacle," Sir Wils returned. "If only we had the time for a proper dalliance."

"If only." She echoed, a certain measure of sadness stealing upon her visage.

"Lirae Thirsby, if you wouldn't mind," Wils said, and the House Mother hooked an arm inside his and helped him back out into the corridor. "Here will do," he added once they put a bit of stone between them and the guest chamber chatter.

"There we are," Lirae Thirsby said as Sir Wils relaxed against the wall.

"You are indeed a godsend, Imogen," Wils said. "Would you allow us some time alone?"

"Of course, milord." Lirae Thirsby presented a slender smile, bowing slightly in Magwyn's direction, before flowing quietly back into the congregation behind them.

"I can mend some of your wounds," Maggie offered once Lirae Thirsby disappeared inside the guest chamber.

"So, it is true then," the councilman said, the azure rings in her irises reflecting back inside his glassy orbs. "You and Emyria are soulbound?"

"We are."

"And you chose this?"

"I did. Suffice to say, without Emyria, I wasn't long for the court of Courowne, and I never would have survived its fall. She proved a rare blessing during my darkest days."

"And for that, I am truly grateful. Though you can't fault an old man his doubts."

"I suppose not."

"The soldier and scribe told me as much, but I was reluctant to believe them. They claimed Remy and Yvemathira bonded as well."

"'Tis true, all of it. And now Desmond and Hrathgon," Magwyn said.

HAVE A CARE, MAGWYN. DO NOT LET YOUR SENTIMENTS FOR THIS MAN CLOUD YOUR JUDGMENTS.

He's harmless, Em. And I trust no other more with my wellbeing.

I KNOW WE ARE NOT ON THE BEST OF TERMS PRESENTLY, BUT SOMETHING FEELS OFF ABOUT HIM. DO YOU NOT SENSE IT?

I sense nothing of the sort. What exactly seems off?

I CANNOT QUITE NAME IT JUST NOW. IT WOULD SEEM HE HAS A RATHER KEEN TALENT FOR MASKING HIS EMOTIONS. DO KEEP YOUR GUARD UP IN HIS COMPANY.

Of course.

"Here, let's walk together." She shimmied up against him, assuming Lirae Thirsby's previous position, sliding underneath an armpit, and wrapping her arm around the small of his back for support as they trailed down the corridor to the next chamber over.

Against him, she couldn't help but note just how much skinnier he'd become. And she was reminded of Rhonyn's tidings a few winters back when Sir Wils fell sick with the flux and nearly found the grave at its presence. She'd prayed for his strength to return for days and quints and months until it became something like a circadian ritual, and even after Rhonyn reported his recovery sometime later, she still kept her heart's desire in her thoughts. She really couldn't help it, all told.

Once inside, she eased him down upon the bed's edge and spanned the room in a wink, whisking back the thick navy and gold-trimmed curtains, allowing a gray pall of daylight to spill past her and into the chamber recesses. A light snowfall drifted down from the heavens beyond, almost in slowed motion, as though the moon itself was trundling to a halt, caught up in its orbit by the nether's emergence.

"Where is it the worst?" Maggie asked as she turned back to take in the councilman.

"My knee, but Lirae Thirsby has made the pain manageable and I won't have you wasting a jot of your gift on me. There are far more important affairs to attend just now, and I will be more than fine in the interim."

"Still putting everyone else first, I see." It warmed her heart to know that Sir Wils still held some measure of honor and decency, especially in the face of his rapidly declining health, and she couldn't help but wonder just how much of the man remained from their days of secret holidays and romantic reveries.

"Putting you first, at least. Like I should have done back when."

"Wils…"

"Whit may have despised me for it, but if anything in this world was worth a king's revilement, it would have been your hand in mine for all these cycles."

The ghost of a grin befell her as she eased onto the bed next to him. "I do appreciate the words…"

"Better late than never, I suppose."

"I never stopped loving you, Wils."

"Nor I, you, Maggie." His voice cracked at her name and slow rolling tears wandered down to his jawline before he quickly wiped them away. "I thought about coming to Courowne every day since. Especially after the coup, but…"

"There were other concerns, I would imagine," Magwyn finished.

"Always and evermore," he said, daubing a sleeve against the wetness forming at the end of his long, hooked nose. "I couldn't just leave the place to House Harver. I wouldn't."

"No doubt your presence kept this place in decent moral standing considering."

"I did my best. But know you were always in my thoughts. Every day since our parting. The first thought I had every morning and the last each nightfall before retiring."

Oh, Wils. It was all coming back to her now. He could certainly pour on the charm when temptation struck.

"Rhonyn promised you were well taken care of," he continued, "and quite honestly, that was all that mattered to me in the end. As you well know, I'm not a man for stirring the pot, and pissing off an emperor falls fairly far down on my list of priorities to accomplish."

"As well it should." He still had that dry wit she cherished so. "Drezhal was an ugly, flawed man, but prize well, he never mistreated me. Not once. Unfortunately, the same could not be said for others."

"It warms me to hear your husband wasn't a complete prat. A fair few stories over the cycles painted a rather unflattering picture of all the Dalivants. Obviously, I had my worries."

"Worry no longer, my love. I'm home now and I have no plans on leaving again." She could almost feel Emyria wincing at the words. "And you should know I never held it against you, Wils. Our parting. It was a dreadful situation my brother put us in, and I understood the ramifications of you bucking up to him. I also understood he was your closest friend and you had to make a hard choice. An unfair choice. Now, do I fancy myself a lady worth fighting for? Yes. Absolutely. But I never would have been able to forgive myself if it came at the cost of your freedom. Or your life."

"And so here we are."

"Here we are."

"Though you are Eld, Maggie, the madwoman will be a problem. She's housing a 'byss walker's essence. One of the Vharyn'ashi."

"...Vharyn'ashi?..." Emyria slithered to the surface. "...Their seed died out centuries ago..."

"Not all of them."

"...How can you possibly know this?..."

"You might recall my studies into black magic lore back when."

"Of course." She'd let him have a black tongue on more than a few occasions regarding the like, nary a curse missed.

"Marrovard's underground archive proved more than plentiful, and that gateway eventually led a daft and curious lad on a jaunt down demonology lane." He cleared his throat. "As you might expect, I met some, shall we say, less than savory folks in the process, folks with knowledge that was very wisely withheld from the academic world, most notably from the Ministry and their ilk, rot, rot, bloody rot, unimportant. One of the few slivers of this knowledge I managed to uncover involved the Vharyn'ashi. Primordial horrors named by the ancient ones as blank-eyed devils, for that was how one could determine their possession of a mortal being."

Magwyn recalled Aiden's transformation under Tetherow's control. The bright, icy-white orbs full of unshakeable malice. And then that of Dysenia Deadeyes in the ritual chamber.

"They are described as chaos hounds, these demons," Sir Wils continued. "They are drawn to it. They feed off of it. And once they find a proper pinch of it, they milk it for all its worth. And this one here survived long enough to luck upon the gift. The very crown of chaos."

"No. This one here found the nether," Desmond corrected from the doorway. "That was how it managed to hide all these cycles. It found the nether and through the nether it found the gift and then it fashioned a way to control a bit of both." The Lanier prince stepped into the chamber, his albino crow walking the length of his outstretched arm to the writing table near the door. "Marsea and I are set to depart shortly. I thought I would apprise you."

"Departing?" Wils asked.

"Aye. We venture north. To The Scar."

"The Scar? Whatever for?"

"To retrieve *The N'therN'rycka* and put your Vharyn'ashi demon back in its box. Most of the others plan to join in with the vanguard or man the battlements, but Remy and Rhymona intend to confront this Dysenia creature in the upper halls."

"The two of them will not be enough for that fiend," Maggie said.

"I argued the same, but they would not hear me. Though, in fairness, I'm not exactly high on either one's list of fucks to bother with, now am I? Mayhaps you might have an easier time gaining their ear?"

"You mean to say *The N'therN'rycka* lies in The Scar?" Wils inquired. "As in the original *N'therN'rycka*?"

"Here's hoping," Desmond said before turning back outside the chamber, and nearly toppling over Lirae Thirsby in the process.

"Apologies, Your Highness," the House Mother stammered.

"Pardon," Desmond muttered before disappearing, Lenore taking flight to catch him up.

Flushed, Lirae Thirsby nodded back at them both, collected herself, and started down the corridor in the opposite direction.

"And I thought I looked ghastly," Sir Wils said. "I can't imagine what all that boy has been through."

"I doubt anyone can." Magwyn brushed a wandering black curl out of her face. "By every account save its actuality he belongs to the grave, and yet—"

She left it hanging for lack of a proper explanation.

"And yet—" Wils echoed. "The gods know, I'm too old for hope and expectations." Maggie felt his hand collapse upon hers. "But you do know how to bring it out of me, don't you?"

"We're off for the uppers," Remy said as he and Rhymona entered the chamber, hand upon the hilt protruding from his waist. "And before you start in, my mind is set and I won't be talked out of it."

"And Thira?" she inquired.

"...I agree with Remy..." His eyes burned with azure grit. "...Dysenia must be put down..."

"Very well." The Empress rose to her feet, Emyria vying for the surface, and Magwyn permitting. "...But we must be smart, sister. Wils has explained the creature is Vharyn'ashi..."

"...Vharyn'ashi?..." Remy glared at Sir Wils. "...The abyss was folded ages ago..."

"True, it was," Wils answered. "But there were yet some of its horrors not within at the folding. Horrors haunting our world. Haunting the other moons. The Vharyn'ashi are parasites, vaporous in form, and they cannot bring mischief on this plane without a host. I presume this one was summoned onto our plane some time before the fold and has been jumping creature to creature since."

"Not only that, but it has found a way to bind itself to this plane through gift manipulation and forging phylacteries," Desmond added as the others joined in their council. "If this Dysenia has one of these Vharyn'ashi in her, as you say, killing her should force it out."

"And then what?" Rhymona questioned.

"And then it will try to take another host. So, you will want to limit how many of you lot are near it when you ax the bitch."

"Fucking come off it," the magus grumbled.

"When I was in the palace library, I was alone," Desmond kept on, "and it disappeared in seconds, likely because there wasn't another living creature within the vicinity for it to attach itself to. Though, by its parting threats about hunting Autumn next, my assumption is it didn't actually die when it dissipated."

"Then what happened?"

"Fuck if I know. Best guess: either it pissed off back to the nether or back to its phylactery for the next poor, unsuspecting bastard to find it."

"Then it should be me and Remy," Magwyn said. "The creature wouldn't dare truss itself to a host housing a dracari soul."

"Yeah, no offense, Mags, but you're fucked in the head if you think I'm playing ghost on this one. I've spent the last thirty cycles of my life thinking I was an orphan, only to find out my aunt has been alive all this time."

"...That creature is not your aunt, I can promise you that. Not anymore..." Magwyn crossed her arms, orbs ablaze. "...I will not keep you from this, Rhymona. Just know, if the Vharyn'ashi comes for you, there will be no hesitation to put you down..."

"I wouldn't have it any other way."

"Then it's settled," Remy said. "No use wasting any more time."

"We'll need to raid the stocks on the way," Magwyn said.

"Assuming there's anything left of it," Sir Wils added.

"May your luck stones prosper," Marsea said from her lean against the entryway.

"And yours to the flourish," Magwyn and Remy returned in unison.

CHAPTER SEVEN

No DOUBT SHE HAS IT," Pion grumbled to Caitlyn as he stepped out into the archives from Marsea's hideaway. "Either Marsea or Magwyn. Gods' wounds, I should have known better than to underestimate her."

"Magwyn?" Caitlyn asked behind the glow of lantern light as the pair started toward the library exit.

"Marsea." *Always playing so coy and innocent.* But Pion knew a practiced manipulator when he crossed one, and the princess proved herself amongst the best, whether she was aware of it or not, utilizing her sweet, comely appearance time and time again to absolute perfection. He'd tried to sway her talents to his advantage only a few short days ago, but he'd come undone a mite after Tetherow's sudden change of plans involving Desmond and allowed his emotions to gain the better of him in the rush, pushing Marsea further away. *The bloody fool I am.*

"She's only one girl," Caitlyn said. "How much of a problem can she be?"

Oh, I do so wonder, my dear lovely Caitlyn, would you say the same of yourself were the roles reversed? She and the princess were not so dissimilar, after all.

"She is giftborn," the warlock winged, "and quite cunning. And she may have a grimoire at her disposal that she's studied for cycles. If she does, indeed, have it, she will undoubtedly become a thorn in our side."

Where are you now, stepsister? What are you scheming? What do you know? His brow furrowed at their last moment together, the anger, the despair, the raw ache in his heart at her spurning, walled off by her bedchamber door. *If only we could speak, if only you'd hear me, I could explain everything. Maybe fix this. We need not be enemies.*

"What's the plan then?" Caitlyn pierced through his pitiful ponderings.

"The only other place I can think to check would be the King's solar. Mayhaps Vaustian got his greedy hands on it first." Pion wiped at his forehead with a cloth. "I'd hoped to avoid mine uncle's company for as long as possible, but it would seem the fates have other ideas."

"I take it you and your uncle don't get on well."

"There's an understatement," he said with a snort. "Though truthfully, no one gets on well with my uncle." They passed the common area and archivist's counter out into the hall. "This way," Pion guided as they made for the stairwell at the corridor's end and a climb the warlock had been dreading since they arrived inside Lancastle's walls.

"How far up?" Caitlyn drew her wand.

"Two floors."

"I'll scout ahead to make sure there's no trouble."

"I won't be far behind," he said as she disappeared up the spiral staircase.

Fucking stairs. Bloody bane of my existence.

Lacking a banister for support, he pressed his palm against the innermost wall, almost hugging it, and followed the wall-walking routine he'd prayed forever abandoned to the past.

Cane first, left foot, then right, stalked by an immediate tremor of searing agony, like stepping on shards of broken glass. *Just like old times.*

Nothing made him feel more ridiculous and utterly pathetic than working his way up a flight of stairs, much less, winding stairs. Such a simple task for most, and yet it took the piss out of him every time.

At least Caitlyn offered to venture ahead, saving him the embarrassment of putting on a hard front, like each step wasn't its own excruciating trial. He clenched his teeth, grinding, four stairs in, a grimace taking shape against his desires, as a fresh stab of pain raced up his entire right side, again and again, every time his snapped twig of a leg took even the slightest measure of weight. And the gods only knew the kinds of foolish expressions his ghastly mug produced under such pitiful conditions.

A few steps higher, Ripley waited on his struggling master, licking at a paw, indifference incarnate.

"Don't mind me," the warlock wheezed as he passed his furry familiar, the backs of his jaw buzzing at the endless waves of discomfort, "just shaving cycles off my life here."

"Hold your ground, sir!" Caitlyn's voice echoed passed him from some rest above. "I said hold!"

Pion halted. "Cait—" he uttered before a shriek of wand magic cut him short.

Shit.

A fist formed and he drove the base of it into the wall, digging himself forward, one punch at a time, forcing himself to move faster, hunting the shots of pain, thrusting himself onward against his warped body's rigid nature.

Go to her! he bade Ripley, staying the impulse to varg into the cat and leave himself open to whatever the hells found Caitlyn.

A mad war cry split the brief silence and a second wand blast wailed out, chased by a third, both thudding into something solid, as torchlight from the open floor up ahead flickered into the stairwell's shadows.

"Caitlyn!" he rasped again, desperation devouring as he crossed a stair over to the outer wall, collapsing hard against it, pushing himself back upright, clawing at the slippery stones, doing his damnedest to propel himself closer to the only person left on the moon he even partway trusted.

Not her. Not now. Take anyone else, you craven bastards.

The center of his palm began to itch, urging him to draw upon the warlock's well, his blood boiling for release. "Caitlyn," he crowed again, fingers pinching a thin strand of the lifeblood pooling inside his missing chunk of flesh.

Here comes the fool's charade.

"Still alive," she said, backing into the stairwell, pale as a hauntling. "But something's not right up here."

I should say. A few steps more and Pion joined her upon the landing, staring into the torchlit phantasmagoria that comprised the King's corridor.

"He just charged at me," Caitlyn whispered as they cautiously approached the motionless body. "And his eyes…"

Pion's face screwed up at the poor dead bastard lying next to a smashed lantern with a pair of apple-sized holes burned through his chest, the smell of over-cooked meat billowing off of him.

Turns out the Lady Ellsbury was a crack spellslinger in the mold of her father. And lucky for her, given this ghastly mongrel's lunatic visage.

"By the dilation and bloodshot in his eyes, I'd say he was hexed, not blighted. Some sort of madness curse. Likely bloodborne." He cast an inquisitive glance over at his companion. "You didn't get any on you, did you?"

"No. I never let him close enough," Caitlyn assured.

"You'll want to keep it that way. If this curse is what I think it is, if it gets inside, it'll devour you in seconds."

"I don't know what's more disturbing. The curse or how it is you know all of this."

Shouts and manic laughter echoed from up ahead, drawing their attention.

"Sounds like this asshole has a few friends," Pion groaned. Though, mercifully, most of the voices were fading further into the distance.

"Should we head back? Is there another way?"

Tap. Tap. Tap. Something else answered from the pitch ahead. The sound of steel kissing stone.

"It might be a little late for that," he answered. *All the other horrors cast upon in this place, what gormless imbecile let loose a fucking madness curse about the lot?*

He and Caitlyn sank back into the shadows between torches, his hand falling upon the kindleblade's hilt at his waist.

"*Lovers twined tempt threads of fate,*" a woman sang, steel scratching across stone anew.

"She comes within spitting distance, you make her feel it, yeah," Pion whispered.

"*Torn asunder, unbound hate.*" The blade came away sharply from the wall, creating an angry spark, and unveiling the woman's position some twenty paces away. "*Of he who dawns the endless night.*"

Pion unsheathed the kindleblade. Not that he would have offered much contest if it came to a clash of irons, though its presence might buy him a few extra seconds were he to require a blood well conjuring.

"Exiled, loathed, cast into plight," she finished on a hard note, holding just short of the firelight.

The warlock's mind began to race with anticipation, a finger trembling over a clasp upon his cane, a clasp that would release the wooden shell for the hidden length of silver within.

"I see you." A knife appeared, trained on them, dragging its mad wielder into view.

Another bluecoat.

Pion recognized her as Ora Mosshart, a Royalguard Captain and one of his father's most trusted. *He must be close. Assuming he's still drawing breath.* And an even darker thought wandered through at that.

What if his father was cursed? Or worse yet, what if Julia was?

"Ora, where is my father?" Pion asked. "Is he alive?"

"As far as I know." A puckish grin sprouted upon the soldier's blood-speckled face, one that betrayed her cryptic words.

"Where is he?" Pion's finger settled upon the cane's clasp. The look in Mosshart's darkly haunters screamed of malefic intent.

Stay in control, his mind whispered. *You're in control.*

"Locked in the King's solar, last I saw. Not that it much matters. The demon's in there with him now."

"Dysenia?" he asked.

"I know what you are, Pion," Mosshart hissed. "Who you are working with."

"I very much doubt that."

"I watched your demon master and the others, butchering any bastard unfortunate enough to chance upon them. You lot should be hung, drawn, and quartered for aligning yourself with such a fiend. The both of you. Your remains set to the flame."

"We don't have time for this, Ora. Let us pass."

She stopped ten paces away. "I don't think I'll be doing anything of the sort."

"It's clear the effects of the curse are wearing off. Why risk your life?"

"Is it wearing off, or have I simply embraced it?"

"Obviously, you have some capacity to reason."

"And who's to say it's my life at stake here?" Her countenance hardened. "I've killed so many, after all, these last few days. My friends, sword-brothers and swordsisters." She held the knife up before her eyes, catching the torchlight in its scant remains of silver, fresh blood dripping off its edge. "I can still see their faces, their terror, as I ran this here blade up and down their bodies, in and out, over and over, against my will. Made a right horrid ruin of my soul, they have." She took a step forward, fixing her fearless dark orbs on him. "But they had to die, didn't they? That's what the voices said. Me or them. Me or them. And the most of *them* were decent folk. Decent enough, at least. Certainly, more decent than you lot." Another slow stride forward. "And yet here you are, one of the most devious scoundrels I've ever come across asking for my mercy." She held again at six paces apart from him. "Now given what I've wrought this past quintweek, and what you deserve, you tell me honest, Pion, why in vaelnation would I ever let you live?"

"Enough from the loon." A bright golden light flared to life next to him as Caitlyn and her crackling wand held his side.

"The loon?" Amusement colored Mosshart's voice.

"Let us pass, or I'll put you down like I did your ugly cohort back there."

"You can try," Mosshart said, reaching behind her back.

"Feint!" Pion cried as the Captain flung a hidden dagger from her offhand.

The sequence to follow was like something ripped straight from the pages of a Chandiian tragedy (or comedy, depending on one's impression of such, shall we say, illogical absurdities).

Mosshart's blade whistled between Pion and Caitlyn, a skinny blur, missing Caitlyn's face by a breath, as she snapped it askew with her father's wand, falling away to the ground in the effort.

The warlock released his cane's clasp, backstepping as he ripped the hidden blade from its coffin and prepared himself.

Only a few strides away, Mosshart lunged at him, her hungry blade growing big as a lance, before something dark and fast bolted across her ankles.

The creature yelped as the two collided and Mosshart came staggering forward, losing her balance, Pion's outstretched blade sinking straight through her jugular, down to the quillons, before she crashed into him, taking them both to the floor in a wild heap.

At once, the violence of their collision and the pain of the kicked creature washed over him.

Ripley!

Gods' wounds, but the beautiful, fat furball actually made himself useful for once. Quite useful.

Though Pion's victory was short-lived, his heart thumping in terror as he felt the warmth of Mosshart's blood begin to ooze over his naked hands, realizing he'd stuck her not once but twice as he made to squirm out from underneath her deathly spasms.

Oh, shit. Oh, shit. Oh, shit. Oh fuck. Blood rumbled in his ears. *Keep it out of me. Keep it the fuck out of me. Not like this.*

A vision passed of him cackling hysterically down the hall, crawling across the castle filth searching for the first random asshole with a cut of steel to put him out of his deranged misery.

You're in control. Stay in control.

"Pion!" Caitlyn cried as she hurried over to him and helped him away from Mosshart.

How long has it been?

How long does it take?

He felt a sickness swell to the base of his throat and began to quiver all over, but did those shakes belong to his mounting state of dread or the all-consuming curse?

Something should have happened by now.

Surely, something would have happened.

Wide-eyed, he inspected the warlock's well, twisting his gore-coated hand from front to back, expecting the madness to have seeped between the scabs of his exposed flesh. There was no way it couldn't have.

And yet…

"Are you?" Caitlyn started.

I'm in control. Still in control.

"Di…didn't see that coming," he said with a crack of the voice, unsure whether to laugh or cry, the shock of it all preventing both.

"No, I reckon not. I can't believe that just fucking happened."

"The madness, it…it should have found me by now. I don't understand how it hasn't."

"Some sort of natural immunity mayhaps?"

"Mayhaps." And almost certainly as good of an explanation as he was like to get, expanding the ever-growing list of fucktittery that no longer made a lick of sense anymore.

Gasping and gurgling, greasy hair in her face and mouth, Mosshart rolled onto a side and brought a palm over the spewing wound in her neck, but became quite still only moments later, her bloodshot orbs disappearing behind half-closed eyelids.

Pion's vision trailed down to his kindleblade protruding from Mosshart's gut then to Ripley, who was hissing and shaking his head as though he'd taken water in the ear, as he wandered unsteadily back to his master's side.

"Fine work, my feline friend," Pion commended, sharing his familiar's ache. And the gods know that barmy bitch kicked the ever-living shit out of him, didn't she? Ripley thought his master walked funny. Well, old lazybones was going to be walking funny for the foreseeable future after this batty little cockup.

"I'll say," Caitlyn added. "I need to get me one of those."

"Trust, the branding burns like a knife-end, but how can I argue against it now?"

In all fairness, the end of his life also meant the end of Ripley's, so his savior's interference wasn't entirely without a selfish thought, though it heartened Pion to know the little sluggard had his back when it came down to it.

Moaning, he dragged himself back over to Mosshart's corpse, mindful to avoid her pooling blood, and slowly slid the dribbling blade back out the front of her neck, where dark fluids continued to spill out thick and copious. He wiped the silver clean with his sweat cloth as Caitlyn handed him the other end of the cane.

"Clever trick, that," she said.

Pion coupled the blade inside the cane again, making sure the spring clicked back into place, and pushed up to his feet, testing that it was reset properly.

"Where does one come about such a sneaky contraption, I wonder?" Caitlyn inquired, as she carefully removed the kindleblade from Mosshart's belly, wrinkling her nose at it.

"I made it myself, of course," Pion answered. "Though I had some study into the design and components from tomes recommended by Tetherow." He held out his palm with the cloth in it and Caitlyn placed the kindleblade atop it. "Though, next time, you better believe I'm tapping the well," he added, as he gave the blade a good cleaning and returned it to its sheath. "No questions asked."

"All this trouble, I'm hoping we're at least near the King's solar."

"It's just around the bend up ahead. With any luck, those other shouts we heard earlier have pissed off in the other direction."

"You'll forgive me if I don't hold my breath," Caitlyn japed as they dared forth into the looming darkness once more.

And despite it all, a smirk befell Pion Harver's hard-boiled countenance. *I daresay,* he mused, *for a pampered richling, this fresh version of the Lady Ellsbury is rather beginning to grow on me.*

CHAPTER EIGHT

SLATTERY," Pion called as the entryway to the King's solar came into view, guarded by a trio of familiar dark-robed figures.

"Harver," Slattery sneered. "Class of you to make the time for us no-name lackeys."

"Your words, not mine," Pion murmured. Though he expected nothing less from the unsavory wretch.

Draven Slattery was of a similar age to Pion and Caitie, which proved about the only positive detail he could rightly name about the man. For, at his core, Slattery comprised every full fucking letter and definition of the word bastard, literal and otherwise. At once bitter and expectant, he gave the Lanier whelps a proper chase for their coin; though, to their credit, at least Seasea and baby brother housed the actual blood of a royal lineage in their veins. As far as Pion knew, by contrast, Slattery was just some wanky whoreson from Bumfuck, Beggarshire, with an unearned chip on his shoulder and a hard-on for the worst breeds of violence.

"And Ellsbury pulls through," Slattery said, ogling Caitlyn, a lunatic smile taking shape. "Good on you, girl. No doubt the old man would be fulsome proud."

Caitie glowered. "I say, Draven, is there not a bucking horse nearby you can readily go place yourself behind?"

"Oof." He caught an invisible arrow in his chest. "And she has one straight for the heart."

"As though you've something of the sort to claim."

"Too true," he kept on. "Terrible shame about your best mate Calem. Had promise, that one."

"Fuck's sake, Slattery," Pion interjected. "Are you quite finished being a bellend just now?"

"Oh, do rein it in, Harver. It was only a bit of humor."

"Because now would be the appropriate time for a bit of humor about the fallen. Have some bloody respect." One of father's old watchwords came round for the call.

For some turds, there ain't enough shine in the sun to get them back even halfway clean.

"I'm quite capable of defending myself, Pion," Caitlyn quibbled, unwilling to give an inch, not even to her allies apparently. "But cheers for the charity."

"Shoo lads, she moves fast, don't she?" Slattery said, winning personality on full display and ever game for a show. "Drunkard Desmond, Mummy's boy Calem, and now Brokeback Harver. I daresay, your standards have dipped, milady." He leered dramatically at her, carving a pinky finger across his cheek. "Though I guess the Misses ain't so fine a fetch now what with the new alterations and all."

Caitlyn flicked her wand up, cutpurse quick, and pressed its end against Slattery's fruits, the pair holding barely a breath apart. "I can make a few new alterations for you as well if you want to keep running your gobshite for the gents."

For obvious reasons, Slattery tensed, stiff as a bowstring, his confidence melting in an instant, as toothless as toothless fuckwits come. "Nope, I'm good right where we're at, thanks."

"I bet you are," Caitlyn withdrew slowly but fixed the wand between them to keep the cur honest.

"Nasty business, these halls," Pion said, fighting the urge to smile at the spectacle. Slattery wanted a show, and by the gods, Caitie bloody gave him all he could handle. "I can assume you lot are responsible for the count of corpses up here?"

"Aye," one of the cultists agreed, removing the half-mask from the lower portion of his face. He was the middle Thorpe brother, the eldest and youngest having succumbed to their bouts with the wretchrot.

"A madness curse," Pion shook his head. "Who would be so daft?"

"Dysenia named it *alzethoth* or some such," Thorpe said. "Said it was like a sickness that lasted a few days. She'd seen it used amongst the wolld in the north beyond The Scar to set the wngar against one another."

Would that he could have the history lesson. But time was of the essence. "I'm assuming our fearless leader is inside?"

"She is," Slattery answered. "But she said no guests were to be permitted."

"I have it under good conviction that my father is in there with her, and I mean to share audience."

"And where he goes, I go," Caitlyn added, a faint bit of light pulsing at the wand's tip.

"Yeah, he's in there. Lost his shit the moment we barged in. Dysenia had to put the surly old tosser down a peg."

"And what is that intended to imply," the warlock took a step forward.

"Don't get all cunt-hurt, Harver. He's still alive."

"Stand aside!" Pion shoved past Slattery and Thorpe, then eyed the third guard, who wore a fool expression, and whose name he couldn't quite recall.

After a moment of tarry, the guard stepped away from the door, motioning for his lordship to enter, and Pion pushed into the chamber to find the gloomy haunt lit dimly by a gutter of hearthfire, his father before said hearth, bound and gagged in a chair in the middle of a blood-drawn pentacle, head hung low as a brigand set to meet the gallows' dance.

Pion fastly perused the rest of the chamber. How long had it been since he'd last graced this room? Nigh on half a decade? Longer? It went without saying really, but the once lavish solar had since taken a turn for the ugly. Banners torn from the walls, sculptures, curios, and wine bottles dashed to bits about the stones.

They met eyes, his father's words muffled through the cloth, and Pion could almost feel the shape of his heart withering in his chest as though it were being squeezed to a pulp by some unforeseen force. He'd never beheld his father in such a weak and vulnerable state before. He hardly knew what to do with it.

But the gods only knew, how many times had he wished for this very scenario to befall him? To have power over his father. To have his father's undivided cares.

Suffice it to say, desperation was not a flattering look on Raelan Harver and satisfaction would not have the heir's company in turn. No, in reality, and for the first time since he could recall, Pion felt something like pity for the man that sired him into this grotty old shithole of a moon only to leave him for the wolves.

"Father," Pion hobbled into the room and ripped the gag down from Raelan's mouth, staring him straight.

"Son," Raelan rasped. "What have you done to yourself?"

Little surprise in those words. "Nevermind what I've done," Pion returned. "Are you infected?"

"I was, but it's wearing off me." Raelan appeared but a shadow of the man Pion left to the rot only days ago. "Though I can't say the same for your cohort over there."

Movement from the balcony drew the warlock's attention as Dysenia slinked back inside from the shifting, slithering shadows, cloaked but for a pair of opaque yellow orbs and a bloodless scowl.

"I know you've the lame leg there, Runt, but going forward I'd appreciate a bit more punctuality, yeah," the ashaeydir carped, drawing back her cowl.

"Dysenia, what is the meaning of this?" Pion groused, eyes darting from his father to the pentacle lines then back up to that of Dysenia Deadeyes.

"Is it not obvious?"

In truth, it was, but he needed to hear the words.

"I need a new host," she said. "And I need you to perform the ritual. I pulled too much getting us here and this saggy bitch is barely hanging on. Considering your father's clout and vigor, he is an ideal choice."

The warlock glanced back at his kin.

Chin up, Pion, his father would say to such a scene. *Eyes hard. Never break. Never show them they've won.*

As much as Pion loathed Raelan for being a ghost in his life, the man was still his father, and he never once actively sought to bring his ghastly spawn any ill-will or ruin, he simply never did anything to prevent it from others. True, it was passive participation, slight after spineless slight, acts Pion would likely never forgive him for, but it didn't warrant a death sentence, and it certainly didn't warrant possession by an entity as cruel and contemptible as that which presently haunted Dysenia Luiryn.

"Absolutely not," he answered, cold as he could conjure, orbs glinting like steel.

You're in control. Stay in control.

"You forget your place, Pion. I am not asking for your permission. My brethren may have taken you under her wing, but you do not defy me my orders."

"Can you not just slag about some other useless halfwit down the corridor and steal *his* life force?" Such had never been an issue before. She took from men and women both, and quite often, regardless of age, race, or disease, fucking them until all that remained was a colorless corpse.

"Of course, I could, you disagreeable little simp. But it would only be a bandage for a death-wound." She stepped into the firelight, her skin both drooping and dried up like that of a sun-beaten husk. "This vessel is nearly hollowed of its gift. Drowning in nether rot. I will require another soon. Before the dawn has her dance. And preferably one of decent standing amongst your people. Considering our time constraints and that most of our options are now blighted, I'm afraid we'll have to settle for the first available. Besides, what has this seditious mongrel ever done for your favor?"

"He is my family."

"He is your *blood*, but let us make one thing clear, he was never your family. None of them were." She drew her wand. "That's why you chose us, remember." The wand leveled on the space between his eyes. "That's why you let us in."

"What's your plan then, Dysenia? Will you murder me here? Then what? Hope you stumble upon a halfway scholared magus with a black heart and a penchant for soul-splicing? Not to mention the five eager souls to bear your transport. Happy fucking hunting there considering the state of this place. As you said. Or is it you actually think you'll last long enough for your brethren to return and summon you on to the next sorry slab of meat you'll burn through before the quint's turn?"

Dysenia held his glare, that ugly, inimitable, lop-sided grin of hers emerging. "I say, for a runt with a malformed backside, you've surely got some spine to you."

"Decent of you to notice."

Dysenia's attentions fell upon Caitlyn. "If not the High Commander, then the spellslinger will have to do. Your choice, Pion, but it must be one or the other."

"His choice my left tit," Caitlyn snapped, whisking her wand up for the defense. "No way in hells I'm letting you run me a ruin like you've done that one."

Fucking hells, Dysenia. Must it always be chaos? Where Tetherow typically exuded calm and order even in the face of failure, the one inside Dysenia wrought an endless maelstrom, destroying anything and everything that stood in its way.

Pion held a hand out at Caitlyn. "Will both of you sheath your cocks for half a second so we can talk this through proper?" He glanced at Dysenia. "I'm sure this squabbling is not what Tetherow would have wanted."

"Tetherow," Dysenia seethed. "I am bloody Tetherow, you feckless halfwit. And Tetherow is not even our true name. It was the surname of the dark seed we attached ourselves to."

"Then speak your true name, lest I forget again," Pion bade.

"You must choose first which one will have me. The absent father or the hard-luck doxy."

"Doxy!" Caitlyn cried.

"I choose neither," Pion followed. "I choose Slattery, or Thorpe, or whoever the other dim fucking shitheel is out there you've got standing idly about. But I won't help you possess my father or sister. Nor will I help you into Caitie. The point of my allegiance was to find family. I won't give up what scant shreds I had of one before all of this began. Do I make myself clear?"

"I commend your chivalry, Runt," the end of Dysenia's wand flickered bright gold. "But you choose one now, or I choose for you. No one is above the slaughter. Everyone must go eventually, down to the rats and dogs."

"Pion," Caitlyn said, fury burning within her honeycomb orbs, the tip of her wand catching the light of her gift. "She so much as makes a move and I put one through her."

"What have we told you time and time again?" Dysenia argued. "If you care for these creatures, if you care for anyone outside of yourself, it will be your undoing." Her hand began to rotate as though twisting a doorknob, the ashaeydir's gift crackling from the tip of her magic-leaking wand. "You knew you were going to have to make some shit choices to get through all this."

Veradon's sake, Pion thought, opening his mouth for a fresh retort as a shriek of magic rent the space in the hallway behind them. *Classic fucking Lancastle. Never a dull moment.*

CHAPTER NINE

If Rhymona recognized any one thing in all the world, it was the leavings of an ashaeydir assassin, and the upper halls of Kingdom Lancastle reeked horribly of the like, no doubt made all the worse by her wicked aunt's macabre pageantry.

Remy glanced back at her after the third set of bodies they'd passed in the King's Hall and she simply nodded. Once you knew the style, once you witnessed its barbarity, there really wasn't much mistaking it. Though she had to admit, something felt off about this particular blood-bath. It appeared rushed and sloppy and lacked the sheer brutality that typically accompanied Dysenia's attendance. Most notably, that she left their faces intact. All but the one thus far.

The magus clutched Fucker in her right hand, squeezing tight, and Val's mae'chii in her left. Somehow the blade's mere presence brought her comfort and renewed strength, however small. And Rhymona whispered its name in her head. A name born from the dust of stars. From the history her kin lost in the desolation of Ashira.

Illuminaria.

Rhymona always named her armaments something daft or vulgar like Cutter, Knifey, or Bitchkiller, at least the ones that stuck around long enough to earn such a travesty, and the gods know she'd gone through her fair share over the cycles. A name was a name was a name, after all.

But Val...Valestriel-shan Alyfain, she always had a certain elegance for even the most violent of things. And this one here bought its song from the highest heavens and their Maidens many, from the very moment Val pulled it from the smithy's forge. And now it pulsed with the ghost of its former master. Of the woman Rhymona loved still. Through this life into the next.

"There's movement up ahead," Magwyn whispered, Eldn energy radiating through the bejeweled scepter she nicked from a hidden panel in her former quarters, the crystal mounted at its head lighting the dark hallway in a pale azure glow. Its recovery began a terribly boring conversation between the Empress and Remy regarding the lost family heirloom long thought stolen by the y'demans during a summit back when.

End of the world and here we are solving decades-old Lanier mysteries like its bloody Mervold Suspense Hour with the nans at book club.

Fortunately, their conversation on the matter was only briefly held.

A wet, wheezing sound rose from the movement and they came upon a familiar face in the Eldn glow slouched against the wall in a puddle of her own fluids, ropes of her insides spilled out across her lap in tangles of red and pink.

"Arkham," Remy gasped, kneeling at her side, resting his blade against the wall.

Amazingly, the woman still drew breath despite a severed arm and copious blood loss.

"High...ness," Arkham labored, glancing up vacantly from her exposed entrails. "Ashaeydir. Raven...holme..."

"Easy then," Remy said.

"Killed a couple...Ki...King's solar..."

"How many remain?" Rhymona asked.

"Fff...four..." she forced the word through her final breath, her orbs growing wide and strained as the death light claimed them.

"Dammit all," Remy cursed, holding a beat before he ran his fingers across Arkham's eyes to close them.

"At least we know what we're in for," Magwyn said.

"By the count of bodies, I'd say they've blasted through most of the mad along with the Guard," Rhymona added.

Remy stood, lifting a Royalguard great shield from between a pair of corpses, buckling it to his arm, before retrieving his watchman's blade. "I will play lead on approach and keep a wall between us. Rhymona you ride my backside until we're close enough for you to do your thing."

The magus nodded.

"Aunt Maggie, you'll keep them busy with Eldn flame until we're close enough to force melee."

"They won't know what hit them." Magwyn patted a pouch at her waist carrying her supply of blood candles raided from the stocks.

"For Lancastle," Remy said, eyes aglow, though not from Yvemathira's presence, "For the Vael."

And Rhymona rather thought the watchman resembled something like a proper King for the first time since...well, since ever.

"For The Vael," she found herself saying, unexpectedly inspired, goose flesh chasing down the span her skin.

Curse these fucking Lanier whelps, she thought. *A surprise every second, each bleeding one of them. Every damn time. And always when I think I'm just about done participating in this poxy-fucked pill of an existence. Bring on the bullshit.*

"RED!" Magwyn howled, a bolt of bright dragonlight shrieking passed Rhymona's wing as they crossed to the left side of the hall, its fever scorching after her shadow's withered shape.

Red was the cipher for left. Green for right.

Fuck, that was close. She could smell burnt leather.

The blast made its mark, setting one of the dark-robed figures aflame, dropping him in a screaming heap as his cohorts drew their wands and returned fire.

Remy bobbed and weaved, collecting wand strikes like a bevy of punches into the lengthy patch of steel, a few angry enough to dent the barrier inward. Dark smoke wafted past them.

Rhymona gripped Illuminaria so the blade trailed down the stretch of her forearm, Fucker poised for the lead strike once they were close enough to cave in skulls.

"Green!" the Empress shouted as they halved the space between the cultists, and Rhymona crouched behind a ducking Remy as they went right and pitched a wall from the ground up. A pair of wand strikes thudded into the other side.

Rhymona glanced behind her and saw Magwyn's great shield approaching. She dropped it to the floor about ten paces behind them as the latest series of wand strikes found her steel wall.

"Move," Remy shouted, and they were racing forward again.

Thonk, thonk, the shield complained.

"Red!" Magwyn called.

They lunged left as one, Eldn flame crackling through the space they held only a heartbeat before, bringing them close enough to smell the burning wood stench of wand magic, and Rhymona twisted around Remy the shieldmaiden, fleet of foot, slinging Fucker end over end at the nearest cultist, the bit burrowing into the middle of his face with a sickening crunch, sending him off his feet backward in a spray of blood, his final wand blast scorching across the ceiling.

Before the remaining cultist could muster a response, Rhymona was on him, growling thunder, a thing most rabid, carving her razorblade forearm across his chest, fastly repositioning Illuminaria to a proper stance as she wrapped around him, before bringing it down full across his backside in confluence with Remy plunging his blade through the bastard's chest.

The poor fuckwit squealed like a pig at a trough.

All the while, from the corner of her eye, through the doorway of the King's solar, across the chamber's hearth glow, she found another wand-wielding figure in wait, one she owed a proper fucking murder to.

"Remy!" she kicked the dying cultist into the prince as a jet of intense white magic wailed passed the others in the chamber out into the hall after them, shredding through the back half of the carved-up cultist's ruined form.

Dysenia! Her heart slammed into the base of her throat.

"Morgandrel," her aunt's voice croaked, rank as a privy pot. "You're still alive."

Backs against the wall, to either side of the entrance, Rhymona and Remy locked eyes.

"How many?" he asked.

"Four, I think," she answered. "Dysenia, Raelan, Pion, and...some girl." Her face was familiar, but Rhymona's mind wouldn't settle enough to conjure a name for it. "I think she may have had a wand as well. And it looked like Raelan was tied to a chair."

"Name yourselves," Pion called out.

"You fucking know who it is, Pion," Remy expelled the name like a mouthful of venom.

"All right, ease up," Rhymona whispered. *We've only room for one loose cannon in this bunch.*

"Stepbrother," Pion answered, rivaling Remy's spite. "Long time, yeah?"

"It's over, Pion," Remy returned. "You're outnumbered. Lay down your arms."

"And what? You'll let me live?"

"Who are the others with you?"

"My name is Caitlyn," the girl spoke.

A spark. *Chuffing hells, that was it, wasn't it? Caitie fucking Ellsbury. The prissy little witling that had a crush on Aiden all those cycles back. Gods' bones, the image was brief, but it looked as though the world had spun her a right proper shitshow since their parting.*

"Caitlyn?" Magwyn uttered as she crossed over to Rhymona's side of the door, drawing another jet of wand magic.

"Fuck this shit," Dysenia's voice rose as a series of flashes followed from inside the chamber resulting in a horrifically chaotic din.

Pion yelled out Caitie's name, Raelan hollered something unintelligible, which ended in a painful cracking sound, and a clattering of objects rang out from seemingly every direction within.

"Is she attacking them?" Remy asked. "Are they against her?"

Rhymona shrugged and poked her head back in to find a return of wand fire coming from their side of the chamber toward Dysenia, who was hiding behind a massive writing table near the balcony firing back.

"It certainly appears that way."

"What the fuck?"

"New plan," Rhymona said. "I'll draw the bitch's fire. She fucks up and shows herself, you and Thira make her feel it, yeah?"

"Are you mad?" the watchman protested.

"I don't even know why you bother to ask anymore." Rhymona held Remy's eyes, thinking of Rill and his awful, but ofttimes useful advice for such darkly scenarios. "Remember, this cunt killed your mum, Remy. Use it."

"I'll watch the others," Magwyn said, scepter aglow. "If they make a move against you, they'll regret it."

"There's a honey." Rhymona grimaced as she backed away from the wall and took a few steps down the hall, digging into the pouch of random potions and playthings she'd nicked from the palace reliquary, pulling out a swamp-green colored vial. "Here." She handed the vial to Magwyn. "Toss this at the back wall behind the writing table."

"What is it?"

"Fuck if I know. Looks ugly as shit though, so hopefully it hurts like a bitch mother."

Remy ripped Fucker from its bloody rest inside dumbarse cultist number two's face and tossed it to her. She caught it, finding her favorite spot upon his spine, huffed in a few heavy breaths, cracked her neck from side to side, rotated her shoulders, and took a couple short bouncy toe-jumps to prepare herself.

This is it, Val. She gently squeezed Illuminaria's hilt. *This goes sideways, I'll be seeing you soon, love.*

She returned to her post at the entryway's edge and peered inside, waiting for a break in the cacophony of gift fire. Though it kept on and on, the seconds ticking by like hours.

Fucking hells, this is endless. If I can just reach her. She sank into her mindscape. *What would give her pause? What would burrow past the demon?* And almost instantly a ploy formed in her head, as though it had been waiting on her to catch up since the fall of her father's House.

A little love letter for Dear Auntie Dreadful.

"Get ready," she bade Magwyn, who nodded. "Remy, when I give the word, toss one of those flaming dragon turds in at the hearth, yeah."

"What are you after, Rhymona?" The watchman inquired as he lay his sword to rest against the wall beside him and conjured an egg of Eldn fire.

"You'll see," she answered, pretend confidence on her tongue as she swallowed down her terror and faced the doorway.

Remy stared at her like she was about to sprout a second head. "Don't die."

"Here's hoping."

"I'm serious."

"As am I."

"Dammit, Rhymona."

"Luck stones and all that shit, yeah?"

"Luck stones," he echoed.

"Burn it at both ends," she returned Halion's final words. Words left her as she held her former lover's sagging body, a dozen arrows chewing through the span of his backside.

And the fates fucking keep us.

"*Blood of the stars,*" she called, "*we war as one.*" How long had it been since she'd uttered the phrase? Hells, how long had it been since she'd even thought it? The battle words of High House Tully. Long enough that they felt foreign upon her tongue and that much more wrong as they left her lips. Long enough that they made her body of scars itch like a rash of ivy.

But almost immediately the wand strikes diminished by half.

"Now," the magus bellowed.

Remy hooked an arm around the doorframe and flung the azure ball of nightmare at the hearth, causing a bright flare-up.

At the disturbance, Magwyn hurled the vial into the chamber and as it reached the space above the writing table, she spat a Chandii curse of her own, and the glass shattered with a sparkle of Eldn fire sending the flaming swamp water spilling down below.

Rhymona entered, chasing ill luck's specter, watching in awe as the contents thickened to a jelly-like substance in midair and began to eat through everything below as it pelted the area like acid rain.

Dysenia rose with a cellar banshee's shriek, a scrawny slip of a thing, nearly as depleted as how they'd found Aiden in the palace library, her flesh now melting down her left arm, portions of her body boiling up into blisters and bursting as her skin spit, warped, and withered. All yellow-eyed menace, she slung her wand arm up at Rhymona's approach, the tip splashing about bright white magic thick as syrup, part of her face dissolving down to muscle and bone, and with a feral cry fired at her niece.

The magus, expecting the reaction, fell into a diving roll, and rose back to her feet narrowly missing the deathbed stream of magic as it left a line of char across the stone floor.

Before her aunt could conjure another strike, Fucker came round like a windmill feasting down into the hag's shoulder.

Shit.

Despite her injuries, Dysenia managed to evade the head blow.

Not again. She'd come in too strong and Fucker gorged too deep inside Dysenia's flesh to come loose, a gout of black and red bubbling out.

Rhymona let go of her husband and circled back on the collapsing woman with Illuminaria clutched firmly in both hands.

Dysenia's wand clattered to the stones as she buckled onto her knees, the one with the acid rot giving out upon impact and dropping her flat to the stones where her left arm spewed into a pool of formless goo. Oh, but how the wretch howled at that, blood spurting from the hatchet wound near her neck, as chunks of her torso melted into a puddle of watery viscera and bone shards.

Rhymona gazed up from Dysenia's writhing at the others in the room. Pion holding a kindleblade, Caitlyn, a wand, and Raelan bound unmoving to a chair on the floor.

Demonic laughter split the silence between them, eerie and disarming, and the magus returned her vision to the fallen woman as nether ichor poured out from her wounds, replacing that which was lost. A malachite vapor seethed off of her as she rose back up, a horridly malformed abomination, her lower body bulging out of her clothes, the seams tearing, replaced by an amorphous mass of nether flesh.

"Rhymona!" Remy shouted from the doorway as he entered, azure burning in his eyes.

And Dysenia spun around in the space between them, facing her, hair clinging to her marred cheeks, froth on her lips, features contorted in pain, her mutilated arm distending at the elbow, stretching out lightning quick, to an impossible length, tendrils growing from the ill-shapen appendage, three long knuckleless fingers, whipping around Rhymona's throat like a hangman's noose, forcing her out onto the balcony.

A flood of visions washed over her upon the impact. Memories, not her own. Memories of all the souls Dysenia devoured to satiate the evil within. Memories of men, women, and children alike, the echoes of their screams desecrating her eardrums.

The nether flesh expanded into a bed of tentacles beneath Dysenia's tattered robes like that of a great sea beast, keeping her anthropoid half upright, as she slithered after her niece, the door to the balcony slamming shut behind them, separating them from the others.

Rhymona clutched at the thick, scaly appendage sucking at her neck and choking the life from her as her feet left the ground, her hand slipping across its slimy coat, unable to find a proper purchase, her consciousness fading inside the carousel of otherworldly images. And with the last of her focus, she found Illuminaria's song, like one of Val's lullabies, latching on to it, as it showed her the version of Dysenia she remembered from her childhood. The valiant swordswoman. Dying. Desperate. Left for the crows. But a warrior true. Dysenia watched, helpless in her death throes, unable to move, as a dark, shapeless entity, not unlike her present form, approached.

By its vibrations, Rhymona understood this thing to be Tetherow...

"Nyaahh!" Rhymona wailed with all the strength she could muster, flailing Valestriel's song blindly skyward, catching something solid, and thrusting up against it, slicing all the way through, severing their hellish union, the waves of unending trauma along with it.

Air filled her lungs anew, crisp and cutting, as she dropped to a knee and pushed back up, breath behind her, riding a swell of momentum into a lunge that took her reeling aunt through the space where its heart once lay, all the way to the blade's cross-guard.

"This is for Larissa and Rill," she cried.

The vapor became more defined as it billowed away from Dysenia's heaving horror of a body, her aunt coming apart like boiled meat off the bone, and Rhymona seized the creature by a shred of its torn robe, slick with nether residue and sloughed skin, whirling it around her into the balustrade, a cold winter breeze scratching at her countenance, drying her watery eyes.

"And this is for my aunt and everything you took from us."

Dysenia's bloating nether flesh weighed her down, folds upon folds of skin, making her difficult to move, as Rhymona tried to force the ever-shifting monstrosity over the edge.

"Your aunt?" Dysenia grated through the one working side of her mouth, the embodiment of enmity, black bile staining her teeth, streaking down from the lone golden haunter the acid jelly left her. "Your aunt chose me over you."

"Fuck you," Rhymona screamed in the fiend's face.

"Oh, but those were Val's last words, too," the creature hissed, her eldritch voice breaking apart into many, "messy as they were. Right before we ripped her throat out."

"Go to hell, bitch!"

"I'll be seeing you there." A black smile.

She was so distracted by the woman's words, so consumed by adrenaline, anger, and hate, that she didn't notice the knife plunge inside her belly until it was too late, and even then, she barely felt it.

Snarling, pushing through the crush of splitting tendrils, into the blade carving up her innards, the magus shoved with all her might as hearth light streamed in behind her and the balustrade cracked, her momentum pulling her over with the creature.

A darkness dug for two.

"Rhymona!"

Something seized her by the back of her shirt collar as the vertigo set in, her throat catching against its front, strangling her, the ledge lusting after her, as an azure inferno burned past her shoulder, and everything slowed. She and Illuminaria came free from the phaedrylax's grasp, coughing blood, holding upright as she watched the monstrous remains of her last living relative catch fire and shrink into the starlit darkness beyond.

Eyes wide as the sister moons, Dysenia snapped a tentacle back up at her, one last dire attempt, its taloned tip missing Rhymona by a nose, as the fiend plummeted toward the ground, the malachite vapor dissipating off her like a trail of stardust in the descent.

And Rhymona caught the gleam of Fucker, still lodged in Dysenia's shoulder, as the mass of flaming nether flesh hurtled through the final span of the massive drop, end over end, shrieking unholy nightmare until it splattered into sauce across the courtyard stones below.

A jerking motion pulled her back off her feet and into the lap of Remy Lanier. He held her tight against him and she leaned back, tears blurring her vision of the sprawling nightfall before them.

"What about don't die did you not understand?" he groused a moment later.

"Remy." The magus pulled the bitch's knife from her belly, wincing at the white-hot pain, muddy black ichor expelling out of her at the ejection site, forming a misshapen fetal-like horror...

CHAPTER TEN

THE NETHER FETUS crawled drunkenly away from her like some beaten mongrel on a bender gone wrong.

It won't have me, she thought as the creature caught flame and emitted a high-pitched alien whine before withering into ash and catching the rush of wind.

"The hateful fucking cunt," Rhymona murmured, pressing a hand to the wound, as Remy helped her to her feet. "She poisoned me." Her voice came out ghastly hoarse.

"She tried to at least," Remy said, Thira flickering in his eyes.

As one, they gazed back over the edge at the massive bloodstain mound below.

"I thought it strange before when you housed both the gift and the nether at once," Remy continued. "But this is quite something else."

"Which begs the question," Rhymona said, blood welling between her fingers and trickling from her stomach, spotting the King's balcony, as they passed back inside the solar where Magwyn had her scepter trained on the others. "What the fuck am I?"

"Would that I could name it," Remy returned.

"And I wouldn't count all your luck stones just yet," Pion said, as Caitlyn cut Raelan's ropes and the General slumped to the floor. "That's not the end of it. Just the end of that particular host."

"What the hells just happened to my aunt?" Rhymona asked, staring into Pion's bottomless black-ringed orbs. "What was all that green shit?"

"The demon was the only thing keeping the nether from consuming her. That green shit, as you so eloquently put it, was the demon fighting to expel itself from its dying vessel. That was its true form. Prize well, that one has a phylactery to keep it bound to this plane. A timepiece."

"A timepiece?" Remy asked. "How do you know this?"

"Oh, you know, Brother. The usual hijinks."

"You were in league with that wretch," Magwyn hissed. "The both of you."

"I won't deny it," Pion said. "I played my part. We can't all be bright and shiny heroes, I'm afraid."

Listen to this insufferable fuckbucket, Rhymona thought, as all of Marsea's tavern rants about the skeevy grotesque began to bubble up to the surface.

"Though it would seem we are freshly expendable now, aren't we?" he continued. "You saw the fiend. All fever and fury. It meant to turn us a fast grave, didn't it?"

"And why was that exactly?" Rhymona asked.

"Have a look around," Pion said, waving a hand to the blood pentacle splattered beneath them. "The entity knew its host was not long for this world and was planning to take a new one."

"Raelan?" Rhymona put two and two together.

"You were protecting your father?" Remy questioned. "The man that mistreated you all your life?"

"It would seem I've something of a tender heart after all," Pion said. "Trust me, I'm just as foxed about all this as you are."

"This timepiece. Where is it now?" Magwyn asked.

"Haven't the faintest. The one in Dysenia was rather cagey, all told, and quite frankly impossible to take at its word."

Remy helped Caitlyn lift Raelan, and they carried him to the divan in the study area. "Let me make one thing clear, Pion." Remy bore a hole through the weaselly charlatan. "I do not trust you." He glanced back at Caitlyn. "Nor you, for that matter."

"The feeling is mutual, Brother," Pion replied with a sneer.

"For the last fucking time, I'm not your brother, Pion."

"Now, now, there's no need for a poison tongue. Trust, I'm well aware of your opinions regarding my House."

"It's my opinion regarding you, apart from your blood banner," Remy fixed the grotesque with a stern glare. "Both of you will surrender your weapons and agree to confinement until we're able to sort all of this."

"You mean to let them live?" Rhymona quibbled.

"Mayhaps, they can be useful."

"Don't be a fuckwit, Remy. This rat will turn on you the first chance he gets," Rhymona said.

"You're one to talk, ashaeydir," Pion was quick to the cut.

"What did you just say to me?" Rhymona lifted Illuminaria at the deplorable shit-stain, eye twitching at the ache of the sudden movement.

"Hand to heart, I promise full cooperation," Pion said, holding up his hands in surrender. "And I'll divulge everything I know about the demon."

"A warlock's well, can't say I'm surprised," Rhymona disparaged.

"I'll wear a gauntlet, if it pleases."

"Mayhaps, we'll take it from you altogether," Rhymona snapped as she lowered the mae'chii and eased down upon the nearest chair not in shambles, utterly spent, her neck beginning to ache. "You talk of promises, as though anything you say would be taken as truth."

"I was going to add, as long as our conditions are met…"

"No one gives a mummer's limp fuck about your conditions," Rhymona griped, resting Illuminaria across her lap before fishing a blood candle from her pouch with her free hand. "Tell him, Remy."

"Say your piece, Pion, and stow the clowning," Remy commanded.

"Fuck's sake, are we really going to entertain this knobend schemer?" The words came out raw and she wanted like fire to massage her scratchy throat, her voice beginning to grate, but lacked a spare hand to do so.

"Allow me to remain with Caitlyn and Father," Pion answered, ignoring her insults. "Here in the solar."

"Shit!" She cried with a start. "What the fuck!" Something wrapped itself around her ankles and Rhymona curled up her feet from the floor, pain shooting through her at the sudden reaction, her mouth dropping at the sight of the creature before her. *Where the fuck?* She blinked rapidly, unsure if she was beginning to hallucinate. "Bloody hells…is that… Grandpa?" She reached down to poke him. *Definitely real.* "What in vaelnation are you doing here, beastie cat?" She gave his little head a rub. "*How* are you here?"

"Grandpa is my familiar," Pion said nonchalantly.

"Now you're talking rot," Rhymona cringed, pulling away from her comforting old companion.

"Don't you wish it so," came the grotesque's smarmy reply.

"Oh, just get all the way fucked then, Pion."

"One should be wary of what they do in the company of others." His smarm grew a wry little smile that was begging to have a blade punched through it.

"Dare I ask, how long?" Her face wrinkled up.

"Long enough," Pion answered. "For your temperament, I suggest we leave it at that."

"And I couldn't agree more," Remy added, eyes rolling at the farce.

Rhymona thought about how many times she and Aiden lay together with Grandpa in the room, and a shiver crawled down her spine.

"I have a condition as well," Caitlyn said. "I request a conversation one-on-one with the Empress."

"You will have to relinquish your sidearm first," Magwyn said, Emyria burning in her orbs, "but I will oblige your request."

Rhymona lifted her shirt and pressed the blood candle into the open wound on her abdomen, grunting back a coming sickness as it melted inside her.

I sure hope Marsea's faring better than all this rotty bollocks. She watched Caitlyn as the girl surrendered her wand to Magwyn and Pion as he handed his kindleblade to Remy.

And then another thought crept back through from the catacombs of her swimming mindscape.

The nether wouldn't have me.

Why wouldn't it have me?

Her eyes became heavy as her attentions fell to the blade wound closing around the last of the melted blood candle, The Spellbind setting its fangs in, its current dancing light upon her skin, drinking away the throbbing that ran the range of her right side, soothing the soreness that had settled in her strangled throat, and something Rill said wormed its way back through her fast-consuming stupor:

There is something greatly powerful inside of you. Something special. Something beyond the means of the most of us.

She let out a vexed groan.

Would've been nice if you could have shared exactly what the fuck you meant by that, you sour old git. Five days to the grave and you're still finding ways to piss me off.

Then came the ashfall…

CHAPTER ELEVEN

As FORTUNE FARED, the ramshackle tanner shop was void of any wandering drylaxes or scavenging ghouls. Still, the Lanier siblings didn't press their luck waiting about for trouble to arrive.

Marsea and Old Boy kept watch, the haxanblade chomping at the bit, while Desmond called forth a fresh ward from the dustiest corner of the dingy shop.

Hope to see this place again, the princess thought as she passed through the portal and into the nastiest blizzard she'd ever experienced.

In the distance, a township named Maidstone slept. Her dark, jagged rooftops carved into distinction by the sister moons despite the veil of snowfall.

Sensing Broenwjar's apprehension about the prospect of townsfolk, she bade him keep to the trees for now while she and Desmond made for shelter.

"Good thing we thought to bring our warm clothes," Marsea said through chattering teeth, the wind blustering roughly about them, the fattest snowflakes she'd ever beheld crumbling to powder upon contact, the snow up to her knees in places and piling.

"You sure you want to leave wolfie out in this weather?" Desmond returned, cradling Lenore in his arms as they trudged onward.

Marsea could barely hear him over the winter's wail, most of his words a muddle she was merely tossing back wild guesses at. "B loves the cold," she shouted. "It's the townsfolk he's not so big on."

To this Desmond simply nodded, bowing his head low to stave off the brunt of the storm.

It wasn't long before they made the empty cobble. Most of the residents had already turned in for the evening.

"This way," Desmond hollered, eyes aglow with Hrathgon's presence as he led them to one of the few structures that showed even the slightest semblance of life; an old limestone barracks with a chained wooden sign blowing above the entryway reading "The Overlook Lodge."

A bell chimed above the door as they entered and Marsea was greeted by the scent of broth and barley, then burning wood, and a faint hint of cloves. Instantly, it took her back to the King's solar and Vaustian's cozy arms.

Only a man. A slab of meat, Other reminded.

Still, the princess exhaled, wishing she could curl up in this scent for a day and just run the gamut of a bookshelf she'd never explored before.

A motley group sat across the dining area huddled around a bottle-cluttered table that had been dragged before the roaring stone hearth. Not a one of the lot lifted their heads from their drink or the card game to acknowledge them. Marsea suspected by their arrangement and demeanor they were townies simply passing the time in the most entertaining way they had available.

The corners of Marsea's lips rose unconsciously as she took in the surrounding quarters, from the deerskin rugs to the long umber banners hemmed in ochre running down from the rafters with a House sigil she vaguely recognized from a distant memory. That of an owl with misshapen horns sprouting from its head.

"This is the oddest innhouse I've ever seen," Marsea said.

"It used to be an old barracks for Royalguard cadets back before the coup," Desmond served Hrathgon's words. "And that field we arrived in used to be a training ground and tourney yard."

"Welcome, travelers," a gruff voice rose from behind the bar, appearing through a cloud of pipe smoke.

"Evening," Marsea managed, shaking the layer of snow out of her hair.

"By the gods, look at you lot," the man said as he approached. He was old as the hills and balding with a bushy brown and gray beard that ran down his considerable potbelly like a flowing waterfall. "Come on in then."

"Long time, Clive," Desmond said, removing his hood and scarf, his eyes flashing azure once more.

The innkeeper retrieved a pair of glasses from his vest pocket, blinking through them at the eldest Lanier sibling. "Curse the devil's cock, is that you, Hrathgon?"

"Pleased to find you hale, old friend."

"And you." The innkeeper spoke with a heavy accent that found most folk who had spent the majority of their lives milling about the backwood townships. "Got yourself a new stooge, eh?"

"This one saved me from the last if you can believe it."

"Never much cared for that Tenbrooks fellow, all told. Dodgy as they come." Clive gave Marsea a proper once over. "And who is this lovely lass then?"

The thought passed through to name herself Selwyn once more, as though the like had become her preferred name outside Lancastle, but she quickly decided against it. If Hrathgon trusted this Clive chap enough to reveal his true presence, then so too would she.

"My name is Marsea," she said. "We've coin, if you've room to spare for the night."

"Room to spare? Heck, this time of cycle, it's usually too much to spare thanks to the elements." His eyes dropped to her side. "But I'll thank you both to keep your steel in their scabbards during your stay."

"Of course," they answered in unison, each giving the other a bashful look at the jinx.

Desmond cleared his throat. "By chance, have you any food or ale for purchase? We're both famished."

"I can imagine. You lot are mad being out in these conditions. But, aye, I reckon there's a bit of stew left. No ales as yet. But we've plenty of mead if you're game for the sweet stuff."

"What say you, sister?" Desmond asked, a friendly smile in tow. "It's about time we have a proper reunion, yeah?"

Not sure bingeing is the best idea right now...

Then again, this could be your last chance...

And there certainly hadn't been much to be merry about lately...

"I suppose it is," she replied with a smirk.

May as well take what you can get. Besides, maybe it'll serve you a decent night's sleep for once.

"Have a booth then, you two," Clive said. "Get cozy. I'll have my daughter rustle up something and bring a bottle for the table."

"Cheers," Desmond said, and he tossed the grizzled innkeeper one of the coin pouches Marsea had kept hidden behind a loose block of stone just outside the Hall of Glass. It was one of a number of places she hid her father's riches around the castle walls and the only one of convenience near the guest chambers.

They found a booth with a window view and Desmond grabbed a candelabrum from the next table over, lighting its three branches with a touch of his gift before placing it on the windowsill.

"This is actually rather nice, considering," Marsea found herself saying.

"Aye, Clive is good folk," Hrathgon spoke.

"Maidens keep me, it's so fucking odd to talk about things being nice anymore."

"Who are you telling?" Desmond said, offering a kindly, but pitiful gap-toothed smile as Lenore comfortably settled into the seat beside him.

"Out of curiosity, brother, which do you prefer? Desmond or Aiden?"

"There's a tough one, yeah." His eyes softened. "Honestly, Aiden feels more real. But Desmond is the truth."

"Well, you're still Des to me unless you tell me otherwise. I know Remy would say the same."

"Remy." Desmond inhaled dramatically. "Not sure we quite see eye to eye, me and little brother. Good spirit, but, between you and me, kind of a wet blanket."

"That's just Remy," Marsea said, shaking off her sodden cloak and folding it into a bunch in the booth beside her, using it to conceal her satchel. "He's dour as they come, headstrong, and he always has to be right. I've had nineteen cycles of it, of argument after argument, so trust it true, I more than feel your pain there."

"I appreciate the charity."

"There's no charity in it," the princess said, working off the glove Elsymir made for her before holding her bare hands up to the candelabrum. "As you said. Remy has a good heart, but he's horribly disagreeable on his best day, a sore sport, and a massive pain in the ass in general."

Desmond let out a snort that made Marsea's soul sing. "He is horribly disagreeable, isn't he?"

"Oh, stars, yes."

"I thought that was just me. Trust, I'm no peach myself. In fact, I'm something of a maven when it comes to putting folk off."

"That may be, but Remy has one way. His way, or it's fuck off, Sally."

"Some mead for the merriment," Clive brought a bottle filled with a honey-gold liquid and a pair of goblets. "The stew is being warmed. We'll have it out soon enough."

"Cheers, Clive," Marsea said.

"Your hand," Desmond said after Clive departed. "Care to share what happened?"

Marsea's eyes fell on his. "You first."

Desmond held up his horror of a hand between them and actually dared to gaze at her through the hole within the palm's center. "This is a warlock's well, obviously. One Tetherow saw fit to prize me with whilst I was suppressed by its possession."

"I have a vague understanding of what a warlock's well is, but what exactly is its purpose?" she asked, filling each glass to the half with mead.

"To pull from the gift at faster and greater volume," he answered. "Warlocks use it like wand magic." He placed fingertips inside the missing flesh as blood began to fill the space, running down his arm onto the table, and he pulled a little blood out like string from a spool.

Marsea covered her bad hand over her mouth in awe. "Maidens' breath."

"Right?" He dragged a length of his blood out and twisted it around the hand before squeezing it into a fist, where it all sank back into the missing chunk of flesh. "Fucked up, yeah?"

"You can just do that on a whim?" she asked before downing her glass of mead to the dregs.

"I can. I just sort of feel it moving within and I call after it, not necessarily by notion, but by will. Then the gift responds. I'll say, if there is any one thing of value Tetherow taught me that the discipline masters at university never did, it's that the gift isn't about thought, it's about being."

"Does it hurt?"

"There's a slight burning sensation at first, but otherwise, no. It's strange. Since Tetherow's possession, I've felt a stronger bond to my gift, like he awoke something inside me that I can't put back to sleep."

"Sounds terrifying, given the source."

"It's unsettling, I won't lie. But look at the state of me. I'm unsettling. I look like one of the fucking blighted. It's a wonder Clive didn't put me to the sword the moment we clamored in." He took up his glass and knocked it back like a seasoned tavern-hound. "Your turn."

"All right, if I'm going to do this, I'm going to see it through properly." Marsea stood, wriggled out of Remy's old tweed jacket, rolled her sleeve to show the bare arm, and plunked the elbow on the table, displaying the whole of her arm from the elbow to the hand.

"Oh, yeah. There she is. And what a lovely lass to behold," Desmond japed, as he gave the eyesore a cursory glance.

"Don't be creepy, Des. This one was well earned, I'll have you know."

"Earned how?" He poured them each a fresh fill of mead.

"An assassination attempt gone awry." Marsea frowned. "Not my finest moment, all told."

"You were the assassin?"

"Indeed. Two quints shy."

"Sod off." He leaned in, studying her nubs again. "This was two quints ago?"

"Not even."

"The scarring is remarkably clean, barely noticeable at all."

"Something about the old blood, I'm told."

"I'll say." He held up his glass. "A toast to what once was. May our missing pieces rest well."

"How very morbid of you."

"You have no idea."

They clinked glasses and swallowed back their contents, and Desmond immediately began to refill.

"Ran the bastard through with a hidden blade." Marsea nudged up her glasses. "Oh, how it sank in with such ease. Nothing at all like what I expected."

"A hidden blade?"

"A spring-loaded vambrace, like in the Chandiian war stories of yore."

"I'll have to take your word for it."

"Make no mistake, he was a real piece of work this bastard in the wood." She was beginning to feel the effects of the mead now. "I was off my head, of course. Had a few pints and a dram of black beforehand to settle the spirit. Then I followed the lout from the tavern deep into The Kingswood, and would you believe he actually stopped to relieve himself?"

"No."

"Oh, yes. Grunts and all."

Desmond slung back his glass. "More drink?"

Wasn't this fun? Marsea held up a finger as she quaffed hers dry and slammed her glass down on the table, drawing the attention of the group huddled near the hearth. "Sorry," she apologized, her rosy cheeks darkening a shade from the embarrassment.

"So, you murdered this defecating cuntlord pre-shit or post? Or was it during? Gods wept, please tell me it wasn't during."

"Post-shit, through some mad luck of the stars. But during the attack, he grabbed my hand..."

"Ugh, no. With post-shit hands? Unwashed?"

"No, I let him have a wash first," she rolled her eyes. "Of course, they were post-shit, hands, you ridiculous tit." Given the madness of the whole affair, she hadn't really thought about the sanitary aspects, or rather lack thereof. "I mean obviously it got mangled against the hidden blade," she held her bad one up again, "and the rest is well..."

"Eh, at least you've still the middle left," he said, leaning back. "'T'-would be a damned shame not to have a spare bird available when needed."

"A silver lining, I suppose."

"And who was this man to you, that had you out in the middle of The Kingswood losing fingers doing The Hood's work?"

"Ganedys Harver."

"Harver? As in the bastard House that killed father and me and usurped our family's throne?"

"As in. And trust it true, I was playing at the rogue's table with this one. Well out of my depths, mind you. But his own brother named him for the butcher's block. I couldn't just—"

"His own brother? Gods, and I thought our House was fucked up."

There's some perspective for you. And just think of what our kingdom will look like if we actually survive all of this, each one of us left a filthy degenerate murderer.

"So, if I'm following then. You were working for who? Raelan? Vaustian?"

"I suppose you could say a little of both, but Vaustian ordered the attack." She glanced away from him as Clive arrived with a pair of steaming bowls.

"Lamb and barley stew," the innkeeper said. "And you can have your pick of the rooms upstairs. My daughter says the ones closest to the stairwell on the right side are the cleanest."

Hrathgon returned. "Your hospitality has been most generous, Clive."

"As was your coin, old friend. Let me know if you need anything else," he added as he backed away to see to the other guests, who'd become slightly more boisterous as the round of Sick Boy was spiraling toward a close finish.

Marsea brought the wooden spoon up to her lips and tasted a small sip of the broth with rice. It was warm and salted, but still a bit on the bland side by comparison to the castle stock she was used to. Though given the circumstances, it would more than suffice.

"As you were saying about working for Vaustian?" Desmond said between bites, shoveling stew in his mouth like a starving savage.

Marsea decided to hold back judgments. Obviously, it had been some time since he'd taken in a decent repast. "I won't sugarcoat it," she started instead. "And I understand you have a dislike for the man, and with just cause, but things became...complex between Vaustian and me over the last few cycles. Especially when he began to see me as a woman."

Desmond's expression soured. "Tell me you didn't do what I think you are implying."

She swallowed. *You may as well tell him.* "We became intimate, yes."

He winced, shoulders sagging as he tilted back in his seat.

"Not that any of that much matters now, seeing as he's dead."

"Vaustian Harver is dead?"

"At the hands of Rhymona, if you can believe that."

Desmond shook his head. "Oh, I can believe it."

"It's actually you," a woman spoke from behind the bar, drawing Marsea's attention. For it was a voice she would never ever forget, not in a thousand, thousand, centuries. The woman wore a simple light tan button-up shirt overlaid by a dark brown coat and matching trousers, all of which appeared scarce better than the garb of the peasantry. But there was no mistaking the voice, no matter what the quality of clothing she wore.

Hilda Veranski. The Mistress of Maidstone.

The ache returned to Marsea's ankles and arches at the woman's mere presence.

"I thought it was another poor jape, but here you are. The stars wept, how many cycles has it been, milady?" Hilda stopped just short of their booth, mouth agape, and took in Desmond, her eyes growing twice as wide. "Great Gilyndroth's ghost. You? But you can't be." Fingers rose to her temple, massaging in circles. "Or has it finally happened?" She gazed out the window between them. "Has the old man finally driven me mad?"

"Mistress Hilda," the princess greeted, standing.

Hilda withdrew a step.

"Are you all right?" Marsea offered a half-smile, her heart thundering across every taut inch of her being.

Hilda's eyes returned to Marsea's. "I don't understand, milady, how are you both here? Better yet, why are you both here?" There was some of that sternness Marsea remembered.

"We mean to cross into The Scar once the storm has blown through," she answered.

"The Scar? Oh, don't be absurd. The Scar is a death pit. Whatever reason could you possibly have to consider such a venture?"

"A grimoire," Desmond said. "*The N'therN'rycka* to be exact. We seek to retrieve and destroy it."

"And you know where this grimoire is?"

"I do. It's a few hours' trek in by foot. Near a monolith. The Tomb of Jostunhorm."

"Jostunhorm?" Hilda propped herself up against the table across from the Lanier's booth and chuckled.

"Well obviously, that's not the reaction I was hoping for," Desmond said.

"Jostunhorm," Hilda replied, glancing back at them. "You've been there before?"

"I have." Azure returned to Desmond's orbs.

Hilda simply shook her head at the sudden presence of a dracari. "Not recently I presume."

"Not recently, no."

"I should say because if you had, you would know a wngar tribe has built their village around it. Scores of them. Mayhaps hundreds by this juncture. Word is they practically worship the monolith. There is no way in hells you would be able to sneak in unnoticed. And you would need a militia the size of the Kingswatch to make a proper run at it. Either that or an actual dragon for distraction."

Marsea frowned, recalling Elsymir's fight with a wngar during her familiar branding with Broenwjar and his subsequent warning about their size and menace.

I've seen some tall as citadel towers. Let me tell you, you see one of those bastards, you run. You run and you hide 'til it's gone.

She turned to Desmond, who appeared just as disheartened as she did. "We don't have a choice," she said. "We need to destroy the grimoire to exorcize a demon inside our sister."

"Your sister?"

"Rather, half-sister," Marsea corrected. "The fourth godsblood needed to recite from the ancient giftblood quartet."

"Now there's a mouthful."

"It is said these grimoires can be used to banish the great nether beast, which approaches Lancastle as we speak and will arrive within days, mayhaps hours. The demon's phylactery is the grimoire buried before The Tomb of Jostunhorm."

"Maidens' mercy, girl," Hilda grumbled.

"Kind of regretting coming out here now, hunh?" Desmond made light.

There was the face, Marsea thought, as a vein creased Hilda's forehead down the center and one of her eyes picked up a subtle twitch.

"Apologies," Desmond added a moment later, "I, uh, use poor attempts at humor to cope with horridly shite situations. Problematic childhood and all."

"And this one is well beyond shite, I'd say," the dance instructor turned barmaid returned.

"Story of my life."

"Desmond, be serious," Marsea made her best attempt at a scolding.

Though, in truth, his gallows humor somehow eased her mounting state of dread, especially whilst in Mistress Veranski's company.

"If you mean to do this, milady, mayhaps I can help," Hilda said.

"I would never ask you to risk your life, Mistress."

"It's just Hilda now, milady. I'm long past my instructing days."

"Very well. And I'm just Marsea." *Long past my princess days.*

"As you wish."

"Don't mind her," Desmond said. "We will take any aid you can spare."

"Cycles ago, after I left Lancastle, I returned home to Maidstone, where I found that some former soldiers and magi had formed a group called The Maidens' Rejects. This group fashioned enchanted masks and gear that would allow them to survive for hours within The Scar. After some time, and many quints of begging from their ranks, they finally convinced me to come along on a mission. And to my astonishment, I rather found that the risk and reward of these absurd undertakings rather suited me. So, I would go ranging into The Scar with The Maidens' Rejects to gather a rare type of mineral that grows there called trezsu. We would partner on patrol with a tool named a death sling."

"A death sling?" Marsea echoed.

"Sounds pleasant," Desmond added.

"The method would comprise of what we called a blade and an anchor. One of us would have a leather harness strapped around our bodies, imagine a belt for the torso that crosses the shoulders and connects at the waist. The other would carry a handheld ballista with a quiver of bolts. These were used in case a wngar were to come along. Which they inevitably did. Once the wngar came within range, the anchor, who is like an archer, would hit the bastard with the bolt, at which point the blade would trigger the harness attached to the bolt and it would propel them up to the wngar's head, where they could quickly deal the deathblow."

"Sounds mental more like," Marsea commented. "This method has worked before?"

"Oh, yes. It's quite effective, in fact. I've nineteen wngar heads to my name."

"Aye, she has," Clive joined them. "My daughter was known as Hilda Giantsbane before the ugly bastards overran the area. One of the best marksmen of The Scar runners."

"You were an archer?" Marsea asked.

"I was," she answered. "And I want to help you in whatever way I can to retrieve this grimoire. I can offer you my skills as an archer, but my blade-wielding days are behind me."

The way she stated the latter, put Marsea off the ask as to why. "As my brother said, we'll take whatever aid we can get. Obviously, if we make it through all of this, you'll receive a handsome purse."

"Let's not count our chickens just yet, milady. Wngar are terribly ill-tempered creatures. Working our way through even a handful of them will be a considerable task."

"A fair point. And I'd be honored to be your blade if you'll teach me the workings of it."

Hilda held her eyes. "You've learned to fight, have you?"

"I have." A few of her victims flashed through her mind. Ganedys, Davrin, Yongrin, followed by a countless number of the blighted.

"I hope your bladework is better than what I remember of our dance lessons."

"Prepare to be gobsmacked."

Hilda Veranski smiled at that. "I hope you don't mind my asking, but how fares your mother?"

"Mother?" Though it shouldn't have, the question hit her like a sack of granstone, and the faceless thing they'd left under the sheet in the guest chamber bed came back for the haunt, sitting ill with the mead swimming around her belly and mindscape.

"I see," the barmaid uttered. Something Desmond did beyond Marsea's periphery must have provided enough answer for Hilda as she produced a horribly mournful expression. "You have my condolences, love. I know your mum was tough on you and Rembrandt. But she had a good heart. She was a good woman."

"Aye," Marsea murmured, doing her damnedest to hold back her welling tears.

"I didn't mean to..." Hilda started.

"I know," the princess interjected, slow wet trails snaking down her puffy, pink cheeks. "You couldn't have known."

"Still." An awkward pause swelled between them before Hilda cleared her throat. "And with that, I think I'll leave you lot to it. Have your drinks and stories, and I will begin preparations." She pushed up from the table.

"Do make sure you're right before the morn though. I'll be waiting in the courtyard out back, and we'll have a test of your bladework."

"Better you than me," Desmond added. "I'm shit with a blade on my best day. But if you need a bit of chaos and Eldn fire, I'm your asshole." He turned up another swallow of mead.

"Thank you for offering, Hilda," Marsea said.

"I made an oath to your father some many moons ago. Back when we were cadets, just starting out. That I would always look after his kin. And, until now, I would say I've failed rather spectacularly in that promise. But seeing as you're both here and in need now, it's the least I can do to try to make up for all that."

"As far as I'm concerned, you don't owe us a thing," Marsea said. "But we're grateful to have you."

Hilda bowed slightly.

"Just one more thing," the princess began. "I've a familiar like my brother, but he's not overly keen on folk and he's had trouble with the wngar in the past."

"Where is he?" Hilda glanced around suspiciously.

Marsea reached into their bond and felt Broenwjar in the wood, padding about, rather enjoying himself considering the ghastly weather.

"He's on the hunt for his supper from what I can tell."

"I'm not sure I follow."

"He's a big ass wolf, is what he is," Desmond clarified.

"Marsea Lanier has a wolf familiar?" Hilda's grin was absolutely obscene.

"She does at that." Marsea allowed a sliver of merriment to peek through.

"I must say, milady, you're nothing at all how I expected you to turn out, given our prior dealings."

Frayed are the threads that cast shadows…

I will not let my past define me…

The scars that bind us…

The old blood must survive…

The name must die…

"What can I say? I am what the moon has made me."

CHAPTER TWELVE

THE EMPRESS KEPT careful watch over Caitlyn as they returned to the King's Hall, making note of the spellslinger's every mannerism in her mental ledger. For all the obvious reasons, the girl's sudden change of allegiances sat ill upon her conscience, but there was also something else there, something she was keeping tightly guarded, Magwyn could feel it in the pit of her stomach, nagging at her like the turn of a bad supper, the empathetic nature of her gift unwilling to let it go untended.

Something screaming for release.

Something potentially useful.

Something worth exploring.

Caitlyn paused beside one of the cultists as they passed, the one that had taken a pair of blades and a wand strike, offering his facedown corpse a gravedigger's scowl, before pressing on to the next doorway down.

"What's in here?" she inquired, dragging a messy tangle of raven-black hair behind an ear.

"Last as I recall, a seldom used council chamber," Maggie said.

The spellslinger turned the doorknob and pale emerald light poured through the window down a long table in the room's center, splitting the shadows within.

Fingers gently trailed the backs of each chair until the end as Caitlyn spanned the stones to the far wall, quiet as a whisper, and halted at the windowsill, gazing up submissively at the sister moons as though they were bestowing their wraith-like guest with a fresh trove of secrets.

The Empress entered and scanned the chamber's obscurities, which had become something of a trophy room in her absence. The severed heads of beasts and wildland creatures preserved and mounted on the walls between High House tapestries and displayed weaponry. Wngar skulls, wildkin hides, a bog troll with bulging eyes and leathery skin, the largest buck shoulder cut she'd ever beheld, monsters she hadn't proper names for, each one more hideous than the last.

She turned away in disgust, gazing into the far corner where a tall wooden dummy lurked, adorned in a suit of gleaming full-plate armor. *The King's piece.* Oh, but she would've recognized the legendary ensemble anywhere. The form of the helm, two narrow slits for the eyes, the intricate engravings on the breastplate, bracers, and greaves. Left to the cobwebs in a room scarce larger than a bloody cupboard.

Keep to the present, Mags.

Magwyn held silent at the table's head, studying Caitlyn's wand in the pastel luminescence, biting her tongue back from the first word between them, following the intuition in her gut and gift despite her mind's want for immediate interrogation.

Some fractious seconds later, Caitlyn sighed, then turned about to face her company, eyes downcast. "We may as well get this done then, yeah?"

"The stage is yours," Maggie said, her tone soft and inviting, prudently placed, as she opened her gift into the girl's emotions.

Caitlyn inhaled and let the breath out slow, forehead creased in thought.

Exhaustion, though not physical.

"You saved me," she began, her voice weary yet almost melodic, the darkness concealing her frontage like a veil as she hugged her arms tight to her chest. "When you pulled me from the apothecary. I didn't expect that."

The Empress studied the girl's body language, every subtle twinge of movement, her posture, hands, and the avoidance of eye contact, allowing her gift to do what it did best. And this one exhibited all of the telltale signs of cycles-long psychological abuse.

"And why is that?" *Just a little push.*

"I'm not exactly the sort for saving, I reckon." Her head lowered, long dark hair spilling down over her shoulders in waves thick as a griever's cowl.

Hopelessness. Fragile as glass.

"Who told you that?"

Caitlyn shrugged. "It's what I've lived. What I've learned. And though I understand my place…"

A pregnant pause.

"…it doesn't make it any easier to accept," Magwyn finished, her gift feeding her the girl's insecurities.

Living with empathic tendencies had never been easy, digging through energies, delving into the burdens of others, unable to scrub away the trauma once it revealed itself, but the like had helped her far more over the cycles than it hurt, especially where Drezhal was involved. It was said amongst the palace pomp that no other could calm His Majesty's temper quite like his oh-so-clever bride.

"I don't know why your actions affected me so," Caitlyn continued. "Mayhaps because you're, well, *you.* A princess, an empress, a proper royal. And I know I was a bitch to you, and I likely deserved it, but then you left me—"

Mistrust. Dense as iron.

"No," Maggie swallowed. "I didn't—"

ALLOW ME.

Em.

I ONLY MEAN TO PROVIDE THE TRUTH.

Do have a care with her this time.

"…It was my choice to leave you…" Emyria answered. "…Magwyn refused, and I thought it put us in danger so I forced her down…"

"Forced her down?" The girl passed through a moment of ponderment. "You mean to say you possessed her against her will?"

"…I mean to say. And though I bear some shame for the deed, it was the right decision at the moment. Those townsfolk would have cut us to ribbons if they caught us, and running seemed a kinder choice than slaughtering innocents…"

"May I speak with the Empress again?" Caitlyn asked.

"I am here," Maggie said.

The spellslinger moved up to the foot of the oblong table, directly opposite Magwyn, and leaned her arms across the crest of the chair's spine, gauging her company.

Magwyn could see the wheels turning behind the girl's gloomy orbs, weighing the decision to confide in her captor.

"Why would you risk your life for me, Empress? Why did you save me, knowing at the time I was your enemy?"

"I cannot rightly say," Maggie returned. "I suppose I simply had a feeling about you, despite your hard words and willfulness. And mine is not a hand for killing, not naturally, despite the particulars of our short and violent history."

"My parents."

Lament. Cold as water under ice.

"I'm told they died of the wretchrot."

"Many died of the like in the ritual chamber scrap," Magwyn said.

"Was it you?"

"No." She shook her head. "Solindiel rather surprised us all with that bit. It could have had any one of us in truth."

"That cursed woman," Caitlyn spat, averting her glower.

"What happened in that chamber, to your parents, you must know, that was not what I wanted."

Caitlyn glanced back at her, daggers in her eyes.

"I wasn't fool enough to think there would be a peaceful resolution, but I wasn't expecting a massacre like that either."

"I expect not," Caitlyn said.

"We all lost something in there."

"The swordsman?"

"He was amongst the casualties. His name was Xavien Ledgermaine, and I will be forever in his debt."

"It's the opposite for me." Caitlyn ran a pair of fingers across the scar Solindiel gave her. *Shame.* "As far as I'm concerned, my debt is paid. My folks aligned themselves with devils and darkly creatures they did not fully understand. To have it true, I still can't fathom why. And now I'll never get the chance to ask it of them."

"For that, you have my condolences."

"I am not a bad person, Empress."

Loneliness. Dark as the ocean's depths.

"I don't believe you are."

"Having the whole of it from Pion, I don't agree with their actions. I don't agree with Ravenholme and what they're doing. What they've done. I don't agree with what my parents made me do to prove their loyalty."

Hello, something. But the way she said it sent a tide of goose flesh down her arms.

"And what did they make you do exactly?"

Her nervousness spiked briefly. "They conditioned me," she said. "Used me. Betrayed me."

Magwyn frowned.

"And I played my part because...I don't know...because of fear, mayhaps. Because they were my blood. Because I wanted to win their approval. What's an appropriate answer here?" She shifted back toward the sister moons, and Magwyn noted the girl had begun tracing her thumbnails against her fingers, index, middle, ring, pinky, and back to index. "Aiden was the worst of it. I courted him at their behest. I lay with him. Let him inside me. Playing the dedicated spy, knowing well and good there was something dreadfully off about him. I knew it was wrong, every bit of it, but I did it anyway. I wanted to be the devoted daughter. That's all I've ever wanted. And, honestly, after a time, I thought if I rebelled, it might bring me or one of my parents harm. To wit, I've never beheld my father so cross and mad as when it came to Ravenholme affairs."

"It is no easy thing to go against family." *If anyone knows the tale better, I'll wait.* "Prize well, I've been through my fair share of trials with my mother and brother both."

"But did they make of you a villain? Did they twist your morals?"

"It's been my experience that love and lineage are the cruelest of weapons." Magwyn placed the wand on the table and approached the spellslinger, halting at the table's end, careful not to overstep. "Caitlyn, you cannot blame yourself for all of this. At least not fully. What your parents put you through—"

"I could have run away. I almost did on several occasions. I had a travel sack prepared that I kept hidden under my bed..." She eased back around to a half, her arms clutched close again. "But I could never bring myself to do it. Even as the requests became increasingly more awful. I still stayed. My choice." Her voice broke at the word.

Regret. A knife through ribs.

"For them, I stayed. I numbed myself. I sat in it. Because I thought it was the right thing to do." Her tawny orbs became shiny with unshed tears. "How could I have ever believed that? How could any sane person ever believe that?" A sniffle. "The gods' wept, but I'm The Vael's greatest simp, aren't I?"

"No, Caitlyn. Family makes all of us do senseless things."

"And then I tried to break it off with Aiden…hoping…gods, I don't even know what I was hoping for by that point…but I just couldn't do it anymore. I could hardly leave my bed, much less the house. And I couldn't stand to look at him any longer. Especially after…" Her breath caught.

There she is.

"After?" Magwyn uttered as she halted before the girl, her gift's aura radiating between them.

Caitlyn's attention rose, knuckles rubbing wet eyelashes. "After his meeting with the masked woman."

"Who was this masked woman?"

"I cannot say. She kept well to the shadows, and they spoke at times in a strange language like nothing I've ever heard. And she had a properness about her and an eerie composure. More dangerous than the giftborn elite. And sharper than any guildlord's bladehand. Enough that it makes my hairs stand on end now just to bear it breath. I had a sense that she knew I was there, watching, but she couldn't have cared less. She spoke of alternate timelines and House Lanier and the Lancastle walks as though she'd lived amongst them for cycles. As though she'd bloody well cobbled them herself."

ANOTHER VHARYN'ASHI?

Let us hope not. One has proven trouble enough.

"Aiden disappeared for a time after that night. For a few days, mind you. Not hide nor hair of him about town and when he returned, it was like he was someone else entirely. Then news came of Stella's death, and he spiraled. I tried to help him at first, but…"

"I think I can deduce the rest."

"I wish I could give more about this woman, but there's nothing for it."

IN DUE TIME, PERHAPS.

"What are your plans now?" Maggie asked. "Do you intend to remain with Pion as he's requested? You know he cannot be trusted."

"My heart cries to the contrary, but my head screams caution. From everything I have witnessed, he is just as lost in all of this as the rest of us.

97

I think Tetherow made him a promise to fix him, his leg I should say, and I overheard something in Marrovard about a place called The Bloodbind, where time can be altered by splicing into alternate realities. Tetherow mentioned a woman named Shelly Manson."

The Empress gazed out the window, across the sea of stars to vast Y'dema, who swallowed most of the lustrous expanse off to the northwest. "I'm familiar with the name. It belonged to Pion's mother. I suppose another conversation regarding his intentions are in order." Magwyn let that sit for a beat before turning back to face the corridor. "I appreciate your—"

"Remy!" a voice called from down the King's Hall. One Magwyn recognized as...

Julia? Her brow furrowed. *What in vaelnation is she doing up here?*

And not a moment later Maggie had her answer in the form of a bloodcurdling screech that reverberated through the castle walls, breaking the skin, and echoing deep inside her bones, settling amongst the butterflies fluttering about the breadth of her belly.

A screech that was unmistakable to her dracari passenger.

No. It's too soon. The Empress swallowed thickly, collecting Caitlyn's wand from the table as she made for the doorway.

"What the fuck was that?" Caitlyn asked.

Magwyn glanced side-long at the girl, wreaths of azure burning feverishly in her darkly haunters.

"...what remains of my brother's corpse..."

CHAPTER THIRTEEN

SHE COULDN'T STAND SORROW. Ever since she could remember. Especially when it came to her own affairs. The pageantry of it. The absurdity. The utter uselessness. She could hardly take herself seriously when the sight of it befell her. She recalled the first time she ever captured her own sorrow, in the reflection of her mother's vanity mirror, four cycles old wailing over the loss of her favorite stuffed animal, Rocky Raccoon, realizing how tragically little her liquid eyes made any sort of difference in its recovery. Accepting that no measure of tears would ever bring back her funny purple friend from wherever he got off to. And, after a time, she would return to that mirror whenever she became sad, and at the spectacle she would giggle at the ridiculous expression her stupid, squishy face made. How silly she looked with wet lashes hanging before her puffy yellow orbs, sobs caught in the bottom of her throat, sniffling about like a bed-sick ninny.

No, sorrow never changed much of anything for Morgandrel Tully, save a body full of scars.

Though what arose in its wake was another tale altogether.

For what arose in its wake was madness.

And madness she rather liked.

It suited her and she it.

It never betrayed her.

Nor did chaos or anger.

Not really.

Thusly, absent expectation, robbed of fellowship, numb to even the smallest slip of affection, she gave herself to the lot. Allowing their dominion. Madness, chaos, and anger. Like a pleasure house whore, ruled by any lord that required bedding. And in this vast hollow, she waited for something to matter. Hoping, all along, for someone to flip the script and prove her empty acquiescence wholly wrong.

And wouldn't you know it? After a time, someone did. At the least, they put in the noble effort to convince her as much.

Valestriel.

The reason to her madness. The order to her chaos. A calm to her anger. A rebel to free her from her darkly rulers.

Only…

…oh, gods…

…no…

…but she'd tried to escape it, hadn't she? Tried to let Val off the hook. Tried to disappear. Even tried to die inside a bottle or behind the black of some blood-mad tavern thug's fist.

But the fates wouldn't allow it, keen to her pitiful ruse.

"Reckon we all have our own shit to smell at one point or another."

The last words she ever shared with her rebel savior. Words she meant like fire at the time. Words she'd eat for every breath yet left her. The gods know, but even a thieving harlot deserved better.

"All this for a boy," Val shouted in reply. *"A fucking human boy?"*

But the poor girl never had a chance.

Not really.

For by the time she and Morgan found one another, her oppressors had crept too far inside. Too deep to be undone by a fancy as fickle as love. Too entrenched to be fooled by a soft body and a tender tongue. No matter how remarkable. No matter how kind.

She was meant to be alone, they said. Madness, chaos, and anger for company. That was how the fates designed her, that Morgandrel Tully. That was how it was written.

But Morgandrel Tully was dead, she reminded, wishing for all the world she'd made the decision sooner, *dead and buried.*

The rift spat her into the shroud of falling ash like a spoonful of poison, its gossamer armor peeling away from her in icy chunks.

And Rhymona Curie says the fates are a pit of wanky arseholes, each one that can go fuck itself rotten.

SHE EMERGED ATOP THE BATTLEMENTS, bleary-eyed from the blood candle euphoria surging through her veins, a spellbound specter to the encompassing bloodbath, as a wave of ghouls and phaedrylax abominations climbed up from the courtyards below and tore a grisly slaughterhouse through what remained of the citadel's defenders, pieces of Lancastle's last scattered from end to end as though by tempest, phantoms emerging from the fallen corpses as the break in the barrier between the living and the dead borne them to the hereafter.

A desperate bluecoat passed through her, his face twisted in agony, as one of his legs became nearly severed at the knee by a sword-bearing ghoul and he spun down violently to the stones, only to be mauled by a pair of rabid blighter younglings an instance later.

Further down, a screaming cloth maiden, smothered in gore, brandishing about a skinner's knife, stepped up inside a crenellation as more ghouls closed in on her, and just as they came within an arm's length, set to make a meal of her, she leapt off, preferring an instant death upon the stones below over being eaten alive.

"Well, it's about bloody time." A familiar voice greeted, her slender figure an inky blur inside the dreary fray.

Rhymona's mouth hung as the figure materialized fully. "Stella?" She appeared quite young, mayhaps in her twenties, certainly younger than when Rhymona first met her in Kanton half a decade ago, and almost a different woman entirely from the most recent version she'd beheld in The Bloodbind, long ruby-colored curls cut of a strange fashion long since abandoned to the past. "But how?"

"Who do you think taught Whit how to soulbind?" She stepped in between a pair of phantoms freshly delivered to The Spellbind and shook her head at the statue of Effie and the lichlord in the courtyard below. "I need you to recover something for me. Something our dear lovely Effie was kind enough to keep hidden all these cycles." She aimed a serious glare Rhymona's way. "It's in the library. Inside an old copy of *Humping Your Nan*. It should be in the center row of bookshelves, the row that lines up with The Cupboard's entrance, seven aisles in from the back wall, fifth shelf up."

"Of course, you're assuming the library isn't already in shambles."

"It isn't, I was just there."

"And what's so gods damned important you'd have me risking my neck for some skeevy dead pervert's rag about stuffing old biddies?"

"It's not about the book, Rhymona. It's about what's inside. Namely, a ring."

"A ring?"

"A ring."

"You're a lovely lass and all, but damn Stella, buy a girl a fucking pint first."

"I see your sense of humor's still intact."

"It's all I've got, really."

"More than most."

"I reckon. And you reckon a bloody ring is going to save us?"

"It may. But, prize well, it's not just any ordinary ring. It's a wishing ring."

"Come again?"

"Like the stories of old, yes. They're real. Wish magic is real. But it's quite dangerous. Far more dangerous than the gift. Thusly, the chandii that came to Vaelsyntheria through the godsgate all those cycles ago decided it best to take its knowledge to the grave with them rather than chance it falling into the wrong hands."

"Sounds like the right call given what all we've done with the gift."

"Right. Well, the Critchlow's were rather known for their, shall we say, defiant nature, and they decided to enchant a number of charms and curios with wish engravements. Two of which were left to me. Though one I spent bringing Tam into the world."

"How's that then?"

"I couldn't bear children, so I used one of the wishing trinkets to do so."

"Fuck's sake, Stella."

"Ancient history. And a lesson we haven't the time to recount. What you need to know now about a wish enchantment is that it can only be used once, and it can only be used to affect its possessor."

"So, I can use it to wish myself the fuck off this shithole of a moon then? Desperate times and all." She added a wink and a fang. Though, truthfully, desperate times seemed rather an improvement on the times that presently found them.

"Rhymona, please be serious."

"I am serious. And for that matter, if you're in The Spellbind now, where the fuck have you been all this time? Where were you when Marsea and Magwyn were here?"

"Suffice it to say, there must have been other matters of import at the time. What with all the goings-on, I've tried to make my stamp where I can throughout the castle walks. Though it's no easy chore for a hauntling. As I'm sure you can imagine.

"And affairs became a mite tougher a few days back when my connection to the living world decided to go and bind herself to a damned lichlord."

Effie.

"She came upon me one day a few months back, sensing my gift through her own, I reckon. And once we had an understanding of each other, I asked her to recover the ring, which I hid in my old chambers while I was head archivist, and in return, she asked me to help investigate some odd behavior involving a few of the other Rin at the Maiden House."

"What odd behavior?"

"Strange noises in the night, darkland scrawlings in the cellars, girls suddenly gone without a trace, the usual bollocks."

"And what did you find?"

"Little to nothing thus far. Whoever is behind it all has proven themselves quite the Clever Sally."

"Of course, they have."

"Neither here nor there now, given all this." She gestured to the encompassing carnage. "At any rate, where are you? Who is still with you?"

"The King's Solar with Remy, Maggie, and a trio of Harvers."

"Dodgy company, those Harvers."

"Now that's being generous."

"What of Tam? Aiden? Marsea?"

"Marsea and Aiden are alive as of a few hours ago. They're headed north for *The N'therN'rycka*."

"Aiden's alive? He managed to expel the demon?"

"He did, though it would seem he was not the bastard's intended mark in the end."

"Tell me it's not her."

"We'll get her back, yeah."

"Bugger," she fired a dark scowl at the far winds. "I figured it was only a matter of time before the fiend unearthed our true lineage."

"Aiden houses a dracari soul that supposedly knows the grimoire's whereabouts. A grimoire believed to be Tetherow's phylactery. So, there's a chance. By the way, found out the root of our little blood curse."

"Did you now?"

"And apparently I'm immune to the nether, so there's a thing."

"A convenient thing."

"Did you know about the alternate realities and time loops?"

"The thought had teeth, but dream dancing is, shall we say, erratic, and horribly unreliable…"

"I'll take your word for it. Long story, short. Me, you, Marsea, and Lita Drufellyn are bound by this curse. And if we all die, it closes the loop and begins again."

"Lovely business there."

"Aye, and there are only two of us left."

"Two of you? You mean to say Lita is dead?"

"So goes the tale."

"You're sure of this?"

"Marsea told me as much. And I have no reason to doubt her."

"Did Marsea see it happen?"

"No. Her father relayed the message."

"Her dead father?"

"Obviously." Rhymona's eyes narrowed. "What do you know, Stella? And why do I mislike your tone?"

"I won't pretend to know Whitman's mind, but I know the story of Lita falling from her mare to be utter horseshit."

"You believe her alive then?"

"I cannot rightly say, but I suspect."

"Why would Whitman lie? And why wasn't she in The Bloodbind with us, for that matter? As I understand it, the curse calls to all of us regardless of location."

"Aye, it *calls* to you. But does it force you to enter?"

A fair point. She'd been off her tits at the time thanks to the ghost blossom in Courowne's underground temple, so no telling what a modicum of restraint might have provided her. "Let's just assume it doesn't, and she's still alive then. Would that not be a good thing?"

"Under normal circumstances I'd say yes, but considering she was there when Tetherow killed me and did nothing to prevent it, I have my doubts."

"She was *what?*"

"Oh, yes. She was there, waiting on my porch, in the shadows, with her wand leveled at me as I found Aiden in the foyer. He'd triggered one of my wards inside and I came to investigate. I admit, my first instinct was to protect my son, not thinking for a second that the pair of them could possibly be in league together. And by the time I realized my mistake, by the time I invoked the demon within him, it was much too late."

"So, it's true then? Aiden killed you?"

He wasn't lying. Not that she thought he ever would about such a thing, and not that she could ever truly forgive him for what he'd done to Val, but maybe, just maybe, she wouldn't bash the fucker's brains in once this was all said and done.

"Tetherow forced my son, the prince, to kill me, gambling I'd not stand against the boy to stop it. Trust, I had the thought to try and fight him, to at least give the bastard a little fuck you to remember me by, but doing so would have caused a commotion and would have risked inviting Tam and Vincent to the fold."

"You just let that prick murder you?"

"I let it kill my body, but as you can see, I'd already made a contingency plan. The same could not be said for my daughter or husband. I had to chance my death would be enough to put them off my family. To put them off Tam's truth."

Rhymona slouched, positively gobsmacked. "Reckon it was."

"Aye."

"So, it's possible and more likely than not that Lita is working with Tetherow? As though we haven't enough fucking problems to sort." Her spirit seethed, a scream pressing for release. "I mean look at this shit," she waved a hand out to the massacre surrounding them. Blood and body parts by the wagonload. "It's like we're in a fucking abattoir out here. What's even going to be left if we do survive all of this?"

"I know."

"What does the bitch look like?" She growled. "I may as well add her sorry arse to my list of fuckwits to punch a blade through."

"She's ashaeydir, appearing middle-aged, I suppose, by midaran standards. Mayhaps around your own count. And she had dark, curly hair. Remarkably plain features. The sort you would likely forget at the passing. Save for her eyes. Her eyes haunt me still, even in death. A ring of dark yellow shaped by a wall of crimson. The number of ashaeydir I've ever beheld, I can count on half a hand, but still, I've never heard of an ashaeydir with eyes like that."

"Nor have I. She was likely possessed then. Tetherow split himself into my aunt, after all. I'd find little surprise if he'd done the same with Lita." *The bastard is a gods damned hydra. Cut off the head and two more grow back in its place.*

"Mayhaps. I thought someone should know as much, since the topic arose, but back to the wishing ring. There's a reason I've been waiting on you specifically, Rhymona. You are the gift's chosen. That is why death won't claim you despite your best efforts. And why you break yourself off from others when they tarry too close. You are the gift's champion and the demon that burrowed its way inside Prince Desmond is the nether's chosen."

"And what exactly am I to do with that?"

"I'm merely giving you what I've uncovered. I don't know their proper names yet, but the gift and the nether, as we call them, are ancient entities, clashing between the stars, presumably the last of their kind, one ruled by chaos, the other by order. And we're just the latest world in their path. The stars only know how many others they've torn through over the centuries. And these beings are well beyond the mere comprehension of mortals. They war with what each world provides them. As such, they have adapted into something we can partly grasp. Though if I'm being completely honest, and try as we might, I don't believe we're meant to understand them at all."

"No, apparently we're just meant to serve them."

"They've given us this world as it is now. For worse and for better."

"And so, what would you have me do then? Bend over and spread cheek simply because the gift demands it? I'm the last bitch you want as your champion, prize well."

"That is where you are wrong, Rhymona. I've seen how you are. I've looked into your mind. Into your dreams. I've seen your truths. You are the perfect choice for a champion. You are fearless, selfless—"

"Don't forget damaged."

"Disinterested in coin or accolades, unbothered by the opinions of others—"

"Well, that one's debatable."

"But mostly because you believe yourself disposable. And foolishly so, I might add."

"Rousing speech, milady," she made a dainty applause like the nobles of court, raising her chin past toff level, "truly."

"The gift is with you now. In this place. Mending your wounds on the other side as it's done countless times before. And you may feel some sort of way about what all it has taken from you over the cycles, but the gift is not going to simply go away because of some societal principles you've a grievance with."

"Oh, fuck you, Stella. It's not that simple." *A new high for you, Rhymona, arguing with a dead woman.*

"Have you not taken as much from it as it from you? All you need do is listen to it. Open yourself up to it. Stop pushing it away when it doesn't suit your every mood."

"I didn't ask for this shit."

"I'm well aware. And no, it's not fair. Nothing about any of this is fair. But you have a responsibility."

"Fuck that."

"You want out of this? You need to open up. You need to let it—" Stella's jaw hung mid-sentence, as though she'd become petrified, and Rhymona followed her abyssal stare beyond the haze of ashfall, into the distance, as a massive twisting creature rent through the night sky, maws bellowing all the hells nine furies.

And here's this wanklord right on schedule...

CHAPTER FOURTEEN

WE BECAME CUT off from the others in the scramble," Edgar explained as the group congregated inside the King's Solar. "Poppy," he shook his head. "Poor girl, one second she was running beside us, the next—" his lips thinned, and his eyes drifted down to his boots.

Remy placed a hand against the arm of his swordbrother, a paltry attempt at comfort, but given the scale of horrors closing in on them, there were no words or actions to truly ease the pain.

"Was Sir Wils with you?" Aunt Maggie asked from the entryway.

"No," Edgar answered. "He remained behind with the cloth maidens. I can only assume they are still in the guest quarters. Hopefully safe. Though it's anyone's guess where safety may lie at this point."

Remy's vision flickered over to Julia. "And what exactly were *you* doing on the battlements? I asked you to remain with Lirae Thirsby."

"I wanted to do my part," she answered, trembling, but with iron in her eyes.

"Aye, and you did at that, little lady," Edgar said. "Trust, I would've been ghoul meat myself had it not been for the girl's fast work with a blade."

"Not helping, Edgar," Remy shot his former lover a withering glare.

"The blight doesn't give a fig if I'm nine, Remy," Julia argued, eyes glittering with Harver grit, sword more red and black than silver. "What do you expect me to do? Distract them with dollies and skip-rope?"

"A point finely made, sister," Pion added.

"Pion?" Julia whispered, taking in her other half-brother, who was leaning over the divan beside... "Father." She rushed past Remy, across the chamber to Raelan's side, all the toughness from only a moment ago evaporated in an instant.

"He's alive," Pion assured, as the sister ran a dirty, shaky hand across her father's sweaty forehead.

"Julie Bug," Raelan rasped as the girl draped herself across his chest, hugging him.

"Not to cut the holiday moment short here, but I think we're all missing the most important aspect of what's happening," Caitlyn chimed in as another screech resonated through the stones. "Namely, whatever the hells that is."

"Dracari drylax!" Rhymona crowed as she burst to life from the depths of her Spellbind trip.

Remy gave the magus a once over as he hurried past her out onto the balcony, Edgar at his side. To the south they found a winged monstrosity spewing waves of azure flame across one of the outer hamlets.

"Piss on my gravestone," Edgar uttered.

The creature landed against the tallest structure in Mythris Pointe, its amorphous mass of flesh shifting around the massive cylindrical bell-tower as it held its position, its antlered head and snout aimed at them.

"Is it just me or is that fucker staring straight at us?" Rhymona asked as she sagged against the castle wall behind them, gently massaging her throat.

"That would appear to be the case," Remy said.

"Fuck's sake, you mangy shit-biscuit. At least buy me a bloody pint first."

"That'll be sure to frighten it off," Pion added as he hobbled through the doorway joining Remy and Edgar at the balustrade.

"Oi, I've already thrown one of you cuntrags off a ledge tonight, don't think I won't add to the list," Rhymona warned.

"So long as you hold me tight in the after."

"If you two are quite finished with the foreplay, mayhaps we can formulate something of a plan here," Remy quibbled, pausing on Rhymona. "And why the fuck are you making that face right now?"

"What face?" the magus questioned.

"What do you mean what face? That fucking face you have there. The bat-shit mental face you wear every time you're about to make an incredibly daft decision."

"I had a visitor in The Spellbind. Stella. She told me about a wishing ring hidden in the library and gave me its location."

Remy blinked slowly. "Go on."

"She believes it can be used against the nether."

"In what way?"

"That part she was rather unsure of. But it can't hurt to add to our arsenal, can it?"

"We don't have the time for another wild goose chase."

"That's why I'll be doing it alone."

"Alone? Don't be daft."

"This isn't a conversation." She backstepped into the solar. "I mean to do this with or without your support, Remy."

LET HER GO. WE HAVE OUR PROBLEMS TO SORT.

The woman has a bloody death wish.

I WAS INSIDE HER WITH THE NETHER, LEST YOU FORGET. TRUST, SHE HAS SEEN MORE HORRORS THAN YOU HAVE QUINTS. IF ANYONE CAN SURVIVE THE HALLS ALONE, IT IS HER.

I don't want to lose her, Thira.

THAT IS NOT YOUR CHOICE TO MAKE, PRINCELING.

Remy sighed.

"I take it Thira agrees?" Rhymona said from inside, already halfway across the chamber.

"I better see you again," the watchman said, following after her. "I mean it."

"Yes, Mother," she called, disappearing out into the King's Hall.

He turned to Edgar.

"Whatever the plan, I'm coming with you," Edgar said before he could start.

"Someone has to watch after this lot." Remy eyed Pion. "They are not to be left unmanaged."

"What, you think I'm going to do a runner?" Pion snorted. "You should've seen me in the stairwell earlier. Nearly shit myself before I hit the halfway mark."

"I will watch him," Caitlyn said as she ripped the cane out from under Pion's hand and fingered the clasp to reveal the hidden blade within.

The warlock barely had the chance to brace himself against the wall and likely only did so out of habit. Remy recalled kicking his cane out from under him on more occasions than he cared to admit. Mayhaps on a different day, in another reality, he might have apologized for his past slights, but not after all the atrocities this wretched version has brought forth.

"I trust her," Magwyn said. "Not that we really have much of a choice here, given our numbers."

"There's my silver. Are you satisfied?" Pion snapped. "Shall I varg into Ripley to keep the peace? Shackle myself to one of the corpses you lot left in the King's corridor?"

"You did this to yourself, Pion," Remy said. "And here's your chance to not muck it up further. I love Julia. More than anything. More than a thousand tomorrows. More than a promise of safety. If any harm should come to her before I return there is no place on this moon or the next that I won't hunt to put you in mud. Is that clear?"

Pion smiled. The bastard actually smiled. "Crystal."

"Remy," Julia met him midway through the chamber. "I love you too." She flung her arms around him, squeezing tight, and he pulled her in close.

"I was wondering if I'd ever get to hear those words again."

"It doesn't mean goodbye," she said, doing her best to mask a sniffle. "And you'd better come back."

"I have every intent to."

"Here," she handed him a pewter flask.

"What's this?"

"Rotgut. For the nerves."

"And what are you doing with a kiss of rotgut?"

"A jape, brother." She held up a second identical flask. "It's actually one of the potions I nicked from Courowne. One for each of us."

Smirking, he clinked his again hers. "I'll cheers to that."

"Remy." Raelan sat up with a grimace. "By the hearth there. You'll find your family's sword."

The watchman followed to where the General gestured, prying apart the shadows to find a familiar smear of white-silver watching.

Exylduin. The blade of Cameron the Conqueror. The first Lanier king. A blade Raelan claimed during the Coup of the Midnight Men and flaunted about the castle walks every day since. A blade Remy had never held in his own hands, not once, in spite of his birthright.

"Take it. It's yours. And well earned."

Another Harver telling me what I have and haven't earned.

Remy strode over to the sword like a sailor at the siren's song, as though the ghosts of his ancestors that wielded it prior were suddenly calling out to him. How often had he dreamt of this moment? What he'd do with such a weapon at his disposal. Truth be told, this was not at all the scene he envisioned at their pairing, but then again, those which derive from fantasy rarely are.

I HAVE BEHELD A BLADE LIKE THIS BEFORE. THE RUNES UPON HER FACE. THEY ARE CHANDIIAN.

A memory shot through Remy's skull like a burning arrow, the same one he witnessed from before, of Darazko LeDrange, Thira's rider, hobbling out from under his fallen dracari's heaving body to face an impossible mob of approaching soldiers. This time the watchman fixated on the massive kindleglaive clutched inside the Chandii warrior's hand, cerulean symbols glowing down its side seething an otherworldly mist.

Do you know what they mean?

THEY ARE ENCHANTMENTS. MOSTLY WARDS AGAINST THE NETHER.

I've never seen those runes on her before.

AND YOU NEVER LOOKED AT HER WITH YOUR GIFT BEFORE, EITHER.

He retrieved Exylduin from her rest, clenching its gray leather-bound hilt in both hands, noting its impeccable balance as he studied the runes beneath bloodstains, each side of the long, sweeping white-steel blade spattered in gore from guard to tip. Though she'd seen many cycles and wielders, her edges held their sharpness, her ornate cross-guard its silver fangs, and her diamond-shaped pommel appeared a weapon all in itself.

If nothing else, Raelan certainly kept the blade in fine repair.

"Continuing the trend of unearthing long-lost family heirlooms, there is one more thing you should see," Magwyn said as she disappeared into the King's Hall. "Fastly then," she called from outside. "We haven't all night, have we?"

CHAPTER FIFTEEN

THE KING'S PIECE?" Remy uttered as Aunt Magwyn swept a hand out to the wooden dummy in the corner. "I thought Vaustian destroyed it."

Verily, he'd had it from a number of folks over the cycles that the spiteful old fuck had fed it to the furnace ages ago. *The lying bastards.*

He crossed the chamber, clutching Exylduin tight, eyes glued to the starlit patch of silver that stood motionless in the dark.

Serves you right for trusting a Harver, you ruddy knob. How many times had Marsea named Vaustian a hoarder? The gods know, he was practically famous for it.

Remy lay his father's sword across the table and marveled at the hanging suit of armor for a beat before brushing cobwebs from the spaulders. "It seems I may have underestimated Vaustian's fancy for defiling other folk's property."

He removed his gloves and traced naked fingers over the griffin engraved across the breastplate's center. Sure, it was a bit dull in places, especially along the sleeves of plated iron, its better cycles long since spent, but for the most, it retained its silver sheen as though fresh off a polish.

Remy recalled the portraits of his father and grandfather donning the armor, and how brave and stoic they looked. Like true knights. When such a thing existed. In their mold, he'd always fantasized about sporting the legendary armor himself, ever since he could remember really.

He retrieved the oval-shaped helm from the dummy's head, studying it in the starlight before fitting it over his dark curls and gazing back at his aunt. It was surprisingly light. Smelled a bit off, a faint scent of oil amongst the musk of its former bearers, but there were certainly much worse matters to quibble over just now.

"It suits you," she said.

"It does at that," Edgar added from the doorway, arms crossed.

Remy blushed as he lifted the helm from his head and sat it on the table, his heart racing. "Will you help me don the rest?" He aimed the question at his former swordbrother.

"'Twould be my honor."

Magwyn glanced from Edgar to Remy, something like an understanding passing across her features. "I'll leave you to it then."

Once alone, Remy's eyes fastly darted to Edgar's, dancing from his mouth to his penetrating gaze. By no means was the Lanier prince any sort of great authority in the language of love and affection, but he thought he found what he was looking for in the man's orbs.

To have it true, their parting hadn't been so pretty. All distant words and cold shoulders. Certainly, nowhere near as pretty as their sessions exploring one another amidst the cupboards and back alleys of Castle Nightsbridge and her seedy hamlets, Remy, lost in a fever dream of thirst, pushing for more whilst Edgar did his damnedest to maintain some measure of reason between them, holding a decade's count in cycles over his smitten lover.

Though, what was love, after all, in a place like The King's Wall? Amongst the hags and heathens and long since forsaken? A pitiless place, hollow and bitter, unmoved by even the smallest moan of romanticism.

At that, his mother's words came back for a timely visit, echoes that felt of a bygone era. Words given when he'd tried to come out to her; the fool he was.

Royals marry for power and standing, Rembrandt. Not love.

Of course, he'd made a shambles of the delivery, nervous as a slag at sermon, so the confusion wasn't completely her fault. But instead of explaining further, or questioning her fidelity to his father, he simply nodded his understanding and got on with his day. Such had been their relationship throughout the cycles. For Larissa Lanier was not one to be quibbled with and, unlike his quarrelsome sister, Remy was scarce one to needlessly start a row.

Little did he know half a quintweek later he'd turn tail from his life-long home, eighteen cycles old, blood on his hands, fear in his heart, venom on his tongue, and by the time he returned, he'd become something else entirely and his mother was a day away from her deathbed.

"I didn't think I'd ever see you again," Remy said, his voice suddenly wanting as he fell back into the present.

"Nor I you." Edgar returned with a warmth that instantly transported Remy back to their tryst in Ravenshire, all heavy heartbeats, moon-eyes, and honeyed words, the pair having stolen away from patrol to some fallen Lord's whore-house at the edge of town.

An endless supply of whiskey and wine had him spinning by the time they made it to a bedchamber, bottle in hand, barely able to keep his legs under him. Edgar to one side, Mia to the other, his breath thick with berries and oak, his chest burning like a midsummer's noontide.

It was the first time Remy had ever lain with a woman, the second with a man, and if ever he needed confirmation over his preference of sexual partner, this experience indisputably provided it. And, make no mistake, for a harlot, at least those Remy had taken company with, Mia wasn't so bad a fetch for the eyes. Good teeth, dimpled smile, and curves that would, no doubt, make any straight man stand at attention regardless of his sobriety. Still, his eyes belonged to Edgar and Edgar alone that eve...Edgar, Edgar, Edgar...Remy recalled the troughs and valleys of muscle beneath his swordbrother's uniform. *Absolutely divine, those troughs and valleys.*

"What happened after I left?" the watchman inquired, words of a vacant nature.

"I'd rather not talk about it," Edgar replied, a wave of guilt coursing the plains of his darkly haunters.

Remy halved the space between them. "You would deny your king?"

"My king, is it? King of all this bollocks?"

"Only a jape. You know I'm not like that."

"Aye."

"And tell it true, what if *this* is all we get? This moment here. Given what we're up against, there's certainly no promise of tomorrow."

"And what exactly are you after here, *my king?*"

"The truth. Whatever the result. You'll catch no judgements here."

"I abandoned my oath, Remy. I deserted your Kingswatch. Left my swordbrothers for the rot. And, truthfully, I'd do it again if put to the choice. Was that what you wished to hear?" Edgar turned away and strode over to the dummy, lifting the spaulders and breastplate from their placement, and set them upon the table between them, his eyes flicking back up to Remy's. "Trust, the decision had nothing to do with our falling out."

"I hadn't thought it would."

"Then why bloody ask?"

Remy stared at his swordbrother, jaw clenched. Physically, Edgar Alewine wasn't anywhere near his typical preference. Sure, he was tall, dark, and mysterious in a rugged, off-the-beaten-path sort of way, made all the more so by his recent bout with the ghoulish horde topping the battlements, but he wasn't exactly conventionally attractive, especially not by comparison to the powdered toffs of court Remy had grown up with or the dandy dreadfuls posting the street corners calling sweet nothings to any noble with pockets and a taste for a dashing young sugar boy. Quite the opposite, in fact. He bore an assortment of scars across his neck and cheek, most that looked to have been made with a blade, and a crooked nose that had clearly been broken at some point, but was never set back correctly...

...and yet there was something alluring about him. Something beautiful and undeniable that Remy could not simply ignore. Mayhaps it was his boldness, mayhaps his confidence and worldliness. Or mayhaps it was merely formed by some mistook semblance of safety he felt within Edgar's company. Whatever it was, it was there, and rejecting it was a feat wholly beyond him.

"Because I care about you and I want to know as much about you as you'll offer. I know my timing is shit, but here we are at the end of all tomorrows so I figured fuck it, why not?"

"Fuck's sake, Remy, you're an odd one, you know that?"

"Duly aware, yes."

"A few days after you left with the Black Stags, Van Wyck had us searching The Scar in hunt of a lost patrol. One captained by his son."

Hugh Van Wyck. The biggest prat in the Kingswatch. Remy recalled how the smug fucker seemed to have it out for him from the moment he stepped foot in Nightsbridge. Making his life as miserable as possible, be it in the tourney yard, the card house, the mess hall...hells, even the barracks. Insults aplenty, empty threats galore, goading and cowing and the like. Intimidations of the insecure and idiotic. Sure, it was a nuisance, but truth was, it paled by comparison to his cycles of dancing around the Harver's unending procession of ruthless head games.

"Sending men by the score into that bloody cesspit. Not a one returned. Most were saying he'd gone mad well before Hugh's disappearance. I'm sure you heard something of the like before you left for Brymshire."

"Something about a curse, if I recall?"

"Aye, a curse by some bog witch they'd butchered outside one of the river villages last harvest whilst on holiday. And, of course, then came all the typical tales of scandal and sorcery that bubble up when shit starts to go the slightest tick sideways."

"Of course."

"Rumor was some dish wench found Old Hughie one night at the Honeypot deep in his cups. This would've been around the cycle's turn. It was said this wench got to sitting in Hughie's lap, twisting about his ear, and proceeded to fuck the young lord's brains out as the night wore on. What little brains he had left, mind you. Then she got on feeding him some ripe old bullshite about a long-lost trinket just inside The Scar containing untold powers. Sounded like a load of hogwash to me, and likely would have seemed the like to any man of a right mind, but we all know the good Lord Hughie was ever a few cards short of a proper deck, yeah."

"Well, that's being charitable."

"Aye, and given all that, I had it from Carrington of all folk so I took the tale with a grain of salt, as you do. There was certainly no telling how much of it was true coming from that tosser, but apparently, there was enough in it to push a rigid old codger like Creed Van Wyck into lunacy's arms.

"Running out of soldiers, he eventually called on Dread Company to walk the gallows. And wouldn't you know it, a couple hours in, we actually found some of our swordbrothers. Hugh amongst them. Walking corpses they were, commanded by a lichlord riding the ugliest horse I'd ever beheld. We swiftly found ourselves outnumbered, so of course we beat path. And before long it was just me and Hawkins left. Somehow, by the skin of our teeth, we made it back to The Wall. But something was eating at me in its presence, begging me not to return, telling me The Wall was a death pit, and imploring me to push south. So that's what I did. I tried to convince Hawkins to abandon with me, but—" He glanced away, shaking his head. "A few days later I came upon a troupe and decided to make some use of my scouting talents. And eventually, we crossed paths with your sister outside Debynshire. And, well, a portal and a hundred cut-up corpses later here we are." A sarcastic grin beat back the ghastly tale as he beheld the princeling once more. "Was that a tale to your satisfaction, milord?"

Remy's hand rose to Edgar's torn eyebrow, a thumb brushing against it. "And what happened here?"

"Caught a branch fleeing the blight. Had me seeing stars for a stretch."

The watchman studied his swordbrother's lips, inching closer, brushing knuckles down the back of his jawline. "I can believe it."

"I've had worse," Edgar answered, a hair above a whisper, a breath away...

...and much too near for Remy to contain himself, apparently, as the hunger from their dalliance in Nightsbridge came back for a quick thrill, causing a swelling between his legs, and he drifted forward pressing his lips against Edgar's, tongue splitting the space between.

"Hoh, hold," Edgar pulled away, eyes large as the sister moons. "What the hells are you..."

"I'm sorry." Remy withdrew a step, his cheeks flushing. "I don't know why I did that." *The lies we tell.* "I thought I..."

...wanted to taste you...

"No, I...I didn't mean it like that. It's fine. I just wasn't expecting it. I mean hell, ten minutes ago I was caught in a shitstorm of ghouls running for my life, thinking it fastly done for, and now..."

"Not to make this about me, but I've lost a lot in the last few days, Edgar. We all have. And there's just so much we can never get back. Prize well, if there's any one thing I understand in all this world, it's losing something you can never get back. So, when I saw you in that doorway, somehow here, somehow alive, after thinking you gone with all the rest, I just...I thought..."

Edgar leaned in, as he'd done so often during their time at The Wall, pressing closer and closer, forcing Remy against the stones, until he had nowhere else to go, their eyes unwilling to part.

"I'm not afraid of us," Remy said. "Of me. Of who I truly ammm—"

Edgar silenced him, his lips crashing against Remy's, crushing against one another, Edgar's patch of facial hair rubbing Remy's stubble raw as they tore at each other like a feast from famine.

REMY.

Not now, Thira.

Their lips twisted about one another, soft then hard, grinding, as Remy pushed back off the wall, their flickering tongues slick and unwilling to part, the prince's pulse quickening as Edgar untied his leather armor and he shook it from his shoulders, leaving him in just his shirt above the waist.

They spun about in their reckless lust until he bumped against the table, wooden legs grating across stone, and Edgar lowered from Remy's mouth to the side of his neck, wet lips nipping gently across the span of his throat before his teeth sank in on the other side and he began sucking deep.

YOU FORGET YOURSELF, PRINCELING.

Gee, Thira, I can't imagine why.

He could hardly keep track of his own spacial awareness, much less offer his dracari passenger anything approaching a halfway acceptable response. Clever fingers trailed from his ribs down his abdomen to the growth in his trousers, cupping his bulge gently before constricting around his throbbing hardness.

Gods, I missed this. He nearly moaned, all but consumed by the moment, eyes rolling back in his head, and for an instant it was almost as though time had stopped. *I could just live in this forever.* A palm slid to his swordbrother's bottom, urging him nearer, Edgar's ample mass stabbing against his thigh. *If only—*

A bloodcurdling screech rent through their stroking and snogging like a blade across glass, its banshee wail coursing through the castle stones and carving a shiver up his backside.

"Fuck," the watchman groaned, his eyes bursting open.

Time resumed as a large black mass tore past the outer wall, sucking the starlight from the chamber, blotting their dalliance in a lightless eclipse.

Without word, Edgar hurried to the window.

"See anything?" Remy asked.

"Nothing."

"This isn't over," Remy promised as he situated his fastly shrinking length.

Edgar shook his head, taking in the prince once more. "I've had more than my fair share of lovers over the cycles, but you..."

"Oh, you haven't seen the best of me yet, gorgeous." Remy wiped fingers across his tender lips. "Now help me into this armor. And for all the stars left us don't you dare go out there and get yourself bloody killed."

CHAPTER SIXTEEN

WITHIN A HALF HOUR, Edgar had him fully armored and they were out the King's corridor and onto the nether-infested battlements, Remy's long navy cape flapping in the storm of magic like a war banner, Exylduin burning bright under kiss of dragon's flame, slicing through blighters like a scythe at field.

Those that didn't get the sword burst apart at Thira's breath, like acid on the wind, curse after curse off their tongue, creating a crimson flood as it spread like a plague amongst the undead legion ahead.

Behind him, Emyria called curses of her own, amplified through Magwyn's scepter, as Edgar and a band of survivors they'd come upon in the upper halls beat back any undesirables from the other side with sword and shield.

Chasing headlong into the sea of combusting ghouls, Remy put some distance between himself and the others, hoping to spin up enough gift use to attract the dracari drylax's attention.

Between blight attacks, he glanced through the narrow eye slits in his helm to the south at the hamlet of Marigaul where the creature breathed bright azure horror from avenue to avenue, tendrils of black smoke rising up from the ruins like fingers from the grave.

Shrieks and shouts could be heard from every direction, hundreds upon hundreds of voices, the hells upon them; though, as ever, it was impossible to tell which belonged to the living and which to the blight.

And the blight proved an endless flood, their bodies mere puppets, dislocating under spriteling invasion, bones snapping and bending into impossible shapes and positions to better endure his ferocious barrage.

Exylduin cleaved through a squealing phaedrylax like a saw through silk, sending dozens of screeching spritelings raining down across the snowy walkway behind him, as he pressed on to the next monster, his movements smooth as quicksilver, spinning away from its massive, hooked appendage and hurling an egg of Eldn flame at it with his offhand. The creature caught flame and began a terrible howl that Remy silenced a moment later with a deft cut that split its temple at a queer angle, and before it could kiss the blood-caked stones, he was past it and hacking through the next unspeakable wretch that needed undoing.

Drenched in gore, he was beyond the gift, practically elemental, melding mantia he knew not a proper name for, as the corpse blood rose up around him, a river of carnage, glistening with bright azure flecks, called to a static pulse by his electric vibrations, and he moved within her humming current, slick as a razorblade tidal wave, ruled by chaos, guided by instinct, dodging and weaving like a madman, hewing through any poor bastard unlucky enough to darken his path.

Until he met a rising black wall.

Hells.

THERE YOU ARE.

Remy halted but briefly, pupils narrowing to pinpricks, blazing azure flame in one hand, shimmering steel in the other, only the snowfall between them, and Thira compelled the Eldn egg at the colossal mass of moving flesh, using the force of its casting to push them back, sliding across the sleet-glossed stones, as a great maw came slamming down into the space he previously held, severing its head in twain upon impact, splashing him in a spray of thick black ichor, as a second bellowing head from the hells only knew where raced in at him.

Following his intuition, he leapt to an impossible height, all gift and glory, by some manner of bat-shit aeromancy, and plunged Exylduin inside its misshapen snout as he hurtled back down like a star thrust from the heavens.

Roaring in pain, the dracari head tried to jerk away from its attacker, but Remy drove the blade down deeper as the beast rose up, snapping its malformed jaw, and shaking its head to throw its unwanted rider, before pushing off from the battlements and taking flight.

Remy clung on for dear life as the world blurred shapeless and another pit of serrated yellow teeth began to form atop its massive head, joined by a pair of thrashing tentacles that sprouted from its forehead like some bastard form of antennae.

"Burn, you fucker!" The watchman pressed a palm of azure fire into it and bellowed bloody hellfire as the nether skin beneath began to spit, crackle, and warp.

At the branding, the drylax emitted a collective wail from its many ghastly maws, and Remy pushed up from his bladed anchor, loping off one of the antennae and leaping from the shrieking half-formed mouth atop its forehead, striding along the length of its melting crown, carving Exylduin through its rancid flesh, leaving a trail of tall cerulean flames seething behind him as he made for its greater mass.

And the gods knew, navigating the beast's twisting body was like running across a pockmarked marshland dampened from a fresh rainfall that reeked worse than a tavern privy after Fairer's Tilt, each step a different feel, one, hard as bone underfoot, the next like soggy earth.

By the citadel's location, he reckoned they were gliding somewhere high above the southern hamlets again, but before he could form a thought as to his next move, the beast hit a quick dive, plummeting groundward.

"Fucking hells!"

Remy's stomach went into his throat at the drop and he nearly slipped off, his helm twisting about his face, blocking his vision, the snapped chin strap flapping across his neck.

Somehow, in his tumble, he managed to plunge Exylduin back inside the shifty miscreation's pulpy flesh and not a moment too soon, as the beast began a series of snaking, spinning maneuvers that surely would have sent him screaming to a fast grave.

Daring a hand free, he ripped the loose helm off, tossing it to the winds, before grasping the hilt again with both hands.

"Come on you bastard!" he hollered, hair whipping about wildly. "That all you got?"

As though in response, he felt a sharp pain in the back of his leg and looked down to find a pair of beady-eyed spritelings clawing and gnawing at the straps of his greaves. "You've got to be shitting me," he growled, kicking at them, sending both flying, their wings preventing them from a messy death below. Though more of the foul buggers were beginning to wake and scratch their way through the surrounding hatchling sacs lining the nether drake's skin.

"Not good."

NOT AT ALL.

As fortune faired, the dracari drylax leveled off as it drifted above the lower city, and Remy worked his way back into a kneeling position checking that the tome holster strapped to his belt remained intact, breathing a sigh of relief when he found *Dusk* still tucked snugly within.

They were soaring roughly twenty feet above the kingdom cobble now, and Remy could make out bluecoats and townsfolk and phaedrylaxes in the shambles below, though it was anyone's guess which side, if either, held the advantage. For every string of gift-lightning crackling through a patch of blighters, there was an equally horrifying drylax shredding through a band of Lancastle defenders.

His gaze rose back to the dracari drylax where he found a trio of ill-shapen heads at one end, then behind at the tail, which was split apart into half a dozen lashing tentacles that were ripping through the rooftops below, creating all manner of havoc for those within the vicinity.

If you've got a plan for what we do now, I'm all ears.

DESPITE ITS ATTEMPTS TO SHED ITS ORIGINAL FORM, THE NETHER APPEARS CONFINED FOR THE MOST PART TO THE SHAPE OF A DRACARI. MAYHAPS THERE IS SOMETHING IN A DRAGON'S MAGIC THAT THE NETHER CANNOT COMPLETELY BEND.

Meaning what exactly?

MEANING IT MAY ALSO BE FALLIBLE TO THE SAME EFFECTS THAT SLAY DRAGONS. OR MAYHAPS ATTACKING THOSE WEAKNESSES MAY BE ENOUGH TO PUT IT DOWN OR WEAKEN IT.

Are you suggesting a good old sword to the vitals then?

I AM SUGGESTING WE DIG OUR WAY INSIDE THE FIEND AND FIND OUT.

Don't suppose you've a spell for conjuring spades.

Dragon's flame razed the kingdom streets beneath them, the screams and battle cries of the warring sides incinerated in an instant, followed by a stifling heat and stench.

"Oi, shithead," he howled, swinging Exylduin round so its tip faced the nether flesh at his feet and with all his might he drove it down into the darkness, twisting and jerking the hilt from side to side, black liquid welling up from the meaty perforation and spilling off what served as the creature's flanks, prompting an ear-piercing cry. "You forget about me?"

One of the dracari heads disappeared inside its torso and a fanged maw formed across its backside, opening up like a swamp-hunting crocodile surging toward them.

"Well, that certainly got its attention." He turned to run, but Thira held him in place. "What are you doing?" he cried.

SOMETHING BAT-SHIT MENTAL, AS YOU SAY.

"Gods tits, speak plainly, Thira."

WE ARE INFESTING THE PARASITE.

"And what part of that is plainly?"

LET IT TAKE US.

"I'm sorry, let it do what now?"

TRUST ME, REMY.

"We'll be torn to bits if we stay—"

I SAID TRUST ME.

At the declaration, Thira's essence burned from vein to heart to artery erupting azure nightmare from the candle scars across his palms, racing up Exylduin's silver spine, as a phantom tempest tore through the natural winds about him, creating a sparkling vortex bubble, his greasy curls and cape floating unnaturally within as though he were drifting weightless amidst the stars above.

And she began carving at the creature's skin, more gurgling black liquid, more bloodcurdling shrieking that soon faded for Thira's witching song, like a lullaby, heard as though from underwater.

Arms working.

Chest heaving.

Lungs burning.

Head swimming.

It's nearly on us.

He could barely hear his own thoughts, such was the intensity of her aura.

Thira!

"*...Drothdae al sheenda,...*" Yvemathira cried, ripping the sword up from its scrawl, a ward blazing bright as a midsummer noontide in its wake just as the maw reached them.

With nowhere left to go, he turned shoulder to the collapsing wall of fangs, a familiar sensation rushing through him as he dropped through the shimmering ward at his feet onto his backside, the spiked jaw crashing down like a great swell only inches above them, confining them inside a darkness black as a drunkard's sleep and cold as a midwinter crypt, Kingdom Lancastle disappearing from sight.

"We're still alive," he breathed into the narrow crawlspace, staring up at the dying ward and sloshing nether flesh above them.

OF COURSE, WE ARE.

"What the fuck did you just do?"

I CREATED A SOURCE WARD AND MAPPED IT TO THE OTHER END OF THE WOUND—

"You can create portals inside of...sentient beings?"

YOU CAN CREATE A PORTAL ANYWHERE YOU CAN SCRAWL A WARD, FLESH OR STONE, THE INCANTATIONS HAVE NO PREFERENCE, NOR DOES THE GIFT.

"Good to know," he said, rolling over and pushing up to hands and knees to inch forward, holding out Exylduin like a torch, her cerulean runes illuminating the void within.

IT SEEMED A DECENT ENOUGH NOTION, CONSIDERING.

"Whatever works at this point."

He quickly found that navigating through the drylax was akin to crawling through the insides of a melting candle, the surrounding surfaces all squishy and waxy, sticking to him like a spill of syrup.

AS I PRESUMED, ONCE ON THIS PLANE, ONCE BOUND TO A CORPOREAL CREATURE, AS WITH OUR GIFT-BOUGHT SOULBOND, THE NETHER BECOMES LIMITED BY THAT WHICH IT CONSUMES, AND MAYHAPS IN THOSE LIMITATIONS...

"It becomes mortal," Remy finished, wiping a hand across his chest, for what little good it did.

PRECISELY.

"I can only assume we're inside the creature's belly then," he said, squinting at dark shapes and serpentine shadows. Though, truly, naught within appeared of the living variety.

A REASONABLE ASSUMPTION.

Movement from up ahead drew his attention and he stared at the space it bothered, swallowing thickly.

Silence, long as an age.

WHAT IS IT?

I thought I saw something.

At their exchange, something pushed up against his hip.

"What fresh hell?"

All at once, the walls came alive around him, various forms taking shape between slithering vines and pulsating red eyes, like figures trapped in mud, as hands and arms and faces pushed inward at him and a clicking sound reverberated about the slender squeezeway.

"Shit. Holy mother of fucking…"

His pulse quickened as he squirmed through the drylax's slimy internal lining, the hands in the walls sprouting arms and hands of their own with odd-shaped fingers, reaching for him from just beneath the surface.

A face pressed in at him, coming for his own, teeth gnashing, and he flinched away from it, unable to draw Exylduin forth in the space given.

PAY NO MIND TO THESE HEAD GAMES, REMY. THE NETHER IS USING YOUR FEARS. YOUR SHAME. YOUR REGRETS. YOU CANNOT TRUST ANYTHING YOU SEE IN HERE.

His heart caught as he turned back toward the path ahead and found the father and daughter from Brymshire laying there before him, a pair of ghastly, chewed-up corpses.

THEY ARE NOT REAL. THINK ON IT. HOW COULD THEY POSSIBLY BE REAL?

"It could be showing me what became of them."

IT IS SHOWING YOU WHAT YOU FEAR BECAME OF THEM. NOTHING MORE. NOW WE MUST BE OFF. WE MUST FIND HRATH-GON'S HEART. I KNOW IT IS STILL IN HERE, FOR THE CREATURE YET BREATHES ELDN FIRE.

A goblin snicker from the space just over his shoulder had him worming forward, kicking and cursing and elbowing, hands slipping about the viscous enclosure as he spewed out into a larger space like a babe from the womb.

"Ugh, what the hells?" He found himself coated to the armpits in the treacly substance that layered nearly every fel inch of the beast's insides and tried with little effect to wipe it off him.

"*Rembrandt...*" his mother's voice echoed past, and a blink later she was there before him, half her face missing, what contents that remained spilling out of the gaping wound as she clawed her way toward him.

His breath held, his face wrinkling up in rage as he rose to a crouch.

USING YOUR MOTHER. IT MUST BE DESPERATE NOW.

A shriek rent through the clicking chorus as a spriteling slammed into the side of his head, pulling at his hair, scratching at his cheek, and spitting black ichor that burned at the touch.

He ripped the fucker from its purchase, smashing it into the space that formed something of a floor, and slammed the bottom of his fist into it, again and again, its little body snapping under each blow like a bundle of damp kindling, as another one leapt atop his back, and a third bit at his leg.

The pests were swarming the nether drake's innards like a mischief of rats. He could hear them all around him, eating through the drylax's flesh in at him.

On hands and knees again, he crawled ahead, fast as his battered body would allow, shifting violently from side to side, crushing as many spritelings against the internal lining as possible until they reached a palpitating wall.

WE ARE NEARLY TO THE HEART. WE MUST GO THROUGH IT.

Remy pulled Exylduin in against his side, before thrusting the shimmering blade through the beating wall, and carving in a circular motion, screaming into the faces of the ghoulish shapes within as he pushed through the oozing wound into the next chamber, which, like the last, appeared nothing at all like how one would expect from the insides of a once living creature.

A thunderous rumble rushed in at him from the space ahead, and he lowered his head away from it as another band of spritelings took advantage. He managed to pick most of them off, fighting from his knees, but one particularly determined bugger avoided him long enough to latch onto his face, where it made a valiant attempt to pry his lips apart and burrow inside.

Madness become him, he bit the bugger's head off at the neck, his back teeth crunching down against its tiny screaming skull, the taste of blood filling his mouth, and he spit its crushed remains over his shoulder, like a cut of bad mutton.

"Fuck's sake," he growled, coughing up part of a broken tooth, his own blood welling and running down his chin.

That little shit Remy would have set to the flame and watched over a drag had he the time for it. Instead, he was slicing frantically through the wall opposite, black liquid spilling from the wound as he stabbed and cut about the fleshy folds inside.

And then he hit something hard.

THERE.

A rhythmic throbbing.

Remy jabbed forward once more for confirmation, and the blade made a sound like stabbing a stone column.

I KNEW IT.

A brilliant azure glow gleamed through the bed of tentacles enveloping it and the dracari drylax heads let out a cacophony of shrill cries from just outside as Remy burned through the folds of nether separating him from Hrathgon's heart, the nether flesh unable to mend itself fast enough to keep the heart from its irksome invaders.

Remy drove Exylduin into the space behind the crystallized heart, wresting it loose like a pearl from an oyster as the scorched tentacles fought to reform.

In full, the heart was roughly the size of his entire torso, dropping like a sack of gold through the creature's doughy flesh, out its belly, and somewhere abouts the kingdom streets below.

His eyes went wide. *Oh, bugger.*

"Was that meant to happen?"

IT WAS NOT.

The night air rushed in at them from the opening, all smoke and death rot as a cluster of spritelings crashed into him.

"Damn it all."

And before he could muster something of a defense, a roar from outside the drylax tremored through him, followed by a collision that bent the world crooked as he slammed violently into the shuddering side wall, holding on for all he was worth as the massive beast began to spin about wildly, seemingly end over end, the absence of proper gravity rattling him about the creature's innards like marbles about a pouch. A second jerking motion sent him sprawling and sliding forward through a host of spritelings, as a third harder quake flung them back against the side wall, before the creature evened out and the sensation of skidding forward became them, coming to a full stop a few heavy heartbeats later.

We've landed.

THAT ROAR WAS DRACARI.

Dracari? But I thought Hrathgon the last.

AS DID I.

Shaking his head through a dizzy spell, he staggered to the opening left by the dracari heart and stabbed at it further until there was enough space for him to crawl through. Covered in blood, nether residue, and goblin guts, he rose to his feet in the middle of a square littered with dead and dying, all Lancastle in sight the color of cartilage.

The bulk of the dracari drylax lay atop the rubble of a burning innhouse, a pile of flaming shit, smashed into mostly cream, chunks of nether flesh squirming about the stones toward its greater portion as a blood-colored dragon crashed down from the sky atop it, bat-like wings spread wide, ripping at the nether drake with massive claws, shredding its amorphous remains further.

Remy slammed Exylduin into a clicking ghoul fool enough to try its luck against him, spinning awkwardly and sending the fiend sprawling bloody off the end of his blade. He whirled around at the sound of snarling and tearing flesh behind him, taking in the great beast fully.

RHYVARIATH, Thira uttered.

It appeared unlike anything he'd ever beheld of dracari of lore, its body built more like a lion than a snake, its skull extensions more bull's horn than antler, though its head and snout bore a passing resemblance to that of Thira and her clutch, at least, its considerable maw of razor-sharp fangs did.

The dracari drylax was not to be undone so easily, spitting black steaming ichor in Rhyvariath's face, as it wrapped tentacles around his wings and constricted about the red dragon's brawny arms, trying to rip him apart.

WE HAVE TO HELP HIM.

Rhyvariath breathed azure flame down into the shifting, elongating mass of flesh, until one of the nether's appendages coiled around his throat, ripping his head skyward.

"Name your order." Remy pushed his way through a swarm of ghouls, cutting at anyone daft enough to come for him, the King's piece shielding him from the few strikes that got past his feints and parries.

THE POTION JULIA GAVE YOU.

"Are you mad?" he cried, taking the scalp off a ghoul's head, before driving Exylduin's pointy-end through the last of a cluster, in and out, quick as a flash. "We have no idea what it will do."

AND IF WE DO NOTHING, THE NETHER WILL ADD RHYVARIATH TO ITS LEGION. A LOSS WE CAN ILL AFFORD.

"What's your thought then." He was in no mood for quibbling. Not now.

WE GO BACK IN.

Back in?

Thira rushed over to the nearest building, where they found a number of bludgeoned corpses lying motionless about the floor, and more flies and roaches than Remy had beheld in all his days combined.

Of course, we're in a literal butcher's shop.

Raw, uncut meats of varying lengths hung from hooks behind the counter at the far wall and appeared to have spoiled days ago by the off color. Others had been ripped to the floor, cut up, and gnawed through.

"...This will have to do..." She leaned Exylduin against the wall.

More roaring and screeching from the clashing beasts outside gave them a brief pause before Thira retrieved a knife from the countertop cutlery, fastly running it across Remy's palm and squeezing the blood into a bowl, where she dipped his fingers in and began painting one of the walls with it. Within seconds, she completed a similar ward to the one she'd cut into the dracari drylax, then spoke the tether into existence, a portal rippling to life behind the glowing bloodstains.

Only darkness looked back from within.

IN AND OUT, she bade, and they pushed through it, back inside the pitch of the nether drake's belly, where its pulverized entrails throbbed and leaked internally from all over, as the two beasts thrashed at one another. Remy held his palm to the ward inside the creature to keep the portal open, and fished the flask from his waist pouch with his free hand, working its cap loose with his aching mouth and spitting it.

"Get fucked, asshole," he breathed, tossing the flask into the squeezeway toward the nether drake's center, and diving back through the portal into the butcher's shop as a bright pink mass erupted, and something flapped over his head spattering into the wall opposite the ward just before the tether closed.

A second explosion echoed from outside, followed by the sound of something large and wet slapping into the building on the wall's other side.

Remy glanced briefly at the viscous mass of bright pink what-the-fuckery sliding down the butchery's opposite wall before collecting Exylduin and dashing back out into the snowfall, cutting the building's corner as a third explosion erupted, further painting the square in pink-glazed nether parts.

RHYVARIATH?

The dracari was nowhere to be seen.

In the avenue behind him, one of the nether beast's blasted tentacles came splattering down from the heavens, followed by more raining chunks of fried drylax.

"Chuffing hells."

He hurried back inside the butcher's shop for shelter, propping himself against the doorway, listening to the drumming of blown-apart drylax innards atop the rooftop as a patch of pink and black goo hit the awning's edge and hung down like poured molasses, oozing thick upon the stones below.

After a few moments of quiet, Remy dared a step out into the grisly snowfall and froze as Rhyvariath caught the corner of his eye, wings beating a wind of burnt flesh and winterdust down the avenue, as he came to a landing in the square but a stone's throw away. Slowly, the watchman turned toward the great red dragon, who stood taller than any of the surrounding buildings with row upon row of razored teeth bared and menacing golden orbs that glared down at him as though he'd pinched a loaf in the beast's fresh baked cobbler.

A breathless gasp.

ALLOW ME.

Oh, by all means.

"*...as always, you have impeccable timing, Rhyvariath...*" Thira started, his body relaxing as she approached the massive dracari with considerably less caution than Remy cared for.

"AND YOU HAVE NOT LOST YOUR KNACK FOR MUCKING THINGS UP, I SEE," came the second voice in Remy's head.

"*...Are there others?...*"

"DOES IT LOOK LIKE THERE ARE OTHERS?" Rhyvariath grumbled. "SAVE HRATHGON, I AM THE LAST."

"*...What you see before you...*" she motioned to the bits and pieces of pink and black flesh caking near everything in sight, "*...is what remains of Hrathgon's body. He, too, has become what the midarans name Eldnumerian...*"

"I SUPPOSE THIS MAKES MORE SENSE NOW." Rhyvariath opened a fist, revealing Hrathgon's heart.

"*...Not that we are not grateful for your arrival, but after all the cycles in hiding, why have you come now?...*"

"A VOICE CALLED TO ME. ONE I THOUGHT GIVEN TO THE GRAVE SOME MANY CYCLES AGO, SUCH WAS ITS SILENCE. A CREATURE FROM ILYNDEROS. CLEVER ENOUGH TO CONSUME THE BODY OF A CHANDII DURING OUR EXODUS AND ESCAPE THROUGH THE GODSGATE UNDETECTED."

Consume?

"*...What voice?...*" Thira pressed.

"THE VOICE OF MY LAST FAMILIAR. A FAMILIAR OF MANY NAMES AND FACES, THEY OF THE CHANGELING MOLD."

"*...A changeling, Rhyvariath?*" Thira scolded. "*You took bond with a changeling? Have you taken leave of your senses as well? There was a damned good reason we left them to rot on Ilynderos...*"

"DO SPARE THE LECTURE, YVEMATHIRA. TAKING BOND YOURSELF WITH ONE OF THE VERMIN SEED THAT MASSACRED OUR KIN TO EXTINCTION RATHER NULLIFIES ANY ARGUMENT YOU BELIEVE RELEVANT. BESIDES, THIS ONE WAS DIFFERENT. THOUGHTFUL. RESILIENT. CAPABLE OF RESTRAINT. AND UTTERLY ALONE ON A FOREIGN WORLD."

"*...Who is it?...*"

"LAST AS I REMEMBER IT GOT DRUNK AS A LORD AND STOLE THE FACE OF AN ASHAEYDIR ROYAL, INTRIGUED BY THEIR ABILITY TO ALTER THEIR APPEARANCE AS IT COULD. I

THOUGHT QUITE LITTLE OF IT AT THE TIME, BUT YOU MIGHT RECALL SOME VISHURA SHIROE BECOME SO RAPT IN THEIR SHINY NEW PERSONAS THAT OCCASIONALLY THEY FORGET THEMSELVES AND WHAT THEY ARE ENTIRELY."

It can't be her. There's no way. I refuse to believe it. She would have told me. In the least, she would have told Marsea, and Marsea would have told me.

"What was its name?" Remy blurted, panic pushing past Thira's possession, heartbeat racing, blood thundering in his ears. "Was it Rhymona?"

"IT WAS NOT."

"Was it Morgandrel Tully?"

"ITS TRUE NAME WAS LITASHOTH ERU. OR SO THAT WAS HOW IT INTRODUCED ITSELF. BUT COME TO FIND, IT BURNED THROUGH THAT ONE WHEN IT JOINED THE ASHAEYDIR LEGION AND BETRAYED OUR BLOOD BOND."

The great red dragon stared him proper.

"I BELIEVE YOU LOT MAY NOW KNOW IT AS A MAGUS NAMED LITA.

"LITA DRUFELLYN."

CHAPTER SEVENTEEN

CORPSES CLOTTED the corridors back to the library, not a one of them blighted, at least none that Rhymona could tell. Small comfort for the dearly departed. Though despite all the blood and butchery, the tour proved eerily uneventful, almost too good to be true considering the past few quintweeks. Though who was she to quibble on about the right side of fortune? Especially given her fuckwit decision to trust a dead woman about a magic ring hidden within some dandy cocksmith's hump diary.

Approaching the hall housing Lancastle Library, the magus leaned against the stairwell's inside wall and peered out into the darkness beyond.

Nothing moved within the pale stretch of starlight.

The only sound that could be heard was the dracari drylax screeching the hells furies from some rest outside the stones.

She drew in a quiet breath and lifted her shirt to inspect the stab wound on her belly once more. The area was still a bit tender, but the flesh had already scabbed over and begun to flake off at the edges. Another candle would surely see it gone forever if she so desired.

The fuck? A sudden draft of shufa invaded her nostrils and her nose lifted skyward, taking in a longer whiff of the unmistakable scent. *Not so alone after all.* She stole a peek back into the corridor's unchanging obscurities, then into the winding dark that led down to the lower corridors.

Stillness both ways.

Knew it was too good to be true.

Brushing down her shirt, she maneuvered Illuminaria so it spanned the base of her forearm, and crept down the hall, skirting the shadows until she reached sight of the library entrance where she found a steady haze of lantern light and a slender figure standing casually inside the doorway blowing out a puff of smoke.

"Are you alone?" Rhymona called to the smoking woman, recognizing her as one of the cloth maidens from the guest chambers.

"Not anymore," the cloth maiden said, releasing a pull as she took in her company.

"What are you doing here?" Rhymona held her guard as she advanced, shedding the hallway's gloom for lantern glow.

The cloth maiden held out the shufa stick. "Having prayer." She held up her other hand. "You caught me."

"Prayer, my saggy left tit. Since when do cloth maidens smoke shufa?"

"Nasty habit, I know, but it helps with the nerves," the woman answered. "If it's all the same though, I'd rather the Ve'Lir didn't catch wind."

Rhymona lowered the mae'chii. "Your secret's safe with me." *Though a bit fucking dodgy, given all that's going on.*

"Imogen," the cloth maiden introduced herself, bowing her head. "And you're the ashaeydir, aren't you?"

"Something like that," Rhymona answered. "And you're one of the Lirae mothers, yeah? Thirsby, if I recall proper?"

"Guilty." Thirsby's sky-blue orbs smiled. "Care for a drag? I hear it helps keep the tits perky."

Rhymona snorted. "Was that a jape?"

"I don't know, was it?"

"A cloth maiden after the clown? Now there's a haunt for the hearth fire."

"The fear has to go somewhere, yeah?"

Rhymona eyed the sad little half cigarillo. *Why the hells not? May be your last.* She took the offer and sucked it down by another half.

"Maiden's breath, no stranger to it then," Lirae Thirsby said.

"You have no idea," Rhymona replied, exhaling a massive cloud of gray before handing the remains back. "Right then, well, luck stones or stars or whatever the hell it is you're praying to," she added before pushing past the cloth maiden into the library walks.

"And where are you off to in such a hurry?" the Lirae mother called after her.

"Have to see a tome about a thing."

"What tome?"

"Keep to your prayers, Imogen."

"Well, now I must know what you're up to."

"How about none of your fucking business, yeah," Rhymona spat over her shoulder.

"Mmhmm, yes, even more intriguing," Thirsby returned, taking to her footpath. "You're awfully bad at dissuading people's interests, I must say."

"Don't you have a flock to attend?"

"I reckon, though I'm quite curious what has you off to the stacks in the middle of…well, in the middle of the—"

"I believe the word you're pissing around is apocalypse."

"Right. And given all that, mayhaps I can be of some help?"

Rhymona halted and she heard Lirae Thirsby's boots come to a stop a few paces behind her. It was clear the woman had no intentions of simply buggering off.

"I can't just sit around in the guest chambers waiting to die," Thirsby added.

Rhymona turned around to face the woman as she pulled the coif off her head, revealing short, slicked-back hair that appeared both silver and lilac in the wash of starlight.

Is this bitch fucking with me?

"I won't." Lirae Thirsby drew on the shufa stick and released a plume of smoke, flicking the roach. "*I won't.*"

"You'll stay out of my way," Rhymona replied.

"Absolutely."

"You fuck up, it's on you."

"Naturally."

She twisted Illuminaria so the blade gleamed. "And I won't hesitate to put my bride through your pretty little habit, you catch a bout of nether sick."

"Of course."

"Of course," Rhymona echoed, before shifting away and striding for the back wall, counting bookshelves. Seven in on the center row, she made a left following the tome spines on the fifth shelf until she came upon a faded copy of *Humping Your Nan.*

There's a honey.

She slid it from its nook, cracking it open, leafing through the pages, front to back and back to front. "The fuck." She shook it, flapping it about, turning it upside down, then right side up, but found nothing close to resembling a ring within. "Fucking hells, Stella." She trailed fingers down the book spines of the fifth shelf up, even adventuring off course to the fourth and sixth shelves, all the way to the other end, but there was no other that read as *Humping Your Nan.*

"Damn fool's charade." She flung the book back down the aisle, spewing through a series of curses.

"Hester's heart," Lirae Thirsby said as the book slid to a stop at her feet. "What did this poor thing ever do to you?" She retrieved it off the stones.

"This doesn't make any sense," Rhymona fumed. "Why would you lead me here? Why would you lie?"

"Why would who lead you here?" Lirae Thirsby asked.

"What?" Rhymona collected herself, staring at the cloth maiden. "Nothing. No one."

Thirsby flipped through a few pages before closing the book and reading the cover. "*Humping Your,* oh my, interesting choice."

"Not my choice," the magus grumbled.

"You do understand how odd this looks, right?" Lirae Thirsby said. "You bursting into the library, tossing about books like a madwoman."

"And you understand how odd it looks, a clothy choking pole by herself while the world burns around her?"

Thirsby cleared her throat. "I don't think I care for your insinuation."

"Then you can fuck right off with your high horse accusations. I haven't asked for your company now, have I?"

"Don't do that. Don't push me away. I'm only here to help you."

The memory of she and Val's last conversation tremored through at the words.

"Help me?" She stomped back toward the cloth maiden. "Help me do what exactly, Imogen? I don't even know why I'm here?"

"Are you having a lark?"

"A lark?" Rhymona strode up within a few feet of the Lirae mother. "Does it look like I'm after a fucking lark here?"

"I haven't the faintest inkling what you're after, you haven't shared anything with me. Now, what are you searching for?"

"A ring." Rhymona held the woman's eyes. "A fucking ring."

"Brilliant." Lirae Thirsby opened her palm revealing a thick translucent band. "Now I can help you."

"Where did you?"

"It was in the book," the cloth mother answered. "When you tossed it, it came loose from the spine fold." She grabbed Rhymona's hand and placed the ring in her palm. "Happy birthfall, darling. You really should learn how to play better with others."

Of course, it was a man's ring. Rhymona slid it onto her middle finger, the only one it seemed to even halfway fit, and thumbed it around, studying the Chandii script etched on the outer band. Size notwithstanding, it truly was a stunning piece of jewelry, likely to fetch a pretty penny at market just for its appearance alone, twinkling fiercely with all the magic it was divulged to possess.

"It's enchanted, isn't it?" Thirsby asked.

"Supposedly, though I'm not exactly—ow!" She shook her hand and clenched it into a fist.

"Everything all right?"

"Bastard fucking bit me." She glowered at the little beastie, blinking through an unexpected dizzy spell, a ringing in her ears like the toll of church bells, slow and sonorous, and she propped herself up against the nearest bookshelf. "...shit..." Her voice came out low and deep.

"Rhymona?" Lirae Thirsby said.

Her head suddenly felt too heavy for her neck and her tongue felt fat with swelling. "Wha tha futh wath in that thufa thtick?" She scratched a hand at her throat, feeling for a bulge, but as with her legs, her hands too had become numb.

Thirsby caught her as she began to list forward and they eased down to the stones together, Rhymona's head resting in the Lirae mother's lap, facing heavenward. "Shufa, of course," the cloth maiden answered.

"Wha thid you do to me?" The words melted together.

"I didn't..."

The rest of her words faded and something swept gently through her hair...

A familiar rhythm...

...like that of a lover's hands. Her eyes closed and opened and she was looking up into the face of...

"Val."

"Morgan," Valestriel answered in dream language, her inimitable smile betiding her from on high.

She lifted a hand to Val's cheek. "I'm dreaming?"

"That you are, love."

"Well, that's not good."

"No, it's likely not. But if anyone can sort it, it's my best girl."

"Out the gates with the romantic tosh, yeah?" Rhymona sat up straight, glaring down the dark, and when she glanced back to Valestriel, she found a cloud of glittery malachite dust in her place.

"Val?"

Rhymona circled about on her knees, passing through the dance of hanging particles as the library blurred and reformed around her.

"What are you doing down there?" A voice called from behind her as a tavern materialized around them.

Cobwebs and candlelight filled a creepy, rundown version of The Brass Lantern Pubhouse. Taking it in, Rhymona half expected to see a ghoulish Trixie stroll up beside her, or, even more terrifying, Wicket's tubby arse trundling out from the kitchen with a steaming plate of the gods-only-knew-what.

Rhymona rose to her feet, eyebrow arched at the sight of her company.

Aiden appeared behind the bar in Trixie's stead, pouring a pair of ales, skin missing off his cheeks where the flesh had been picked at with a blade and widened at the edges of his mouth, a grotesque grin sliced into permanence.

He gazed at her, orbs awash in demonic possession, smile cracking apart and rising up his mutilated face.

"You poisoned me?" she said.

"I had to make sure it would be only us," Aiden answered as he slung the mug down the pine to her.

Scowling, Rhymona let it pass her by and it shattered on the floor at the bar's end, echoing into oblivion.

"And poisoned seems a bit harsh," Aiden said. "Though, all told, you look like you could use a proper pinch of shut-eye."

"A proper pinch of shut-eye?" A sickness invaded her dreamscape like the whine of violin strings, one long sour unending note, moths filling the hollow of her belly. "Who the fuck are you?"

Aiden chuckled, staring down at the bar top, rapping knuckles against it like one of the good ol' boys at banter.

"Something funny?" Rhymona carped.

Aiden returned his attention to her, his face warping, eyeteeth smile on full display. "That smug bitch Critchlow," his voice came out riven, "she actually thought she could keep a wishing ring from me."

"All right, enough with the pageantry, arsehole. Name yourself and let's have it proper."

"Oh, don't play the shit-brained dullard now, Morgan. You know damn well who you're speaking to."

"Mmm, Tetherow, I presume."

"And there's the burn." He slowly approached, fingernails dragging down the bar top. One long drag, then a *tap, tap, tap.* "Good Old Malthus, good for a wank, but otherwise an absolute waste of flesh."

"How?"

"I told you I'd be seeing you, didn't I? I'm everywhere, Morgan. Always closer than you think."

"You arranged this?"

"Though not without some degree of difficulty. You fuckers don't ever sleep, do you? It's really quite impressive."

"What's the matter?" She pouted. "Poor wittle dream demon can't get its nut."

The fucker actually had a snort. "Something to that effect. And I do apologize for my other's rather unbecoming behavior. Not our finest moment, I must confess. Though after a time in possession, we begin to take on some of our host's, shall we say, personality quirks, and suffice it to say, Dysenia Luiryn was as ill-tempered and mistrustful as they come. Hells, she was practically feral when I found her."

Rhymona backed into the tavern dining area as Tetherow stopped a few feet away from her, tapping a long talonesque fingernail against the wood, matching the beat of her hammering heart.

"How about you don't talk about my aunt, yeah," she hissed.

His smile shrank to a smirk. "It would seem I've been underestimating you all this time, Morgan. Oh, but if I'd known what you were. What you had become. What a pain in the ass you'd prove to be. I would have ripped you back through that dead man's rift the boy buggered up and bled you to the bone."

"Mmm, straight to the villain monologue then? Spooky shit, truly. Don't suppose you'll regale me with your master plan next?"

"There's no plan, Morgan. Only destiny. Only what's written. It's really quite easy once you have her song."

"And more's the pity, yeah?"

"You know, I fucking hate the ashaeydir. Vile filth down to the last." Aiden rounded the bar's end out into the tavern after her, each step slow and deliberate. "But you, Morgan. You surprised me. You, despite our feuding, I actually like."

"Aren't I the lucky girl?" she returned, scratching at the razor wound on the inside of her forearm. The gods only know, even in her dreams, the bastard itched beneath her skin. "Oh, but that's right, I couldn't give a sloppy wet whiskey shit about what you like."

"Rot, rot, bloody rot, and another jape for the round." He spread his arms out wide like a carnie showman for an invisible audience, spinning about for that extra bit of flair, before halting on her again. "I get it, Morgan, you're pissed. Join the fucking club, I'm its founding fucking member. But I thought mayhaps we could shelve all the ill will for a scrap of discourse, champion to champion, chosen to chosen. And mayhaps we can come to an understanding over all this."

"An understanding?" She scoffed. *The stones on this sicko.* "I understand you're killing a fucking world for no other reason than its gods damned Manafell."

"You mean this world that you despise? This world you condemn behind every breath? Excuse me while I go shed a tear."

"Now, who's being the clever cunt?"

"You are blind, girl. You only see what you are told to see."

"Is that *you* telling me? For, right now, all I see is a prick talking out his arsehole."

"You need to let this go, Morgan." All semblance of playfulness evaporated from his expression. "This hero turn you think you're on. The gift has fooled you. Led you astray. Suckered you in with its charms and vanities. But you're smarter than all that."

"The gift has allowed me to survive all the shitfuckery you've thrown at us."

"The gift is a curse," the wretch growled. "An abomination. You've said the words yourself. I've had them from you how many times?" He glared into her. "Or have you already forgotten our little late-night dalliances? Our drunken walks on the shore playing windup with the liftboy. Our whispered oaths shacked-up in that shithole Ashborough named as living quarters.

"There were a few times I thought you'd found me out, all told. About my possession. That Aiden wasn't really Aiden. Those random looks of confusion on your face. Oh, how they sent my host's used-up heart to the races. And I came so close to killing you. So many times. But you never said the words. You never asked. Not once." He shook his head. "Not even after you peeped the old mean mug inside our dead man's rift."

Baka! Memories of her cycles with Aiden in Kanton flashed with Tetherow's descriptions and dread filled her. "No..." she uttered.

"Those nights, those conversations, they are the only reason I let you leave that rift. And the only reason you remain alive presently." Tetherow shifted away from her, arms tucked behind his back, smug as a lord at council. "As for the nether, this was all coming regardless of my influence. The gift must be quelled. The fates demand it."

"Damn the fates," she spat. It felt a proper response given the echelon of fucked her world currently fell within.

"Why can't you see it, Morgan? What you truly are. All of you. You all act the same with the gift. Like fiends. Addicts feasting on a corpse. The nether merely shows you a reflection of the gift, controlling you behind the mask of choice. What's it going to take to make you see? To make you accept the truth? You are the villain of this story. And not even that. You are the villain's whore. But you don't have to be. You can reject your master. You can still—"

"You!" Rhymona snarled. She could tell Tetherow was becoming impatient, so she decided to expedite the inevitable. "You are the villain, Tetherow. And you fucked up killing Val. Butchered any chance at discourse you'd ever gain out of me."

"Mayhaps you fucked up giving her so much power over you," Tetherow argued. "Prize well, Morgan, it won't get any easier from here."

"No, but I'll get better at dealing with whatever comes."

"Will you?" In a blink, the Aiden-Tetherow mongrel disappeared and a shadow thing appeared in his place. Cut like the figure that saved her when she ran a blade down her arm and found her gift. A creature dark as night save for the rows of jagged yellow fangs curled up in a beastly snarl.

"You?"

"Us." The maw returned, drooling a slick, mucousy fluid.

"That was you in the stables?" Rhymona shifted away from the shadow thing, fist driving into the tabletop beside her. "No." She whirled back around. "Fuck that. It can't be. Fuck this dream world bullshit."

"*I* saved you, Morgan. *I* kept you from dying that night. Not the gift. *I* showed you what you were capable of."

"Piss on that. There's no way."

"You don't think I see your shadow everywhere I walk? No matter how many times I split my essence, there you are, a pale white horror in the corner of my eye, staring me rotten, wailing like a broken banshee on her blood moon. You and I, we are the same. You haunt me every measure as ugly as I haunt you."

"We are not the same."

"We are chosen. Blessed by entities beyond our comprehension. Intended as enemies. But it doesn't need to be this way. We can rebuild this world, you and I. We can choose. We can remake it proper, so that no one need suffer."

"Just like all the other worlds that ate shit to the nether's feasting? My ancestors' home included."

"Your ancestors?" Fury deformed the shadow thing's smooth, featureless face. "Your ancestors slaughtered mine. Your ancestors are the reason I'm here in the first place. But I can look past their slights if you can look past mine."

It's a trick, her mind screamed, unwilling to allow the thought of an alliance with such a fiend fit inside her head.

"You must think me The Vael's greatest simp," she argued. "That I'd ever entertain even the smallest sliver of a demon's rhetoric. You'll not reap an ounce of pity from this soul for my haunting, Tetherow, so go vomit your heresy in someone else's ears. Long live the banshee queen. May she skullfuck your every memory from here to eternity."

A plague of silence fell between them, thick as storm clouds.

"Are we done here," Rhymona spat after a time, wishing away the incessant itch from the razor scar down her inner forearm.

"It would seem we are," Tetherow answered, a gash of rotting teeth in the shape of her shadow. "I thought I'd give you one last chance. I thought you worth at least that much. But I am done asking. I am done pitching you the same old argument. When you're at your last breath and your precious gift spurns you for another, I hope you remember this conversation."

"Already forgotten."

"You're well out of your depths with these Lanier whelps, Morgan, and doubly so with all this godsgate business. It will only lead you to ruin."

"Cheers for the tea, bitch."

And then she had it. Long after she'd had enough of Tetherow's gaslighting. A glimmer in the gloom. A floating disk in the distance. She imagined herself before it, closing her eyes, and reopened to find her twisted reflection in the mirror staring back at her, *into* her, the one with the big black eyes, the dramatic cheekbones, and the upside down cross carved fresh into her forehead, a trickle of blood running down her nose from its endless weep, grazing her lips.

She reached out toward the fiend in the looking glass, the panic consuming, hands collapsing around its throat. A tightness upon her own. A cramping in her stomach.

Followed by a hoarse gasp of air...

CHAPTER EIGHTEEN

DAMNED IF YOU DO. *Damned if you don't. All out of options.* Pion leaned back, drawing a long breath as he took in the solar, blank expression in tow, letting those same words eat their tail in his head once more.

The chamber was eerily peaceful, horrid smells aside. Almost normal. Almost like old times. That is, of course, if you ignored the wand marks and splotches of Dysenia Luiryn strewn about here and there. Not to mention the pile of corpses in the corner by the hearth. Slattery, Thorpe, and shitheel number three.

On a positive note, you're not rotting with them, Pion thought. *Though jury's still out on just how grateful I should be for such a blessing.*

It went without saying really, but, as usual, everything was well and truly fucked. And he felt an even greater fool for believing it could have ever fallen any other way.

You could just go numb again. He was practically at the precipice presently. *You could just go away. Bury yourself within. It's easier to hide, remember? It's easier to just disappear. Become a ghost. So much easier to be nothing to nobody.*

Cycles of toiling and preparation, *poof,* gone in a span of minutes, everything that he'd worked so hard for pissed to the four winds. And what's more, he'd done the pissing, and for a father that never accepted him, much less loved him, and a girl he'd hardly spoken more than a handful of sentences to.

Reckon I'm scarce better than these loathsome Lanier's at the end of the day, he mused. *Heart pulled in a new direction every second despite the head's desire. And where has it brought you Pion? Where has it spat you out? Where it always does. Back in Lancastle at the mercy of the fates. Caged. Alone. And reviled.*

Pion made a passing glance at Caitlyn, who leaned inside the solar's entryway, staring down the King's corridor, clutching his cane, finger on the clasp, ready for anything.

Well, mayhaps not entirely alone.

Pion hated that he liked her. That he cared about her and her opinion of him. She made him weak, after all. But he couldn't simply ignore his feelings. The truth was a hungry blade ever eager for a bite of his flesh. He saw how his insincerity went with Marsea, and he'd be damned before he allowed Caitlyn to catch Marsea's aversion to him.

His vision flicked back over to his father and Julia. They remained seated on the divan talking in hushed voices, both in better spirits than he. Though it warmed his heart to behold it. Especially of Jules. He wanted to join them but remained sitting in a chair against the wall beside the balcony egress, the winter winds cooling him from just outside.

So, what's your play, Pion? He asked himself for the thousandth time in the last hour, rubbing Ripley's head, the cat familiar perched in a ball across his lap. *Where do we go from here? Let's run the gamut one more time. Make sense of it all.*

One: Our alliance with Tetherow is likely gone. No doubt the split that left Dysenia a floundering phaedrylax will find a way to return and report your betrayal to the other essence fragments. And given your current predicament, the chances of you not only finding, but destroying the timepiece phylactery in a timely manner is practically slim to none. Which means your chances of convincing the split inside Autumn to correct your deformities are likely off the table, assuming they were ever there in the first place. Which now makes your pact with Tetherow all but useless. Besides, even if you thought there was a chance Tetherow might have you back, could you truly trust it?

Simple answer. No.

Moving on.

Two: There is still the possibility of a time loop splice, thanks to Marsea's haxanblade. Not that meeting some alternate version of your mother is terribly high on the agenda anymore, especially provided the state of things, but perhaps you're thinking too small, and a goodly bit more could be accomplished with the prospect of time alteration at your fingertips. Marsea wouldn't be an easy sell, though. Hells, consider it a miracle if she ever deigned to enter the same chamber as you again, but mayhaps she wouldn't have to be a sell if you proved your worth and loyalty.

There's a laugh, he thought. *More fairytale bullshit. What would the girl that shits gold need from a broken grotesque still begging for ordinary?*

He glanced from his father, to Jules, to Caitlyn again. This time she met his gaze and his head became stuck between a shake and a nod. Caitlyn pursed her lips and returned a nod then resumed her glare into the torchlit beyond.

A few minutes later Julia grabbed a chair and dragged it up beside him.

"You're awfully quiet back here," she said.

And you're awfully calm for a girl of nine cycles in the middle of a massacre. "I've been thinking."

"Anything interesting?"

"Not really."

"I know you think you're alone, brother," Julia said. "But I'm here."

Pion shifted his attention back to Caitlyn as she paced out into the hallway to the opposite wall of the King's corridor. He couldn't stop himself. Subconsciously she kept calling to him.

"You like her, don't you?" asked Julia.

"What?" Pion glanced back at his sister.

"Caitlyn. You fancy her. I can tell. You're pretty obvious, honestly."

Little sister, ever the observer. 'You've the mind of a girl twice your age,' he recalled overhearing Marsea once tell her out in the courtyards on one of their morning walks together. He scoffed at the like back then, but mayhaps she was on to something.

"She saved my life earlier," Pion said. "What's not to like?"

"Yeah, but you 'fancy her' fancy her." She shrugged. "I can see why. She's quite bonny, isn't she?"

Caitlyn strode back across to the entrance as he opened his mouth to answer, catching the pair of them staring directly at her and stopping. An eyebrow raised.

Julia unleashed an awkward smile and Pion followed suit prompting a quizzical expression before Caitlyn propped herself back against the doorjamb, shaking her head.

"Brilliant, now she thinks we were talking about her," Pion whispered.

"We were talking about her," Julia answered.

"You know what I mean."

"Right. And Dah's doing better if you care to know," she said, changing the subject. "I think he'll be able to stand and move about soon."

"Glad to hear it," Pion mustered.

"Pion, what happened to you? Why did you leave us? Why were you helping Tetherow?"

Straight for the heartstrings like a true Harver. "I was confused," he answered, unsure of what else to really say. And honestly, it wasn't too far off the truth.

"Marsea and Remy said not to trust you. That you were bad. That you might hurt me."

"No," Pion found her waiting orbs. "Never." He shifted in his chair so he faced her, and Ripley jumped down off him, none too pleased about the sudden movements. "I will never, ever hurt you, Jules. You know that, right?"

"I…guess…"

He took her thin, grubby hands in his. "I may not be a good person, and Marsea has seen the worst of me, I woefully confess, but I love you more than anything on this moon, do you understand?" He waited for her response.

"I…understand…"

"You can count on me, Jules." He let her pull away. "Whatever it takes, whatever it is, I've got your back. Even if it means my own."

Liar, a small voice whispered from the back of his mind.

"Say you believe me."

"I…I believe you," said Julia.

He hated the words. Hated his insistence. *No, Jules. You don't. And if you do, you shouldn't. You should be telling me to bugger off and beat the road. Find a cliff and keep walking. Disappear and never return. I don't deserve your company. I don't deserve your trust.*

All told, he hadn't the faintest inkling what he would do in a situation where it was him or Jules. He knew what he should do, but that didn't mean he would. Fifty-fifty he sacrificed her life to prolong his. Same went for his father. That went without question really. And likely Caitlyn too.

Welcome to the bright side of minimal expectations.

Welcome to the silver lining of being shunned and unloved.

What did he care?

He wasn't raised as a knight. He wasn't raised with honor. He wasn't raised to protect anyone other than himself. And even that bit was a decision he made entirely of his own volition for his own continued survival. Not that anyone feigned half a toss anyway. Else he would have likely been beaten, stabbed, or strung up ages ago by some nameless whoreson looking for a quick schill and a back alley burn name. Such was the cruelty of the cretins outside His Lordship's walls.

Truth was he was still here battling these fucked up contrasting thoughts because he and he alone willed it so.

Raelan coughed, drawing their attention.

"I think you should go speak with him," Julia said in a low tone. "I think it might do you both good."

"I will," Pion said.

"Fantastic." Julia stood up in front of him. "I'll see you over."

"Eventually," he added. "I will eventually."

"No time like the present," Julia said, hand waiting.

There was a time, not so very long ago, her meddling would have pissed him off. Though nowhere near as much as her kindness. Her innocent outstretched hand, he would have taken as pity, slapped it away, and made a fool of himself hobbling across the chamber. But what little pride he had before left when he fell turncloak and told Dysenia to go fuck herself. He'd made his bed with these people. Chosen a side. For better or worse.

He took her hand and she turned his over, briefly studying the warlock's well in his palm. Then she pulled him up to her and didn't say a word about it as she wrapped herself under his arm and walked them over to the divan.

Raelan cleared his throat at the company. "Son," he greeted.

"Father," Pion said. *You look like shit*, he fought the urge to append.

"I'll go check on Caitlyn," Julia said dismissing herself.

"Thank you," Raelan said once they were alone, his voice gravelly. They both looked into the charred hearth across the room before them. "I know it's a little late in the game for me to pretend at fatherhood with you, but you've earned the words, Pion. In spite of my shortcomings. In spite of my absence." Raelan turned to him. "I am sorry, son. For what it's worth. For all of it."

Pion's head turned, brow furrowed, and he held his father's gaze.

Am I dreaming? Did I die? Who is this imposter wearing my father's husk?

"For making you feel less." Raelan kept on. "For not believing in you. For taking you for granted."

Fuck you, old man, Pion wanted to say. *Eat shit and choke.* The words slammed into the backs of his teeth as his jaw clenched. *Stay in control.*

"I did this for Jules," Pion said.

"I deserve that."

"This isn't about deserve. And it's certainly not about *you*." He landed hard on the 'you.' "It's about Julia." He turned away from his father before the scowl took hold.

"As well it should be."

"I'm not a Harver," Pion said. "I'm a Manson."

"So you are."

"Don't do that. Do not placate me."

"What would you have me say then? Would you have your mother's story? Gods willing, I'd have it plucked from my mind, every memory, and place in yours just so you could know her. So you could know me. Before I became this. Before I let my anger win and blamed you. I loved her, Pion. Please understand. And I hated you for robbing me of our future. And I was wrong. Horribly wrong. And wrong again when you came through that door looking a madman's horror from what I let the moon do to you." His voice cracked apart at the end. "Why did you save me?"

"Because I knew what Tetherow would do to you. And as rotten as you've been to me, I couldn't allow her to—"

A hand fell on his and Pion tensed. His father's palm was cold as the crypt. "Pion."

Pion stared down at his father's pale leathery hand.

"For as long as I draw breath," Raelan said. "I'll do my best to earn it. To earn my fatherhood back."

Pion swallowed, frozen below the neck, feeling awkward, wishing he had a bottle of absinthium to drown inside.

"We've got incoming," Caitlyn called from the King's corridor.

"Blight?" Pion asked, almost thankful for the interruption.

"Not sure yet," Caitlyn answered.

"It's Aunt Maggie," Julia announced.

Maggie? Pion worked his way up from the divan and shambled over to the doorway, shoulder collapsing against the wall as the Empress and Edgar arrived, bloody and winded.

"We have to move," Magwyn managed through panting breaths. "A few survivors have helped barricade the western entrance, but the blight's topped the wall and it won't be long before they take the King's corridor."

"How long?" Caitlyn asked the obvious question.

"I'd give it a half hour at most," Edgar said.

"Where's Remy?" Julia asked.

"Um…" Edgar started.

"He jumped on the nether drake, the bloody loon," Magwyn said.

"What do you mean he jumped on it?" Pion inquired.

"I mean, it came after him. He literally jumped on top of it, stabbed it in one of its nasty heads and it took off flying with him still standing there like an idiot."

"Classic Lanier foolishness," Pion muttered.

"I don't doubt Yvemathira put in her fair share with that decision," Magwyn said, azure in her eyes. "Nothing to be done about it now. We need to raid the upper reliquary and barricade ourselves in the guest chambers. At least there, we can portal out if need be." She returned Caitlyn her wand.

Caitlyn found his eyes and offered his cane back.

Julia drew the sword at her belt.

Edgar ranged over to Raelan and helped him up. "You good?" he asked.

"Good as I'm going to get," Raelan answered with a wince.

A shout echoed down the hall as Pion entered the King's corridor. He glanced into the pitch from whence the noise came.

Footsteps approached at a fast pace, and a man appeared, mace in hand.

Pendrith? Pion recognized the dark-haired magus as he neared, hair and chewed-up skin clinging to the bloodied instrument at his side. Pendrith was dressed in Royalguard attire, having apparently stripped a corpse of its decency to fit in, but this asshole couldn't be further from a noble knight of Lancastle. No, Howard Pendrith was one of the nastiest bastards in Ravenholme. A killer through and through.

Devils beside you, demons within, came the old Covenant watchwords, as Pendrith's eyes landed on Pion.

"They've broken through," Pendrith said to the group. "The others were overrun. We have to go now."

Overrun or did you ambush them? Pion couldn't help but think.

"Damn the reliquary," Magwyn said. "Straight to the guest halls. Do not stop for anything." And she turned back west, aiming her scepter at the ceiling, calling her gift, blasting it down to rubble, one strike after another.

Pion hobbled next to Caitlyn, wiping his head against his sleeve and shoulder, sweating pouring off him.

"I know that man," Caitlyn eventually said, stopping at the stairwell behind the others.

"He's Ravenholme," Pion said.

"Is he a problem?"

"I don't know."

"It's a fairly simple question, Pion. Should I put him down?"

He gazed into her honey-gold eyes. And not for one moment did he doubt she would if he gave the order. "Not yet. We should speak with him first."

"I'm over the politics, Pion. I'm over the games. We've no more time for it. Now either this fucker's a problem or he isn't. So, which is it?"

"Problem."

"Grand." She started forward, out of sight in a blink.

"Caitlyn," he called. "Caitlyn, what're you going to do?"

But she was already well beyond his reach.

Fuck. He kissed the outer stairwell, hugging the wall close, and worked his way down. Before he could reach the next floor down he heard a wand blast, followed by a second.

"What the hells are you doing?" Edgar growled. "What did you do?"

"He was Ravenholme," Caitlyn argued.

Shit, gods dammit. "Stop. Hold." Pion cried, his feet hammering down atop each step as he juttered forward, the stones driving through him, grinding up from heel to brain, until he met the landing of the guest chambers, and he slammed shoulder first into the door jamb and hung there. "Edgar, wait. She's right."

"What?" Edgar backed into the wall between them, Raelan still held up over his arm.

"I knew him," Pion said. *Stay in control.* "I told her to do this." He glanced down at Pendrith's unmoving body, a shoulder and half his head painted across the opposite wall. *Bloody hells, Caitie.* "He couldn't be trusted."

"And you two can?" Edgar shouted, basically defenseless.

"Edgar," Julia said, eyes wide as the sister moons. "I trust him."

Edgar glared at Julia, hefting a slumping Raelan back up, eyes darting back and forth between the three of them.

"And I trust Caitlyn," she added.

"Sorry to make this difficult," Pion said. And he truly did feel sorry for the poor bastard who was clearly in over his head. *Welcome to Lancastle, lad. Where comes a knife for every alley. And a death for every doorstep.*

"Difficult?" Edgar groused. "Difficult? You just blew his brains all over the wall."

"Edgar, you're fine," Raelan rasped, hanging around his neck for dear life.

"Why the fuck aren't you lot moving?" Magwyn crowed as she hurried down the stairwell behind him, stopping at his side and taking in the fresh patch of murder.

"He wasn't a soldier," Pion said, as though a point existed. "He was an asshole that was likely to find us all a fast grave."

Magwyn turned sidelong at him wearing an expression for the ages. *Summon the nearest magus for a burning glass.*

It was a shit explanation to be sure, a holiday gush of an explanation, but he was quite done with trying to explain himself. Pion simply cleared his throat and pushed forward, past Magwyn, past Caitlyn, past Pendrith's corpse, past Edgar and Raelan, taking his sister's side, and they started forward into the torchlight ahead.

"Sister," he said.

"Brother," she answered.

Still in control.

CHAPTER NINETEEN

C<small>ARE TO EXPLAIN</small>?" Magwyn asked Caitlyn, turning away from the soldier missing the better part of his head.

"He wasn't Royalguard," Caitlyn replied.

"And you thought that deserved a killing?" Maggie studied Caitlyn. Mayhaps she'd read the girl wrong in the council chamber. Her eyes trailed down from Caitlyn's tawny glower past Solindiel's razorblade memory to the wand leaking bone-white magic onto the flagstones at her feet.

"He was Ravenholme," Caitlyn added.

"So, I heard," Magwyn said. "And so were you."

"Against my will and better judgments. But he was Covenant by choice. And he would have caused problems for us, I know it."

The gods know, there was no bend with this one.

"He helped us hold back the blight in the upper halls," Magwyn argued as she faced the stairwell and put a pair of scepter strikes into the surrounding stones collapsing the entrance behind them.

"He did what was necessary to survive," Caitlyn said, backstepping down the corridor after the others. "I understand you're disappointed in me, Empress, but I couldn't risk it. Not now."

"I know the world is in tatters, Caitlyn, but we cannot give in to lawlessness, striking each other down for what-ifs and could-happens."

"We're all killers now, milady. The blight saw to that. Made us choose. Kill or become legion. And Ravenholme brought the blight, so in my eyes, one of their lot cross my path, they find the grave."

"Grab a torch," Pion ordered from up ahead.

"Was it him?" Maggie asked. "Did Pion put you up to this?"

"Pion's nothing to do with this. The decision was mine," Caitlyn answered. "I recognized his face from the ranks in Marrovard and I made a gut call. If you want my wand back." She stopped. "Take it."

Magwyn halted, glancing down at the pitch-black stalk aimed back at its wielder, the antler hilt held out begging for repossession.

An uncomfortable hush hung in the air between them.

Is she testing me?

"The wand is yours," Magwyn said, stowing any further harping, and pushing on into the pitch. They could argue the point 'til the cows came home, but, end of day, Caitlyn was far more useful to the group with a wand at her disposal than not. And assuming the corpse was indeed a Ravenholme conspirator, he likely deserved a goodly measure worse than what found him.

"Stay behind me," Edgar's voice carried from the dark down the corridor.

"Jules, keep watch over father," Pion said.

Magwyn and Caitlyn caught up to the others as Edgar and Pion halted before a guest room with its door missing from the hinges. Entrails and appendages bestrewed the stones at their feet, ranging into the far corridor past the firelight.

Edgar turned away from the guest chamber with a grimace, coughing into the top of his fist. Pion simply stood there, slack-jawed.

"Fucking drylax," Edgar groaned.

"Bug, stay here with me," Raelan bade Julia.

No.

A terrible chill stole down Magwyn's spine, sharp as a knife through skin, culminating in a cold, ugly fear that blossomed in the pit of her stomach.

"Wils!" she shouted, mayhaps louder than was wise, rushing past the group, heart bashing against her ribcage.

The smell hit her well before she made the doorway. The unmistakable stench of death rot. Of piss, shit, vomit, and rust.

"Wils!" she cried again as she crept through the crowd of cloth maiden corpses, far too many severed limbs to sort through, though not a one of them looked to belong to her missing beloved.

"Maggie," Wils's voice echoed from outside the chamber and she navigated the carnage back out into the hall.

"Poppy!" Edgar called, his eyes wide as dinner saucers.

"Wils," Magwyn breathed.

And there they were, Wils and Poppy, as though she'd only just imagined the guest chamber bloodbath behind her.

"How are you still alive?" Edgar asked as Poppy approached.

"Luck," Poppy replied. "Dumb luck, some random bluecoat, and this." She held up the frying pan. "I swear it's been blessed or enchanted by some mad deity or some such."

"I'll say," the huntsman said, shaking his head.

"I heard a ruckus out in the corridor," Wils added, "and we all came out to check. Next thing I know the girl here is pushing me back inside and slamming the door behind us. We hear screaming and tearing and bones snapping outside. And I called forth a deception ward on the back of the door, hoping I got it right, praying it would be enough to send the creature away."

"It was," Poppy said. "Thank the gods."

"I only wish we could have saved the others." Wils frowned at the lower half of a cloth maiden's body splattered against the wall between them.

Magwyn wrapped Wils in a hug, and he returned her affection. "I know it's selfish," she whispered, "but I'm glad it wasn't you."

"Where is Remy?" Poppy asked.

"He's fighting the nether drake," Edgar answered.

"Fighting the nether drake?" Poppy echoed. "Alone?"

"For now," Magwyn said. "Given the state of these quarters, I think we need to find shelter elsewhere. Mayhaps the library."

"I agree," Raelan replied.

"And that's where Rhymona went," Julia said. "Maybe she's still there."

"Caitlyn, on me," Magwyn ordered. "Edgar, you watch the rear. I caved the stairwell, but there's no telling what fel sorcery may lie in the shadows."

Onward they crept, hugging the walls, rarely speaking, and only in whispers when required. All the way to the end of the corridor and down one more floor to the mage's quarters, which opened to a small courtyard used for study that led to the library wing.

Starlight found them as they stole across the tranquil courtyard and Magwyn couldn't help but notice just how far away everything sounded, as though they'd somehow stumbled upon the eye of the storm.

Impossibly, the library wing proved even eerier than the courtyard, ghostly quiet and devoid of any violence or damage. So quiet she could hear every movement the others made, so quiet she could almost hear Vaelsyntheria's subtle revolution.

Anything? she asked Emyria.

NOTHING.

Something isn't right about this place. I can feel it in my bones. It's like the nether is avoiding it.

She halted in the library doorway.

"You feel it too, don't you?" Pion asked from a few feet in front of her. "The vibration."

"Do you know what it is?" Maggie questioned.

"I was hoping you might educate me."

I CAN HEAR IT FAINTLY. I HAVE HEARD A SOUND LIKE THIS BEFORE, BUT NOT IN CENTURIES. AND NEVER ON VAEL-SYNTHERIA.

Then where?

ILYNDEROS. BEFORE WE LEFT HER. SOMETHING IS SHIFTING THE ORDER OF THINGS, CAUSING A FRICTION IN THE LAWS OF NATURE.

How do you mean?

"Care to let us in on the dracari's ruminations?" Pion asked.

"Em says the vibration may be a shift in the order of things."

"Well, that's not ominous," the warlock said. "A shift in what exactly?"

"Would that I could name it. All we know is that something momentous is taking place somewhere on Vaelsyntheria right now and it's disturbing the fates, creating the global tension we're feeling."

"Could it be a cataclysm?" Pion pressed. "Could it be the endless night?"

"Your guess is as good as ours," she closed the double doors to the library behind them and began to bind a ward to it.

"You lot stay together," Edgar said. "I'll check the stacks for survivors."

"I'll join you," Caitlyn offered, gazing back at Magwyn.

The Empress nodded her head in approval then returned her attention to Pion. "I assume between all that dark-dabbling you learned how to scrawl a ward?"

"I know a few defense spells, if that's your ask."

"Brilliant, you take the left and I'll run the right. Meet on the back wall."

CHAPTER TWENTY

RHYMONA GASPED AWAKE, still clutching at her own neck, froth caked to the sides of her lips, blinding pain coursing her insides, head to toes, ancient and unrelenting, her ring hand burning and throbbing as though it'd been smashed by a smithy's hammer.

"Shit," she croaked, the real world returned to her in waves, walls of books disappearing into the shifting shadows above. She lowered back down to the stones, praying the sudden surge of adrenaline would soon usurp her crippling agony.

How long was I out for? She wiped spittle from her face with the back of a sleeve, her heartbeat pounding inside her brain, rattling from ear to ear.

A click-clicking sound joined the pulsing cacophony swelling inside her head and she swallowed something that tasted metal.

What is that?

Her head rolled toward the end of the aisle.

Footsteps?

"Imogen," she rasped, her throat still uncooperative.

The footsteps doubled. There was someone else with her.

Rhymona tried to push herself up but caught a bout of queasiness and immediately dry heaved, having little to nothing in her to give up. *Bitch did a fucking number on me.*

"Who's there?" a voice called. "Rhymona?" It belonged to Edgar.

"Here," she nearly choked on the word, lowering herself back down beside *Humping Your Nan*, her vision unwilling to settle, fever pouring off her.

The shivers found her around the same time Edgar did, Caitlyn Ellsbury right by his side.

"No," she said, suspecting the worst, not knowing if these two were in cahoots with Imogen, and not knowing if Imogen was in cahoots with Tetherow. The gods know, she didn't know who she could trust any longer.

Then there was Julia, standing behind them at the end of the aisle.

"Munchkin," she croaked.

"They're with us," Julia promised, kneeling down beside her.

"She needs a candle in the worst way," Caitlyn said overtop her.

"All out, I'm afraid," Edgar returned.

"Just stay with me," Julia told her.

"I'm going to get the Empress," Caitlyn said as she disappeared.

Rhymona felt hands sweeping through her hair again, brushing strands out of her eyes, as Julia eased her head into her lap.

Julia kept talking to her, but Rhymona wasn't hearing the words properly.

Fia stood behind the girl, watching, and Rhymona stared, expecting the shadow thing to unleash a devilish Tetherow grin at any moment.

What felt like ages later, Magwyn arrived. And Pion was there with Grandpa at his ankle. And Raelan, and Frying Pan Girl, and the dusty old geezer from the guest chambers who Magwyn fancied for whatever reason.

"Rhymona, if you can hear me, I'm pulling you into The Spellbind," Magwyn said. "I'm not sure what this is or what you've done to your hand, but it's rotting."

"It's what?" she slurred.

"Turning gangrene."

"Gangrene?" *The fuck?*

"The rest of you see to the warding," Magwyn ordered.

Rhymona's tried to lift her hand back up to examine it, but it wouldn't obey. *Tetherow, what did you do?* she thought as The Spellbind rift rolled over her and her eyes rolled back into her head.

"Fucking hells, like someone placed all the world's hangovers in my head at once," Rhymona said as she and Magwyn materialized in the courtyard by the statue of Effie and the lich.

"Rhymona, what happened?"

"Lirae Thirsby bloody happened. I think. Then Tetherow."

"Tetherow?" Magwyn returned. "It's in Lancastle?"

"I'm not sure. But I think the House Mother may be one of its spies. The fucker drugged me into a dream state and tried to recruit me."

"Recruit you?"

"You heard right. Said we could remake the world. Said a bunch of weird shit about a connection to each other." A phantom passed through her. "I think it's getting desperate."

Rhymona could feel the giftwell flowing into her now, nursing her aches. Though her hand with the ring still burned like hellfire.

"What happened to your hand?"

"Guessing Tetherow swapped out the wishing ring for a cursed one." She held up her hand her middle fingers melded together at the base and darkening. "Some bit of necromancy, I reckon." It appeared a wretched horror of a thing, darker than the skin above her wrist and rising. "I can barely move it. Hells, I can barely feel it at all."

Magwyn gave it a once over. "I think it's actually a carnomancer's curse, some kind of flesh-eating spell. Something the gift can't heal. We may have to amputate."

"Eat my arse, amputate."

"It'll likely become worse the longer you let it fester."

"Where's Remy?"

"He's fighting the nether drake."

"What?"

"You heard me. And before you ask. Yes, alone. And definitely his decision."

"Fucking idiot."

"Another few minutes and you should be decent enough, but you'll need to make a decision on the hand."

"We're not taking it, end of discussion."

"Your hand, your choice. But again..."

"I know, you'll put me down if I become a liability. Right back at you. What's the plan from here? Why are you all in the library?"

"We're holed up for now," said Magwyn. "The upper halls have been overrun and this was the best defensible spot left while we await Des and Marsea."

"Yeah, I've seen what the nether does to libraries. Your warding spells better be goddamn immaculate. I doubt there's a hidden temple below Lancastle we can escape to if it goes tits up."

"What else did Tetherow say to you?" Magwyn asked.

"Its usual fare. More about the gift being evil, rot, rot, bloody rot. But all it's fucked anyway, you know. I mean I don't completely disagree with the bastard. The gift is a problem, always has been, and most folk that use it turn rotten at one point or another. But killing a world is not the answer." She glanced at Magwyn, who stood with her arms crossed. "What does Emyria say? How does she feel about the gift?"

"...Though I understand why it was necessary at the time, I believe there has been enough evidence to prove my sister was wrong about sharing the gift with the Midarans. And especially so given what horrors your ancestors would eventually bring to this moon. It all just seems so hopelessly inevitable, does it not?..."

"No argument there." *Less and less a fight about morality, and more and more a war for survival.* "Though Tetherow brought up an interesting observation. One I didn't indulge, but one I believe to be at the crux of all of this. What is good and what is evil? In my mind, the answer is completely subjective. We are all villains with the capacity for heroic deeds and likewise heroes with the capacity for unmitigated horror."

"...Agreed..."

"Tetherow said the nether is merely a reflection showing us for what we truly are. And he named the gift an addiction and its users...us, fiends. And honestly, is it wrong?"

"...As you said, it is all subjective..."

"Before all this. Before I learned to use the gift to defend myself, I would have agreed wholeheartedly. I've seen the worst of the gift, prize well. And it's as ugly as what the nether does to us. But the gift stole my family from me long before the nether arrived. Then it stole my personality, my future. And it spat me out like this. Cursing it, hating it, defying it wherever I could, but needing it all the same. And now look at us here, standing with our cocks out in some bastard version of it. Letting it drink of us as we drink of it. What the fuck is it healing me for? What does it want from me? Why have I been chosen?"

"Because you have nothing left to lose," a voice spoke from behind her.

"Stella?" Magwyn uttered.

"Hello, old friend," Stella said. "Long time."

"Too long," Magwyn said.

"Nothing left to lose because the gift took it all," Rhymona hissed. "I'm not it. This barmy little puppet clusterfuck the gift desires and I never will be."

"Rhymona," Stella began.

"Stow the debate, Stella," the magus interjected. "Fuck the gift and fuck you too if you mean to lobby."

"Oh, love, we're well past the part where I convince you of one side or the other," Stella said. "But you already know this. Regardless of your wishes, you have been chosen as a powerful pawn in the game to come. The game for control of this moon. You, me, the Laniers, we've all been chosen, the gift's stratagem masquerading about The Vael's denizens as chaos. From what I know, the nether has won the past few games on Ashira and maybe even on Y'dema, and Vaelsyntheria is on to the final stage now. The pick your poison stage. Live with the gift, as endless as it is, as mad as it is, as unpredictably fucked up as it is, or do nothing, become nothing, conform and die with the nether."

"Shit choices."

"That's life in a nutshell, isn't it?" Stella ventured a desolate smile. "But every now and again there's a barely-there nugget that makes some measure of the suffering worth it. And that is why I chose the gift and will always choose the gift."

Table scraps, Rhymona thought. *Is that all life is meant to be?*

"Tetherow found your little wishing ring by the way. All your haunting in this place, you didn't sense any malfeasance from the House Mother?"

"Obviously not."

"Tetherow, he knew everything. All of it." Rhymona held up her hand. "And now I'm stuck with this shit."

"I'm sorry."

"You're sorry? That's it? How do I fix it, Stella?"

"Like any hex. You find a way to reverse the spell or create a salve, elixir, what-have-you to treat it."

"Cheers for the empty advice. Any more useless errands you can have me go fuck myself over with or are we good here?"

"It's some form of carnomancy, yes?" Stella said. "Mayhaps there will be something in *Noon*."

"Assuming Marsea and Desmond are able to recover it. And that doesn't even broach the fact that Tetherow now has a wishing ring in its repertory."

"I fucked up, Rhymona," Stella said, locking eyes. "I apologize, and I'll do what I can to help you fix it, but I'm just as surprised about this as you are." She shifted her gaze to Magwyn. "I thought I felt a breach in The Spellbind, so I came to check, expecting one of you. I came to apprise you of Remy. I found him in the lower hamlets."

"Is he alive?" Magwyn asked.

"Alive and well, actually. He managed to slay the nether drake with the aid of another dracari. A beast named Rhyvariath. He and Remy have since rallied the troops and they are now fighting back toward Lancastle Citadel, clearing the streets of blight. There is hope yet."

"You can move anywhere around the kingdom?" Rhymona asked.

"Most places, yes. Though there are some areas warded away from a hauntling's presence."

"Can you hunt for Lirae Thirsby and let me know where you find her?"

"I'll certainly give it a go. Can I assume you're still in the library?"

"For the time being," Magwyn said. "Though I plan to find Remy. Where did you last leave him?"

"The Daggerstone Walks twixt Marigaul and The Coldwater."

"So, the arse-end of Uglytown," Rhymona murmured. "Why am I not surprised?"

"I'm sure Edgar will want to come with me," Magwyn said, her attentions befalling Rhymona. "Though you should keep watch over the others."

"And miss out on the carnival of fuckery?" Rhymona scoffed, immediately questioning her expected exclusion, Stella's words from only moments ago sinking back in. She hated being told what she was, hated being forced to participate, but above all else, she hated not being given the choice.

And that is why me, she spoke to her gift. *You are the choice. For better or worse.*

The magus thought about the others. From a threat standpoint, she wasn't terribly worried about Julia, Gilcrest, or Frying Pan Girl, but Pion, Raelan, and Caitlyn were another tale altogether. Each offered a distinctive slice of danger she'd have to be wary of. Not that she trusted any of the lot, all affairs considered. She was loath to admit it, but she even had her reservations about Julia now that her father and brother were back in the picture.

"Someone has to keep watch over the Harvers," Magwyn said.

"Are you saying you trust *me* to do that?"

"I'm saying of everyone left in my life you are perhaps the person I trust most outside of my own blood."

"Don't know if that's wise."

"I don't know either, but I'm willing to risk it."

Rhymona returned her attention to her hand. "It's your funeral."

"Shall I close the bind then?"

The magus shook her poisoned hand to loosen it and squeezed it into a fist. "Kill her pretty and let's be on with it."

CHAPTER TWENTY-ONE

THEY'D CARVED a crooked path to the upper kingdom by dawn break. Men, women, children, soldiers, citizens, all banding together behind his gift and blade, cheers and cries of *Hail King Remy*! and *For Lancastle*! making the rounds of the grand, unyielding mob.

From above, Rhyvariath burned through the bad streets, affording them an advantage the nether lacked, try as it might to meld together and volley aerial assaults at the merciless beast.

Remy and Thira took turns in control, switching between his gift and her dragon essence, as the other neared depletion, alternating pairs of Royalguard officers occasionally breaking through the blight ahead to buy them a few breaths of rest. Dirty, bloodstained, unrecognizable faces, faces without names, a problem the watchman prince meant to rectify provided they all survived.

Back at the reins, Remy hewed through a charging bluecoat ghoul, all adrenaline and forward momentum, swatting aside a blade thrust by a second blighter, spinning around it, and whipping Exylduin across the back of the fiend's skull.

An arrow whizzed past him into a third set of clicking noises and Remy whirled around to face his assailant finding a ghoulish scullery maid with an arrow jutting out of her temple.

The bastards were growing smarter by the second, becoming more cohesive, more like a hive mind, forming strategic challenges and clever little sneak attacks, gaining ever closer to a deathblow.

Remy watched the scullery maid drift away from him, toward a boy nocking a second arrow to his bow, but the ghoul collapsed face first in the snow well short of the young bowman.

"Clear," Remy shouted. He nodded at the boy, who couldn't count much more than a dozen cycles. *Tough way to cut your teeth at war, this.* "Brilliant shot," the watchman commended.

"Thank you, Highness," the bowman said with a heavy backwoods accent, sprouting a sheepish gap-toothed grin.

"What's your name, boy?" Remy asked as some of the mob began to trickle in from the avenue behind them.

"Clara, milord," the boy answered and Remy realized his mistake.

"Clara, is it?" He sniffed back phlegm. "No boy at all then."

"It's all right, Highness. Most folk that don't know me make the mistake. And rightly, I wear the part well."

No argument there. "How old are you, Clara?"

"Fourteen."

"Are you from Lancastle?"

"Nay, Belhurst, milord."

Belhurst? An eyebrow raised. Belhurst was two, mayhaps three days north.

"Pa sent me and my sister south when word of the blight came through." She looked down. "But Kira didn't make it long. A soldier named Jory saved me. Jory Evers. He's the one got us here."

"Is Jory still alive?"

"Yer fuckin' A right I'm still alive," an unmistakable voice roared from the swarming crowd, breaking through the ranks, looking a right proper pile of shit, as they all did, eyes still bulbous, bloodshot, and twitchy. "And here I now find ye. Ain't no useless Toff no more, are ya? But a fuckin' King, yeah. Gods save 'em."

"What the absolute hell?" Remy breathed at the frail, pasty-faced swordsman. "How?"

The last he saw of Jorem Evers, the bastard was killing townsfolk in Brymshire to feed his blighted brother. He appeared deranged, a liability, a lost cause, brandishing his blade about, threatening violence at his swordbrothers. Thusly, Remy and Dennings left him to his lunacy. And yet here he now stood.

It's truly all random, isn't it?

"Lady Fortune, I reckon," Jory answered. "After you all left, I saw the lichlord, and Al had a go. Tried to make a meal of me. His own brother, the ornery shit. And I nearly let him have his way. It would've been a mercy, to have it true. But then some mad bitch with a glowing knife brained him and..."

"REMY." Rhyvariath landed atop the nearest building and most in attendance glared up at the great beast, gasps and whispers making the rounds, none of them having ever seen such a monstrous creature before.

"THE PATH IS OPEN TO THE CITADEL," Rhyvariath said, his thunderous voice echoing inside the courtyard stones. "DO NOT VENTURE EAST, THEIR NUMBERS ARE STILL CONSIDERABLE THAT WAY."

"Cheers," Remy replied. "Shall we meet atop the western battlements near midday?" *Assuming, of course, we're all still here.*

"AGREED." Rhyvariath clutched Hrathgon's heart in his claw. "I WILL FIND A SANCTUARY FOR THIS, THEN FLY SOUTH TO LOCATE THE NETHER BEHEMOTH."

"Luck stones, friend," the watchman prince said as Rhyvariath took wing, glancing over at Clara afterward. "How many arrows left?"

"Four."

"Stick close, yeah?"

"Of course, milord," she answered. "'Scout's honor.'"

The watchman returned his attention to Jory. "You take a half, guard the right flank."

"Aye."

Remy's gaze fell upon a female bluecoat soldier that appeared to be wearing the most blood of the lot. "And you, soldier, what's your name?"

"Cadet Telfair, milord." She stood tall, wielding the Royalguard regimented sword and shield.

"Telfair, your half take the left flank. We're pushing onward to the north entrance, should be open ground, but we all know that means exactly shit the way things are, so keep your eyes peeled and your blades hungry."

"Hail King Remy!" Jorem shouted.

"For House Lanier!" another roared from somewhere amidst the crowd's belly.

"For Lancastle!" a third.

Remy couldn't help himself, his father in the back of his mind, as he lifted Exylduin high, riding the pulse of Lancastle's survivors, pushing his gift into its steel to create a great azure beacon of hope.

"For Lancastle!" he joined in, pumping Exylduin to the heavens with each cheer.

And the chant went on and on as they advanced into the labyrinth of courtyards separating the great citadel from her many hamlets.

King Remy, they called him. And the gods know, he never thought he'd see the day. And he certainly never expected this sort of response. Through it all. The coup of the Midnight Men. The loss of his father and brother. The cycles of torment and mockery. Somehow, he'd come full circle. Somehow, they sang his name.

If only there was the time to enjoy it.

He thought about Marsea then, and Desmond, and how they might change things moving forward. Mayhaps they could govern together. Mayhaps they could be an actual family again. Mayhaps he and Des might get on like old mates and he'd finally know what it felt like to have a true brother. Mayhaps he and Marsea could walk the high halls side by side and simply talk of their day without worry of some vile cutthroat over-hearing.

Remy raced from stone to pitch to stone again, a dream of peacetime dancing in his head, dodging the unmoving body parts strewn about the yards and arcades, occasionally peering over his shoulder to check on the mob. They followed, still. They battled, still. They cheered, still.

"Hail King Remy!"

"For House Lanier!"

"For Lancastle!"

"Fuck the blight!"

Amongst a host of other indecipherable war cries.

A shimmer of white light in the courtyard ahead caused him to slow by a hair and he prepared Exylduin.

"Ready yourselves," he howled as he trailed under the arcade passage to the next courtyard over, the snowfall quickening, his heartbeats thundering, expecting some Ravenholme mongrel on the other side or something far, far worse, but instead finding...

"Edgar."

His footsteps hastened, but everything else slowed around him as he stuck his Eldn-lit blade into a snow drift and they slammed into each other's arms in the courtyard's epicenter. Without waiting, without care, without abandon, they embraced and Remy brushed a hand across his love's cheek.

"Still alive, I see," the watchman said.

"Did you doubt me?" Edgar returned.

"Gods, I could kiss you." Remy countered.

"You could."

And without delay Remy did just that, pushing through the cold clouds between them, crushing his lips against that of his heart's desire, forcing his love's words back down his throat.

The watchman prince was done with the charade. Done with hiding, done with pretending, done with everyone else's expectations of him. Man, woman, lowborn, high. He felt how he felt, loved who and what he loved, and right now, at this moment, despite it all, Edgar Alewine was all he could think about.

"Heard you're into slaying nether drakes now," Aunt Magwyn greeted.

Remy and Edgar pulled apart, taking in the surrounding survivors. Some gawked, some glanced away, but a few appeared genuinely glad for them, Magwyn included.

"I had help," Remy said.

The Empress nodded. "Rhyvariath, I'm told."

"And not a moment too soon. He's gone to scout the nether's location. We're to meet again around midday and assess." Remy glanced into the dark castle entrance. "How's the citadel?"

"The lower quarters are mostly clear for now, but everything above the guest hall is lost to the blight. Some have holed up in the library."

"Julia?"

"She is among them."

"Any sign of Desmond or Marsea?"

"Not as of yet. Though they may have waited until daylight to push into The Scar."

"Likely a wise decision," Remy said.

"Your Highness, some of the blight from the kingdom walks are pushing into the rearguard ranks," a bluecoat shouted as he broke through the crowd. "They'll be on us any moment."

"Get inside," Remy said, retrieving Exylduin. "Everyone."

"I'll seal the entrance behind us," Magwyn said.

The survivors burst into action, scurrying into the castle depths. It was nigh impossible to count the heads in the stampede, but eyeballing, Remy guessed they had nearly a few hundred. A few hundred left from thousands. It made him ill to give it any more thought than that.

"You too, Clara," he ordered, realizing she hadn't yet left his side.

"I won't leave you, Highness."

"I need you to go, Clara." He used a stern tone, not unlike his mother when she'd made a pass at actual parenting. "Follow the others until you're inside the library."

She offered a hurt expression but obeyed.

"Tough kid, that one," Edgar said.

"And a perfect draw with a bow and arrow." Remy smirked. "She might even give you a run for your coin if put to the contest."

"We all make it through this, I'm game for a round through the old target yard."

They waited, side by side, swords at the ready, until they heard the clicking sound of the blight resonating through the arcade passageway, and watched, steady, as the last of the survivors trickled into the courtyard, a pack of ghouls hard on their coattails.

"Be ready to blast the doorway," Remy commanded Magwyn.

"On it."

"Don't die," he said to Edgar.

"Right back at you," Edgar returned as they held their position in the courtyard's center.

A half dozen ghouls spilled in from beyond, chasing after a trio of hobbled bluecoats.

Remy rushed past the bluecoats and buried Exylduin in the first ghoul's face, as Edgar sliced through the second ghoul's neck, beheading the gnashing fiend.

With one hand on his blade, Remy parried a blighter's strike, sending it past him, and conjured an egg of Eldn fire to his offhand, flinging it into the next ghoul, screaming a Chandiian curse at the encroaching horde, and turned around to find Edgar stabbing his sword down into the third blighter's face as its cohorts burst into bloody chunks behind him all the way back out the passageway into the next courtyard over.

"Should buy us some—"

"Remy! It's here!" Magwyn cried from the citadel entrance, eyes wide as the sister moons, expression warped in confused agony, coughing up blood, a blade poking through her chest.

"Maggie!" Remy howled as the blade retracted and she dropped to her knees, her scepter clattering to the stones, the world spinning on its head again.

Behind her stood Jorem Evers, eyes the color of hellbent winter, black grin on full display.

How did I not sense it?

How did I not see it?

Tetherow...

Jory's blade ate through Magwyn's throat, twisting and ripping out the side of her neck.

EMYRIA.

"End of the line, sunshine," Jorem spat, summoning Magwyn's scepter to his offhand psychokinetically, disappearing into the pitch as he sent a series of scepter strikes into the entrance, collapsing it behind him, preventing them from following.

Magwyn slumped, her head bending unnaturally to her shoulder, hanging on by a sliver of muscle and skin, an azure mist billowing from the opened flesh as the black substance lacing Jorem's blade expanded across Magwyn's shoulder, seeping inside her.

She's gone. She's actually gone.

KEEP YOUR CHIN UP. WE ARE NOT OUT OF THIS YET.

"What the fuck?" he heard Edgar say as Magwyn's body began to writhe, wail, and vomit nether ichor all at once.

"*...She is becoming a phaedrylax!...*" Thira shouted as they raced toward her, ghouls pouring into the courtyard behind them.

A tentacle burst from Magwyn's neck wound, followed by a second and a third, lifting the rest of her torso off the ground like a rag doll appendage, spritelings hatching from the nether flesh's spawning sacs.

They halted.

EMYRIA CAN STILL BE SAVED.

"Fuck!" Remy barked.

"What now?" Edgar asked as they collided, back-to-back, a phaedrylax to one side, an army of blight to the other.

I don't know if he's gifted, Remy argued.

THERE IS NO OTHER CHOICE.

"You have to accept her," Remy said.

"I have to what?"

"Emyria, you must accept her. And yes, it's going to hurt."

"Fantastic."

"There's no other way."

"What do I need to do?"

"Trust in your gift. And trust in me."

"Is that..." Edgar's words became cut off by a mad scream, the azure mist snaking around him, infesting his body.

Remy burst into action. *You motherfuckers let me live this long. I'm not dying like this. You stars, you gods, you heathens, you horrors, you see him through this. Whatever it takes.*

Remy conjured an egg of Eldn flame sending it shrieking into the sea of blight, calling curse after curse, a hex for every corpse he rent through, working a circle around Edgar as Emyria invaded his orifices and forced their union.

Crimson, black, crimson, sometimes meat, sometimes bone, sometimes liquid, his blade never stopping, tongue in full-tilt summon, bartering, badgering, begging every last entity the fates would allow.

And then his aunt arrived in the maelstrom, a six-limbed tentacle squirmer from hell.

Exylduin blazed across the bulk of her slithering black flesh, dragon's flame screeching, crackling, boiling pus bursting after him, as he split through a ghoul fool enough to bugger about his path, and he conjured an Eldn egg kissing it ugly in the face of the next fuckwit in line, blood slop chasing his dancing shadow.

It was everything Remy could do to keep the blight from reaching his beloved. Cutting a black and red circle of body parts around them, Edgar's howls like daggers in his soul.

But this is what the fates decided, the fucking assholes.

This is how it had to be.

His love was on hands and knees, the snow melting around him, damn near catching flame, as Emyria forged their soul bond, his veins radiating with dracari essence.

You can do this, Edgar. If anyone can do this, it's you.

Another curse, another pooling of blood in his wake. Aunt Magwyn again. Exylduin branded the nether flesh with a fresh scar. Ghoul, hack. Ghoul, slash. Ghoul, curse. Black, crimson, black.

An explosion of white-azure light from inside the ring of carnage. Remy slowed.

Edgar dashed past him, azure-eyed, slamming the edge of his shield into a ghoul's face, caving in what remained of its diseased brain, and racing toward the only exit, a passageway into the northern courtyards.

"Edgar!" Remy called, giving chase.

"We'll go through the library directly," Edgar yelled over his shoulder. "It's warded against the nether."

THEY ARE AS ONE.

Brilliant deduction, Mervold.

THIS WAS THE ONLY WAY.

So you keep saying.

"I feel incredible," Edgar shouted from up ahead.

Add Jorem to the list of Tetherow's puppets. How many is that now? The bastard could be anyone at this point. And Aunt Magwyn. Remy's heart caught. *She was right there. She was with us. She kept a dracari within. And Tetherow still fooled all of us.*

BUT WE KNOW HE IS NOT IN EDGAR AND THAT IS ENOUGH FOR NOW.

No, fuck that, Thira, Remy quibbled. *We're not just pawns for you lot to blow through as you please.*

WE ARE TRYING TO SURVIVE ALL OF THIS JUST AS YOU ARE, REMY. WE ARE DOING OUR BEST.

I know.

TETHEROW IS AN UNKNOWN. YOU NAMED HIM VHARYN'ASHI. I HAVE NEVER FACED SUCH A CREATURE BEFORE. NEITHER HAS EMYRIA.

Edgar flung his shield through one of the staff quarters' windows and leapt through the gap of broken glass.

AS FOR YOUR FRIEND, IT WOULD SEEM HE HAS TAKEN WELL TO HIS NEWFOUND ABILITIES.

Remy dove through after, rolling up to his feet as Edgar began to scrawl a ward across the opening.

"Thank you, Remy," Edgar said, eyes burning with Emyria's presence.

"I am sorry about Magwyn. We did not always see eye to eye, but I cared for her as a sister."

The first blighter slammed into the magical barrier seconds after the sigil wrapped, followed by another, and another, forming a wall of gnashing maws and bloody claws scratching and beating against the flickering ward between them.

"We need to leave," Remy said, "before they realize other windows exist."

CHAPTER TWENTY-TWO

By DAWN, the blizzard had blown through, though snow still floated down from the heavens with a slow, quiet charm like in the old holiday stories.

Marsea greeted Broenwjar as he came padding up to her at the edge of the field they'd arrived in the night before. Considering his relative calm, she presumed the nearby wood was clear of any wildkin watchers or worse.

"Did you enjoy yourself, B?" she asked, taking to a knee before him and ruffling an ear. By the fresh bloodstains running down his muzzle and chest, he'd filled his belly on some poor forest critter after a game of hunt and the rush had put him in an uncharacteristically good mood. Marsea reckoned for all the madness he'd been through since their bonding, sometimes it was just nice to go out and be a wolf in the wild for a bit. Her nose wrinkled up as his breath hit her. "Oi, you certainly smell like you did."

The urge to bend her mind into his and check in on him had been strong, especially after she sank into her pillow with nothing but her thoughts for company, but something told her to let him have his solitude. That he'd earned it and needed it as badly as she needed a few hours rest. So, she clung to her prayers and songs and visions of *The Kingstome's* pages until slumber eventually steered her into a dreamless sleep.

Standing, she stared off into the distance, west of the field where the remains of a tiltyard lay still as a backwoods cemetery. *Is this where you earned your spurs, father?* she couldn't help but wonder. She'd had the tales aplenty over the cycles. That Whit Lanier was amongst the best to ever tilt a lance and took down more than his fair share of tourney jousts back when. At the recollection, she became profoundly aware of her father's grimoire inside the satchel hanging down against her backside.

"Look at this beastie here," Hilda called as she approached beside Desmond, carrying a queer-looking harness that was laced with a thick russet wire in one arm, and a giant-sized crossbow in the other.

"Broenwjar meet Hilda. Hilda, Broenwjar," she made the requisite introductions.

"Stars alive, he's a biggun. A wngar wolf through and through," Hilda replied. "Haven't seen one of his kind in ages."

"A wngar wolf?"

"That's what we name them because of their size. They're known for prowling the extreme northern territories, well beyond The Scar, beyond even the wngar kingdoms, feral as any creature scouring The Vael." Hilda eyed Marsea. "They rarely hunt this far south though. Do you know how he came to be tamed?"

"His previous master, I believe. A man named Elsymir Beldroth. Elsymir brought him back from a terrible injury and bound him to his own life force to keep him from the grave."

"I recall the name from my cycles at court," Hilda said. "He's y'deman, yes?"

"He was. The stars rest his soul." Marsea let her silence answer any remaining questions of the man.

"Lenore's doing good, too, thanks for the ask," Desmond quipped before taking a drag from the bent cigarillo he'd won off one of the card players the night before playing three card brag.

"And how are you faring?" she asked. The state she left him in the night before it was a wonder he was standing, much less conversational. She'd never seen anyone drink as hard as her brother, not even Rhymona, excusing herself from the festivities, once he got in with the locals. And thank the maidens she had the wherewithal. Another shot or two and she would have been painting the walls in fresh sick all the way to her bedchamber.

"Never better," he replied.

"Never better my eye," Hilda grumbled. "I found him emptying his guts out in the greenhouse not an hour past."

"No judgments, yeah, but the jasmine needed watering."

A few others began to fill in the space behind Hilda and Des carrying the same armaments. Marsea eyed the soldierly group, four in all, two of which were a part of the gambler's table from the night before.

"We've a few reckless halfwits willing to join in our little suicide mission," Hilda announced.

"It's an honor, Highness," the one on the far left added. She was a bonny thing, the only female of the four, and the youngest by a fair few cycles.

"You have our gratitude," Marsea said.

"That's Daisy," Hilda introduced. "And her father Gareth." He offered a bow, curtains of long blonde hair trailing down well past his shoulders. "You've already met my nephew Asher, and Rufus, who we keep around for some ungodly reason."

"Somehow, I keep waking up not dead, how's that my fault?" Rufus muttered between puffs of his corncob pipe.

"It's certainly not for lack of trying," Gareth added, clapping his gray-maned friend on the back.

"Daisy, can you help Marsea with the harness?" Hilda asked. "Once you're secure, we'll go through a trial run with it." Hilda handed the harness to Marsea, which she found lighter than expected. "Daisy and Gareth will go first, show you the workings. We'll practice on the redwoods down yonder."

Marsea handed her satchel to Desmond and fitted the harness over her shoulders, tightening the buckles at the shoulder blades and waist to fit her form.

"Looks good," Daisy said, tugging in a few places to make sure the harness was safe and snug. "Sure you've never done this before?"

"Positive."

"See this pulley here?" Daisy noted a strap that hung from the front padding of the harness, which hugged over her chest, taut as a corset. "Once the bolt has found its target, you'll yank it hard as you can. You'll feel a snap then the harness constrict, but don't be alarmed, that's how it's supposed to be, it's just the wiring running its course, then make sure you're clutching your sword tight cause once you pull it you'll have about two seconds before you're flying, and a blade works a heck of a lot better on a wngar than a row of knuckles."

"You've slain one before?" Marsea asked as they walked toward the opposite side of the field where a cluster of redwoods rose up tall as citadel towers.

"I've three to my name. Four, if you count one I stumbled on half-dead from a wildkin attack. Best way to down 'em is the neck. Front or back. Whatever your fancy. Don't make much difference from what I've wrought."

"Once you're up there, you have to move swift," Gareth added. "You've got about three seconds before they're on you. So, you've gotta be ready to plunge steel midway through the air."

Marsea could sense Blind Widow salivating in her scabbard at the mere mention of bloody murder.

They halted about twenty paces away from the first redwood.

"A crown for the lady," Hilda fished a strip of cloth from out her travel sack.

"What's this for?" Marsea asked.

"Your hair. Get it in a knot and tie it back. You can thank me later."

"All right, now you watch me," Daisy said. "I usually give a five count after the bolt has been fired, then pull."

Gareth grabbed the end of Daisy's harness wire, and Marsea found hers. It appeared almost like a key. He fitted it inside a lock-type apparatus at the end of the bolt and twisted until there was a clicking sound. "You ready?" Gareth asked, nocking the arm-length bolt inside his oversized crossbow.

"Ready."

And Marsea took note of every little detail about Daisy's posture as she unsheathed her sword, from her stance and squat to her offhand clutching the strap to her bosom.

"Luck stones, lass," Hilda said.

"Keep'em," Daisy returned, mugging a harlequin's smile.

Click. Click. Went the cocking stirrup.

"Happy trails, darlin'," Gareth bid.

Crack!

The shot went off, easy as you please, and Marsea found herself counting with Daisy as the bolt soared through the snowfall and burrowed into the tree about twenty heads high. On the five mark, right as it sank into wood, Daisy sprinted forward, jerking the strap away from her, and she became airborne a blink later.

Holy shit! Marsea's eyes grew wide at the sight.

Daisy gripped the hilt of her blade in both hands as she flew at breakneck speed toward the tree, all the resemblance of a human arrow, sticking the landing on a thick branch where she moved like water around the trunk, stabbing once to the front and a second time to the back, before spinning back to her audience with a fish-eating grin and theatrical bow.

Good gravy. The scene was like some farce ripped out of a mad-capped carnie act.

And the princess would have clapped at the sheer audacity of it, but awe quite found her fixed to the spot she presently filled, mouth agape, heart racing, her palms sweaty despite the cold. Maidens' breath, she'd never witnessed anything of the like before. It was mental. It was reckless. It was brilliant. And quite honestly, the most beautiful thing she'd ever beheld.

"What do you think?" Hilda asked, eyebrow arched. "You up for it?"

"Oh, yeah," Marsea answered, pushing her glasses back up the bridge of her nose.

Fuck a ballet lesson. This here is the dance I'm meant for.

"We'll start simple—" Hilda began.

"No," Marsea cut her off. "I want it exactly where Daisy's was. That's about the height of the most of them, yeah?"

"Roughly."

"Then that's where we start. Unfortunately, time won't stand still because we wish it so, and just now it would seem we are tragically short of it."

"Dick on the table, I like it," Desmond added as he flicked the end of his cigarillo. Lenore croaked her support from her perch upon his shoulder. More and more he was proving himself less of a royal, but to have the tale, he'd graduated crown of his order a few cycles back and in the days since, oversaw the university's archives. Marsea had so many questions she wanted to ask her brother, about his life and his experiences as a student and scholar, but there simply wasn't the time.

Daisy returned to the group, tossing the bolt back to her father. "Think merry thoughts, Highness," she encouraged.

"You let me know when to loose," Hilda said.

The princess gripped the hilt of her haxanblade, letting the sword's enchantment merge once more with her gift, before tearing it free from its confines, her blood boiling at their bond, bad hand choking the harness strap against her heart, and she dug her boots into the same exact place Daisy did, facing the redwood.

All you've been through, this should be easy as pie.

She ran her tongue across the pink scar rising off her upper lip and a smirk followed.

"Loose!"

Famous last words, those.

Click. Click.

Crack!

The bolt caught wind.

Two.

Three.

Four.

Her jaw clenched briefly, and her pulse raced quicker as she squeezed the shit out of Blind Widow in her good hand.

"Fuck!" She cried as she sprinted forward, ripping the pulley back, and she felt the harness shrink around her like a closed fist as the wire snapped from the strap and began to slither through, one step, two, and before she could even think to let the detached strap go, she was airborne, off like a shooting star, the tree coming at her fast as a three-story pitfall.

Much too fast.

Much, much too fast.

Fucksake...

She was two-thirds of the way to the tree by the time she got anything close to a proper bearing and she hurled Blind Widow like a spear at the mark as she slammed into the same branch Daisy landed on, full body collision, air punching out of her as she scrambled to find purchase before her backward momentum could drop her down through the sea of branches below.

Hugging onto the limb for dear life, she gasped for breath, in and out, her mind a maelstrom of curses as she labored to secure herself, feeling the bruises swell on her arms and chest from the impact, and a cheer rang out from whence she'd come.

The hells?

Clinging on like a drunken buffoon, she shimmied toward the trunk and used it to leverage herself back upright on the nearest bough to her feet. Once settled, she ripped the haxanblade from its cut, then jerked the bolt loose, dropping it to the snow drifts before navigating the branches back down, her body aching all over.

"Well done, milady," Hilda said.

"Well done? I'd say I buggered that one pretty spectacularly."

Broenwjar was the first to reach her, nudging at her bad hand with his snout, licking her fingers.

"I'm all right, B," she assured him.

"You did as well as any other I've seen on their first pull," Gareth said. "I missed the branch entirely, flew right on past, landed about ten paces yonder with a broken arm and shoulder out of socket. Took a season's turn before my next attempt."

"It just came at me so fast," Marsea said.

"I'd have given you better warning, but there's truly no words to do it justice," Hilda said. "I've found letting folks suffer it first hand is the best recipe for success."

Same old Mistress Veranski, Marsea thought, recalling the former instructor's words from back when. *Anything worth learning is done through discipline and determination, and if that doesn't make the mark, then it's rinse and repeat 'til it creates the reminder. Train the brain to accept a new reality and the body will believe it.*

Marsea may not have cared much for Hilda Veranski, especially back then, but she damn well respected the woman. She had little doubt, her footwork, despite the pains she still endured, would be anywhere near the quality it was now without those dance lessons. It certainly helped her in her sparring sessions with Vaustian and Cas, and that much more since her release into the Vaelsyn wilds.

Train your brain, Marsea.

"Again," she said, holding Hilda's stare. "Same as last time."

AGAIN. Again. Again!

It was around the fourth attempt when she found her gift and everything began to slow.

By the sixth she was positively feral, Other oozing from her pores, Broenwjar giving chase.

On the eighth, after a bevy of bruises ran the length of her, she finally landed the death sling proper.

And on the tenth go, she was practically dancing circles around the horribly pockmarked redwood.

Hilda Veranski held a thumbs up in the distance. And Marsea beamed, despite the times.

Not bad, old girl. Not bad at all.

CHAPTER TWENTY-THREE

Fucking hells, H. What did you lot do to this place? Aiden asked from The Scar's edge, pulling up the front of his cloak to shield his nose.

The expanse distended before him in the late morning pall, more scab than scar, all sulfur, smoke, and snow, its stench just as stifling as was her ghastly appearance.

Hrathgon remained quiet, having dug himself into a darkness within during the nightfall whilst Aiden was busy drinking the innhouse dry. Quite intoxicated, the archivist somehow managed to retain some of the dracari's worries. Words like void, emptiness, hollow, absence, and severing, echoed through his drunken memory.

Say one thing for Aiden Ashborough, say his alcohol-addled brain was sharp as a whetted blade where it counted.

H, if you can hear me. We're here.

He waited a moment before glancing at Marsea and shaking his head.

"Not to worry," Hilda said from behind her mask, black down the left side, white down the right with a red line like a tear running down from the eye to the jawline, "we know the location of the tomb. Obviously not where the dragon buried the thing, but we can at least get you to it."

Aiden nodded.

"Lead on," Marsea bade, Wolfie at her side padding along majestically.

In just their short time together, he'd rather grown a fondness for Marsea.

A lament formed in the wake of this fondness, however. Of all the cycles he'd missed spending with her. Though he had to wonder, had he not been murdered, had he simply been left to the Lancastle cage as Marsea and Remy were, would they have been so keen on each other now? Hells, would he even still be alive to ask the question?

A few paces in, he noticed The Scar felt different underfoot. It was soft, like going from stone to sponge. There was a slight sinking sensation to it. Almost like it wanted to swallow them up, but for the surface to shield them. Though, he reckoned, if creatures big as wngar walked the moor, he'd likely get on without too much trouble.

"It's quiet," Marsea said.

"Aye, the wngar have rid the land of most of its former inhabitants, wolld and wildlife alike," Daisy said behind a mask. As with Hilda's, it covered her entire face, bearing the style of the masquerade. Porcelain-white skin from the lips down, the top portion displaying the detail of the half-masks worn at a gala, black ivy on a field of gold.

"Hilda," Rufus said. "Ten o'clock." A giftborn and former battle-magus, he was the only one of the Maidstone crowd to remain unmasked.

Aiden followed their stares to the west and found a pair of massive silhouettes bobbing up and down on the horizon.

"I see them," Hilda returned.

"Ain't never spotted the bastards this far south," Rufus grumbled.

"Is this a problem?" Marsea asked. "Should we prepare?"

"Not as of yet," Hilda said, squinting hard, "they look to be running away from us."

Or from something else, Aiden thought.

THE SCAR WAS STILL for a while as they pushed further inward, an eerie hush rolling over the barren landscape, save for the soft crunch of their boots over snow. They stopped for a brief rest after an hour and Aiden just stared into the pale horizon before them. Something sat ill in his stomach, rotting his heart and clogging his head with doubt. A dalliance with destiny. A knowing that Tetherow was close by. A sense of impending doom.

Dread caught his breath as a fresh group of shadows bled into the distance, the first activity they'd seen since they first entered The Scar.

"Movement ahead," he called over his shoulder at the others.

They all watched in silence. The minutes passed like days.

"It's wngar," Rufus said. "Something has 'em in a pother."

"Or someone," Aiden replied, turning about to Marsea.

"You think it's Tetherow?" she asked the obvious question.

"I know it is. I can feel the bastard's presence like a phantom limb."

"Do you suppose it can feel yours?" Marsea asked.

"I don't know. I reckon it's possible. We were a part of each other for however long, and given its abundance of arcane abilities, it wouldn't surprise me." Lenore croaked from her perch on his shoulder before taking flight into the winds ahead. "She certainly believes it's her old master."

Marsea nodded. "Then we must make haste."

THEY CAME upon the village outskirts within minutes and found a legion of wngar warring with their own, massive black appendages bursting from some of their bodies only adding to their horrific appearances. One writhing corpse nearby sprouted a series of legs from its torso like that of a giant mountain spider. Gareth fired at a wngar that approached them, the bolt taking it through a roaring mouth mid-battle cry as Daisy launched after it, alighting the creature's upper chest as it came crashing down to the muck, sliding to a halt.

"Nice shot," Daisy cheered as she spun back toward the group and leapt down from the dead wngar's sternum

"Daisy!" Gareth bellowed as a blood-soaked tendril twisted up from the dead wngar's face behind the daughter, slick and gleaming, and pierced through Daisy's backside and out her belly.

Red leaked out from inside her mask as the tendril expanded like that of a Kraken's tentacle and lifted her into the air, spritelings bursting from the egg chambers upon its flesh, ripping off her mask, and burrowing into the poor girl's eyes and mouth just before she became riven at the entry wound.

Gareth crumbled to his knees in horror, removing his protective mask. "Dai...Daisy?"

"We have to keep moving," Marsea shouted, sprinting into the glut of mutating giantfolk toward the towering monolith, Hilda at her side, and Asher chasing.

Just then, Aiden became aware of the crows. Hundreds of them. Circling, watching, conversing, dining on corpses, Lenore among them, slicing through the fetid winds.

"You heard the girl," Rufus said, gravebone wand crackling, leaking piss-colored magic from its tip. "Keep moving."

The archivist drew his sword and glanced at Gareth, who slumped in disbelief, eyes vacant. "Gareth, we have to go."

"I...I killed her," he uttered, staring ahead at the expanding nether beast that rent his daughter in twain. "I..."

"Get it together, Gareth."

"She...she...she..."

"Bugger this." Aiden was off before the man could complete whatever response was stuck in his mind, fastly realizing the futility, and unwilling to mind a broken father in this manner of bedlam, especially with Marsea having run off into the fray already, and doubly so with Autumn so close.

Hunting the cherry blossom trail left by Marsea's haxanblade, he raced headlong into the sea of carnage, crashing from body to body, spinning, stumbling, barely able to keep his legs under him, narrowly avoiding spears both black and silver, until the snowfall became thick with the Blind Widow's mist, severed appendages, and chunks of swelling, snaking, hemorrhaging nether flesh and larvae everywhere.

At some point he caught a snap of chain lightning, finding Rufus at the other end, and chased after the practiced sorcerer, who proved quite ruthless with a wand, and that much more dangerous with a bag of potions at his disposal.

Wide-eyed, blood thundering in his brain, Aiden somehow kept his feet, calling forth every ounce of the gift that would have him, leaping limbs and skirting steel, a lash of screeching magic here, an explosion of some bastard concoction there, trudging through the snowy muck, sword slashing and chopping awkwardly at anything in his way. Plenty to count amongst them. Wngar. Wildkin. Ghouls. Spritelings. And enough crows that to merely name them a murder would be an insult, for by their number they were more akin to a massacre, pursuing Lenore in lead, like bees to a queen, eventually forming a swarm around him like a shield against the flooding blight.

"Don't be a tit. Don't be a tit. Don't be a tit." His paltry rally cry echoed.

Packed in the spiraling melee, the blight practically stacked on top of each other, he lost Rufus to the splintering, spreading, congealing horde and found a phaedrylax spider-wngar hybrid skittering toward him.

"H, you feel like not dying, you may want to consider unfucking your host's current predicament."

He hadn't slung about a proper patch of iron since...well, since the first time he died, and faced the approaching drylax in what he recalled of a defensive stance, preparing for an ungodly amount of pain, as the fiend leapt at him from ten paces ahead, Lenore's flock too far away to offer even the smallest semblance of support.

Hilt choked in both hands, he suddenly felt cold and not from the fall of snow as the sword caught flame, and before he could even comprehend his possession, he was spinning next to the passing fiend, hacking it in half midair, releasing the sword from one hand, the Eldn fire remaining in his open palm as he slung the flaming sphere into the blight ahead, immolating another pair of the mutating bastards.

Hrathgon.

"...**Never stop...**" the dracari shouted as a feral collision transpired behind them. He reeled about to find Broenwjar ripping the throat out from a maul-wielding wngar.

Wolfie, you big, beautiful, mad bastard.

And the gods only knew, nothing in his studies had prepared him for battling nether-infested wngar.

Another mishappen wngar charged at him on all fours like a monkey possessed, massive forearms painted in gore, yellow teeth gnashing, and Aiden readied his blade, preparing for impact, but before it could reach him a wand strike surged into the side of its head causing an explosion of blood and bones across the span of its face. The abomination hit the muck with a hard thunk and slid forward the rest of the way, inches from

Aiden's feet, a spill of boiling wngar brains slopping onto the edge of his boot.

"You're welcome," Rufus said from up ahead, where the path suddenly appeared quite open to the monolith.

Almost too open.

"**...Move!...**"

He raced after Rufus once more, catching sight of Marsea off to his right slamming into a wngar, haxanblade opening the goliath's throat end to end as she danced across a shoulder and plunged the angry end through the creature's nape.

Broenwjar passed him up, stampeding back toward his master, ramming into a wildkin, crushing it under paw as they hit the mud, and with an easy roll the beast was back up on all fours and on to the next.

As Hilda's support, Asher had already fired his quiver empty and ripped a hatchet from his belt, braining a ghoul inches from his aunt's backside as she nocked another bolt, preparing Marsea's harness for another launch.

"**...Keep going. We cannot help them...**"

He pressed on, swinging his sword wildly, chasing Hrathgon's whispered curses, ghouls bursting to pieces around him, blood and body parts splashing across his footpath from every direction, one after the next, until he was inside the village where he found within a hemomancer's pull to rival his own, blood rising from every corpse in count like his chant aboard Blackhall's Banshee, multiple streams pooling midair and flowing in the direction of the great monolith.

A blast of gold screamed out from up ahead and Aiden found Rufus again. He followed the second strike and found...

"Autumn..."

Aiden's eyes lowered to the mold-colored grimoire in Autumn's hands as she shoved it inside a satchel at her side. The monstrosity appeared as though something pulled from the depths of a swamp.

She twisted around a wngar's backside, a carnomancer's hex melting the wind, dragging cloth and unspooling flesh from the bellowing giant's bones as though flayed with an invisible knife, stretching out into a skin shield before her, absorbing the battle-mage's strikes.

THE OLD FOOL IS NEARLY TAPPED.

Strike after strike came from the howling magus, each smaller than the last, as Tetherow spellflayed anything in sight to withstand the onslaught, the call of corpse blood replenishing the demon's endless incantations.

"Rufus!" Aiden shouted as a phaedrylax rushed for the magus.

"...**Thas'kon ech vira dhu leckt!...**" Hrathgon followed and the nether creature burst apart, spattering Rufus.

Another hex left the lips of Autumn Ashborough an instant later, and the distracted mage's wand arm bent at an impossible angle, the bones within splintering apart, breaking the skin. A terrible cry ruptured through the sorcerer, as both legs cracked backward at the knees, dropping him to the muck where his body twisted the wrong way at the waist as though a rag being rung of water, and a third crack silenced his agony, as the top of his spine cut through his throat and snapped out the side of neck, his spouting lifeblood joining the many streams of floating plasma.

"Thought quite well of himself, didn't he?" Autumn greeted.

Words betrayed the archivist as he watched Rufus's body wither to a pale husk in seconds.

"And then there's you, Desmond Lanier," Autumn smirked, Tetherow's demon mask twisting her facial features as it had once done his. Waxen complexion, cheekbones cut hard as razors, little worm shapes crawling beneath the taut skin of her face. "You know, I'm actually impressed you're still here, especially after watching you dither about uselessly for all those cycles. Though, I suppose, that is what cockroaches do, isn't it?"

"You going to run your gob all day or are we going to get to it?" Aiden snapped.

"You never should have come for my shit, boy. Favored or not, I am your end."

"Your shit?" Aiden sneered. "Your fucking shit? You sick hateful fuck. She's just a girl. And you do this to her? You make a ruin of her. My sister?"

"Oh, don't act so noble now, Desmond. We both know you're a selfish, manipulative piece of shit. Or have you already forgotten? I was you. Hells, we were so close for a time I nearly forgot where I ended and you began."

"Allow me to remind you." A hand reached for Rufus's wand, the gravebone horror snapping up from the mud beside the old man's broken corpse into Aiden's possession, catching flame upon thrall of its new master, and a jet of azure-flecked gold shrieked from its spitting maw at the abominable fiend.

Autumn clapped her hands together, ripping out a string of blood from the warlock's well cut inside her palm, and dragged her hands down to create a scarlet shield wall before her, the rippling puddle of gore absorbing the furious wandshot.

"You smug little prat," she called, multiple eldritch voices echoing out of her. "I wasn't good enough? But you'll whore yourself to the dracari, will you?"

"Fuck you."

"And not just any dracari, but the very dregs of their society. I'm assuming that is you, Hrathgon."

"Hrathgon didn't murder the people I love," Aiden argued.

"Still sore about the ashaeydir slag, are we?" Autumn tutted. "Some part of you must have wanted her death or you would have found a way to stop me." Quick as a whip, she darted out from behind the wall of nether flesh, palm opened toward a nearby wngar corpse, fingers splayed out as the massive corpse split apart like an axe through wood, black swallowing the skin, red bulbous sacs rising and bursting pus globs that formed little devilsprite hatchlings.

A wngar drylax sent one of its barbed appendages stabbing after him, and Aiden dove into one of the nearby huts where he found a younger female wngar cowering in the corner, head tucked into her knees.

"The fuck?"

A black mass smashed into the hut's side wall, a crack pushing inward from outside, which appeared to be made of mud. Another tremor from beyond and the wall fractured, letting a sliver of the daylight in, followed by a giant wngar eyeball appearing in the middle of the dark flesh staring directly at him.

"...**Barigos thae cauza,...**" Hrathgon crowed, rising back to the surface, and a bubble formed around him, stretching out beyond the hut and creating an iridescent azure barrier roughly the size of a castle's great hall.

"There he is," Tetherow cackled from outside. "But you know this little carnie trick won't hold me. Or have you already forgotten our dance inside the palace stacks?"

WHEN THE TIME COMES, YOU STAY OUT OF MY WAY, DESMOND.

When the time comes for what?

I WILL DO WHAT I MUST TO END THE THREAT.

You'll not kill my sister if that's your intent.

Hrathgon offered no reply as they marched back out into the chaos, wand in one hand, blade in the other.

I meant it, Hrathgon. She's not to be harmed.

Outside, a massive glowing dome shimmered overhead, like a glass turned on its head, trapping them inside, and casting a pale cerulean light about all within.

Nothing moved around them save the streams of gore. Everything contaminated by the nether appeared frozen in time. Whispers called from every direction like the land had come awake, like those that were buried beneath during The Dragonsfall never truly died. At least not fully.

A wngar drylax stood between the siblings, kept at bay by Tetherow's will, Autumn waiting beside her flesh shield, an impish expression painted across her once delicate features, floating blood trails weaving around her like a spider's web, crows caught within the magic globe circling overhead, Lenore amongst them.

"The rest of this is not going to go how you think," Autumn warned.

"Story of my life."

"You believe your people deserve this world? You pathetic parasites."

"Parasites?" Aiden scoffed. "You're a fucking fart that possesses people. You can barely survive without one of us parasites to infest. By your definition, you're vermin possessing vermin. I wonder if there's even a word yet for something so low."

Blood slapped down to the muck from the hanging streams around them and from the corner of his eye, he could see Marsea outside the bubble, covered head to toe in gore, ripping her sword from the nape of another wngar's neck.

Sensing him, she rushed to the magical barrier and pounded the bottom of a fist against it, sending undulations over its surface, though unable to enter.

She stepped back, preparing the haxanblade for a strike, by her expression, intending to carve herself through the barrier to him, but before she could try, another wngar was upon her and Hilda fired a bolt into its chest that Marsea chased skyward in a high arch, plunging her blade through its face, riding it down to the muck as it toppled over backward.

"Autumn, if you can hear me, you must fight back," Aiden called. "You can do this. You must remember who you are."

"Oh, so very touching," she returned, deranged smirk bending to a glower. "But the girl is a ghost."

"You underestimate her."

"I own her!"

"You don't own shit. I know exactly where she's gone. Where you've put her. Away in that freaky-ass memory loop nether pit of yours. But Autumn is twice as clever as I am, and that much more defiant, so, if I was able to break through it, you know damned well she can."

Aiden pushed his gift in at her, hunting for her, for anything.

Tam, I love you. You must remember. You must trust me. This is your brother. You must fight back. You must buy me time.

"Aiden." Her sweet voice sang softly as one of her vineyard lullabies. "Aiden, it's me." She slid a step forward.

The archivist raised his wand, channeling his gift from the warlock's well into the gravebone, sparks igniting at its end, raining golden tears into the bloodstained snow.

The flesh shield immediately darted in front of her.

"Nice try, asshole," Aiden snapped.

"End him," Autumn bade, and the frozen nether creatures came to life all around them.

An energy hummed within him, without him, as Hrathgon burrowed to the surface, shrinking the magic barrier until it surrounded only him, absorbing the nether's onslaught, then he compelled what remained of the azure bubble into the scorched fray and Aiden was out of his body again, pissing through the astral plane skyward...

Oh, fuck.

Oh, fuck.

Oh, fuck.

What the hells?

...halting at a measured drift about twenty paces east of himself, the dance of colors snapping from slaughterhouse rainbow to a black and white blur as he weaved through the massacre of crows around him.

Shrieking below.

Burning flesh.

Did he just force me to varg?

A bolt shot through the air between him and his body, plunging into the mass of smoking drylax creatures now melding into one another, forming one colossal beast, and Marsea followed, sopping vermillion, soaring past him, Tetherow's conjured bloodstreams flowing into the screaming, seething haxanblade, as she reared it back for a death strike, Broenwjar giving chase through the herd of blight below her.

She landed atop the creature, stabbing one of its many faces through its forehead, springing down onto a pair of fusing shoulders to a second head, piercing it through the side of its neck and slicing it across the throat, before leaping off.

Hrathgon sprinted along the opposite side of the amalgamating nether colossus, dodging spritelings and nether larvae, blasting holes through wildkin ghouls, all the while peppering Autumn with wandfire, but Tetherow was not to be outdone so easily, the floating flesh shield collecting any shot that came even remotely close.

He's going to kill her to get to Tetherow.

Aiden forced Lenore to dive, and the crows mimicked her movements.

Bridge the gap. Regain control.

Aiden passed Marsea as Hilda and Asher caught her up, bolt quiver empty, each one hobbled, heaving, and bloody, descending into range, watching Autumn pull from her warlock's well, conjuring a glowing string of obsidian that swelled into an egg inside her opposite palm.

What in the fuckmother of all demon-hell-shittery?

He'd never beheld anything like it before, like some bastard union of the nether and the gift, and Hrathgon was running them straight toward it.

The wretch is going to get me dead again.

He beat wing once more, croaking Lenore's balls off, everything he could muster for warning, skirting and swerving through the suffocating blight between until he slammed into his own face.

Hrathgon swatted at him. "**...I said stay out of my way...**" the dracari grumbled.

But Aiden kept after him, digging Lenore's talons into his cheek and neck, finding purchase as a wildkin ghoul plowed into them from behind, taking them all to the muck. The fiend's head imploded a moment later as Hrathgon sent a wand pulse through the side of its half-eaten face.

"**...Bastard fool...**"

He scrambled back up to his feet, steam pouring off him, and began carving a scar of conflagration around them to buy a few moments of reprieve.

Damn it all, Aiden thought, realizing what the steam signified.

Despite their physical separation, he could still sense Hrathgon's aura waning, the dracari soul pulling from his host's fastly dwindling gift, boiling his blood, burning him alive from the inside out.

"Desmond!" he heard Marsea calling, finding her in the distance, cutting down anything Broenwjar missed, as the blood-caked beast made a ghastly trail of the dead like nobody's business.

He inched Lenore up from the snow, a wing hanging limp, crushed in their fall.

"**...This ends now...**" Hrathgon said to him with a scowl before leaping the knee-high wall of flame into the legion of nether.

Numb to the pain, Aiden tried to move Lenore's broken wing, working it about to snap it back into place, but the infernal thing wouldn't budge.

Trapped in a bird that can't fly. Seems about right.

An instant later, he heard a terrible sound, a shriek of magic like nails on glass, and watched as Tetherow's sphere of gift-nether nearly engulfed a diving Hrathgon, incinerating everything in its path.

Incredibly, Hrathgon rolled back up into a sprint, somehow maintaining his balance, slicing through a fold of nether tentacles and disappearing beyond, as the sound of steel colliding resounded.

Hopping and hobbling through the sea of kicking legs and twisting nether tendrils, he managed to find the clashing pair again, Autumn returning every measure of savage horror Hrathgon gave, their swords burning azure and obsidian, sparking, spraying about gift and nether residue thick as magma with each connecting blow.

Then he was rising off the ground, plucked up like a chicken from its coop, his little crow's feet kicking, clutched tight on both sides so he couldn't escape. The grimy, blackened hands turned him about to face his captor and he found a cloudy-eyed ghoul staring at him, its head tilting in confusion as it studied him, knife scars weeping down its forehead and cheeks, as its jaw unhinged, and the fucker's breath hit him hard as an overturned privy bucket.

It was around this juncture his predicament truly registered and Aiden realized the blighter was going off diet for a bit of fowl.

Oh, you've got to be fucking shitting me.

No, no, no, he croaked for all the hells furies, over and over, squirming madly and snapping his beak at the ghoul, but it did little to deter his ravenous foe.

And as he neared the fiend's widening broke-tooth maw, a mist appeared behind it, and a dark-colored spike burst through the ghoul's mouth, nearly skewering him along with it, before it retracted, and a dark, watery blur passed them.

He twitched away and the ghoul's grip loosened as it wilted to the muck, and Aiden shifted to the blur, finding Marsea, and watched as a tentacle coiled around her ankles, and pulled her up into the whipping winds away from him.

"Marsea!" he squawked, wriggling from the ghoul's hands and a prickling sensation halted him in place.

"Uck," his bird belly cramped, and he coughed up something of Lenore's insides.

The familiar bond.

At the thought, a surge of azure energy raced past him and Autumn and Hrathgon were dueling over top of him, hacking and slashing wildly at each other. It was all he could do to simply wobble out of the way.

He watched himself, growling, cutting the air around a floating shield of crackling Eldn flame, impossibly fast, his veins radiating through his very skin, bright as the snowfall, steam pouring off him thick as cauldron stew.

All the while, Autumn played off his every movement, as though she'd written the tale, ever a step ahead.

She's winning.

She's going to kill him.

She's going to kill me.

Aiden cried out from a sudden phantom pain, shaking his head as though he'd taken a fist to the face and when he glanced back up, he found Hrathgon whirling violently toward him, a nasty black gash having opened up across his countenance, carved across his nose, forehead to jaw, and he crashed down to his knees, the two desperate souls in wrong bodies glaring something awful at one another.

The floating magic shield dissipated behind him, as Hrathgon stabbed the sword down into the snow to keep some measure of balance, forcing himself back up, glowing white-speckled giftblood pouring from the split in his face.

"No!" Autumn shouted as her blade came in for the kill, halting, shaking inches from the side of his skull. A deathblow in limbo.

"Autumn!" the archivist rasped through Lenore, flapping his one good wing like a loon.

She's done it. She's managed to push Tetherow back down.

"Aiden, run!" she bellowed, Tetherow's demon mask gone, her sword falling to the snow.

Wait, what?

She remained frozen like a hare turned prey. Save her lips. Trembling.

As though she...

"I...I can't keep him back," she cried, tar-like tears burning down her porcelain cheeks, and out her nostrils, their mother's amethyst pendent shimmering from its place about her chest. "You have to run." Her head twitched to the side, a clicking noise expelling out of her.

Silent as the stone, Hrathgon adjusted his grip on the sword, angry end out, no intention of running, no intention of letting her live, shifting back toward Autumn...

Nooo! Aiden's voice echoed through the astral shift as he drew upon his gift, begging off every ounce of it that would have him, sending every prayer he'd ever harkened, calling any favor that would take pity.

Burn it all and kill me pretty.

One last time.

For Autumn.

Though if wanting were wishes and wishes were real, this one hadn't quite made the mark, falling inches short...

No...

Wresting back control of his body, he faced his sister, hilt unsteady between them, half its blade lodged inside her belly.

Horrible inches...

"Tam," a chill stole through him.

So close.

Yet…

"You have to kill me," she whispered. "You must do it…" tick, her head jerked, "…now. It's the only way."

"Fuck that…"

"I've seen what Tetherow can do with my gift, Aiden. I can't…" tick, "…hold it back…"

"Yes, you can." He met her eyes, the one twitching horribly. "You will."

"Bugger all, Aiden, don't be stupid." Tick. "Gods tits, we're so fucked."

"Oi." Her vulgarity caught him by surprise. "When did you start gabbing about like a harbor-end whore?"

"There's a jape coming from you." Tick. "You and mother both, always keen for a scolding."

"What? No. That's not what this is." His attentions lowered to the sword and the waterfall of red oozing down her waist and leg.

Fuck.

"I need to pull the blade out," he said.

She placed a hand on his shoulder for support. "You save me, it'll eat the world," she said, her lips spilling nether residue, joining the thick streaks of black leaking from her eyes, nose, and ears like raindrops down glass.

"It can eat half the stars into the next galaxy over for all the fucks I give." Aiden gently inched the blade from her belly, mindful of her grunting as the steel came free and he let it fall into the snow beside them. "I can't lose you, Tam. I won't."

"You will…" Tick.

"I won't," he said defiantly.

"Aiden…" Her poisoned eyes opened wide, pupils glacial and nearly eclipsed by that of her haunter. "…it's coming…"

"I'm not leaving you, dammit. If you die, I…"

…*die*, he meant to say as a thin gleam of silver rose up from Autumn's side, quick as a cutpurse, and entered his neck, robbing him of the word's passing.

She stabbed me, he thought, twisting away from the blade by instinct, forcing it awkwardly out the front of his throat, as an obscene grin befell his sister's sallow countenance once more, nether residue pouring between her blackened teeth as though she'd swallowed the contents of an inkwell.

"Sneaky little cunt," the many eldritch voices spoke, marking Tetherow's return. "What a fucking circus, you Laniers."

Aiden stumbled backward a step, clasping at the gushing, gaping hole in his neck, blood spewing out, as Autumn raised her palm at him with the warlock's well cut inside it, chanting, calling to his brimming, boiling blood spill.

Vision dimming, choking on his own fluids, Hrathgon, roared to the fore, pushing what remained of his host's gift to its limits, doing his damnedest to seal the wound and keep him upright, but Tetherow's incantation would not be so easily undone, fighting tooth and nail against the laceration's closure, draining them ounce by ounce.

Crows cut about their showdown like a drove of knives, more than a murder, more than a massacre, The Hood in delight at the sheer power thrumming between them.

"Desmond!" Marsea shouted from somewhere nearby, but all he could do was gurgle in response, agony consuming, his skin burning and warping as Hrathgon's soul began to devour its host to stave off their impending damnation...

CHAPTER TWENTY-FOUR

BLADE FROM FLESH. In and out. Rinse, repeat. One slab to the next. Sever. Eviscerate. Consume. Blurring black, gray, pale, gray, black again. Shape to shape. Torso to torso. Ritualistic. Animalistic. Devouring. Blood everywhere. Splattering into her. Running off of her. A sliver of howling steel emanating deep scarlet, drinking from misshapen shadows in a dense rose-colored mist.

She hadn't the time to unpack it, to breathe it in, to let it digest. For she was all bite. Gnashing, tearing, gnawing momentum. The haxanblade's appendage. For however long. An endless maelstrom of ruthless, unbridled, impulsive butchery.

Until she wasn't, Blind Widow's rage-hex rolling off her with the dwindling blood flow, its aftereffects pounding behind her temples like a heartless hangover, and her vision settled, the haxanblade's vibrations relenting, leaving her muscles aching and her gift to clean up the mess.

Panting, Marsea spun about, scanning the bloodbath hellscape beyond her dissipating breath clouds, the snow churning around her, but finding nothing unblighted. It was just her and Old Boy and an ocean of nether creatures.

No Hilda.

No Asher.

No Maidens' Rejects.

And no Desmond.

Fearing the worst, she shouted her brother's name across the heaps of corpses and cut-up nether flesh, over and over again as she slogged back toward the crooked monolith, until her throat became dry and uncooperative.

No response.

Not a peep.

A spark of magic drew her attention from the shimmering spindrifts ahead and a sigil began to carve through the air as though by an invisible knife, a rippling mirror expanding from its source once the symbol was complete, and a figure vaulted through it, all bright ruby carnage.

The heck...?

Huffing and puffing, Broenwjar at her side, they passed through pockets of horrid heat and bitter cold chasing after the sylph-like figure.

Her guest proved remarkably quick, a marvel of mesmerizing motion, and that much more proficient with a blade, slicing a path through anything that dared impede, and before Marsea knew it, she'd found Desmond again and a girl that could only have been Autumn in the distance.

Desmond tottered away from the silver-haired hag-child, sinking to his knees, clutching at his neck, smoke billowing off him in waves.

Autumn approached, knife in one hand, the other drinking blood from Desmond's wounds.

She's going to kill him.

Only a man. A slab of meat. Other put in her two coppers.

The figure split through a wngar torso creeping about with a series of long arachnid-like legs, a pink mist pouring out from her wake, as she ran up an enormous mass of charred nether flesh and leapt off, dropping down to sever Autumn's outstretched hand, sliding round, slick on her knees, sword plunging into the snow like an anchor, as she spun back up to face her foe, throwing up a warlock's well of her own in the turnaround, blood shooting out of hers like silk from a spinneret, coagulating midair, sharp as an arrow, piercing through Autumn's chest and taking her to the ground with astonishing force.

Good gravy!

The figure closed its hand into a ball, snapping the bloodshot off at the well, and tossed its hood back, unveiling a horribly disfigured face twixt curtains of eggshell-colored hair, where there were noticeable clumps missing in places. In one smooth sequence, she fished a collection of little glowing curios out from her jacket pockets and tossed them about the area, bright azure lines sparking to life in the muck from their placement, connecting one to the next, until it formed the shape of a pentacle.

Totems, Marsea thought, their humming presence keeping the encroaching nether creatures both distracted and at bay as she slid to her brother's side within the ward, glasses sagging to the end of her nose. "Des, I'm here." Her heart broke at the sight of him.

He murmured something of a response, but the wounds across his face and neck kept him from proper speech. "*Kill...kill...kill...*" it sounded like.

"Absolutely not," Marsea dismissed the request. "You don't get to leave us."

"S...sorry..." he managed. "Thi...think I might've fucked up a little bit."

"Don't you dare," Marsea bade, Broenwjar joining them.

"Back to the hells with you, godless heathen," the disfigured woman spat before dousing Autumn in a strange, dark liquid from a pewter flask.

Immediately, the youngest Lanier sister let out a ghastly wail, kicking and wriggling violently around the bloodlance pinning her to the mud, clawing out at the woman as a malachite vapor began to materialize overtop her.

"*You,*" a series of demonic voices rasped out.

"That's right, fucker. Me." the woman answered, as one of the totems clicked open beside the writhing girl.

"*Traitorous whore,*" Tetherow seethed.

"What are you doing to her?" Marsea questioned.

"Exorcism, darling," the woman said, calm as you please.

"You're killing her."

"I'm doing what needs doing, Marsea." Her eyes shone a frightful shade of crimson-ringed yellow. "It can't be helped."

She said my name. She knows me? "Who are you?" Marsea asked.

The woman began chanting in the old tongue, a pale purple glow emitting from inside the totem sucking the screeching, cursing malachite vapor toward it, the vapor pulsating, fighting its fate and ultimately losing, as it disappeared within the strange wooden box, the top snapping shut and catching flame once the demon was trapped therein.

Autumn shrieked, her body withering to ash in sequence with the totem's burning, and before Marsea could properly process the scene before her Autumn was gone, her remains little more than dying embers twirling almost majestically amidst the four winds' wander.

"What did you do?" the princess hollered.

Desmond slumped down against her, hand slipping away from the wound on his neck, falling to her death sling harness, shaking, his glowing lifeblood leaking onto her chest.

"Des." She let go of the haxanblade and pressed her bad hand against his seeping neck wound, where the surrounding skin began to melt and blacken, stinging her at the touch, as though she'd just dunked her fingers in boiling water.

He gazed up at her, his eyelids heavy, and she could feel his body going rigid and shriveling in her arms.

"Stay with me," she said, thinking herself obtuse for uttering such useless nonsense.

"It's...done," he wheezed, breathing slow.

"No, it's not done." Her frown deepened. "We still have Lancastle to save. I won't let you—"

"Do...don't think you've much choice in the matter," her brother interrupted.

Damn you, Desmond. "But we've only just found each other." It was arguably the most selfish thing she'd ever said to anyone and that included the untold number of spiteful digs she'd flung her mother's way over the cycles.

"They both must pass on," the woman said.

"Stay back," Marsea barked at the woman, and Broenwjar padded into the space between them, lowering to a prowl, hackles raised.

"I'm not here for you," the woman said. "Only possessor and possessed."

"Then you've done your job, haven't you?"

"Not yet I haven't. There's one more." She retrieved Autumn's satchel from the mound of ash and bone, her eyes landing on Desmond.

"You cannot have him," Marsea said, hand crushed against her dying brother's weeping neck, wishing for all the moon Rhymona or Thira were here with her. They would know what to do. They would know how to save him.

"I only need you to let him die."

Tears trailed down Marsea's cheeks, the pressure beginning to release from behind her face, and she took a steady breath.

Suddenly, the wind died and the snow fell lazily around them in big, fat clumps.

"The Vharyn'ashi cannot be killed," the woman continued. "It's split its essence so many times there's no telling how many versions of it exist. Splits upon splits, that one. Scarcely a thing at all any longer. As for your brother and half-sister, none who have housed the essence of a demon can be allowed a gravedance. The demon etches itself inside their flesh, branding itself onto its host, placing trigger words within their unconscious minds, where it festers, rotting them from the inside out, causing unusual, violent behavior, even against their loved ones, even after exorcism.

"Desmond and Autumn betray you once the nether's put away. You and Remy both. That's when the real horror begins. You think this shit's ugly with the nether? This is a fucking cakewalk compared to what comes next. Trust, I'm doing you the favor here. I'm doing the entire fucking moon the favor," she glanced up at the stars, "for those still keeping count."

A thousand questions stormed the gates of Marsea's mindscape, though not a one passed unto her lips. Not a one beat past the bud of numbness.

"Allow me to correct this mistake," the woman implored.

"Mistake?" said Marsea. "They are my family."

"This is the only way to be sure."

Marsea studied the woman. Despite her facial deformities, something about her shape and demeanor rang familiar. "I know you, don't I?"

"You know me, yes, but you cannot trust me. Rather past me. You likely know her as Imogen Thirsby."

"Thirsby? As in Lirae Thirsby? The House Mother of Lancastle Abbey?"

"As in. She is but a face I've worn and prize well I've worn many. You cannot trust her. Nor can you trust Rhymona."

"Rhymona?" Marsea swallowed. "Why?"

"She is not all she appears to be," Thirsby said, pulling a dark green grimoire from the satchel and tossing it onto the muck between them, retrieving her haxanblade before approaching.

Marsea glanced down at *The N'therN'rycka* then back up to Thirsby. "She is ashaeydir. I'm aware."

"She is so much more than ashaeydir, Marsea," Thirsby said. "She is the gift's chosen. And the gift is pure evil. She is the most dangerous being on the moon right now. More dangerous than the Vharyn'ashi. More dangerous than the nether. Or Rhyvariath. Your brother there. In the future, he is her lover. Her slave. Her personal assassin." She glanced sidelong over her shoulder to the pit of ash and ember that remained of Autumn. "And the girl there was the one that put a wand blast through the back of your head. So much for all that."

"The future?"

"1836. Seven cycles from now." Thirsby stabbed the haxanblade into the muck and lowered to a knee before the Lanier siblings. "Where I'm from."

"If you're telling it true," Marsea began, "that means we win. We defeat the nether."

"In my version of the timeline the nether was sent back beyond The Pale, yes, but as I've said, what comes as a result is far worse. That is why these two must be put to the flame. And why this particular phylactery must be transferred."

"Transferred? How do you mean?"

"The demon's spell cannot be undone. At least, I haven't the faintest inkling how to undo it. But I do know how to transfer it. Old Girl here," she twisted the haxanblade deeper into the dirt. "She's, um...well let's just say she's a problem and a problem solver. She eats the codex, the bind comes into me, I puff a little Poison Sally, call up The Hood, and its permanently unwritten from the chrono sequence. Corruption achieved."

"You mean to kill yourself?"

"This was always a one-way trip." Thirsby stood, picking her blade out from the muck.

Marsea felt a strange current coming from her haxanblade.

"All you need to do right now is nothing," Thirsby said. "Let the dragon soul devour him."

"Your sword," Marsea reached for Blind Widow.

"They are one and the same," Thirsby answered. "The death crone's hangnail. It can sense you. Its old master."

"Old master?"

"As I've said, your kin betray you." The blade trained on Desmond, prompting a growl from Broenwjar. "I am undoing their misguided malice. I'm giving you a second chance to unfuck your future."

Desmond groaned, pushing away from her, lying flat in the snow, body all sticks and knobs, blood running down his face and neck, eyes rolling about their sockets, icy blue and bloodshot.

"It's done," he repeated.

"Des," she whimpered over him, wanting to scream at the stars like she would never stop, but the pain only burrowed deeper within.

"I'm done, Marsea." Words like fire despite his throes, forced through the whistling hole in his throat by the last of his gift. "I don't want to be here anymore. I don't want to be brought back. I don't want to be saved. I want to be done." His head was pointed toward her, but his eyes were faraway. "Let me be done."

And Elsymir's omen regarding loss wormed their way back through her thoughts.

To survive what is to come you will eventually have to abandon someone, a lot of someones more than like, and yes, some of them will be your family and the folk you've come to love most.

Lenore waddled up next to her master and Desmond's head listed to take her in, his body shrinking to bone, skin flaking, rising off him like dust motes.

"You deserved better, Lenny," Desmond said, Lenore croaking something in return.

Thirsby dropped another totem next to them and Marsea met the woman's darkly haunters as it clicked open.

"For the dragon soul," Thirsby answered. "Unless you want to share the same fate one day, best not to let it in. And make no mistake, this one would have your skin in a heartbeat, whether you wished it so or not."

"Marsea," Desmond's head rolled back to her. "I'm glad we found each other."

"Me too." She felt his ruin of a hand brush against hers. The maidens know, he was wrecking her something awful. *Why does it hurt so much? I barely know you.* She moved her hand under his. *Given the last few days, I should be better at goodbyes by now.*

And yet...

"I believe in you," he whispered, the words strained, nearly dust on his tongue. "I'll always be with you, Marsea."

"Always," she echoed.

"At least...I didn't die alone..." His eyes stared through her, as though unable to take her in properly. "T...tell Rhymona...tell her..." The giftlight receded from the wound in his throat. "Tell her, I—"

Marsea waited breathless for her brother to finish, but the words never came.

She watched helplessly as the glow beneath his skin began to fade, and he wasted away before her eyes, his flesh rotting, lips curling back from his teeth, hair falling out, wilting down to nothing but bone and soiled clothes, Lenore withering silently as one at his side.

A bright azure ball of vapor rose off him and she stared into its grasping crackling nebulous, desperate to claim her, in the few seconds they shared before it became entombed in the totem's hollow and caught flame.

A hush fell between them as Marsea's head hung. *One day*, she thought, directing her anger toward the star maidens. *That was all you could offer us? One bloody day together. What was the fucking point? It would have been less cruel if we'd never met at all.* Her vision rose from the red-dappled snow to the wall of nether creatures and ghouls encircling them.

"He knew," Thirsby said, after a time. "He likely still felt the bastard in there with him somewhere."

"I suppose," Marsea mumbled, refusing to process the host of emotions welling up within.

"The haxanblade will see you from this place," Thirsby said. "It's a portal key."

"Portal key, my eye," Marsea said. "I've beheld more than enough of its lair."

"You've seen the hag, I take it?"

"Unfortunately."

"Any others?"

"Others?"

"Is The Bloodbind the only portal you've opened with her?" Thirsby asked.

"Aye, and I'd rather keep it that way if it requires a life for trade every time."

"The Bloodbind is but a taste of The Widow's powers. Her doorways are endless, you only need know their name or properties."

"How do you mean?"

"She's a repository. A gift sponge. Like a blood candle that never melts. And the blood she stores amplifies her abilities. The Bloodbind is but her hearth ward. Flesh from flesh, blood from blood."

"Hearth ward?"

"Think of it like a call to home. But she's absurdly intuitive. Always hungry for more. Trust, she'll use you for every ounce of knowledge you own. It's likely she already knows everything about you. She'll open a portal to any ward you've given her. You only need name it.

"I wasn't standing in the middle of The Scar in the future. It's not even possible in 1836. But I knew the name of Tetherow's ward here, so I called it once I traveled back to 1829."

"Sylvoth'yka," Marsea said.

"The Lancastle Library," Thirsby nodded. "Lancastle has a number of them. Usoma'umae will take you to the scullery. Jhara jhahara will open in Alistair's Courtyard. Hera'schikta will place you in the churchyard. Pick your poison if Lancastle's your destination."

"And what do I do once I name it?"

"Let your gift loose. Imagine a door and where it leads to. Speak its name and act as though the blade were a key and the ward its lock, carve it into the air like you're using an oversized pick set."

Thirsby settled the fang of her bright cherry haxanblade against *The N'therN'rycka*'s face. "And now it's my turn."

"You're leaving?" Marsea asked.

"Don't want to risk mucking up anything unnecessary. I've likely already done a number killing your killer and chatting with you here." She wiped her forehead with the back of a sleeve. "Trust only yourself, Marsea, and beware of Rhymona and Imogen."

"Rhymona is my friend," Marsea said. "She would never betray me."

"Rhymona is no one's friend. She is a powder-keg. And you don't want to be anywhere near her when she goes off."

"Then why not kill her, too, if she's so awful?" Marsea asked. "You've already come this far."

"I'm too close to her now. My past self, I mean. And I can't afford to trap myself in an eternal coil. Given the circumstances of my present timeline, this was the best I could manage without running into my past self and risking a suicide paradox, and this particular phylactery simply could not be allowed to persist."

"I still don't understand," Marsea said.

"It's not for you to understand," Thirsby answered. "It's for you alter."

"Alter how?" Marsea gripped Blind Widow and stood, nudging up her gran glasses. "You portal here out of nowhere, talking nonsense about a buggered future, throw a totem at a demon, butcher my family, and then what? What am I meant to do with all this?"

"Would that I could name it, but banishing the nether is not the answer. At least not fully. In fact, the nether may be your best defense against the gift."

"I need more." Marsea glanced up at Lirae Thirsby from under her brow, blond bloodstained curls clinging to her face, sticking to her glasses like seaweed, feeling utterly defeated, heartsore, and alone. "I need something." *Anything.* "It's not enough, what you've given. And it's certainly not worth the lives of my brother and sister."

"Nothing will ever be enough, Marsea," said Thirsby. "But understand, you are not as alone as you think."

Her dreadful orbs rose up to the heavens, and the princess followed her gaze and found a sky gray as the sepulcher.

Fitting, Marsea thought. For living in this place had become something akin to being buried alive.

"The gift is a part of me," Marsea said. "It's protected me."

"The gift is a drug. An addiction. A parasite. It gave you what was necessary to earn your favor and keep it. That is what it does. And once you've found it, once you've had a taste, there's no way around calling it forth, it latches on to your impulses and desires, of which you have little control over, and it never lets go. But now that you know its truth, mayhaps you can work to temper it."

Marsea glared at Thirsby. Her gift pulsating through her, through Blind Widow, through Broenwjar, embracing her, keeping her together.

The gift was everything. Without it where would she be? How would she be?

Would she be?

Thirsby drove the haxanblade into the book of flesh and it let out a terrible, hellish whine. She removed it and dug in again, stabbing down into the screeching grimoire several times, blood leaking out of it, the blade wailing as it drank Tetherow's words dry from its parchment, the warped ancient flesh-binding wrinkling, blisters bubbling up and bursting as the sword ate it alive.

Marsea remained frozen to the spot, Broenwjar at her side, the nether all around them. Still. Watching. As though in mourning.

Releasing the haxanblade, Thirsby collapsed to her knees and plucked a cigarillo from her pocket fitting it gently between her lips. "Reckon this is it," she said, snapping a tiny flame to the tip of a finger and lighting the cigarillo's end. "Keep your distance." She spoke between little stokes and drags. "You don't want to inhale too much of this shit."

A stench like burning flesh began to pour off her and she removed the cigarillo from her lips, taking Marsea in, eyes narrowed. "Never thought this would be it. The final thing I see. You of all folk, the final person I talk to." She coughed and snorted back phlegm. "You ever meet the old me, tell her Litashoth Eru says, 'go fuck yourself.'"

"Is that you?"

Litashoth Eru took another pull and nodded, ash rising off her. "Keep a pair of totems on you and the nether won't bother." She swallowed. "Maidens' breath, this shit is—" She slouched, her body sinking all at once, arms falling limp to her side.

Marsea remained silent, somehow both numb and angry, as she watched the poison eat through Litashoth's disfigured throat up into the pockmarked ruin of her face, holding still until it devoured the light from the woman's sinister orbs and she dissolved into a mass of unrecognizable pulp, her version of the haxanblade melting right alongside her.

Slogging past catatonia's call, Marsea unbuckled the harness and pulled it over her head, before collecting the satchel containing *Dawn* and *Noon*, then shoved a pair of glowing totems in her jacket pockets and another pair in with the grimoires.

Ready, B? she asked Old Boy in their special familiar language as the wall of blight and black began to shrink closer with the ward's disturbance.

He let out a low grumble in response.

Same, she thought, glancing back at her brother's remains one last time. *I'll save our kingdom, Des, if it's the last thing I do.*

She gripped Blind Widow in both hands.

Here goes.

"Sylvoth'yka," she cried, stabbing the blade into thin air, a bright red spark igniting the ether like a struck match...

CHAPTER TWENTY-FIVE

THE STAFF QUARTERS had become a jungle of nether growth; flakes of ashy skin floating in the static patches of hot and cold, strands of blackened sinewy flesh coating the walls as lichen to a rock, spriteling sacs pulsating between the dark tissue like a colony of cysts on the verge of bursting.

What a pain, Remy grumbled at Thira. *How could Tetherow possibly be this organized?*

Every corridor leading to Lancastle Library proved a dead end, twixt thickets of nether flesh walls and doorways blasted into impassable piles of rubble.

CALM YOURSELF.

Calm myself! That bastard may well have my sister not to mention one of my best friends.

AND HARPING ON IT DOES NOBODY ANY GOOD.

I can't lose anyone else, Thira. And especially not Jules.

YOU CAN ONLY CONTROL SO MUCH.

Gods, I'm sick of those words. But after nearly two decades of having little to no control over his life, he'd now gained back enough of it to understand its true worth.

Remy and Edgar were on to option three in their attempt to get to the library, risking the blight back on the third floor, where they could scale the outer castle wall down to the rear of the library. Assuming this went to plan, Emyria could then splice them through her defense spell and back inside the library.

Though, the gods only knew, in the time it took them to get this far, and given the state of the staff quarters, anything could have happened in the library.

Remy pushed the cluster of horrific thoughts to the back of his mind as they arrived at one of the chambers above the library, and he warded the door against the approaching clicking noises behind them as Edgar pushed open the double doors leading out to the balcony on the opposite wall.

Together, they stared out across the sprawling kingdom, finding a hellish landscape beneath the sister moons' fade, marred by patches of conflagration and smoke. Gods' breath, but between Rhyvariath, the nether drake, and the blighted horde there wasn't much left unspoiled.

Frowning, Remy shifted his gaze below them where there was about a ten-foot drop from the balcony to the protruding arch of the nearest library window.

"Don't suppose you can make us fly?" Edgar said, and Remy realized he was talking to Emyria. "Too bad." He turned back inside the chamber. "We'll have to manage with a bit of skullduggery then."

"A bit of skullduggery?" Remy followed, watching as Edgar flung pillows and pulled the coverlet from the bed, stripping the sheets below and began knotting them together. "Is this you then revealing your sordid past?"

"It's what we've got."

"And how many times have you done whatever it is you're about?"

Edgar offered a wry smile. "I'll thank you to let that one lie."

"Oh, good, well at least you've some experience then."

Back out on the balcony, Edgar looped one end of the sheet around one of the stone balusters, checking the fit to make sure it was snug, then wrapped the other end around his waist like a belt before tightening the knot that bound the two sheets together. "Think we're good."

"Well, I should hope so. It's a good fifty-foot fall if you fuck it up."

"I've had worse."

"A burglary gone wrong, I take it?"

"Keep it up, you."

Remy reached for Edgar's hand, pulled him in, and kissed him. "In case you kill yourself."

"Ye of little faith."

Edgar eased one leg over the other side of the balustrade, followed by the second. Remy gripped the other end of the sheet as Edgar bent to a squat and maneuvered himself beneath the balcony.

"Give a little more," he called after a few seconds, "almost there."

Remy let a little more sheet slide over the edge.

"Oh, fuck," Edgar said.

Oh, fuck? "What, oh, fuck?"

"South wall," Edgar returned.

Remy glanced over the edge and saw a couple wall crawlers making their way toward them. "I've got them," he called, conjuring an egg of Eldn flame to his hand and pelting the nearest one with it. The bastard shrieked all the way down, landing awkwardly in the grass, its body broken in several places. The second crawler fared little better.

The watchman could hear Edgar chanting below as a white light began to radiate and a crackling sound like burning wood grew louder. A scent of rotten eggs wafted up to him as more wall crawlers appeared on the far wall.

There was a snap as the light disappeared. "It's done," Edgar shouted. "I'm in." He tugged the sheet three times and Remy pulled back until the other end came to him.

The crawlers were closing in on him, growing in number.

"Shit, shit, shit, shit, shiiit." He worked the end of the sheet around his waist and tied it like the sash of a robe, squeezing it as taut as it would allow.

He grabbed Exylduin as the first blighter arrived and jammed it through the fucker's face, ripping it back out as it went limp and dropped from sight. Quickly, he backstepped inside the chamber to give himself room for the coming madness and dashed forward, past three ghouls that were crawling onto the balcony, leaping over the center balustrade, into the ether, free falling for what felt like ages, until the sheet caught at its length, jerking him back toward the castle wall and the split in the ward where a blighter was waiting, gazing curiously inside.

Remy slammed into the unsuspecting bastard with his feet, kicking the ghoul through as he followed, gripping the sheet in his offhand, and singeing it with Eldn flame as his momentum carried him inside the library's depths.

Edgar had a sword waiting for the wall crawler, putting the fiend down as Remy landed further down the aisle and spun back around.

"Hell of an entrance, that," Edgar said.

"And hopefully never again," Remy replied.

Emyria resealed the splice in her ward to keep anymore ghouls from stealing in after them.

All the while screams and shouts and shrieks of magic echoed from every direction in the stacks before them.

We're too late.

Twenty paces down the back wall ward light illuminated from behind the bookshelves.

"Ready yourself," Remy whispered as an area of the wall slid forward revealing an unmistakable bladed figure and a massive beast.

Marsea! His brain howled and before he knew it, he was racing toward her, calling her name like a loon.

"Remy?" Marsea answered, a vision of absolute horror.

"Is it just you?" he asked. "Where's Desmond? Autumn?"

She shook her head. "But Tetherow's gone. *The N'therN'rycka* destroyed." She gazed ahead toward the sounds of battle. "What's happening out there?"

"More Tetherow bullshit," Remy said. "He's possessed a watchman named Jorem Evers."

"Then what the fuck are you two doing here?"

"We had to break in through the back window."

"Come on, we have to help the others," Marsea said before rushing into the center aisle.

Brother and sister dashed toward the fury and wandfire screeching about the library's common area, side by side, blade for blade. His, blazing an azure inferno. Hers, cast in a crimson nightmare, drinking in every ounce of bloodshed lost to the dark of the stacks.

"Go back! Keep going, girl!" a voice Remy recognized as Raelan's ordered from down one of the rows as they came into the first wave of the onslaught. A blighted noblewoman wailed at him and he cut her down, the blood spill leaping off him into Marsea's blade as she hacked through a ghoulish bluecoat.

"Fuck, he's already turned them," Edgar yelled, conjuring an egg of Eldn flame to his offhand.

"I heard Raelan this way," Remy shouted before he darted off in that direction.

"Remy!" Marsea hollered after him. "We have to stick together."

"This way!" Remy returned, smashing the face of a clicking fiend into a book-shelf, shoving past a pair he believed unblighted, before coming to the break in the row to the next aisle gap.

"I won't leave you!" he heard Julia's voice up ahead in the next row over.

"Jules!" he cried.

"Remy?" he thought he heard her voice return.

"They're still here!" He called over his shoulder at Marsea and Edgar.

A wand strike lit the stacks at the end of the row and Remy kept full steam ahead, one row away from where he believed Julia to be.

"He's turning," Raelan's voice.

"We have to leave him," Caitlyn agreed.

"Where the fuck is Rhymona?" Pion bellowed.

"She went after the spellslinger, the mad bitch," Caitlyn answered.

"Damned fool!"

"Remy," Julia again.

"Julia," Remy returned, swiping the tomes from the shelf to peer into the next row over. Books disappeared from the shelves on the other side and they met eyes.

"Remy," Julia breathed.

"Run to the end of the aisle," Remy said. "I'll meet you there. Tell everyone to keep running. Leave anyone unable."

"Listen to your brother," Raelan said from the shadows behind her. "Pion, get her to Remy."

"What do you mean to do?" Pion asked.

Remy was already racing toward the row's end.

"I mean to protect my family," Raelan answered.

"No," Julia cried. "You can't stay here, there's too many."

"Jules, I love you. And I am sworn to protect my kingdom and kin. Now go!" her father barked.

Remy ran into Caitlyn first, the tip of her wand burning bright and angry.

"What happened?" Remy asked. "Who's still with you?"

"We let in some survivors from outside the library. Only, some of them were infected. They started attacking each other and then a man with a scepter showed up and..." her gaze shifted between Remy, Edgar, and Marsea, back to Remy, "...where's the Empress?"

"She's gone," Remy said.

"Gone?" Marsea questioned.

Remy forced himself to meet his sister's eyes. "Tetherow killed her. I should have seen it. I should have known an ignorant dullard like Jory couldn't have survived the blight this long on his own."

"I am still here," Edgar said, his orbs burning with the dracari's presence. "Cheers for the ask."

Julia slammed into the back of him as the others arrived and he wiggled around her hugging her tight.

"What the fuck?" Marsea said, the haxanblade leaping up from her side inches from Pion's face.

"And a fair hello to you, too, Seasea," Pion said.

"Any particular reason we're not putting this deplorable wretch down where he stands?" Marsea quibbled.

"No time to explain," Remy answered. "Where's Rhymona?"

"Where do you think?" Julia huffed.

THERE IS NO TURNING BACK NOW, REMY. WE CANNOT RISK IT.

I'm aware. "She's made her decision then. We need to figure a way out of this place."

"I've got us," Marsea said. "I know a few more wards around the kingdom."

"I told Rhyvariath we would meet upon the western battlements around midday," Remy said. "Any wards near there?"

"I've one for the churchyard."

"Close enough."

"Stand aside," Marsea bade as a series of horrible cries tore through the clicking stacks behind them. "B, you stay with Jules, no matter what."

Broenwjar let out a low growl.

"*Hera'schikta*," Marsea called, piercing the open air behind them and carving a ruby-red ward into the aisle that rippled out to form a watery rose-colored portal.

"That's new," Remy said.

Books began exploding out from the stacks in the rows behind them as though by a phantom wind, coughing out into the aisle, the dusty old bookshelves complaining from the sudden rise in attention, as they came toppling into each other.

"And that's our cue," she answered.

The others entered leaving just Marsea and Remy.

"Dammit, Marsea. No." Remy said.

"I have to." And she did that annoying nose scrunch face that meant there was no arguing. "I can't leave her to die. She's family."

"Then I'm coming with you."

REMY.

"You can't," she said, hard as a coffin nail.

"Like hells."

"One of us must carry on in case this all goes to shit. Here." She passed along the satchel. "*Dawn, Noon,* and *The Kingstome.*"

He took the satchel.

"I trust you still have *Dusk.*"

He patted the tome holster at his side. "Marsea…"

"I'm doing this, yeah. And you're going with the others."

"I better see you again."

She punched her glove into the heart of his breastplate. "The King's piece." She smirked. "It suits you."

"I mean it, Marsea."

"I know," she said as she backed away. "Make sure Old Boy behaves." She added before disappearing inside the crumbling stacks.

CHAPTER TWENTY-SIX

STAY CLOSE," Rhymona ordered Poppy, who held the magus up from under an arm.

"They aren't attacking us," Poppy said. "How is this possible?"

"Would, that I could name it," the magus muttered. "Some fuckery about being the gift's chosen."

Together they navigated the bloodbath, the ranks of the undead growing with each hobbled step taken toward the library's entrance, toward the fiend that wrought it all.

Not her best decision, all told, going after a creature that can command the grave-ridden, especially in her present condition, but she wagered it was Tetherow amongst the lot, and she needed answers. Not to mention this fucking cunt ring off her finger.

She tried once more to push her gift into her rotting hand, if not to heal it then to at least bring some measure of feeling back to it, but the gift refused her commands, as though it couldn't cross the threshold of infected tissue, as though the bloody thing weren't a part of her at all anymore.

A sphere of magic bobbed between the cracks of battling blight and survivors.

"There," Rhymona commanded. "Toward the light." She drove the tip of Illuminaria into the stones to keep herself upright and made an effort to pick up the pace.

"Watch out!" Poppy cried, and Rhymona reacted, swinging Illuminaria up at an attacking ghoul, just enough to keep the bastard's blade from splitting her skull.

Poppy lunged out from under her arm and walloped the fucker across the side of its head with her frying pan.

The ghoul held still for a moment, one side of its temple dented in something dreadful, an eye popped from its socket, the other twitching grotesquely, seemingly taking them in, before Poppy cracked the fool again for good measure, pissed as a prizefighter, sending it falling back loose-legged to the flagstones.

"Well, I've seen that now," Rhymona rasped. *And I'll never cook the same again.*

Fastly, Poppy returned to her side to keep her upright.

"You pack a helluva punch, lady."

"Cheers," Poppy breathed.

The glowing scepter broke through the wall of staggering ghouls and movement froze all around them, the few remaining survivors scrambling for safety at the strange halt in butchery.

Rhymona scanned the sea of clicking, twitching ghouls, not a one of them advancing from the spot they held, coming back round to the one with the glowing white glare, her mind unwilling to accept the face it wore.

"Shit Breath?" she uttered, taking in Jorem Evers. The state of him.

"Morgandrel," Shit Breath answered, blackened broke-tooth grin on full display.

She let out a pathetic little chuckle, defiant as her body would permit. "Well played there, Dick Cheese, possessing one-half of the dumbest hick this side of The Scar. Clearly, you've done your research."

Shit Breath's netherfiend smile grew, Tetherow's haunt contorting his inbred features into a warped demon's mask. "Beggars can't be choosers, as they say." And the gods only knew, it was disturbing as fuck watching Jorem Evers address her with a halfway civilized tongue. "Speaking of which, any chance you've come around to my little offer yet?"

"Still thinking on it." She eased away from Poppy and held up her ring hand, which had become black as char, bloody, and pus-ridden, covered with all manner of boil and blister. "Care to explain?"

Tetherow started slowly toward them, narrowed eyes, studying her hand as it approached, as though it actually gave a toss. "Oh, that thing is looking ripe."

"What the fuck did you do to my hand, arsehole?"

"Hmm, let's have a think," it scratched at Shit Breath's misshapen chin. "I seem to remember something. What was it? Ah, yes." He lifted a hand, curling his fingers inward, leaving only the middle up, and her hand did the same, against her will.

"What the shit?" Rhymona dropped Illuminaria to the stones, as Tetherow began to wiggle his fingers, and she clutched the wrist of her bad hand as it mimicked everything that Tetherow was doing, a burning sensation shooting throughout with each little twinge of movement like a thousand angry little pinpricks.

"Now, I'm no physician," Tetherow started, "but I'd say you've got yourself a good old-fashioned fingerfucking going on here."

This fucking clown.

"You ever hear the tale of the dead man's ring?" Tetherow asked.

"You better not be about to spout some ruddy Mervold cockery at me."

"But the old codger must've pulled the thought from some truth, yeah. Binds on pickup, don't it?" The fiend's dialect fluctuated between that of Tetherow's noble tongue and Jory's busted-ass bumfuck half-language.

"You bastard," she snarled, barely able to form words against the searing agony.

"Yes, yes, I'm well aware of your feelings toward me. Oh, but robbing the grave can have some pretty damning consequences, can't it?"

"Rhymona, what's he talking about?" Poppy uttered.

"My hand, it's...it's not obeying my commands," Rhymona answered, clutching the fetid eyesore into her stomach as Tetherow abandoned whatever devilry he'd used to control it.

"You see what your chaos has bought you, Morgan? And where is your gift now?"

"Fuck you and fuck the gift," she gritted. "I'm done with it." She commanded her gift into the hand once more, but it wouldn't obey, her gift halting midway down her forearm.

"But it's not done with you, now is it? Not unless you let it in."

"You can stow the nether propaganda, yeah. I'm done with all of it."

"No, you're not done, Morgan. You're not done until I say you're done."

"Go bathe in acid, fuckface."

"Now there's a lovely little chestnut from the gag bag," the demon mocked, bending Shit Breath's backwoods twang. "Look at you, girl. You can barely stand," it sneered, puffed as a lordling.

She felt his fever twisting about inside her hand again and groaned back the pain, swallowing it down like a gob of mucous, unwilling to give the fucker an ounce of satisfaction.

"I could kill the gutter rat," Tetherow aimed Magwyn's scepter at Poppy, the crystal seething with dark energy. "Or I could simply have you do it."

Her bad hand wrenched away from her body against her will, blade-hand quick, skin bubbling afresh, flailing this way and that before it leapt out after Poppy's throat.

"No!" Rhymona jerked her hand back, the black skin cracking, the abscesses leaking, trailing down her arm, fingers squirming. "Fuck you!"

Poppy dropped to the stones, terror in her rheumy eyes as she stared up at Rhymona in disbelief.

"A close one there," Tetherow snorted.

Rhymona kicked Illuminaria over to Poppy. "Grab the sword, Poppy."

"What?"

"I said pick up the gods damned sword," she croaked.

Poppy retrieved the blade and returned to her feet. "Why?"

The magus froze, finding movement in the crowd beyond. *Fiandrel?*

"Rhymona!" Poppy again.

"Because you're going to cut this fucker off me," Self-destruction answered. "Fuck this boiled turd of a day!"

At the words, her diseased hand shot away from her body and slammed against her face.

"*Fuuuck*," she screamed into her wet, putrid palm, as nails dug into the skin of her forehead and cheeks pushing for skull, drawing hot beads of blood from within. She swung about wildly, half-blind, trying to rip her own hand from its clutch, but the wretch wouldn't budge.

Something crashed into the back of her and she staggered into the sea of blight. Fluids splashed the side of her as she caught a gleam of silver cross high to low then spear forward.

"Stay back!" Poppy bellowed.

"*Ca...can't breathe!*" Rhymona cried, bouncing from one body to another, hysteria's harlot.

"Hold still!" Poppy shouted and Rhymona felt something settle against the back of her forearm. "Are you sure?"

"*Yes!*" A muffled shriek.

"I'm starting," Poppy said.

"*Shit, fuck, shit, fuck, shit, fuck, shit,*" the magus yowled into the stink of her rotting demon hand, breath be damned, realizing the girl was actually going to take it.

"Don't you do it, whore!" Shit Breath's eldritch voice hissed in her ear as her vision began to dim from the lack of oxygen. "Don't you cut me out..."

Her skin began to crackle and whine as the front of her shirt became damp, then heavy, then soaked.

Oh, fuck. It's coming undone.

"You stupid one-armed slag!" Shit Breath jeered, cackling.

"Gods!" Poppy yelled, carving back and forth, a malachite vapor billowing from the lacerated flesh.

"Don't do it.

"Don't do it.

"Don't do it," Shit Breath chanted faster and faster.

"Let it in.

"Let it in

"Let it in."

It's only a hand, a slab of meat, Rhymona thought as the bone snapped and her arm fell limp to her side, gore slinging out its opened end, and she dropped to her knees, the world spinning, the demon hand withering to bone and ash with the amputated curse.

She gasped, the sound of metal against stone before her, and lowered to a hand, tucking the remains of her severed arm into her stomach. A beat later, her stomach contracted and she puked blood and cinder atop the glowing ring.

Baka.

Baka, baka, baka.

Tetherow began to slow clap as she spit the remains of bile from her mouth. "Do you see it now, Morgan?" the fiend flouted. "What the gift has made of you."

"How 'bout you hop off my cock, you manky-arse fuckweasel," her voice blistered out as a pair of glowing cubes landed in the space between them, ticking like a child's toy before snapping open.

Tetherow recoiled at the pale purple light as a banshee began slicing through the halo of ghouls surrounding them, hacking the blight limb from limb, dashing about the unsuspecting legion like a wildkin savage off a rip of spriteling dust.

"Marsea," Rhymona heard Poppy cry as her blood and vomit rose into the air before her chasing after the bright crimson blade, a pink mist curling about them.

She glanced back to Shit Breath, but the devil was gone.

"Get her up," Marsea ordered from somewhere in the mass of clicking heads, figures dropping two at a time.

"Here," Poppy arrived at her side and helped her back to her feet.

You do this to your chosen? Rhymona thought as Poppy took her up under her good arm. *Maybe now you can find someone else to go fuck themselves in your name.*

The blight closed in behind them as they followed the trail of ruined corpses into the library depths.

"Hera'schikta," Marsea called in the mist before them, carving a scarlet letter into the ether that splayed out into a churning pool.

Not The Bloodbind again. She was barely holding on to consciousness.

Marsea passed them to keep the chasing blight at bay, and they caught eyes briefly, just before Poppy guided her through the portal and into the churchyard.

"Rhymona!" Remy hurried over to her as she and Poppy flopped down in the snow between gravestones. "The Stranger take me." He conjured an egg of Eldn flame to his hand. "What the fuck happened to her hand?"

"Tetherow possessed it," Poppy answered. "I think."

"Rhymona, I'm going to cauterize it."

"Wait!" Pion shouted.

"She's bleeding out, Pion. There's no time."

Let him speak, Rhymona meant to argue, but her tongue refused the words, lost in the fluids filling her lungs. Instead, she slammed the bottom of her fist into Remy's leg, gurgling her ire.

"I can give her a new arm, so long as you leave it open," the warlock explained.

"What the hells are you on about?" Remy spat.

Marsea appeared through the portal just before it swallowed itself.

"How?" Rhymona managed.

Marsea dropped down next to her, opposite Remy, a bundle of bruises.

"Carnomancy," Pion said. "I've dabbled with the like before aiming to correct my own…deformities."

"Which appears to have gone over swimmingly given your present state," Remy quibbled.

"Obviously, I haven't performed any of this on myself. Only a dullard would be so rash. But I thought to at least learn the craft so that I might train another to it."

"If not yourself, then what did you practice on? You know what, no. I don't even want to know."

"Probably for the best, that."

"And here I thought we'd already reached peak levels of batshit," Edgar added.

You have me take my hand and immediately present an answer? she spoke to the gift. *Fuck you if this works, you messy cunt.*

"Do it," Rhymona wheezed.

"Rhymona." Remy's eyes hardened.

"Let the fucker try," she squeezed the words past the lump in her throat.

"I'll need unblighted flesh," Pion said.

"This is madness!" Remy fought.

"Search the bodies," Marsea ordered.

"Rhymona, this is absurd," Remy said. "You mean to let Pion bloody Harver experiment on you?"

Absurd went out the fucking window with my goddamn hand, the magus thought, staring up teary-eyed at the faded moon of Ashira, a vision of she and Valestriel dancing the loon amongst the Rheshian dregs. Her eyes trailed over to Remy, the princeling dour as ever.

"Fine." He shook his head. "Help me get her inside."

Where's a barkeep when you need one? Her thoughts were drifting. And it was around this juncture that she began to lose time to memories of Val.

———

THE NEXT THING she knew she was lying on the altar, next to a severed arm, a blood candle seeping into a gash inside the palm of her remaining hand, the grotesque chanting above her from Autumn's grimoire, Fiandrel's shape watching from the corner of her eye, a murder of crows leering down at her from the church rafters, bent in a crooked spiral.

That can't be right.

Her head tilted.

How the fuck did you lot get in here?

She'd never seen so many together in all her days.

Hood must be close now.

She blinked.

Just float away...

Into obscurity...

Eyes drooping, her attention returned to her side down her arm past the missing portion to the severed hand that now occupied the space where hers once resided. At first glance, it appeared roughly the right size, in the least, it was female, likely noble given the jewels that wreathed its fingers.

Wait a tick. She closed an eye to focus better with the other. *I recognize that hand. Those jewels. The massive diamond on the ring finger.* Butterflies flitted about her belly as her head rolled back toward the congregation settling on a body in the front pew, the top half of it wrapped in a blood-stained bedsheet.

The queen's ring.

They meant to bind her to Larissa's hand. She let the thought stew for a breath, head listing back to the severed hand. Which meant they actually mutilated their mother's corpse for her. Which in itself would be a sweet gesture if they weren't talking about chopping up bodies here.

Is this what you want? she asked the gift, Dysenia's words from the shop swirling about her mindscape. *Honestly, it's as though the more you suffer, the more adversity you face, the less control you have, the better you somehow become, and the more you somehow defy the odds.*

Is this what you desire? she pressed.

Blood pooled between her aching stump and Larissa's pale white hand, merging, coagulating, Pion's incantation coming faster now.

Something spoke to her then, something more sound than voice, its will caught somewhere between a current and a pulse, azure, electric, unruly, and a twinge of movement followed, fierce as a crack of lightning.

Fingers. Her synapses screamed.

Wait...fingers? Her brain caught up to her gift.

Larissa's fingers were obeying her commands across the blood spill.

Somehow...

Impossibly...

This can't be real. She rotated her arm, and the hand followed as though attached. *No fucking way.* She pulled her phantom hand into a fist and Larissa's hand closed. *I've beheld some batshit mending spells in my day but this...*

"Stars alive," Julia uttered. "Did you see that? Mum's hand just moved."

Larissa's fist bloomed.

"There it goes again," Julia sprang from the front pew and raced up the trio of steps to the pulpit.

"Incredible," Poppy gasped.

"Rhymona, are you doing that?" Marsea asked.

"Yes," she answered, a ghastly grin forming as she focused on the magic thrumming between the foreign pieces of flesh.

Chaos, she thought, understanding Tetherow's fear of the gift a little more clearly now. *It craves this shit. The less right it is, the more it thrives.*

Her blood leeched into the pale hand as though it were a glove, twisting about the narrow spaces inside, channeling between flesh and bone, restoring the life to its cells, the blood spill glistening as the static hum of the gift drew Larissa's wrist into Rhymona's stump, stretching the skin, as the melding pieces mutated to an anatomical compromise, and set to their new constitution.

A prickling sensation radiated from the fusion point up her arm and across her shoulder into her chest, the blood pumping like a banshee through her veins, spiking her adrenaline, and she shot upright like waking from a nightmare, gritting her back teeth at the thrill noting the distinct differences between the old flesh and new. The smaller grooves and arches, the softer skin texture, the thinner bones, the lack of scars, as though the woman had never lifted a thing in all her cycles. Nothing fit correctly. Nothing at all. And yet...

Rhymona raised her arm up, squeezing Larissa's hand into a fist then splaying the fingers out wide before curling them into a fist again.

Madness.

Pion stopped chanting and her gaze shifted to take him in, meeting his unnatural orbs. Clearly, she had underestimated this one. They all had. And without reason, he'd given her *this*. Without reason, he'd decided to help her.

"Why would you do this?" she asked him, jabbing the thumb of her true hand about the palm of Larissa's, feeling every bit of the pressure as though it had always been her own. "Why would you give me this?"

"I didn't do it for you." His eyes moved past her to Marsea and Julia. "I did it for them." Back to her. "And I did it for me. If we survive all this, you owe me a spell. I hear you're quite the healer so carnomancy should come quite naturally to you."

The grotesque thought she could fix him. His mistake.

She swiveled her wrist, still in awe of the binding. It was nearly flawless on the surface, a slight pigmentation difference, but nothing a few days under the sun couldn't amend. She had both hands again. That was all that mattered. "I reckon that's a fair trade."

"I could do the same for you, Marsea," Pion said. "I would have before, in fact, but Vaustian..."

"He asked you not to?" Marsea asked.

"Asked is not the term I would have named it, but effectively, yes."

"Does it hurt?" Julia asked.

"It's a bit tingly," and that was an understatement, "but surprisingly, no," Rhymona answered. "Jules, this is your mother's hand. I..."

"We couldn't find any unblighted in the courtyards," Julia said.

"It was our best solution, given the time we had," Marsea added.

Rhymona gazed past the royal sisters finding Poppy and Broenwjar at the bottom of the stairs and Caitlyn across the nave keeping watch near the cathedral's barricaded entryway.

"Where is Remy?" she asked Marsea. "And Aiden, for that matter? What happened in the north?"

"Remy and Edgar have gone to the western battlements to meet with

Rhyvariath. Aiden," her mouth bent weirdly and she swallowed. "He and Autumn, they didn't…"

Rhymona pushed off the altar, grunting, her body screaming seven shades of sore from toe to scalp. Words betrayed her.

Aiden's dead?

Tam…

"He fought bravely," Marsea said. "We have the grimoires and banished Tetherow. At least that part of him. The godsgate is still an option."

"But there are only half of you."

"Pion took to *Noon* fairly well, I'd say."

"And I have some familiarity with *Dawn*," Caitlyn said.

"You do?" Marsea asked as the group all turned to the approaching spellslinger. "How?"

Caitlyn's eyes locked on Rhymona. "Aiden and I were together."

"*Together*, together?" the princess asked.

"Yes," Caitlyn said. "I've read through *Dawn* countless times in the wee hours of the night, Aiden passed out wherever the drink led him. Prize well, I'm more familiar with its text than any other grimoire across the gods' great Vael."

"Marsea, we need to discuss this with Remy and Thira," Rhymona said.

"I agree," the princess answered. "In the meantime, I'd like a chat just you and I, if you're up for it."

"With that sort of buildup, how can I possibly say no?"

What else happened up north, Marsea?

"Jules, come with us," Marsea said, leading them toward the Lirae Mothers' private sanctum. "B, keep watch."

CHAPTER TWENTY-SEVEN

RHYVARIATH WAITED atop the western battlements, wide as the patrol path, thrice as tall, and motionless, as though carved from the very stones he warmed, exuding all the grotesquery of a belltower gargoyle. Charred corpses muddled the snowy walkway leading up to him, not a one moving, a stench like overcooked meat and burning leaves on the winds warring between them.

Remy and Edgar approached the great beast with caution, rime frost caking near everything in sight. He appeared uninjured, but one couldn't be too careful given what the nether did to Hrathgon.

"The gods know, Em, it's something quite different viewing you lot from up close," Edgar said to his passenger and Remy was beginning to get a sense of how awkward it must have been for everyone else these past few days as he randomly spoke aloud with Yvemathira.

Any read on this expression? Remy queried his dragon companion.

NOTHING OUTRIGHT. THOUGH HE APPEARS TO BE MEDITAT-ING, WHICH KNOWING RHYVARIATH LIKELY DOES NOT BODE WELL.

Remy marveled at the massive dracari. Enormous wings wrapped like a shield wall around his body, collecting the snowfall, only his reptilian head visible. A pair of golden pools appeared from the space above its snout as its eyes came open.

"AND WHO HAVE WE HERE?" Rhyvariath's voice spoke inside Remy's head through the gift, his wings unfolding from his burly torso, his garnet scales shimmering majestically with each movement.

"Emyria," Edgar spoke the dracari's greeting, eyes glowing bright azure.

"WHAT OF THE EMPRESS?"

"She didn't make it," Remy replied, spitting the answer sideways. "Another one of Tetherow's ploys."

"MY CONDOLENCES."

"Oh, the bastard will get his," the watchman prince promised. "Mark my words."

"Damned right it will," Edgar served Emyria's ire.

"And what of the nether beast?" Remy pressed.

"IT WILL BE HERE WITHIN HOURS, LIKELY AS THE DARK SETTLES. AND IT HAS GROWN CONSIDERABLY SINCE LAST I BEHELD IT. YOU WILL NEED TO DECIDE SOON WHETHER TO STAY OR RUN."

It's too late to run. At this point, we're either fucked or we're not. "We're not running," the watchman said. "I won't leave Lancastle to Tetherow and its rot."

"YOU BELIEVE YOU CAN DEFEAT THE BEAST?"

"I've a mind to send it through a godsgate, yes."

"WHAT SAY YOU, YVEMATHIRA?"

"*...I say we ran on Ilynderos, we ran again when the Midarans came for our heads, and if we run now, with what little remains, we will always be running. We must make our stand here. As one...*"

"ETHEREALITY HAS MADE YOU BOLD, MY QUEEN." Rhyvariath bared his jagged fangs, producing something like a grin.

"*...There is but a fine line between bravery and foolishness, but here we have The Spellbind for a brace and a few capable warders. It may be the best opportunity we get to banish the fiend...*"

"YOU KNOW THE GODSGATE RITUAL?"

"*...I do not, but my host does. And his family. They possess the old Chandiian grimoires and need only piece the spell together...*"

"STILL BRANDISHING ABOUT THAT RECKLESS HOPE OF YOURS, I SEE."

"*...And you are still the consummate pessimist...*"

"IT HAS KEPT ME ALIVE THIS LONG."

"*...Will you stay, brother? Will you eat your fear and aid us in this?...*"

"YOU HAVE NOT GIVEN ME MUCH CHOICE IN THE MATTER, HAVE YOU?"

"*...Obviously, I cannot force you. And I would not, even if I could. We want you with us, Rhyvariath, but it must be your decision...*"

"Please, Rhyvariath," Emyria said. "Yvemathira may be too proud to say it, but I am not. We need you with us. You may be what sways this war to our advantage. Your defense during the ritual would be invaluable." Edgar lowered to his knees before the great dragon. "I beg of you, brother, stay with us, help us see this out."

Rhyvariath let out a contemplative groan, his attention diverting from Edgar to Remy.

Remy bowed his head. "We need you, Rhyvariath."

"I NEVER THOUGHT I WOULD SEE THE DAY. THE IMPERIAL CLUTCH BROUGHT TO HEEL BEFORE A WHELPBACK."

"Does that mean you will help us?" Emyria inquired.

"I WILL STAY, YES. BUT THERE IS ANOTHER MATTER I MUST ATTEND TO IN THE TIME WE HAVE."

"Mayhaps we can be of aid?" Remy said.

"TAKE NO OFFENSE, PRINCELING, BUT THIS IS A MATTER I MUST SETTLE ON MY OWN."

"Understood," Remy said. "The others are holed up in the abbey below. That is where we will meet before we depart for The Spellbind in the central courtyards. I will send off a flare of Eldn flame once we are set to begin the ritual."

"I WILL KEEP AN EYE TO THE SOUTHERN WINDS AND WARN ONCE THE BEAST IS NEAR." His wings spread out wide behind him preparing for flight. "AND THOUGH IT IS UNLIKELY, IF YOU CHANCE UPON LITA DRUFELLYN, WILL YOU SEND A FLARE FOR IT?"

"Of course," Remy said.

"*...Watch your wings, Rhyvariath...*" Thira added.

The dracari unleashed an amused snort. "AND YOU WATCH YOUR HUMAN, YVEMATHIRA." Claws crushing crenelations, Rhyvariath leaned over the edge, dropped down out of sight, and reappeared a few seconds later, twisting up high into the heavens.

"Bit of a dick, isn't he?" Edgar asked.

"...*You have no idea*..." Thira answered as they turned back for the stairwell. "...*But he was amongst our scrappiest warriors and he has never once betrayed my trust*..."

"I know that name," Edgar said. "Lita Drufellyn. Rather, Emyria does."

"She is Rhyvariath's familiar, apparently," Remy said. "And a changeling."

"A changeling?"

"She came through the godsgate on Ilynderos disguised as a Chandii. So says Rhyvariath."

"I reckon that makes sense for the rest here."

"Go on." Swiftly, they started down the stairwell.

"She's also the Wyrmstower Witch and a chronomancer. And the reason Marsea's blade is haxan."

"...*Chronomancy? No doubt Rhyvariath had some influence then*..."

"Oh, without question," Emyria answered. "And he better keep his word."

Remy slowed as they neared the first floor, drawing Exylduin and listening intently, quietly descending the last few steps and holding fast against the wall just inside the stairwell entryway.

"Blight?" whispered Edgar, blade in fist.

"Unsure." The urge to conjure Thira's Eldn flame ate at him something fierce but would likely ruin their surprise advantage.

He extended Exylduin before him, turning it slightly, working its face like a mirror, hoping to catch a reflection of the disturbance...until he had it...twixt specks of blood, a cloth maiden, only, the figure wasn't a cloth maiden. Hells, it wasn't a maiden at all.

What fresh fuckery?

His eyes grew wide as it stared into the stairwell's pitch, squinting.

It was him! The bloody cloth maiden was him!

"*What?*" Edgar mouthed.

"*It's me,*" Remy mouthed back.

"Is someone there?" something like his voice called out to them.

Remy shook his head, orbs pouring out of his sockets.

"Best to come out then," the double said. "I've an assortment of oddments at my disposal I've been itching to use."

WE DO NOT HAVE TIME FOR THIS, REMY. WE MUST MEET THEM HEAD ON.

The watchman inhaled, squeezing Exylduin's hilt. *"Hold here,"* he mouthed to Edgar, conjuring an azure egg to his palm as he twisted into the opening.

"Oh," the double said, "it's you." A devilish smirk rose upon its face. "Well, isn't this awkward?"

"Who the fuck are you?" Remy stepped into the corridor, gift crackling the hells' nine furies at his side, aching for release.

"I'm you, obviously," the double said. And the gods only knew, it looked exactly like him. All save the posture.

"The hells you are," the watchman prince spat. "You're the changeling." *How small has our world become?*

"The changeling?" the double chuckled. "Gone a bit mad then, haven't we?"

"He's looking for you, your old master."

"I've no master." A snort. "I'm the fucking King of Lancastle." The double backed away as Remy approached.

Gods, is that how I actually sound?

"The dragon outside would beg to differ," Remy raised Exylduin, pushing back all of the insecurities about himself the double was bringing to light. "Lita Drufellyn, is it?"

The double held as though petrified by the call of its true name. "Well, here we are then."

"Here we are," Remy echoed.

"Are you going to kill me, princeling?"

"Why do you look like me?"

"You really have to ask?"

"I really do."

"Because she trusts you. I thought wearing your skin, my best play to put her in the ground, since you lot saw fit to keep her going."

"You might want to be more specific."

"Morgandrel. She needs to be put down. Or she'll be the death of all of us."

"Yeah, not happening." *Rhymona bloody Curie, a walking gods damned death wish. Is there a soul alive that doesn't want you pissing worms?*

"She is the gift's chosen," Lita hissed. "Pure evil. Chaos incarnate. The death crone reborn."

"Tosh, she's practically a puppy once you get to know her." He matched the double's intensity.

"You need to listen to me before it's too late."

"And you need a better excuse."

"She will take everything from you, Remy. Everyone you've ever loved. All of it. You let her live, she'll ruin this moon from sea to shining sea."

"Remove your mask."

"Not happening." She mimicked his tone and inflection impeccably.

"Why are you wearing a cloth maiden's habit? Who were you?"

"Why do you insist on asking insipid questions? And refusing crucial answers simply because they do not suit your preference?"

"I thought changelings had to consume their prey to wear their appearance," Remy said.

"Foolish Midaran folklore," Lita said. "While some of my, shall we say, less civilized ancestors consumed their victims, it was done more to destroy the evidence of their proxy than out of any necessary corporeal requirement. There were a few daft enough to believe that the consumption of the flesh would transfer the powers of their prey. Silly Vishura shiroe superstition. In truth, we only need the blood of the being we wish to imitate to begin the transformation."

The double's eyes trailed beyond him and Remy felt Edgar advancing into his shadow.

"Should I send a flare?" Edgar asked.

"...*Not just yet...*" Thira pushed into possession. "...*We need our brother on guard. Undistracted...*"

"I won't let you take me," Lita said. "I've far too much yet to accomplish."

"...*I am afraid you do not have much of a choice...*"

"I've dealt with dracari before," Lita spat. "Long before I played have-not to your barmy brethren. Proud as a princeling, that one. Though I suppose, you'd know something about all that, wouldn't you?" Lita opened a fist, revealing a tiny wooden box. "Do you know what this is, dracari?"

Remy toed forward a step, ready to immolate the meddling wretch at the slightest wrong move.

STOP! Thira screamed in his head. Remy had never felt such a terror in her before.

What?

SHE CARRIES A SOUL CASKET.

"You do recognize it then," Lita snarked, his double showing yellow irises ringed in rusted red.

What the fuck is a soul casket?

YOU HAVE HEARD OF A GENIE IN A BOTTLE, YES?

Of course.

SIMILAR CONCEPT. ONLY INSTEAD OF GRANTING WISHES, A CREATURE LIVES INSIDE THAT BOX THAT SIRENS SOULS FROM THOSE IN ATTENDANCE AND DEVOURS THEM. I THOUGHT SUCH A CONTRIVANCE LOST TO THE RUINS OF ILYNDEROS.

"You let me walk, you keep your souls," Lita said, backing away. "Sound like an even trade?"

"I won't let you harm her," Remy called after his double.

"You won't have a choice, princeling." The darkness of the corridor's depths stole the changeling from sight. "I'm just getting started."

CHAPTER TWENTY-EIGHT

"You know we can't trust them," Rhymona said, turning the key of an oil lamp as Marsea drew the sanctum's door closed behind them.

"Sister to sister," Marsea glanced from Rhymona to Julia, "to sister. No matter what, we watch our own. Just us three and Remy."

"Munchkin Club," Julia said.

"What's that then?" Marsea's eyebrow arched.

"Inside joke," Jules clarified.

"It's our little cipher," Rhymona added. "In case shit goes sideways, munchkin's the secret word."

"As in 'Marsea Munch' munchkin?" Marsea aimed the question at Julia.

"What other munchkin is there?"

What other munchkin is there? "A fair point. And to your point, Rhymona, no, I don't trust them. Caitlyn seems a decent sort, but Pion's..." She shook her head. "...well, he's a Harver, isn't he? And he's long since worn out any measure of integrity he once held. No matter what fancy devilry he pulls from his pockets to aid us."

"My thoughts exactly."

"But of the nether and Lancastle and our lives, if it comes down to a godsgate ritual, and he's willing to put his neck on the line beside the rest of us, I don't know what other choice we have. It's obvious given your...

fresh alterations, he has a connection with *Noon*, fucked up as it is. Mayhaps, he's meant to help us."

"Help himself, more like," Rhymona said. "End of the day, he is the enemy."

"He was the enemy," Julia argued. "But he's changed."

"Changed my arse," Rhymona scoffed. "He turned cloak to save his own skin is what he's done."

"I'm not saying you have to trust him and I don't expect you to ever like him, but he's with us, he's with me."

"Jules," Marsea started.

"Once a turncloak, always a turncloak," Rhymona said.

"We can argue allegiances until the nether comes," Marsea said, "or we can accept what help is offered and deal with his past slights another day."

"Fine," Rhymona grumbled, "but this," she raised Larissa's hand, "only buys him a brief truce. He fucks around or goes against one of us, I've a cut of steel waiting. Speaking of which..." She pulled the rings from Larissa's fingers. "I believe these belong to you."

Marsea took the fistful of jewelry, stuffing them in her trouser pocket. She hadn't the faintest inkling what put the thought in her head to take her mum's hand, or why she actually agreed to go along with it, but, somehow, she knew it was the only way. Remy wasn't so easy to convince at first, but Rhymona was Rhymona, he literally owed her his life, and though she looked a corpse, she wasn't yet beyond The Hood's Door and their mother was.

Besides, she was family, bloodkin or no. She'd earned her place in Marsea's mind, and thusly the princess would go to the ends of The Vael to keep her going, even if it meant trusting a wretch as dodgy as Pion Harver,

She'd lost enough already. Mother, father, Desmond, Aunt Maggie, Autumn, Hilda, the Maidens' Rejects, Elsymir, Dags, Klaus, Cas... Vaustian...

So it came to pass that Rhymona now wore their mother's left hand.

A line from Viv Llewellyn's *Winter Cycle* memoir rose to the fore. *For better or worse. Fuck it. Who cares? Fail horribly.*

Famous last words, those.

"Now on to the order of business." Marsea nudged up her glasses.

"And the primary reason I pulled you all back here. We need to discuss what all went on in The Scar. Namely a certain Lirae Thirsby…"

"Thirsby!" Rhymona sneered. Not exactly the reaction Marsea expected.

"She came back from the future," the princess began. "She's the one that buried Tetherow. Bandying about all kinds of oddments and opinions all the while."

"This ought to be rich," Rhymona said.

"To start, she said I shouldn't trust you. Or her. Rather past her."

"Did she now?"

"Aye. And she was rather adamant about it. She mentioned something about correcting a past mistake. And then she killed them. All of them. Tetherow, Autumn, Desmond, and then herself."

"Herself?"

"Said it was a one-way trip and that she'd done what needed doing." Marsea stepped toward the firelight. "What do you know about her?"

"Honestly? I don't know what I know about her. A few hours ago, I thought she was just some dull god botherer with a stick up her arse. Then I find her smoking shufa in the library, slicker than Sally Switchblade, all honey-eyed and soil-tongued and…well, she was there when I fell out, and I'm not exactly sure what happened after that."

"How do you mean?"

"For one, I think the bitch poisoned me, forced me into slumber, so Tetherow could have another tiresome monologue. And when I came to, she was gone as the ghost. Reckon I should count my ruddy luck stones she didn't serve me a knifing in the interim."

"I should say so, given the violence I watched her dish out in The Scar, a knifing would've been a kindness."

"Tut, remember when shit surprised you?" Rhymona asked. "'Cause I don't. Not even a time traveling cloth maiden assassin in cahoots with a dream demon."

"Trust the one that came back from the future had a bone to pick with Tetherow. And likewise, Tetherow named her a traitorous such-and-such."

"All right, hold right there? Tell us about this future Lirae Thirsby?"

"She named herself Litashoth Eru, but told me I'd likely know her as Lirae Thirsby." Marsea's hand dropped to the hilt at her hip. "She had the haxanblade here. My haxanblade. And that was how she carved a ward back to 1829."

"Back from where?"

"1836. Where evidently, you've become a tyrant worse than anything the nether has done us."

"A tyrant?"

"She also mentioned I was dead, killed by Autumn on your order."

Rhymona leaned back against the wall, arms crossed, lips pursed, clearly perturbed.

"I'm only telling it like I heard it," the princess defended.

"Did I say anything?"

"It sounded like bollocks to me too," Marsea said, "but that's why I'm telling you now. Even if we entertain her story, even if it *was* all real, it couldn't possibly happen the same. My killer is dead..." *Rest in peace, Autumn.* "...which means almost everything I do from here on out is uncharted territory. And maybe it means you'll make different decisions as well."

"Let us make one thing clear right here, Marsea. I would never order your fucking head."

"I know."

"I love you. And I mean that. I love all of you. Remy. Julia. You're all my family. I may be your mother's age, the gods keep her, but you are my sister, both of you. And Remy my brother. You're all I have, you lot. You're the reason I haven't fucked off from all of this ridiculous bentcockery already. And the gods know, if I had my way, I would've done so days ago."

"I know. Trust me, I know. And I know we can make it all different."

"1836," Julia interjected. "That means we survive all this."

"Aye. Apparently, we put the nether back in its box."

"Then there's hope yet," the youngest sister said.

"Yes. But we all must stick together," returned the eldest. "No matter what."

"And we will," Rhymona declared.

"Here." Marsea fished a totem out of her pocket and tossed it at the magus.

"What the fuck is this thing?" Rhymona studied it.

"A totem that eats demons."

"No shit."

"I have one as well. I figure it may come in handy."

"Especially with another one of Tetherow's puppets roaming the castle."

"Indeed."

Rhymona's eyes rose back up to meet hers. "The haxanblade. You cut a portal from the library to the churchyard."

"Blind Widow is a key, as Dagmara explained," Marsea said. "Only it's far more powerful than she ever knew. It's how I got back home so quickly. And, evidently, I've only just begun to scratch the surface of its abilities. Thirsby told me it's some sort of gift sponge, which is why it drinks the blood from its victims. Though it's not actually the blood its after."

"It's the gift."

"Precisely. It stores the gift within to amplify its powers."

"Mervold would shit a brick at the telling," Rhymona said.

"Mervold would shit an entire fucking kingdom. As far as the portal cutting, the blade is a key to any door with a name, any door written with the gift. All the wielder need do is know it's calling and Barb's your auntie."

Rhymona shook her head, a grin creeping across her face. "I don't care what they named you before. You're a bad, bad bitch, Marsea Lanier."

"Pot meet kettle."

"You too," Rhymona aimed the words at Julia.

"How could I not be with you two for company?"

"All right, all right, that's enough with all the mushy stuff, yeah," Rhymona said.

"Hey, you started it," Julia returned.

"There's one more thing about Lirae Thirsby," Marsea said. "I believe she may also be Lita Drufellyn."

"Oh, shitting hells." Rhymona scratched Larissa's fingers across her forehead. "Bugger me blind. That's it, isn't it? It all makes so much more sense now."

"It does?"

"Baka. Baka. Baka." the magus began to pace. "Lita is Thirsby. And she's been right under our noses this whole fucking time." Rhymona held mid-stride, orbs meeting Marsea's. "And if Stella's stories were true, and

Lita is actually ashaeydir, she may well have a trezsu implant in her, which would have allowed her to change her appearance as I do. The Stranger brain me, I'm such a bloody foolhard."

"I would say we were all fooled," Marsea said. "As many times as I sought her guidance and attended her prayers." The words sank in. *As many times as I confided in her my darkest thoughts, my most selfish transgressions.* "Oh…" Her face scrunched up. *Good gravy, the woman knows near everything about me.* "This conversation stays between us, yeah?" Marsea added. "Our best leverage may be that she doesn't know we all know."

"What conversation?" Rhymona replied.

"Not a peep," Julia added.

What I'd give to know her location right about now. Her thoughts wandered. Not that she could actually act on such a whimsy if the answer fell from the heavens.

Focus on what you know you can control, she chided. "We get through all this, I want to bury mother, have a proper funeral. Same goes for everyone we've lost. Desmond, Autumn, Aunt Mags…"

"Father," Julia whispered.

"Jules, we don't know…"

"I know," she answered, eyes fighting back a film of liquid.

"*If* Raelan is gone, then yes, of course."

"And Uncle Vaustian? And Uncle Gan? And Aunt Sylvie. And Aeralie?" she asked.

Marsea met Rhymona's eyes before locking back on Julia. "All of them. We'll have a great ceremony for *all* of those we've lost." This seemed to satisfy her.

A commotion started up from inside the cathedral.

"They've returned," Marsea said, pushing through the door to the others.

Remy marched down the center walkway between rows of pews, snow in his hair, a look of agitation scrawled across his guise. Edgar and Poppy placed the pew barricade back against the entrance.

"What do any of you know about Lita Drufellyn?" Remy inquired.

Rhymona glanced at Marsea.

"Fuck it, may as well tell him." *So much for between us.*

"We believe she's Thirsby," Rhymona answered. "And I think she's ashaeydir."

"Not quite," Remy answered. "She's Vishura shiroe."

"A changeling?" Marsea uttered.

"Aye, and she was last seen wearing my face and carrying some contraption called a soul…" His eyes fell to her hand. "…casket." His eyes rose back to hers. "Marsea, where did you get that?"

She held up the totem. "Yeah, we've got some catching up to do."

"It would seem so."

"Wait?" Rhymona said. "Did you just say she was wearing your face?"

CHAPTER TWENTY-NINE

OFF WE GO to summon a godsgate! Pion mocked as they pushed eastward into the courtyard labyrinth toward The Spellbind's location. *And they name me the mad one?*

Dusk would soon be upon them, the sister moons bleeding through the dreary horizon once more, slowly gobbling up all but the brightest of stars.

Though you agreed to it, didn't you? The mad fool you are.

Caitlyn glanced over her shoulder at him, wand seething in one hand, *Dawn* gripped in the other. Pion found he could no longer read her expressions. They all sort of appeared the same now. Caught somewhere between fear and fury, and when she beheld him, mayhaps a hint of pity.

"Keep going," he answered what he presumed to be a scowl, cold clouds forming at his words. "I'm fine."

Though, in truth, he was anything but. The flesh spell took a mite more out of him than he could have ever anticipated. More than even a soul-splicing ritual. Sure, he'd performed a few carnomancy casts before, little harmless experiments here and there, but certainly nothing on the level of reverse amputation.

All affairs honest, he was just as surprised at how well it all turned out (not that he'd ever admit to it). Minding the queen's decomposed flesh, lividity had long since set, the blood all but blanched, only scant traces of gift residue within, but it was like something else—something fated—something from beyond the incantation was guiding his hands and tongue throughout. Hours later, he could still feel its aura here with him, scratching at his shadow like a hauntling playing at windup.

The stack of Chandii-stock blood candles in his waist pouch beckoned, his nerves begging for their union like a desperate resinhead itching for a quick fix, but it was much too soon. Much, much too soon. And his thoughts wandered to the chest of elixirs and tonics locked away in his bedchamber and the skin of celebratory absinthium he'd left assuming he'd actually see it again…with a corrected spine and leg and something like a mother by his side.

Only now, those dreams somehow seemed an age away. And death was breathing down his neck, all but certain.

At least, regarding the godsgate ritual, they were evenly paired. He and Caitlyn. Remy and Marsea. Not that he completely trusted Caitie, but she was far less likely to serve him a knife than the brainsick ashaeydir. No, thankfully, his barmy lab mouse Rhymona would remain with the others inside the citadel, making for the King's Reserve Chamber outside the officer's barracks.

Given the ugly elements and possible danger, he bade Ripley to protect Julia, and Marsea ordered the same of her wolf companion. As well, it was decided, if the ritual went bollocks up, at least he and Marsea might be able to varg inside their familiars to potentially aid or warn the others.

Classic Lanier hopefulness, that. But truly, what else was there anymore?

The warlock passed under an arcade into another courtyard, minutes away from destiny. Bodies and limbs lay everywhere, most torn through viciously and growing in number the nearer they gained to The Spellbind. So many they almost seemed staged, the gentle fall of snow only adding to the theatrics. He left their rot to the furthest corners of his vision, refusing to take any of them in directly. The smell, however, would not be so easily dismissed. It quite reminded Pion of the animal carcasses he'd found strewn across the woodlands during his family hunts. The sound of feeding flies all that could be heard for leagues.

He clutched *Noon* tight to his chest, the ferrule of his cane hammering down atop the stones underfoot, coercing him forward, the memory of his father's hunts distracting him from the pendulum pain shooting all throughout his broken form.

Pion had always reviled his father for forcing him out at the ass-crack of dawn for a bit of useless sport. A sport he could never hope to master. Hells, he could hardly stand on his own, much less naturally, what made his father think he'd be capable of aiming a gods damned bow and arrow with any degree of quality? It was fucking demeaning is what it was.

Unless...

Regret bubbled up inside the pit of his stomach.

Well, there is that...

Realization briefly stole away the agony of his hurried footsteps.

Was that your attempt at bonding, old man?

Stones to crunch of snow.

Bugger all. Their unexpected reunion had thrown him for a loop. Though such seemed precisely the sort of backward-ass good-old-boy bullshit his father would likely confuse with caring. *I think I preferred despising you...*

A thunderous bellow rumbled across the winds overhead as war horns trumpeted in response.

And so ends the calm before the storm.

The behemoth was close, almost on top of them, its horrible battle cry soaking through his clothes and skin, rattling about his bones and into his shriveled black soul.

Seventy-four, he reminded. The page of *Noon* his quarter of the gods-gate ritual began on. *Stay in control.*

It took the better part of the afternoon, but they all managed to find their parts.

At least they hoped.

Skimming through his portion, the spell's recitation wouldn't take much longer than a few minutes between the four of them to complete, assuming the distractions remained at a minimum. Now what came about once it all started was anyone's guess. Neither Thira nor Emyria were present at the conjuring of the last one on Ilynderos and Rhyvariath was still in the wind. And then there was The Spellbind to consider and the havoc it would wreak on their bodies if the nether forced them to hide physically within. He'd had a dozen different tales over the cycles, presages most ominous, all ending with the same horrific warning. That walking within The Pale was a suicide quest, aging those fool enough to test its power decades in the span of minutes.

The others stopped at the end of a courtyard and he felt the majestic hum of The Spellbind's invisible barrier nearby.

"We're close enough," Marsea said, nudging up her spectacles.

Through a pair of dirty glass circles, their eyes met, her glower snatching the breath from his lungs.

Oh, but those lovely haunters, Pion thought. And within Caitie's company, he'd almost forgotten about her inexplicable hold over him.

Eternity in an instant.

Iron eyes.

Grudge eyes.

'You're dead to me' eyes.

Seasea hadn't spoken two words to him since their nasty dialogue through the door of her bedchamber over a quintweek past. Though honestly, her eyes said more than enough. He'd topped his fair share of shitlists over the cycles, but this one hit hard as a gallows sentence.

"In case you were wondering, she fucking hates you," Caitlyn murmured as Marsea marched off after her brother.

"Puzzled that one out, did you?" Pion said.

"For a High House princess, she seems rather plain, you ask me."

You don't know her like I do, he wanted to say, but what would have been the point?

"Is that your attempt at a rally on then?" he asked instead, acting at court decorum as though it still had a place in this utter miscarriage of an empire.

"Is it working?" she returned.

"It's not *not* working."

"You could do better, is all."

"A girl after my own heart."

"Oh, don't you wish it so."

They shared a daft smile.

"And what are you two grinning about?" Marsea asked from the court-yard's edge, her expression a most exquisite terror.

"Nothing," Pion answered. "A bit of hangman's humor."

At the center of the next courtyard over, Remy fired a sphere of Eldn flame high into the heavens where it sparked inside the dance of snowflakes, angry as a combusting comet.

Despite the brilliant spectacle, Marsea's iron glower never left him. "You better not fuck us on this, Pion." Her hand dropped to the hilt of her sword where she exposed a sliver of steel. "Or you'll find a messy one at the end of old girl here."

His heart shriveled at her icy words, and he swallowed back a sneer. More and more she was gnashing on like the ashaeydir gutterwitch, wasn't she? All insolence and irrational confidence.

"You worry on your own shit, yeah," he replied sharply. "Mine's all sorted." Not his best look given the turn of things, but he'd be damned to the darkest pit of the nine before he let himself be cowed like a cockless craven in this his final hour.

You're in control.

"For your sake, I hope that's true." Marsea shifted to Caitlyn. "Let me know when you're ready to begin."

Caitlyn's attention trailed from Marsea to Pion. The warlock sucked in a deep breath and nodded.

The spell would need to be spoken in sequences. *Dawn, Noon, Dusk,* then *Haunt.* As such, each would have a turn while the others did their best to protect the chanter from whatever came at them. Worst-case scenario, if the nether found them, they would shield themselves inside The Spellbind to complete the incantation.

Another beastial roar rent through the coming night, this one wholly different from that of the nether behemoth.

Pion swallowed as something large came crashing atop the stonework behind them.

As he turned about, his vision rose to the most magnificent creature he'd ever beheld, its massive claws dug deep into the lower battlements overlooking the courtyard.

The Stranger take me.

Pion could feel his eyes bulging out like boiled eggs, jaw hanging slack.

"WE ARE OUT OF TIME," Rhyvariath spoke inside his head, more sensation than sound. "AND THE NETHER IS UNENDING."

"Godsgate unending?" Remy asked.

"YES."

"You're sure?"

"IT MAY BE THE ONLY THING THAT CAN STAND AGAINST IT," the dracari returned, beating its enormous wings down and catching a fresh wind. "BLIGHT APPROACH FROM THE SOUTH AND EAST. I WILL BURN A PATH, BUT YOU MUST REMAIN VIGILANT. THERE ARE MANY MORE THAN BEFORE."

And with that the dragon disappeared, a fiery screech following.

Toll the requiem bells.

"You heard him," Remy said, shifting toward them. "It's now or never, Caitlyn."

Caitlyn holstered her wand, then cracked *Dawn* open and leafed through to the spell's page.

"Pion, you watch her," Marsea said as the warlock fished a blood candle from his pouch. "Wait for the end and start your section. Once you're done, Caitlyn, switch guard with Remy. Remy, you then watch Pion. If shit goes sideways, run through the north exit to the outermost courtyard. Halt when you see ghostlight and phantom ichor and you'll know you're in The Spellbind. If you're reading when we run, for stars' sake do not stop. No matter what."

A wall of smoke rose up from the southeast where Rhyvariath was burning through the advancing nether legion.

Heart pounding, fingers stiff and uncooperative, Pion clawed *Noon* open to page seventy-four, dropping the blood candle in its center like a bookmark.

We're actually doing this then? You're actually doing this?

The Lanier siblings spun away, nearly in unison, drawing their swords side by side as they approached the courtyard's eastern entrance and prepared for hell.

Pion shook his head at the pageantry, every range of emotion he'd ever conjured over the highborn pair chewing through him as he watched them man their positions.

Anger. Hate. Jealousy.

Relief. Admiration. Awe.

All the tomes he'd scoured regarding the godsblood, and not a one described their true potential with any measure of accuracy. Never in his life did he expect to see Marsea or Remy slinging silver through the dregs like tourney yard champions, and certainly not while simultaneously melding multiple mantia within.

"Vael to Pion," Caitlyn said, wresting him from obsession's embrace.

"Hmm." His eyes shot up to hers.

"You ready?" she asked, eyebrow arched.

"We've got this," Pion answered against his gloomy nature. *And the gods know we're all properly fucked if I'm the bloody voice of optimism left us.*

"Kittens and cupcakes, yeah?" Caitlyn said with a fetching smirk.

"Kittens and cupcakes," Pion echoed, the combination of words triggering a flash image of the day he found Ripley mewing his tiny furry head off in the alleyway outside the Aft Street sweet shop. His mother and siblings dead and dying around him. Some bastard mutt having gotten after the litter in their sleep.

And before Pion could finish the thought, Caitlyn began, honey orbs sparkling, amber light rising from the tome chased by a phantom wind that intensified with each passing word, her hair flowing smartly in the breeze behind her, the snow swirling about her ankles, rising like a tempest.

A shriek like a blade down ice pierced his eardrums, and it took everything within him not to drop his grimoire and cover his ears. A massive chunk of stone sailed overhead from some rest beyond the citadel and as it disappeared into the lower hamlets Pion realized it was the top half of one of Lancastle's watchtowers.

"Sodding hells," he uttered. *It's here.*

Another maw cried out from further east, more of the citadel catching air and smashing somewhere abouts the kingdom below.

"Keep going," he bade Caitlyn, his teeth starting a chatter, body trembling, betraying him as it always did in times of trouble.

Stay in control.

As for Caitlyn, she held her form marvelously, never once straying from the incantation despite the horrific signs of impending doom surrounding them. It was at once the most beguiling and inspiring thing he'd ever beheld, inciting a swell of confidence within that forced his shivers back down.

You've got this, he told himself, wetting his lips, swallowing back the lump of fear in his throat, adrenaline spiking with anticipation.

Not long now. From what he recalled of her portion, she was near the passage's end, only a few lines away.

"Brace yourselves," Remy shouted as the first wave of ghouls surfaced, demonic clicking closing in all around them.

Marsea stabbed her blade down into a nearby corpse and twisted, drawing blood, and her sword lit up like a crimson torch, pink steam trailing her movements as she fell into one of Uncle Vaustian's sparring stances.

In chorus, Remy called an egg of Eldn fire to his off hand, kissing the palm to Exylduin, dragon's flame coursing her steel from cross-guard to point.

Almost time.

Caitlyn was screaming the words now, amber-gold glyphs tearing out from her pages accompanied by a dense morning mist and creatures not of this plane.

The Pale is open.

A heavy breath.

Here it comes.

He crushed blood candle to warlock's well, flapping *Noon* open before him.

Page seventy-four.

Remember who the fuck you are.

You're in control.

And he caught the last of Caitlyn's curse, a perfect conjunction, her maelstrom bending up from the wailing tome, as the amber morning mist gave way to noon's golden glory, the words rising from the parchment, forming gilded sigils in the air before him, disappearing one into the next as the midday miscreations from beyond The Pale began to populate the surrounding courtyard. Monsters of the flesh, corpses sewn into one another, abominations so foul even the hells wouldn't have them, their misshapen brides twice as ghastly.

Caitlyn darted past him, ripping her wand from its rest and firing at the courtyard's mouth, leaving him all alone inside the crowd of encroaching eyesores, their ruined forms, at the edge of his vision, blurred into a pulp of rearranged appendages.

Throat in shreds, the warlock shouted word after word, giving himself to the tome's dominion, wondering if the curious presence from his flesh-altering spell with Rhymona would make its return.

"We can't hold them!" he heard Caitlyn holler out. "There're too many!"

Shit. The thought crept into the spell's cast as something black slammed into the snow beside him.

Followed by another similar shape to his right; the refrain of, "*Control. Control. Control,*" echoing.

This one he caught at the corner of his eye. *A crow?* Chased by a third and a fourth, their bodies slamming into the ground with breakneck force.

Suddenly the heavens were raining crow corpses, as though the nether beast had swallowed them up from the sky on the way north and was now regurgitating them across the kingdom like a volley of arrows.

"Move, Pion!" Remy cried as a hand grabbed his sleeve yanking him forward. "Don't stop reading, I'll guide you."

The warlock nearly lost the spell in the pull, pushing through it by memory's count until he resumed his proper place, control forsaking him. Remy hacked and slashed his flaming sword at the distortion beyond, through any ghoul that made a run at him, painting the path in blood and marrow, cape flapping, dashing to and fro, before him, behind him, calling up energy walls above and around him, anything to keep him reading, anything to keep him untouched, leading him from courtyard to courtyard, through the intensifying crowstorm, and The Spellbind's song rang in Pion's head all the while, the noonfiends screeching after them, golden letters bursting like bubbles as he summoned them up from the grimoire's glowing guts.

His part ended as he passed through a faceless phantom inside The Spellbind's barrier.

"Remy!" He barked with the last of his voice, and the prince ripped *Dusk* from his tome holster and began his set.

Scarce halfway through and the shit's already fucked.

Pion drew another candle from his pouch, one melted around a razor, and plunged it into his bad leg.

"Fuck!" he screamed at the ghostlight, the limb exploding into fire as the foreign giftblood rushed through his veins, mingling with his own, Chandii stock, and it felt like fingers were burrowing their way into the muscles of his thigh and beginning to tear outward.

A mad glaze stole over his eyes, drool running from the corner of his lips, as he gave in to the chaos, pushing past the torrent of excruciating pain, spinning about Remy, through a floating cloud of milky-white phantom ichor, and aimed his cane at an approaching blighter, clicking the latch as it came within range and firing it into the bastard's face, sending the swine sprawling off course into a crowd of Spellbind phantoms.

Remy kept reading, lavender sigils exploding into little puffs of dust around them, feeding the spell's expanding vortex, as dusk creatures bled in from The Pale, joining that of the noonfiends and the morning mist.

Hobbled, Pion dodged another ghoul that caught inferno as it passed him by.

The hells?

But there was no time to mind it.

The warlock swayed backward as a crazed bluecoat's blade whistled past him, narrowly missing his chin. And a moment later, a wand blast took the bastard's head off, dark fluids splashing across his frontage.

He spun away, through another clot of phantom ichor, blood in his eye, hair clinging like seaweed to the fresh gore upon his face, flailing his cane blade around, the half-melted Chandii candle jammed in his albatross of a leg, the only thing keeping him upright.

But the blight was legion and there were far too many and more closing in.

Control.

He collided into someone and swung wildly at another in the whirlwind that followed, plunging his steel through a third that made clicking noises, the bastard clutching his cane blade into its chest, trying to pull him in as it staggered past. He let go and, somehow, kept standing on his own.

Tosser.

Immediately, Pion's fingers dug into the scabbed ring of missing flesh upon his other palm, drawing forth a stream of gore which he slung out like a lasso at a gleam of silver in the snow, forcing his giftblood around its hilt before yanking it back to his hand.

I'm in control.

Fresh clicking rose from behind him and he flung the blade out in its direction like a chain sickle, ripping the blood strand back after he felt it connect with something solid, a gash of dark liquid spewing across the snowdrifts.

Fucker, he thought as something warm, wet, and copious spattered across his backside and he whirled around to face it, expecting to find his end.

Only what he found in place of death was a thousand times more horrifying.

Oh. His words became choked.

The creature loomed above him, twice his height, reeking worse than a dead man's privy pot, bare as her birthfall, bending low to sniff his head, mangy white hair hanging, saggy pale gray breasts pushing in toward his face, nearly touching.

Pion held still, staring the fiend dead in its fucked-up face as she leaned away. One eye was rolled back inside her skull so only the white appeared, and the other revealed a barely visible pus-colored iris staring up and to the right. After a beat, it posed a savage smile, red-tinged slobber running down her blood-caked maw.

Dagger meet heart.

It can't be.

It was a smile he recognized.

A smile he could never forget no matter what fresh horror it fixed itself to.

"Spared by the bitch of a bastard's seed," he uttered as the smile of Rhymona Curie tore past him, her skinny frame bending unnaturally through the ghoulish onslaught, taloned fingers splitting any patch of flesh that filled her path, a river of frayed appendages and blood spill curling in the air after her, his own blood in pursuit.

"For fuck's sake." He stabbed the sword into the dirt, severing the call of his warlock's well before the bitch drank him dry as well, and gazed back at the spectacle as Caitlyn appeared through a cloud of floating phantom ichor, a crow nearly impaling her, but for the hell hag's madness, Rhymona reaching up and yanking the bird from the air mid-dive as she screeched past, where it disappeared inside her tousled mess of hair and came out a blink later a half-eaten glob of ruffled feathers.

Did she just bite that fucker's head off raw?

"What the shit is that thing?" Caitlyn asked, seven shades past the loon herself.

"A blood wraith," Pion answered, watching it leap from ghoul to ghoul, a shitstorm of entrails and blood swirling after her.

"Your face…"

"It's The Spellbind," he explained. "It's like a dead man's rift. Standing within it will age our bodies."

"How long do we have?"

"Quarter-hour, give or take."

"Brilliant."

"He's nearly done," Pion rasped, his attentions befalling Remy, then flitting toward the mist-laden courtyard entrance they'd come through. "Where the fuck is…Mar…sea?" The name trailed off as his vision rose to the mass of black flesh flooding over the arches and eaves of Lancastle Citadel, tentacles slamming across the patches of rooftop, gripping towers, dragging the bulk of its shifting, sinewy shape forward, its countless mouths emitting an ear-splitting din as it rose over the castle like a child playing dollhouse.

CHAPTER THIRTY

Light as a feather, **Marsea Munch.**

The princess picked up her pace, as the ground began to tremor, pulse throbbing behind her eyes, twisting, twirling, contorting, the haxanblade wailing ugly as a hillside haunter as a stream of gore chased her through the host of ghouls, one courtyard to the next. Twenty, mayhaps thirty of the bastards in pursuit, dense as a mischief of rats, with a pair of drylax horrors to boot.

Her mind wavered in and out of consciousness as Blind Widow chewed through an endless herd of flesh and bone, the haxanblade racking her body for every ounce of gift within, Other filling in the cracks of her faltering form, drinking up her pain and dumping it down inside the furthest depths of her vast internal ocean.

Smooth as silk, she jerked away from a blighter's overhead swipe, the evil-looking great sword missing her by an inch as the death crone's hangnail tore across its wielder's belly, spilling its innards out like a bundle of wet rope around its ankles.

Flowing with the ghoulish current, something clever fast caught the crook of her eye, its impossible shape suddenly filling the space to her left. *Phaedrylax,* her brain screamed, and she flailed Blind Widow out into the void, deflecting a flash of silver, sending it out long, its shifting black mass stumbling past her, landing with a damp thud in the muck some-where behind her.

She pushed on to the next slab of meat, a housecat made stray, a stray amongst rats, swallowing down her panic, running through every attack Vaustian ever taught her, and slashed at the ax-wielding ghoul guarding the passage between courtyards, screaming at the top of her lungs, the gift blistering through her bloodstream, her body reacting faster than her eyes could follow, sparks flying as Blind Widow met with the ax head, kissing vibration's end, and quickly reversing course, hooking the wretch below its armpit, gorging through ribs and muscles and organs upward out the opposite side of its neck.

Maidens' mercy.

His body began to slide apart as she rushed past him and into the narrow connector between courtyards.

She'd split him in half like it was nothing, slick as a sickle through satin, The Widow's steel gushing a most grotesque manner of garnet.

But she couldn't stop now. She had to find the others. Her part of the incantation would soon be upon them.

All momentum, Marsea dashed through the passage, skewering Blind Widow through a waiting ghoul's gnashing maw, cross-guard to teeth, brains and blackened blood exploding out the back of its skull into the snowy garden nook at the other end. She drove the fiend down to the ground, never slowing, and jerked the haxanblade free as she pressed on into the northernmost courtyard through gobs of gore, blazing snowfall, and waves of bright floating phantom ichor.

Viscera painted the stones just ahead as the blood wraith passed, one ghoul to the next, and Marsea rushed into the courtyard stretch, working Blind Widow back into her sheath before wrestling *Haunt* from her satchel, and narrowly beating one of the pursuing drylax horrors into The Spellbind barrier, where The Pale ate through its netherflesh as though the fiend had fallen inside a vat of boiling acid.

The Spellbind could keep the drylax creatures at bay apparently, but not the blighted as evidenced by their unending presence within. Marsea reckoned there wasn't enough nether in their system to eat them up on impact; instead, it was roasting them slowly from the inside out (as though affairs hadn't already become macabre enough).

A chorus of shrill cries and howls filled the air, and she glanced back to find the nether behemoth cascading over the citadel.

Fear crackled down her spine, jarring as a bolt of thunder. *Keep moving, girl. You have to find them.*

As the thought passed, a fretful voice bellowed her name from somewhere within the cauldron of corpses, so close, and yet, in this manner of bedlam, it seemed such a woefully far distance away.

A wand blast shrieked out and the princess spun around toward it only to find a bluecoat ghoul in her path making that awful clicking noise, arms bent at obscene angles by the spritelings controlling it, officer's blade poised for murder, its sinister scowl almost intelligent. Her hand dropped to the haxanblade's hilt, preparing to draw, but as the fiend took a step toward her, a crow impaled itself atop his crown, dropping him limp onto the muck in an explosion of feathers.

Loon-eyed, Marsea snorted at the unexpected break in fortune, trudging a step forward, where something took her off her feet, *Haunt* flying from her grip in the impact.

Bugger.

She crunched to the ground next to someone nearly twice her size, the wind knocked out of her, half her face dragging in the snow and ash, the rim of her glasses cutting into her cheek, as intense, fiery pain stabbed down the length of her body.

"Marsea, if you can hear me." Pion's voice. "He's on the last line!"

Fuck.

Stiff, aching, face throbbing, worse than what Ganedys gave her, she forced herself to move, rolling onto her side.

Get up, Marsea.

Dizzy and desperate, her vision distorted, breathing choked, she searched for the grimoire in the few seconds she had before her attacker clawed atop her, forcing her down into the dirt on her backside. "Dammit!" she rasped, unable to reach Blind Widow under the bastard's weight, catching the ghoul under its bearded jaw as it dove in to bite a chunk from her face, bloody slobber running down from its nasty sawblade maw, dribbling across her forehead and glasses as she pushed at the clicking wretch, scratching, gauging, pulling out chunks of its hair, clubbing it with her gloved hand, unable to wriggle free... until a keen wind hissed by them, reeking of rotten fish, removing the fucker's head from its eye sockets up, blood, brain matter, and bone shards coiling out like soup from the hollow of its freshly severed scalp.

The princess rocked to her side, the headless bluecoat thumping onto the red-stained snow next to her. *Fuck.* And she grunted up to her feet, disoriented, turning wild circles about the slaughter field in hunt of the grimoire, unable to locate it.

"Fuck." Her eyes darted about frantically. "Come on. Where are you?

"Marsea," a voice answered, and she stopped her spiraling at the ghost of her father a few feet away from her, Stella beside him, a cadre of hooded phantoms filling the space behind them, each one in magian attire.

Another ghoul raced in at her, its neck bent wrong, and she shoved past it, plumb exhausted, stumbling toward her father, knowing *Haunt* would be nearby. It just had to be.

"It's in you, Marsea," her father said. "You don't need the book."

"Yes, I do. Where is it?"

"You know the answer," he returned. "You've read the words. How many times now?"

"What?"

"Draw your blade, girl. Defend yourself and speak the damn words."

"I…"

"Now," the king barked. "I will lead you to the others."

"Marsea!" Remy howled from some rest over her shoulder.

"This way," King Whit said.

Out of time.

She ripped Blind Widow wailing from its coffin and charged into the carnage once more, racing after her father, her mind instantly snapping to *Haunt*, page twenty-nine, in from the back. Without hesitation, she began the incantation, the words flying off her tongue like a dream language, cerulean sigils both foreign and familiar forming around her and evaporating into the ether over her shoulder as she hewed through a ghoul she recognized as Ursula Essengale, one of her mother's best loved house servants.

A breath later, a blighted scullery maid replaced Ursula's ruined shape and Marsea cut through the girl, pirouetting around its falling corpse to brain another, the haxanblade wolfing through what stretch of skull her strike did not split, until its head rolled to the dirt, leaking its insides across the snow like a cracked egg.

By this point, Marsea may as well have been unconscious, such was her possession. She was all instinct now, all gift, some haunt beyond elemental, her voice overlapping with Other's, ten lines into the chant, the words flowing through her as though from a tavern song, words she'd read a thousand, thousand times before, thinking them her father's, thinking them some barmy half-spell he'd thought up in a fever dream, never once believing them stolen, never once believing them this crucial.

The grass rippled like waves beneath her boots, an edge thrumming through the drizzle of snowflakes, coupled with a static cling...

...her ears popped and the world began to slow...

...a crow plowed into the snow next to her...

...a body dropped on her other side missing its lower half, blood and guts coiling up at Blind Widow's behest from the pile of loose meat at the severed end...

...another wand blast screamed out from the mist just past her father...

...and the world began to warp...blurring...bending...slipping off its axis...

...the heavens bleeding an endless prismatic rainbow, the color of riftlight...

All the while, she never quit the incantation despite the seeming shift in reality, through hauntling, dusk wraith, and noonfiend, she brandished Blind Widow, slicing about the congestion of corpses to keep the fel creatures at bay.

"Get under something!" Pion commanded from up ahead and Marsea caught a gleam from Remy's armor. They were headed for the arcade and nearly there.

So close.

Suddenly she was running downhill as the world began to tilt sideways, her feet leaving Vaelsyntheria's surface, momentum suspended as she became airborne and weightless inside the petrified snowfall, everything in the courtyard drifting cut-string into empty space. Spluttering the last of her lines, Marsea floated through a gauntlet of crows and viscera toward The Spellbind's end, as a frothing maw appeared.

Good gravy.

262

It was right outside The Spellbind, an abyss of waiting fangs, boiling its flesh against the magical barrier to reach her, to stop the ritual, The Pale somehow keeping it at bay.

But she couldn't stop herself from moving toward it, try as she might to kick away. There was nothing to grab onto, nothing to slow her plight, and soon she would pass beyond The Pale's sanctuary, the nether's hellmouth trailing her movements, its thousand crimson eyes slavering in anticipation.

Cerulean sigils danced about her, dissolving like faeling dust as she bit off the last of the godsgate incantation and glanced over a shoulder, gazing back at the ground, some twenty odd feet below her, trying to locate her father in the eldritch maelstrom.

"Father!" she cried out unable to find him.

"Stay calm, love, he's coming for you," the king assured, as though he'd become the very wind itself.

Who's coming for me? she thought before a bright flickering light appeared on her left, strafing the nether flesh with Eldn flame as Rhyvariath scorched through a thicket of lashing tentacles and passed inside The Spellbind's shell just before the endless behemoth closed around it like a palm over glass.

"Sweet mother-of-pearl."

Marsea clenched her teeth and tensed up preparing for the impact. One of the two creatures would have her in a matter of seconds.

The nether beast's bog breath hit her like a tidal wave causing the glyphs of The Pale to glimmer white-gold and her stomach to turn.

Inches away...

Closer than Rhyvariath...

Hurry, hurry, hurry, she pleaded.

But as fast and willful as the great dracari was, he wasn't going to make it.

You have to do something, Marsea. Buy him some time.

She gripped Blind Widow in both hands, adjusting the blade to her side, and prepared to thrust it hilt-deep into the horizon of flesh. Death be damned, if she was going out, she would make bloody well sure the fucker remembered her. As she readied for the strike, a fresh gout of gore began to spot the haxanblade's steel, the drops swiftly becoming a steady stream.

The fuck?

Her heart jumped to her throat as she expected a ghoul attack from behind.

"Marsea!" a voice shouted instead, and the princess whirled about sidelong to take it in.

"Pion?"

Giftblood poured out of his mutilated hand in both directions, into Blind Widow and down to another sword buried in the dirt at the other end.

Of all the absurd devilry surrounding them, this by far took the cake. The maidens know, she could hardly believe her own eyes. Like something ripped straight from the pages of fairytale folly. The wretch who had made her life a living hell for cycles was putting it all on the line to save her.

She felt something impossibly cold brush up against her arm, toiling to burrow beneath her skin, using her fears against her, and she froze, imagining herself lying naked on a patch of ice, shivering, curled in a ball, the glacial surface sticking to her, burning through her, flaying the skin from her muscles as she tried to pull away from it.

"I've got you," Pion said as he caught her arm and pulled her into him, the blood tether holding as globules of gore blossomed out around them from the collision.

Furious, the nether beast slammed its rabid maw against The Pale's threshold, a hair's breadth away.

"How?" she started with a shiver. But before Pion could answer, Rhyvariath swooped in and gathered them up, curling his immense wings around them as he corkscrewed away from the ghastly leviathan, skirting The Spellbind's boundary.

"What the hell is going on?" she cried, cradled in the dracari's massive arm. "Did something go wrong with the spell?"

"YES AND NO," Rhyvariath spoke inside her head as his wings unfurled and they landed near the others. Gravity still in flux, he dug his claws deep into the muck to keep them grounded.

"What did we do?" Marsea shouted over the nether's baying, stabbing Blind Widow into the dirt and hunkering down next to Pion beneath the dragon. "Is this not a godsgate?"

"IT IS, BUT NOT LIKE WHAT MY KIN CONJURED ON ILYNDEROS."

The nether beast continued to bludgeon itself against the shimmering barrier, shrieking all the hells furies, thrashing about wildly, flattening itself around the unbreakable Pale, trying to find a way in as it swallowed up all the riftlight from outside The Spellbind's ghostly glow.

"IT IS ALMOST AS THOUGH THE CONCENTRATION OF GIFT AND NETHER SURROUNDING US HAS CONFUSED THE INCANTATION."

"Confused it how?" Pion asked, wrapping his bloodstained hand with the sash from his robe.

"WE OPENED A GODSGATE, YES, BUT INSTEAD OF IT APPEARING LIKE A NATURAL PORTAL WOULD, IT HAS INSTEAD, SHALL WE SAY, FUSED WITH PART OF THE KINGDOM."

"The maidens know, Rhyvariath, speak it plainly," Marsea grumbled.

"LANCASTLE IS THE PORTAL. AND IT IS NO LONGER ON VAELSYNTHERIA."

"What do you mean no longer on Vaelsyntheria?" the princess asked. "Where are we?"

"WOULD, THAT I COULD NAME IT. I WATCHED THE LANDMASS CRACK APART FROM THE SURFACE SOMEWHERE IN THE WOOD OUTSIDE THE HAMLETS AND THAT WAS WHEN I CIRCLED BACK."

"Care to speculate?"

"OBVIOUSLY, WE ARE IN A RIFT OF SORTS. THOUGH WHERE IT TAKES US IS ANYONE'S GUESS."

The nether screamed from above and Marsea dared another peak up at it, clinging on to Rhyvariath's scaly arm, each scale the size of her hand.

Something from outside The Spellbind was eating it alive, its blackened skin bubbling up and blistering, pockets of flesh exploding like boils under lance, its many orifices withering to ash and flaking away, pillars of sunlight shimmering into The Spellbind through the freshly made holes in its frying torso.

"There's sunlight," Marsea said. "How is that possible?"

"IT WOULD APPEAR OUR NEW HOME SERVES A DIFFERENT CIRCADIAN RHYTHYM THAN THE VAEL," Rhyvariath answered matter-of-factly.

"On a floating island fuck knows where, sounds about right," Pion murmured.

Marsea met his black-ringed glower. He'd already aged a number of cycles in the few minutes it took them to complete the godsgate incantation, a cruelty of The Spellbind's protection, marking him with crow's feet and deep marionette lines. "You're a bloody fool, you know that?" she said.

"Well aware, yes."

She shook her head. "Why did you come for me?"

"You know why," Pion answered, casting her a puppy dog gaze, like she'd hung every star in the heavens. "I may have acted a jealous prat from time to time, but I like to think I've made no secrets about my feelings toward you."

She may not have cared much for his affections, but she certainly couldn't deny them.

"You're still on my shit list," she said.

"And you're still on mine."

Marsea felt the butterflies vacate her belly as the ground settled beneath them.

They waited breathless for a moment.

"I think we've stopped," she said as the first body came splattering down into the snow a few feet in front of them.

Maidens' breath, she thought as another followed, and another, the undead raining down all around them, dozens upon dozens of them, their corpses crunching violently about the pre-existing courtyard carnage.

It was the most awful thing she had ever beheld, and yet strangely she could not look away. Though, in truth, the whole affair was concluded in a matter of seconds and they were thereafter claimed by the kiss of a bastard sun as what remained of the great nether beast melted down The Spellbind's barrier.

The sound of a skirmish drew Marsea's attention to the southern walks, and she found Remy and Caitlyn battling their way through a cluster of ghouls that had either been lucky or clever enough to hide under the arcade during the godsgate rift.

She hurried toward them, Blind Widow at the ready, though the pair needed little help dispatching the threat. "Thank the maidens you're alive," she said, fighting back tears as she passed outside The Spellbind's border.

"And you," Remy returned.

"I daresay, you look as old as father," she added. And he did. Nearly twice his actual age, silver streaks running through his hair.

"Stand the mirror, sis, and you'll find our mother's sister."

"We can crack on about being geezers later, yeah?" Pion said, as he hobbled up behind her. "Right now, we need to find the others and figure out where the hell we've landed."

CHAPTER THIRTY-ONE

Stars alive, what's happening to the floor?" Poppy shouted from behind as the left side of the corridor began to slant askew, turning clockwise.

Rhymona crouched as the hallway began to rotate and the right wall became the new floor, the castle sloping topsy-turvy like the wander home after a turn through the tavern dregs.

They were greeted by a cacophony of glass breaking and wood sliding across stone from inside each chamber as the furniture within creaked and cracked against the rooms' inner walls.

"We're spinning," Julia answered, navigating the moving stones, clever as a stage dancer, seemingly unaffected by the change.

"It's almost like the moon's losing gravity," Edgar added, glancing back at the party from up ahead, as the wall-floor gave way to the ceiling-floor and the torches dumped out from their sconces darkening the hall.

"And here I thought shit couldn't get any more mental," Rhymona said, adjusting to the shifting corridor behind Julia, literally crawling the walls, gazing through the window at her feet for light as it passed into the new wall.

She leapt a closed doorway upon the floor, floating unnaturally for a beat before holding atop the stones on the other side to make sure Julia made it to the stretch of floor-wall between chamber doorways and they held beside another window as it crossed their feet.

"It must be the godsgate spell throwing the laws of nature out of sequence," Poppy said.

Gee, you think? Rhymona thought. "All good?" she asked Julia.

"This is mad!" the girl answered, giddy and glowing. "But kind of fun."

Grandpa poked his ruffled head out from the satchel at Julia's side with a 'kids these days' glower, meowing his disagreement.

"I know, love," Julia pouted. "I know. But we'll get through it, yeah."

They waited for the new floor, which was the actual floor, to settle then hurried ahead to the length of stones Edgar occupied, pacing the makeshift footpath until the floor became wall and wall floor once more.

Rhymona turned back to Poppy and Broenwjar.

"Hurry, Priscilla," Edgar encouraged.

The spinning hastened, becoming more erratic.

"I'm doing my best," Poppy replied.

Broenwjar effortlessly leapt at the rotating space of wall and landed casually beside them.

"Show off," Poppy called after him.

The light through the windows suddenly, mercifully began to brighten.

"What the hells?" Edgar grumbled.

"Anyone else seeing rainbows?" Poppy lowered herself to the window in the floor, and together she and Rhymona glanced down into the unmistakable light, its colors fluctuating like the insides of a glass prism.

"Do you hear water?" Julia asked, hanging close behind her.

Rhymona walked the wall to the ceiling with Julia, listening intently. *Fuck me.* She did. It almost sounded like waves lapping ashore.

"What have they done?" Poppy asked before she crossed over to them.

"Fucking—" Edgar yowled from behind them and when Rhymona circled toward him he was gone.

"Edgar!" Poppy shouted, as the hallway suddenly began to rotate counterclockwise.

The sound of glass shattering inside the opened doorway Edgar disappeared through echoed past them and Rhymona scrambled toward it as it rose up to the ceiling. A marshy scent poured out from within as a patch of thick black goo drooled down from the door frame.

"He fell through!" the magus howled. "He's out the window!"

"Why the hells would he open the door?" Poppy questioned.

"I don't think he—" Rhymona started before a shriek of magic pierced her ears, nearly causing her to tumble into the chamber after Edgar. She kept her balance but barely and Julia pulled her back on her arse. Scrambling about, she rolled with the rotating hall, halting on her knees, gazing behind them.

"There she is," Shit Breath greeted from behind Poppy's smoking corpse, smiling smugly, "on her knees before me yet again."

Not good.

"You bastard!" Julia yelled, taking a step toward him.

"Jules, no," Rhymona croaked, reaching after the girl and catching air, forcing herself into an awkward shamble after her.

This bellend. Every fucking time.

"Oh, she was deadweight anyway," Shit Breath said, unaffected by the corridor's curse, levitating as though by some bastard form of aeromancy, and appearing decidedly more skeletal since they last held company. It went without saying really, but Tetherow had almost wrung the poor fuckwit dry of what little gift he may have once possessed.

"Stay behind me," Rhymona ordered Julia, stepping between the girl and the demon, sliding with the rotating wall, regaining some measure of balance as she worked Illuminaria free from her belt holster.

"It would seem my apprentice has finally gone on and betrayed me," Shit Breath said. "Though, I reckon it was always inevitable, wasn't it? It really is hard to find good help these days."

"There's a crackup coming from your ilk," Rhymona spat.

"Oh, but I do so wonder, my dear Morgandrel, have you allowed Runt to remain graveside for fixing you?"

"He didn't fix me."

"Oh?" Shit Breath turned up a hand, hers remaining hers. "Is that not a new paw I see? Did you at least get her name before having her butchered?"

"Piss off."

Shit Breath had a laugh at that. "He's special that Runt, isn't he? A mind every measure as daunting as his body is broken."

"Don't care."

"You should."

Broenwjar prowled up into the space at Rhymona's side. "Hold, boy," she ordered. "Stay with Jules." The magus crawled the rotating walls, splitting the space between her and Tetherow's latest corpse costume, each step becoming more and more bouncy until she too was floating.

"And what will you do, Morgan?" Shit Breath asked. "You cannot defeat me. Not as you are."

"Tell that to the last piece of fuckwit pie that had a go."

"Fuckwit pie," he chuckled, "I like that." He leveled Magwyn's scepter on her. "And she's far enough there."

She met his icy white orbs. "Do it, fucker." Rhymona held beside Poppy's floating corpse, the scent of burnt hair and fresh blood spill filling her nostrils as it leaked out from the hole in the back of her friend's skull. "Oh, that's right, you can't. Some batfuck nuttery about the fates, isn't that right?"

"I could." His lips curled back in a snarl of blackened teeth.

"I'm ready," she spread her arms out wide, releasing Illuminaria so it floated forward between them. "No one's stopping you."

Is this what you want? she asked the gift. *You want the self-destructive hell hag?*

"What are you playing at?" Tetherow asked.

"Every end is a beginning, yeah?" She grabbed Poppy's shoulder, maneuvering the body between her and Tetherow like a shield, and ventured closer beside her drifting mae'chii, riding the wings of chaos, dipping her toes into the madness, catching the corridor's spin as though it were the most natural thing on all the moon. "Isn't that what the last of you cunts pitched me?" Silence. "Well, I'm ready to begin not giving a fuck about this existence anymore. And I'm done pissing through the same tedious conversation with you lot. Honestly, if I have to hear one more arsehole tell me about myself, I'll do the deed myself."

"Now that's dark, even for you."

"Comes a time you get sick of it. Sick of the games. Sick of the lies. Sick of being a thing. Sick of fighting. Sick of failing. Sick of blaming yourself for shit you didn't consent to. Sick of pretending like your feelings don't matter."

"I said that's far enough," Tetherow snapped.

"Read the room, dipshit," Rhymona bobbed forward. "I don't care what you do."

"I'll kill her." The scepter shifted over her shoulder to the space she presumed Julia presently occupied.

"Broenwjar," Rhymona called, knowing the wolf would honor Marsea's bidding and protect the girl at her calling.

Shit Breath's piercing orbs flitted back to hers.

"Julia, I want you to keep going," she ordered, her eyes never leaving that of Tetherow's. "Don't stop until you get to the rendezvous."

"Rhymona, I won't just—" she started.

"I said go, dammit!" the magus shouted back, every measure as ugly as she meant, watching from the corner of her eye as the girl disappeared at a bend in the corridor. "Just me and you," she began again once they were alone.

"Now you're on to it."

"On to your desperation. I can smell your host rotting from here. You really put it on old Shit Breath, didn't you?"

"Oh, I did him the favor, trust it true," the demon's voice fluctuated between Tetherow's elegance and Jory's bumpkin. "The state I found him in. At least I gave the wretch some measure of purpose."

"Jory may have been dead from the neck up on his best day," Rhymona said retrieving the strange wooden box Marsea gave her from her waist pouch. "But he was a Black Stag, one of my swordbrothers, and as such, I reckon he's owed a proper release. In the least, he's owed a damn sight better than what you've put him through."

Shit Breath's eyes narrowed on the box then grew wide.

"I'm assuming by that dumbarse fucking look on your face you know what this is."

"Aye, I know what it is, but do you?"

She gave it a once over and shrugged. "I'm told it eats souls, even crusty old limp dick turd biscuits like yours."

"Oh, but she's a fetching way with words, hasn't she?"

"So, she's been told," Rhymona spat. "And now it's her turn to play the bully."

Shit Breath sneered, nostrils flaring.

"Yeah, that's about the right visage there." She toed against the stones another step forward and held. "You make one wrong move, Tetherow, and it's bitch box island for old boy, yeah." She clutched the glowing trinket. "I'm assuming I have your attention now."

"Say your fucking piece, whore."

"Explain to me what the fuck is going on out there?"

"Oh, this?" He spread an arm out. "Would that not be the godsgate ritual you allowed the Lanier whelps to bugger on with?"

She chopped off another few stones between them. "You'd do well not to piss me off right now, fuckface."

Diseased orbs of curdled milk bore a hole straight through her. "I am merely giving you what you've asked of me."

"The castle's off its tits shitting a circle inside a fucking rainbow. What the hells did they bloody do?"

"They fucked around with sorcery they don't understand," Shit Breath hissed. "What else did you expect would happen?"

At his words, the prismatic effect of the riftlight pulsing through the wall-floor window between them altered to a bright golden pillar, ascending as it rotated to its proper placement as a wall and the corridor evened out. Gravity restored, Illuminaria clattered to the floor, a sharp, metallic clang, and Rhymona lowered Poppy down to the stones before her.

"And would you look at that." Shit Breath murmured.

"Sunlight," Rhymona uttered, retrieving Illuminaria and rising to her feet.

"We're not on Vaelsyntheria anymore," the demon quipped.

"Yeah? And where are we?"

"Hell, if I know. I'm in the same fucking boat as you now, aren't I?" Shit Breath took a step closer. "I do know it would be a mistake for you to open that box."

"Tut, you think I'm going to just let you carry on after all you've done? You killed Val, murdered Poppy, Aiden, Rill, Magwyn, Dysenia, however many thousands of others. The least you can do is crawl your sorry arse inside this baby bitch coffin and burn for it."

"I'm the only one of you that's lived beyond the moons of Dalynisa. You lot have no idea what's out there."

"I think we'll take our chances." Her thumb settled under the box's metal clasp.

"I can bring her back," Shit Breath blurted. "Your precious Valestriel."

Rhymona's heart stopped and her mouth bent sour. "Bring her back?" she worked through the frown. "Aiden said you hacked her up."

"A different slice of the fuckwit pie took your lover. Not me."

"Don't play that shit with me, Tetherow. You're all the same sodding anus in my book."

"And there you go again, pretending to understand things beyond your comprehension." His icy orbs flickered with menace.

Mouthy fucker. Rhymona leveled her sword between them. "Not a good look your slagging the girl with the death box in her hand." And the gods know, she still hadn't quite adjusted to an uneducated twatwaffle as was Shit Breath whinging about with a noble tongue.

"The haxanblade is not of this moon," he continued. "Hells, it's not even of this galaxy. It's forged of an ancient material your kin have come to name trezsu. A material perverted by your ancestors on Ilynderos ages ago. By your Midaran mask, I trust you're at least somewhat familiar."

The bollocks on this slick bastard. She squeezed the ever-living fuck out of Illuminaria's hilt, her chest burning like a furnace. "I'm familiar," she answered.

"And you've seen what it can do. You know it doesn't obey the laws of nature. Nor of time and space. As such, it can be used to carve through timelines. I can teach you how. And then you can play skeevy nursemaid to whichever version of Valestriel you wish."

"The haxanblade has chosen Marsea."

"Then we get rid of Marsea, don't we? Train the blade to a new master."

"She is my family."

"She has done nothing but use you. All of the Laniers. That's all they've ever done, Morgan. Use you."

"And is that not what you're playing at right now?"

"I am offering a service for a promise. You destroy that box and I'll return Valestriel to you."

"It won't be her though, will it? It'll be some other fucked up version. And I won't go against my family for a ghost. No matter how much I loved her." Her thumb twitched against the metal clasp, a rush of gift to the brain, everything in her telling her to awaken the thing within the box. "I told you I'd get better at dealing with what comes." She flicked open the clasp from its notch and tossed the totem at Shit Breath, where it hit him in the chest and fell innocuously at his feet.

They both stared down at it.

What the fuck, Marsea.

Shit Breath snorted. "You dumb bitch, you must speak the key to unlock its power."

Bugger all.

In the hallway behind him, a doorway opened and a figure staggered forth, azure-eyed, huffing and puffing, caked in nether residue, sword slick with slaughter at his side.

Edgar?

He spoke at them in a strange esoteric chant and the totem guttered to life, radiating a pale purple glow from inside, sucking out Tetherow's malachite vapor from every orifice across Shit Breath's body.

Shit Breath reeled back, aiming his scepter at Edgar, but the power of the box proved too strong, and the scepter blasts hit the floor and wall before the demon wrenched back around onto his hands and knees, a slave to the soul-eating totem, bones popping out of place upon impact, compliant as kindling, their sharp ends ripping through skin and uniform.

Now who's on their knees, she thought, Fiandrel's dark shape standing her side.

Sensing the soul casket's growing hunger, Rhymona stepped back from it, watching as Tetherow fought against its expiry, spitting obscenities, words from a language she'd never heard before yowling out from the pulsating cloud of demon essence. The stones beneath Shit Breath's fists spiderwebbed out like a cracked mirror and the air caught a sickbed stench causing her eyes to burn on contact.

Eldn flame caught in Edgar's hand, swelling to the size of a cannonball as Shit Breath's withering glare snapped up to meet her, the reeking malachite vapor spilling from his eyes and mouth.

"You'll never be rid of me, Morgan." It promised, a ghastly mad, defiant grin on full display. "No matter where you run to. No matter where you hide. It's me and you, love. Until the crows delight."

Dragon's fire engulfed him at the vow, singeing through Shit Breath's tangle of stark-white hair, melting the flesh of his face, skull peeking through in places as it ate him alive. Still, his icy white orbs and snaggle-toothed smile never left her, choked laughter echoing inside the conflagration, even after the host's corpse was purged of its possessor, even as the soul casket burned to ash, sealing its curse.

CHAPTER THIRTY-TWO

STRANGE SUNLIGHT SHIMMERED across the grisly courtyards of Lancastle Citadel, the sound of the ocean in Remy's ears as he rushed across the last square leading up to the officer's quarters, cutting Exylduin through any blighter that crossed his path.

None of it made a mite of sense. The ghouls remained, but the drylax creatures were charred to a crisp. Not that he was complaining. As for the nether behemoth, it appeared a motionless corpse, it's gooey, smoldering mass oozing down the castle walls like burnt honey.

According to Rhyvariath, the spell worked and yet it didn't. Even Thira found it all confusing. Though, Remy supposed, they were still alive, wherever the hells the godsgate ritual spat them out. And the answer wasn't somewhere on Vaelsyntheria, as evidenced by the unfamiliar horizon, which wore a much larger sun to the east and a single white faded moon off to the far west.

A wand blast shrieked out from behind him and he glanced over his shoulder to find Caitlyn keeping the pace, ghoul parts painted across the wall just inside the doorway. They were headed for the King's Reserve. He could only pray the others made it there safely. He couldn't imagine losing a one of them, Jules, Edgar, Rhymona…

He shook the thought from his head, unwilling to allow its company.

If the past few quints had taught him anything, it was that worrying over the uncontrollable was utterly useless.

Marsea and Pion remained with Rhyvariath. They would survey the damages and report back their findings. Remy could only hope they returned with something positive.

He slowed as a slumped body came into view in the corridor up ahead. *No.*

Despite the gruesome injury he recognized her as Poppy. She'd taken what appeared to be a wand strike to the back of her head that cauterized all the way through the middle of her forehead down to her upper lip.

"Shit," Caitlyn said as she arrived beside him wearing a pained expression. "Poor girl."

"Someone propped her up like this," Remy said.

"Had to have been one of the others."

Remy studied the area, starting with the pile of ash and bone beside Poppy.

DRACARI FIRE, Thira said.

Which means Emyria was busy.

"There was another here," Remy relayed Thira's thoughts. "Put to the dragon's flame. Likely the person who attacked Poppy."

Caitlyn shook her head, her eyes darting about the hall. "There's a bit of blood, but it would appear to be Poppy's."

"Hopefully that means the others are safe." Remy started forward again. "This way."

He'd never run so fast in all his days and a minute later he had the scent of wet dog followed by the hulking shape of its owner. *Broenwjar.* Remy's heart leapt at the sight of the great beast, and this time for all the right reasons. Another breath and Edgar paced out into the hall from the King's Reserve Chamber, stopping as they met eyes. He looked awful. Truly awful. His clothes smeared in what Remy could only guess was nether residue.

"They made it," Edgar called into the room with a smile.

"Remy!" Julia squealed, shoving past Edgar, a waterfall of raven-black hair.

Remy permitted himself a grin at the sight of them and held her close as she crashed into him.

"I'm so glad you're safe," he said, pressing a cheek into the top of her head.

"You look old," she said, pulling away. "Your hair's all gray."

"The Spellbind aged us," he explained, his eyes rising to Edgar. He'd completely forgotten about his new appearance and though he hadn't actually beheld himself outside of Exylduin's warped reflection, he knew it wasn't pretty. He felt a child at the thought, but he hoped the gray wouldn't put Edgar off of him. "I think Marsea and Pion may have gotten the worst of it."

"Where are they?" Rhymona asked from her lean against the doorway.

"With the dragon," Caitlyn answered. "Assessing just how boned we are."

"And the nether?"

"Far as we can tell, the beast is dead," Remy said. "As are the drylax creatures. But the ghouls still persist."

"Because of course they do," Caitlyn grumbled.

"We found Poppy," Remy said holding Edgar's gaze.

"Aye," he managed, clearly still struggling with it.

"What happened?" Remy questioned.

"Tetherow," Rhymona said. "The one in Jory. He followed us."

"Is he…" Remy began.

"Dead as fuck," Rhymona finished. "Yes." She pushed up from her lean. "Swallowed up by one of those soul boxes Marsea brought back from The Scar."

"Good riddance," Caitlyn spat as she disappeared inside the King's Reserve Chamber.

"Are you?" he started.

"Still here," she said. "Come along, Jules. Let's give these two a moment."

Remy watched his sister trail back into the chamber, Broenwjar following.

A soft breath and then Edgar was before him, inches away.

"How bad is it?" Remy asked. *Best to go on and get it out of the way.*

Edgar nodded. "A little worse than Caitie."

"How much worse?"

"I'd say forty-six, maybe forty-sevenish."

"Fuck me," Remy raked a hand through his hair. "Forty-sevenish?" *I really thought I fared better than Marsea in all this.*

"You make a fit forty-seven though, yeah." Edgar's hand cupped the side of his face. "Trust it true."

"Evidently we're near the ocean, wherever we are," Remy said. "It'll be good to wash off the stink..." *And get you alone in a bedchamber*, his mind suggested, despite the state of affairs.

"All in due time," Edgar returned. "I'm itching to have a scout about though. Being cooped up in a castle isn't really my cup of tea."

"We can go now if you want?"

ARE YOU SURE THAT IS WISE?

No, but we won't venture far.

"The battlements are covered in nether..." he worked for the right word. "...carcass."

"I caught a glance, briefly," Edgar said.

"Oh?"

"A gnaudrylax pulled me from the hall outside during the ritual. Fortunately, we," he paused, "me and Em, caught the upswing of the castle wall as it spun and were able to jump through into another chamber before it dumped us into the yard. I'd have been done for if not for Emyria's quick reflexes. And she burned that drylax bastard down a few layers before it dropped away."

"Gods, I could have lost you," Remy uttered. *Shit, did I just say that out loud?* Though Yvemathira felt the same of Emyria.

"Could have, should have, would have," Edgar answered, far too cavalier, "but we're through it now. Mostly."

"Mostly," Remy echoed. "We're going to have a scout," he called to the others.

"Is that what we're naming it, then?" Rhymona returned.

Same old Rhymona, he thought.

"Bring us back some figgy pudding," Caitlyn added. "And wine. All the wine."

Remy shared a look with Edgar and they started back the way he and Caitlyn had come, walking in silence until they arrived at Poppy's body.

"I know you cared about her," he said. "Once we get everything sorted, we'll have a funeral for the heroes that helped us stand against Tetherow and the nether."

"It should have been me," Edgar answered.

"It shouldn't have been anybody," Remy replied, placing a hand on Edgar's shoulder.

"She was relying on me to protect her," Edgar said. "She didn't want to stay in Lancastle, but I convinced her. I was selfish."

"No."

Edgar's eyes cut to his. "I knew she would stay for me. She was…she had feelings…feelings I couldn't reciprocate. I never told her…I…"

"Edgar, you did what you could."

"Not enough, obviously." He folded his arms, glancing away. "I thought she was safer here with me than out on her own begging about some dodgy backwoods hollow."

"I think you're being unfair to yourself. This whole cycle has been nothing but one impossible situation to the next. And you've done your best. You've done right by—"

"Have I? Would that be why I keep losing the people I care about the most."

Remy swallowed, weighing his next words carefully. It was clear Edgar had hit his threshold, some patch of mourning that had been building up since the gods only knew when.

A pregnant silence befell them, stretching for what felt like hours to Remy before he cleared his throat and said, "I'm here for you, Edgar. Whatever you need."

He knew it was a weak attempt at comfort, but it was the best he could offer. Truth was, he hadn't even approached his own mounting bundle of traumas yet, how could he even partway pretend to unpack Edgar's?

"Apologies," Edgar answered gruffly. "I don't know what that was."

"I do," Remy said. "Those feelings are valid. I have my own brand, trust it true. And I fear the day they finally rise back to the surface. But I won't deny them when they do. And I won't deny you yours now. Sometimes it just hits when it hits."

"Aye," Edgar said, little more than a grunt, sniffing back the surge of emotions.

WISE WORDS FROM ONE SO YOUNG.

Words I wish I didn't have to speak.

"Do you think we saved the Vael?" Edgar's eyes flickered azure, announcing Emyria's presence.

"...*From the brunt of it, I have to believe so...*" Remy answered, allowing Yvemathira control. "...*I hope Rhyvariath is able to gain some sense of where we have landed...*"

"The air is unlike anything I have ever experienced," Emyria said as they started forward.

"...*There is certainly a notable difference in gravity. And that smell...*"

"It is oddly familiar," Emyria said, raising Edgar's nostrils up and inhaling. "Yet, I cannot place it."

Remy arched a hand over his eyes as they passed back out to the courtyard walks. The sun was beaming bright and angry, almost instantly soaking through his armor and layers. It quite reminded him of late summer on the Vael. He spun a circle, taking in the heavens until he came to the castle, topped by a layer of scorched nether flesh that hissed and billowed into a lively wind.

Edgar worked off his coat and draped it over the arcade baluster before joining Remy out in the courtyard's center, staring up. "Looks like someone dumped a chamber pot overtop her."

"I haven't the faintest how we'll ever get her clean of this."

A clicking sound echoed from the next arcade over and Edgar drew his sword. "I've got this one."

The blighter appeared in the passageway at the words, a bloodstained bluecoat staggering toward them, half its face clawed off, skin hanging, its lone eye the color of curdled milk. It held at the entrance and studied them, its head ticking violently.

Edgar stopped a few feet away. "Bit odd, this one, yeah?"

"Indeed," Remy replied.

"You recognize him?"

"I don't. But he was a captain by his accoutrements."

The creature dropped to its knees, eye to the stones, ticks jerking its head to the right as though something was pulling it by the hair.

"I think it's one of the rebels," Remy said.

"Rebels?"

"We've come across a few blighters like this. That seem to know what they are and linger about idly."

The bluecoat's eye began to bulge until it popped out of the socket and a smoking spriteling dug its way out of the hollow within, covered in brains and fluids, flopping onto the cobble like a fish out of water before catching flame and withering to dust. The ghoul's body sank down into its kneeling position and remained motionless.

Remy and Edgar waited for a beat.

"Shit just keeps getting stranger and stranger," Edgar grumbled, as he drove his blade into the blighter's open eye socket, unwilling to take any chances.

Remy's attentions returned to the sky where they found Rhyvariath soaring in the distance, southward.

"I can't imagine its good news," Edgar said.

"Likely not," Remy answered. "Let's make a round to the west. I want to check on mother."

"Works for me."

"I'm assuming they'll have returned by then and we'll have a better handle on precisely how fucked we are."

REMY FOUND Larissa laying in a painful position in the middle aisle between rows of pews, one of her legs bent at an awkward angle, the sheet twisted tightly about her upper body, discoloration where her head rested. He winced at the spectacle, ashamed they'd left her to find such a state.

"Help me get her on the altar," Remy asked, placing Exylduin in the pew behind him.

Edgar delicately moved her legs back together as Remy reached beneath her armpits and they lifted each end together, sidestepping up the aisle and stairs to the altar where they gently set her down atop it.

He stared down at the patch of red in the sheet. He couldn't imagine what it looked like inside. How much of her was still recognizable. His hands curled into fists.

Fucking Tetherow.

"Want to talk about it?" Edgar asked.

Remy's attentions trailed over to his companion. "No, not yet at least. Though I appreciate you asking."

"Of course." Edgar raked fingers through his disheveled locs. "Wish I could've met her."

For some reason this drew a smirk from Remy. "No, you don't. She would've hated...us."

"I could have charmed her."

"Make no mistake, no one charmed Larissa Lanier without her say so."

"Did she know about your preference?"

"Yes and no. She most certainly knew, nothing got past my mother, but we never properly spoke on it." He pulled some of the sheet out from under her so it wasn't so snug against her form. "What would have bothered her about you is not your gender, prize well, rather that you are lowborn."

"She was like that?" Edgar asked, eyebrow arched.

"Station was king to her, yes. Everything else came second. To have it from her brother, my Uncle Rho, they came up hard, pretty much came from nothing. I think it was her worst fear to ever return to that life."

Edgar shook his head. "From nothing to the highest of royal houses, I can't imagine how much that would have fucked with my head."

"Yeah? And try going the opposite way. Not that this is about me."

"I reckon everything's about to change though, isn't it?"

"It already has." Remy felt a ripple from Yvemathira at the question. She'd tucked herself into another meditation session as they crossed the courtyard labyrinth to the abbey.

"Highborn, lowborn, does it even matter anymore?"

"A fair question, that. And I can only hope wherever we've landed, whatever's out there, it's not against us. We can't afford any more enemies."

"There's the understatement of the cycle."

"Another issue I'm concerned about is available resources in relation to the count of survivors."

"Rhyvariath mentioned some of The Kingswood came with us. Worse comes to worst, we have wood for fire and repairs, possibly herbs for alchemy, hopefully wildlife for the cook."

"All fair points."

"We can't get too far ahead of ourselves, Remy. One step at a time, yeah?"

"One step at a time," he echoed, straightening the ruffles in the bedsheet covering his mother. Of course, he was glad for Edgar's company for all the obvious reasons. But of this Remy was most grateful for his ability to keep things positive and in the present.

"You up for clearing the lower quarters?" It was all he could think to do to distract himself while they waited for news from Marsea and Rhyvariath.

"I suppose we've got to start somewhere, don't we?"

CHAPTER THIRTY-THREE

THE WIND RUSHED through her chopped mess of hair, her glasses shielding her eyes from the brunt of it as they charted the incantation's damage. Marsea estimated the landmass was roughly half a league long and a full league wide.

If put to the ask, Rhyvariath could probably span the island fully in a couple minutes. It included Lancastle Citadel, her many hamlets, most of which were overrun with blight, and a sizeable chunk of the Kingswood north of the kingdom.

From a dragon's eye view, the nether behemoth lay burnt and putrefying in the sunlight like a beached sea creature, stretching from the castle, south a quarter league, to the end of the island, where its mass had become severed by the ritual, the rest of it left to the maidens only knew where.

The princess felt arms draw tighter around her belly as Rhyvariath arched back toward the castle proper. Pion sat behind her, some mad blood spell spilling out from his warlock's well keeping them saddled to the soft space behind the dracari's neck.

"How're you holding up?" she shouted back at him.

"Not dead," he answered in his typical glass-half-empty demeanor. "I've got another candle if we need it."

"I think I've seen enough for now," she said, patting Rhyvariath three times, which was the signal for him to take them back down.

There was nothing but ocean in all directions, and a time would come when they would need to pick a path and have Rhyvariath scout it for civilization, but the ocean wasn't what frightened her most, nor was it the nether beast and its rotting army, but rather the stars above, who held a much larger count than those of Vaelsyntheria's heavens; though they were shaped unusually and appeared in eerily unfamiliar patterns.

Rhyvariath landed in the courtyard at the western edge of the citadel near the officer's barracks, lowering himself so Marsea and Pion could dismount safely. The princess had to help her riding mate down as he struggled with his malformed leg and winced at the smallest twinge of movement.

"Thank you, Rhyvariath," Marsea said once they were back on solid ground.

"I MEAN TO HUNT FURTHER WEST," the dragon answered inside her head. "I SENSED SOMETHING IN THE FAR WINDS. A MOST CURIOUS AURA."

"Anything you can provide would be greatly appreciated," Marsea said. "Shall we meet here again in a few hours?"

"I BELIEVE THAT WILL BE SUFFICIENT," Rhyvariath answered before taking wing and leaving them.

Marsea turned back to Pion, who greeted her with a grave expression. Try as he might to mask it, she knew he was putting on airs. He looked exhausted. Beyond exhausted, really. And after their turn through The Spellbind, older than his father. Yet, despite it all, here he was. By her side. Enduring. And for the first time since their volatile relationship began, she was confounded by him; caught somewhere between annoyance and appreciation. "You should rest, Pion."

Something like a smile crossed his lips as he dragged dark gray curls from his face. "I'll rest when you rest."

"Suit yourself, but I won't be stopping anytime soon."

"And I like a challenge."

She shook her head. "Let's find the others, yeah. I want to make sure Jules is okay. And I know Broenwjar's worried about me. I can feel his unease growing with every second we're apart."

"Would, that I could say the same of Ripley," Pion said. "Though I am relieved they are both still with us."

The princess inhaled as they started across the courtyard toward the nearest citadel entrance. The air sang of summertide, the snow and ice melting fastly around them.

"It's strange to me that you've had a familiar all this time," she said. Pion didn't exactly exude the animal-loving sort, after all. Though mayhaps some of that belonged to her knowledge of Vaustian's disdain for pets.

And you really need to stop lumping all of the Harvers together, don't you? she scolded. Appearances aside, there was a world's difference between Pion and Vaustian individually and, thanks to the godsgate ritual, quite literally.

They passed inside the castle's depths, stepping cautiously around a pair of blighter corpses near the entrance.

"I felt a connection with him when we met and hid him away in my chambers until he was big enough to fend for himself." He tapped forward, his blade cane scratching rhythmically into stones with each step. "But by that point, I couldn't seem to get rid of him. Trust it true, he's the laziest little co-dependent fucker you'll ever meet, and the gods help you if you try to get in the way of his comfort."

The housecat and the stray, Marsea mused, disgusted with herself. "And so naturally you thought to make such a creature your familiar?"

"That bit came cycles later. Admittedly, it was a desperate, foolish, and reckless affair, binding Ripley to my giftblood, but at the time it felt necessary."

"Necessary? For what reason would binding your soul to a cat be necessary?"

Guilt ran the course of his gaunt features. "For Tetherow reasons," he answered, a hint of regret in his tone. "Namely, it needed a spy at Perciya University."

This response took her off-guard. Brazenly forthright and decidedly un-Pion-like.

Is he actually opening up to me? For better or worse, she had to find out. "A spy?" She pulled at the string, ever so slightly.

"It required a way to keep tabs on its host when it wasn't—"

"How was it you came to meet Tetherow in the first place?" she cut in, genuinely curious, as a thousand questions beat at the forefront of her mind. If Pion was willing to share, she'd go through every one, be it weeks, months, or even cycles, she was ever game for a rabbit hole jaunt. And the maidens know, she wished she had a quill and parchment handy to jot them all down.

"It came to me during a bout of fever, back when it still ate dreams, back when I first began dark-dabbling. A dream I awoke from understanding how to summon hearth demons."

"And how long have you been dark-dabbling?" Before the nether, she'd regarded him as a lech and a schemer, amongst an assortment of less savory titles, but a warlock bending through black magic was never one of them.

"Seven, eight cycles."

Eight cycles? The number pulled her eyebrows up. *He would have been... fifteen?*

"I'm just trying to wrap my head around all this." She gazed at him as they paced the corridor side by side. "Why would you do such a thing?"

Guilt bled to shame. "A multitude of selfish reasons," he said, "but mostly because I wanted to correct my disfigurements. So, I stole a few tomes from Uncle's hoard and started singing spells. One of which I believe gained Tetherow's attention. And in the days to follow, the demon burrowed its way into my brain, into my dreams, this ghastly voice, pestering me, cursing me, threatening me, threatening to end those it thought I cared for most, growing worse with every nightfall, for weeks on end. And I tried to fight it. I tried to ignore it. With everything in me, I tried to push it away. For Jules. For father. For you. Because, quite honestly, you'd been through enough, even back then. But in the end, I wasn't strong enough. And I wasn't ready to lose you. Any of you. Of course, I'd had the thought that it was just a demon planting seeds in my head to drive me into madness. To control me. But then other things it promised began to occur. Things it couldn't possibly know if time were linear and alternate realities were rubbish."

The princess stopped and Pion held a step ahead of her. "Such as?" she asked.

He shifted partway back to her, dragging a skeletal hand across his chest. "It began with our parents' engagement. I'm sure that hit you as suddenly as it did me. Almost as though they'd become bewitched."

"And were they?"

"I don't know. But Tetherow spoke of its passing months before the announcement."

"What else?"

"Next, I found out about Desmond's resurrection and his attendance at university under the name of Aiden Ashborough. That was when I performed the familiar ritual with Ripley. And through Ripley, I found out about the ashaeydir assassin and Stella's blood pact. Like ducks in a row, just as the demon prophesied. And it told me the false heir would vacate the throne upon his passage day and wouldn't you know it…"

"Remy," she followed. "He abandoned us on his eighteenth birthfall."

"That was the one that sold me. Up until then, I clung to my doubts, claiming happenstance after happenstance, but knowing Remy and how obsessed he was with the throne and family legacy, never in a thousand cycles would I have believed he would desert it, and especially not on the eve he aged into rightful possession. I was gobsmacked by it, as you might imagine, as I'm sure you were."

"Oh, yes," she agreed. And Marsea recalled the tirade her mother launched at Raelan upon finding out. She'd never heard her mother curse in all her days, not once, and in a matter of seconds, she'd heard enough swearwords to fill the rest of *The Kingstome's* pages.

"As for you," Pion continued, "it named you as the Red Shrike. One of the most feared bladehands the Vael over."

Such as she was. Such as she would become.

And you will know her wander by the endless trail of corpses.

"Now that one threw me," said the warlock, "especially after you took injury. All the way up until the godsgate ritual when I watched you inside the maze of corpses wielding that wretched sword of yours like a tourney yard champion." He shook his head, his eyes falling to her belly.

"What?" She didn't care for this expression at all.

"Nothing. It's not important." His eyes flitted back up to hers. "Things are different now. They're already different."

"It's important to me."

"Marsea—"

"Say your bloody piece, Pion. Enough with the secrecy." She stepped up to him, feeling her hand reach for The Widow's blessing as her other gripped the collar of his robe and forced him against the wall. "I won't take no for an answer."

Dread replaced shame and he dared to place a boney hand atop hers. "All right then, steady on."

Her grip loosened.

"As I said, the demon knew about alternate realities," the warlock began afresh. "It knew about the powers of the sword you now carry. And it promised me it would fix my form and cut my mother from a timeline where I would be appreciated as her son."

"Your mother?" Marsea let go of his robe.

Shelly Manson. Stars alive, this went far deeper than she ever could have predicted. How could she have missed all this? Naturally, her thoughts drifted to that of her own mother again, who they left lying on a pew in the abbey worship chamber. The maidens only knew what the rift did to her body inside those hard stone walls. She shook the thought from her mind. *Stay focused.*

"So, it wasn't entirely about fixing your bad form then?" she questioned.

"Not entirely, no. And yet I still nearly broke my oath to the demon a dozen times over. But for every occasion, it held a tempting new vision and promise. The last of which involved—" The word hung in the air thick as a storm cloud.

"Involved?" she urged him on.

"Apologies. I spoke out of turn."

"Like hells, you did." Marsea nudged up her glasses, highborn chin rising, Blind Widow calling for a fresh topping of blood. "You don't get to do that, Pion. Especially not now."

"And you don't want to hear this. Trust me, I'm doing you the favor here."

"Yeah, and fuck your favor." A hand slid up Blind Widow's scabbard to her cross-guard, her thumb releasing a sliver of steel.

"Let me rephrase, I don't want to be the one to tell you this."

"And I couldn't give a frosty old fig what you want, Pion. Out with it."

"Us, all right. It showed me a vision of us."

"Us?"

"Me and you."

"What about us?"

"We were together."

"Oh, come off it." *Never in a thousand lifetimes.*

"We were," he said weakly, averting his gaze. "We were lovers. Mates. Betrothed. All the pretty, pretty things we as humans ever lust heedlessly after."

The thought made her skin crawl. "It was fucking with you, Pion." *It had to be.* "We are talking about a bloody demon here."

"Was it?" He stepped away from her. "Is it truly so far-fetched, Marsea, that we..." His words drifted mute as he glared back at her, sorrow in his night-colored orbs. "Am I truly so awful?"

"I mean..." *The stars save me, what in the bloody nine is happening here?*

"Am I truly worse than what Vaustian was to you?"

Oh, now we're getting down to it, aren't we? "I don't know how to answer that." A shit response at best, but it was all her brain would allow for amongst everything else it was trying to process.

"You didn't know him," Pion snapped back. "What he was."

"Then educate me, Pion." she pressed. "The maidens know, must you be so terminally irritating about everything?"

"Tell me how you really feel then."

"I don't care how awful it is. This is what I require of you if you wish to worm your weaselly way back into my good graces. I need you to be honest with me. With all of us. Without hesitation."

"I know you think me a craven and a turncloak, but everything I've done, every deception, every betrayal, every cruelty, has been to protect you."

Protect me? The absurdity of it. "From what?"

"From it. The demon. Tetherow," he whinged. "I should have told you. I admit that." He leaned against the wall, clearly embarrassed by his high-pitched outburst, and took her in, his brow creased in frustration. "I wanted to tell you, Marsea. But you weren't ready to hear me and it said it'd kill you if I did. A risk I wasn't willing to chance."

"All right, Pion, before we continue, don't you ever, *ever* tell me again about what I was or was not ready to hear. Savvy?"

"Savvy."

"Brilliant, now why me?"

"I don't know. The world is fucked and the fates are assholes. It's something to do with the gift in me. It disregards my brain when it comes to you. It screams for me to defend you. At any cost. Even at my own expense. Why the hells do you think I came after you in The Spellbind? I mean you're a fetching lass and all, but no one in their right mind would've risked so much with that level of bedlam at play. And yet there I was, showing my ass, ready to die so long as it meant your survival."

"Cheers for the offhanded compliment. Truly."

"You know damned well that's not how I meant it."

"I'm messing with you, Pion. Obviously, I don't care."

"Right, you don't care."

"Precisely. Now, why was Tetherow targeting me?"

"It wasn't just you, Marsea. It was targeting all of the old blood. Desmond and Remy too. Those it deemed the greatest threat. But you were the biggest obstacle because it believed you were the Red Shrike."

"And how does Vaustian play into all of this?"

"Because he's the one that let the demon in."

Knife meet chest. *He what?* "What the fuck does that mean, he let it in?"

Pion let out a miserable groan. "It means your dearest Vaustian wasn't always Vaustian. I won't pretend I understand how, but Tetherow had some strange form of symbiotic triad possession between Desmond and Vaustian."

Symbiotic? "Meaning what exactly?"

"Meaning the same demon essence could possess both your brother and Vaustian independently of one another. Or so that's how I understood it." His attention dipped back to her belly.

"Why do you keep doing that?" Marsea questioned. "Why do you keep looking at my...my lady bits?"

"Your what? I..." His eyes cut away from her. "I'm not looking at your lady bits, Marsea. I...dammit, I don't want to fucking do this with you anymore. I don't want to argue. I don't want to pass you ill tidings. I don't want to be your enemy. Every second we are at odds..." His eyes became glassy as he stumbled for words. "Gods, can't you see it's destroying me?"

"Too fucking bad. Now explain."

The wretch appeared to gather his wits at this, pinching the bridge of his nose and clearing his throat. "Tetherow said this would happen." His gaze steadily rose to meet hers. "That we would leave Vaelsyntheria and you would bear a fatherless child amongst the horrors of a distant land."

Fatherless child? Maidens' mercy, did I hear that right?

Her hand lowered to her stomach.

But I'm not...

I couldn't be. I haven't felt any of the signs. I'm not showing...

She thought back to the last time she and Vaustian lay together. The night before her duel with Ganedys in the woods. Her memory stretched the span of the three to four months prior when they shared a bed at least a dozen times.

Through it all, she'd never considered a child. It seemed impossible given the state of her life. *Oh, but what a fool you are.* She noticed Other's sudden conspicuous silence. Had her gift hidden this from her? Blinded her to it? She wanted nothing more than to channel her inner ocean and confront Other about it, but, of course, there wasn't the time for it. There was never any time.

Stars alive, this is all so supremely fucked.

She didn't know what to believe anymore. Who to believe. She held Pion's solemn, otherworldly orbs, searching, and a bone-deep terror befell her. She might not have cared for his premonitions, but there was no doubt he thought them true, and so too did her feral heart despite her head's denial.

"I hope this is one of the things that are different now," Pion said after a long silence. "I will gladly eat the words. I only want the absolute best for you, Marsea. And I'll help you in whatever way I can."

"Why the fuck didn't you start with this?" she snapped, the haxanblade shrieking for carnage, feeding off her ire.

"You mean given our history? And the fact that a few hours ago you weren't even speaking to me? It seemed a right decent decision not to start off with the old 'hey, I think you might be pregnant, and also it might be a half-demon.'"

Shit on a fucking stick.

A word rattled through her at the telling. One she'd only heard spoken between Vaustian and Cas and only once before. One she'd scoured the library stacks for in the after and still only unearthed a single paragraph about it.

Cambion.

It settled thereabouts the pit of her stomach, and suddenly she felt a few pounds heavier. She eased herself down onto the ledge of a nearby windowsill and let out a slow, even breath, her vision swimming, panic soaking through her clothing.

"Marsea," Pion took a step toward her.

"Stay back," she bade him, closing her eyes. "I need some air."

"You don't have to—"

"Can you please shut the fuck up, Pion? I need a moment to think, all right."

She sighed as a somber hush fell across the space between them. Endless seconds, eating her alive, until finally… "Fuuuuck!" The word exploded out of her. "Fuck you!" she pushed up from the window and paced the pillar of sunlight pulsing through it. She'd never screamed like this in all her days, as though all the horrors of the past few quints, hells, of her entire life, had caught up to her all at once.

To Pion's credit, he held his tongue as a series of less intelligible swears followed, erupting out of her like a firestorm.

By the time she concluded her profanity-laden tantrum, she was huffing and puffing, her cheeks burning, her throat achy, her eyes wet and itchy.

"We don't know that it's true," Pion said calmly after a time, clearly sitting on the response.

"I know," she said, wanting to slug the shit out of him, but rubbing a hand across her belly instead. "But I can't just ignore it now, can I?"

The image of a milk-eyed grotesque wailing out of her made her queasy, and she forced herself to swallow the rising sick back down.

"As ridiculous as this is to say, I can't have a demon baby, Pion." She sat back atop the windowsill and stared down at the worn leather glove clutching her abdomen. "I don't even know if I want children. And I certainly don't want to raise a child, half-demon or not, in our present circumstances."

"I'm not really sure what to say here."

"No, I don't suppose you do. Heck, I don't suppose anyone would."

"I know I'm probably the last person you wish to confide in or rely on for anything, but I am here for you, Marsea. Come what may."

She found his black-ringed orbs again.

"Why?" she asked.

"Why?"

"Why now? After all these cycles of you being a jealous prat, suddenly you're the knight in shining armor? What do you want from me, Pion? What's your game?"

"I want to see you hale and happy, as daft as that is to say given all this. It's all I've ever wanted. But I could only control so much."

"So, you're not just using me?" she jabbed, fangs fully whetted. "You don't want me carving up timelines to find you a mother?"

"A childish reverie, that. And one I'm set to let sail." He held just outside the pillar of sunlight. "Besides, who's to say we're not already in another timeline she rightfully belongs to?"

"Oh, for Seren's sake. Is that truly Pion Harver I hear speaking on hope's behalf?"

"I am nothing if not a hopeful foolhard," he said. "As for us, I have no expectations of you, Marsea. And I certainly don't expect you to just suddenly start trusting me. I understand that I must earn your trust first and that I'm a long way from it. I only ask that you give me an honest chance. I don't wish to annoy you, but I also don't want to leave your side. Or rather my gift doesn't, but that's on me. It's how I feel. It's what I want. I'm tired of fighting it. I'm tired of fighting you. I want to protect you and help you in whatever ways possible from here on out."

"Laying it on a bit thick, aren't we?"

"I feel how I feel."

"And your words *feel* a little too good to be true."

"I could say the same of you indulging my company."

"What can I say? Desperate times and all."

"Oh, but she's a fancy old dagger for the kill, hasn't she?"

They shared a pair of crooked smiles.

"We broke the fucking world, Pion."

"You say broke, I say saved."

"I'm worried about what's inside of me." Her smirk faded. "About birthing that bastard's heir."

"Well, I'm not going anywhere. As long as you'll have me."

A sigh whooshed out of her, and she shook her head as she tried to come to terms with Pion Harver as an ally. *Who is this person?* she couldn't help but ponder. All this talk of demons, 'twas almost as though he'd become possessed of another persona entirely.

"You can't tell the others." She pushed up from the windowsill, doing her damnedest to maintain control. "And especially not Remy. He won't understand."

"As you wish."

She studied this hobbled, hunched creature before her, prematurely aged by the godsgate ritual, trailing the contours of his misshapen Harver features down from brow to the cane handle cupped smartly before his waist in both hands.

After everything, this is what was left her? Keeping secrets from her own kin with one of her worst enemies?

You could always kill him, Other said. **I bet he'd let you.**

Oh, now you have something to say, do you?

Only a man. A slab of meat.

We're not killing him, Marsea returned. *And where were you?*

Approaching voices from ahead drew her attention and a beat later her brother turned the corner next to his lover, sullen masks scrawled upon both of their faces.

Her hand came away from her belly and settled upon Blind Widow's hilt as she started toward them.

Frayed are the threads that cast shadows…

I will not let my past define me…

The scars that bind us…

The old blood must survive…

The name must die…

Words of another world. Another age. Another reality.

Famous last words, those…

CHAPTER THIRTY-FOUR

ONE HUNDRED SEVENTY-SIX survived the godsgate ritual at last count. Dozens with injuries and a handful fighting the grave hereafter.

One hundred seventy-six out of thousands.

Mostly folk from the northern hamlets where the blight nary bothered and the nether beast hadn't yet reached. They were amongst the poorest of the kingdom folk; the common folk, as it were, the tough, hard-working, grind-it-out folk that saw to the fields, the shops, and the menial grunt work. The perfect lot to weather the utter shitshow the dead man's rift had cast them into. The hope was that they would find more survivors over time, but three days had already passed since they'd arrived on this new world and they'd scoured nearly every inch of the island, from the castle cellars to the outermost woods.

Pragmatism told her they likely wouldn't reach two hundred. Hells, they likely wouldn't reach one hundred eighty.

Rhymona Curie wiped her brow with a linen cloth from the guest chamber she'd claimed as her own and stared up through the canopy of trees to the flicker of sunshine beyond. She reckoned it was around midday on this world based on previous rotations. Which meant the next few hours would only become more humid. As though her dirt-stained tunic hadn't claimed enough stink already.

She'd ventured out with a hunting party that morning, but fastly left them to their squabbling, Marsea included.

Speaking on Marsea, the princess had changed considerably in the godsgate aftermath. Becoming quite cagey almost overnight, like she was hiding something awful, mayhaps many somethings, despite her promises to the contrary. And this wasn't even broaching the topic of dodgy-arse Pion, who had rather suddenly become her new best mate, scarcely leaving her side. Another Harver in her ear, whispering nonsense. A menace Rhymona meant to sort in due time, but for now, she needed time to herself. Time to recharge. Time to gather her thoughts. Time to process this new reality in which she was in all likelihood the only one left of her kind.

Grunting, she massaged at a crick in her neck. Who would have thought sleeping in an actual bed for once would've stiffened her up so? Silver lining though, she did actually manage a full night of sleep. A blackout hard, dreamless, drool on the pillow night's sleep before Marsea woke her with a rap at her door.

There appeared to be a clearing up ahead, and she forced herself to trudge on through the creatureless wood, her mind wandering to yestereve and Rhyvariath's tidings.

Apparently, there existed something like a mainland to the west with many strange towers that displayed peculiar burning glass images of humanoid creatures like he'd never beheld before. He also described an assortment of other curiosities that got the Lancastle survivors going. Namely, large cross-shaped airships in the sky and long metal serpents that slithered across the earth atop glowing bars.

He claimed it would take about an hour to reach the city of towers and he could take two. Naturally, Remy volunteered to join on the next venture out, Edgar by his side, which made sense considering their coupling. And the gods know, she'd sell her left tit to have Thira and Emyria's opinion on the matter. Did they just dissociate any time the pair hit the sheets? Did they get into it too? Was it something like a two-person orgy?

No, she smirked at the range of her smutty mind. *Not what we focus on today.*

She reckoned they would have made landfall by now as they were set to depart not long after she and Marsea's hunting party hit the trails.

"Hope you're being smart, Toff," she muttered as she came into the clearing before the island's boundary, the trees nearest the edge slanting this way and that, like jagged teeth, as their roots became twisted up and severed by the godsgate incantation.

She inhaled the salty ocean air as she unhooked Illuminaria's sheath from her belt and found a spot atop one of the fallen trees.

"I can almost feel you," she spoke to the sword, *even though we've never been further apart.*

An image of Val found resonance. One of Rhymona's best loved memories. And she let the scene wander against the backs of her eyelids. Her Valestriel on stage dancing to a tavern turner in the firelight of the Lowly Lantern Innhouse during their tryst in Rhesh. 'Twas a dance for her despite the modest crowd, Val at her most sultry and seductive, twirling about and throwing hips she didn't rightly have.

Rhymona let out a sigh, getting hot at the flashes from the hours that followed.

I can bring her back. Your precious Valestriel, Tetherow's eldritch voice crept between her thoughts as it had a thousand, thousand times since their standoff outside the barracks, and a chasm opened in her gut.

Sick fuck. She seethed. *Had to leave me with one more haunt, didn't you?*

"But I made the right choice," she promised Illuminaria, eyes fluttering open. "A choice I'd make again and again, no matter the timeline, no matter the consequences."

Her chest tightened at the words, a wave of sorrow washing over her, as the blade scar running down her forearm prickled anew.

A scratch a day, keeps the demons away. And she had the notion to mend this particular wound properly once everything settled down. Assuming settling down was an actual possibility.

"Who are you talking to?" a voice split the quiet from behind.

Rhymona bolted up, hand falling to Illuminaria's hilt as she rounded on her company. "Remy?"

"Rhymona," he answered with a screwy face, stepping out from the tree line, all royal swagger, arms tucked neatly behind his back.

"Why are you still here?" she questioned.

"We pushed the trip back another day."

"Why?"

"Rhyvariath said he wanted one more pass through. The gods only know his reasoning."

"Mmm, he's an odd one to be sure."

"Took the words right off Thira's tongue."

Rhymona's grip loosened from Illuminaria's spine. "No offense, yeah, but I came out here for a bit of solitude."

"Understood. But prize well, I am here if you need to talk."

"I don't know what I need right now, Remy." She resumed her place back atop the fallen tree. "I'm still trying to work through it."

Remy halted a few feet away, staring at her, head tilted queerly, watching her with a strange expression she'd never beheld of him before. "You know you don't have to be alone, right?" he returned, echoes of Valestriel ringing in her ears…

…pissing her off. "With all due respect, Toff," she started, glaring at him sidelong, "can you sod off for a song, yeah? I just need some time to myself."

"Tut, what crawled up your ass?"

"What crawled up *my* arse?" she rose back to her feet. *Let's have a count, yeah. I've outlived everyone I've ever loved. I've…*

And before she could gather her thoughts for a proper retort, Fiandrel appeared beside Remy mouthing something and Rhymona stared hard into the tiny abyss of her mouth, willing the gift to vocalize her noiseless words…

"What the hells are you looking at?" Remy asked, following her gaze.

:not remy,: Fia's whisper found a wind.

"Not Remy," Rhymona repeated, and her eyes widened as they flitted back to the watchman prince and she recalled Remy's warning about the changeling wearing his face in the abbey worship chamber.

"What did you say?" Remy questioned.

Her gift began to boil. "You're not Remy."

Within a blink a wand thrummed to life at Remy's side, angry as a buzzsaw, spitting bright white gift honey from its tip. "Toss the iron," the watchman bade, eyes like something spun up from na night terror, bristling with a crimson-gold malice that screamed of demons, daggers, and a thousand ditches.

"Get fucked." Rhymona went for the draw and Remy fired a white-hot curse at her, inches to her left. The magus froze mid-pull, shaking, heart racing, breath heavy.

"You know what I am?"

"Obviously," Rhymona answered.

Vishura shiroe. The creatures her ancestors slaughtered and tortured to learn of their trezsu's properties.

"Another reason you've got to go, Morgan," the changeling said, "I can't see any other way around it."

"I just wanted a little peace and quiet."

"Aww, the chaos queen wants a little peace and quiet, does she?" Imposter Remy pouted. "There's one for the stage." The changeling motioned its wand down to the ground then back up at her. "Now, on you go then."

"You're going to have to pry it from my cold dead hands, I'm afraid."

A wand strike wailed past her head, chased by a second that sent shards of wood biting into the side of her leg, forcing her down to a knee.

"Must you always be so bloody quarrelsome?" the changeling scowled, the silver rod in its hand humming with a ghastly crackle of the gift, channeling far more magic than Rhymona had ever beheld of a wand before.

Not good. "What can I say? I'm a simple girl and I give what I get." Rhymona lowered her head, bone-white bangs hanging down, hiding her eyes. "Lita Drufellyn."

"Look at you, knowing things. It would seem my reputation precedes me."

"It does at that." Rhymona groaned up to her feet. "The cloth maiden mask. Damned clever, I'll grant you. Right under everyone's noses, all this time. Had Marsea eating out of your hand like a fucking pigeon."

"When you're the last of your kind, you learn to adapt."

"Is that what you've done? Or are you just another piece of the fuckwit pie?"

"The what?"

"Are you one of Tetherow's puppets?" Rhymona expounded. "Bastard's got its hand up just about everyone's arse these days, figured I'd go on ahead and clear up any confusion."

"I am not possessed by the vharyn'ashi," Lita answered. "Quite the opposite, in fact."

"Well, you certainly sound like the skeevy old tosser, don't you?" Rhymona hissed.

"Tetherow lost the plot and I'm fixing its mess. I tried to warn it you couldn't be reasoned with. That you were mad as a cut snake and twice as unruly, but it formed some queer obsession with your bond to the gift."

"I think we've all lost the plot given our present state, wouldn't you say?" She gazed back toward the sea.

"Everything that's been done to you, and you still manage a sense of humor. I can appreciate that about you, if nothing else."

"Warms the heart, truly." Rhymona's eyes met the changeling's. "Now are you going to kill me or can I have my fucking solitude back?"

"You welcome death?"

"I welcome change. I welcome an end to suffering. An end to my oppression."

"Your oppression?"

"My lack of choice. Nothing has ever been my choice. And I'm done with playing Table Scraps to everyone and everything."

"At least you understand your place. But we are all at the fates' mercies in this."

"And what's your place within the fates' mercies? You were part of The Bloodbind curse too. I'm assuming you're aware of it."

"Woefully aware, yes. And I mean to reverse it."

"Reverse it?"

"The blade must be purged of the souls fueling its hex." The changeling reached inside its coat and retrieved a soul casket. "Once they are removed and the blade is destroyed, the loops will end."

"That easy, hunh?"

"Here's hoping."

"And why kill me?"

"Because you are the gift's chosen. And you are not worthy of such a title."

"This shit again. How about fuck the gift? You can be its new champion. Here take it." She pushed a middle finger in the changeling's direction. "All yours. I relinquish my claim."

"If only it were so easy. But you are it's chosen until you are not. And the way I see it, the person that kills the gift's champion claims the right to bear its mantle."

"Fetching tale, yeah." Rhymona inched back a step toward the cliff. "Don't suppose you've another shufa stick to burn for it?"

"Fresh out."

"Mmm, reckon I'll die disappointed then, I won't?"

"Let me see you, Morgan. Show me the heathen beneath the veil. Let me see what the cycles have done to you."

The hells? "You can go fuck yourself if you think I'm leaving a corpse in that cursed skin."

"Oh, sweet child, there won't be anything left by the time I'm done with you." Lita-Remy licked its lips and his jaw appeared to unhinge slightly.

At the spectacle, an image struck Rhymona from the old ashaeydir scripts of a snake-like maw large enough to swallow mouthfuls big as pumpkins and she was reminded of how the Vishura shiroe were said to dispose of their victims.

"What's the plan here? You going eat my sad, little, used-up carcass and wear me about the courtly catch next?"

"That predictable, am I?"

"They'll know you're not me."

"Oh, I don't plan on letting them live long enough to find out." A monstrous eyetooth grin parted the watchman's grizzled features like a scalpel through sutures.

Gods.

The illustrations and old stories scarcely did the changeling's horror true justice. And to see it for the first time on the guise of one of her nearest and dearest...

Fuck this. She could abide her own death. But not that of her family. Not Marsea. Not Remy. And not Jules.

Not her Munchkin Club.

Rhymona made to draw Illuminaria once more, but a wand bolt tore through her before she could pull a single finger of silver, spinning her round with a force that nearly sent her over the island's edge. *Baka, shit, motherfucker,* her mind howled, blood spiraling out of her as she landed on her knees, Larissa's hand catching her before she ate dirt, as her right shoulder sagged nearly boneless, crackling and smoking from the missing chunk of cauterized flesh.

The agony was such that she went numb from the neck down, her scream coming up bitter red vomit, tears leaking from her eyes, as her gift set to repairing what it could around the ghastly wound.

"If you won't obey," Lita rasped, "I'll simply rip the thing out of you."

It was everything within her to keep upright.

"Eat my arse, bitch," Rhymona growled through the blood filling her mouth from where she'd apparently bitten through the side of her tongue.

Trembling, she inspected the fist-sized hole that chewed all the way through the space of her right clavicle, bone into meat, and out her shoulder blade at the other end. A whimper escaped at the sight of it.

"I'd say your manners could use some work, but what would be the point?"

Rhymona gazed out at the ocean, her right arm unresponsive. "Is this what you wanted?" she addressed the gift.

"What's that, then?" Lita inquired, stalking ever closer.

"Screw it," Rhymona cried out, a ruby river trailing down the corner of her mouth, Larissa's hand clutching Illuminaria's hilt.

I'm not going to take this shit sitting down.

She slung the blade outward, pitching the sheath into the sea.

Me and you, Val.

Rhymona drove the blade into earth, pushing up. *You want to wear this busted-arse mug for a gown, you can dig it up from the depths.* She hobbled the distance to the island's threshold, back to her butcher, and as she reached the kingdom's end, hurling herself to the crush of waves below, two things happened...

One, she heard the shriek of another wand blast.

And two, she heard a voice call out her name.

No!

Falling...

The world slowed to a crawl...

Excruciating seconds...

Heartbeats loud as thunder...

Thirty...forty...feet down...

Half a breath at most...

Just enough time for her fear to claim its stake...

The ocean's surface punched the air from her lungs, the impact briefly paralyzing her, surging through the smoking hole in her dead shoulder, invading her mouth and nostrils, drowning any chance at a response.

"Marsea!" She tried to scream back as the cold kissed the bone, throat raw, grasping for the heavens with her one good arm, kicking her legs like mad.

But it was too late.

Much too late.

And a void dark as obsidian's shadow dug its claws inside her, dragging her despondently deeper into oblivion's waiting embrace.

GLOSSARY

GENERAL TERMS

Blight, The – Sentient beings reborn as ghoulish creatures by black magic incantations. They are typically controlled by a lichlord or a necromancer and operate in a hive mind.

Charonisk – A man-made concoction with similar effects to eldn fire.

Dragonsfall, The – The event comprising both the fall of dragons by man and the spreading of the gift into the elements that would result in The Giftborn Age.

Drylax – A physical curse of the nether. There are two forms: A gnaudrylax, which is a being fully consumed by the nether. This form is fluid and ever-shifting. And a phaedrylax, which is a partially consumed being. This form still experiences some confines of the host's body.

Eldnumerian, The – A chandiian term. "eldnu" meaning ancient, "meria" meaning master. They are also known as the old ones.

Nether, The – An ancient cosmic entity that feeds off of the soul and the gift. It can be physically manifested on the mortal planes using reverse wards and necromantic incantations. It incapacitates its victims using their fear until madness consumes. The result of the madness, once the soul and gift have been purged from the body, is known as the blight.

Oathsworn, The – The knights of the round. They are a clandestine order formed to serve the realm of men. There is no head or foot. All are equal. The Oathsworn was founded decades ago by King Cameron Lanier. They protect the realm against darkly creatures and the supernatural.

Quintweek (quint) – A fluid term indicating a general passage of time. There are five days in a week. Six weeks in a month. Nine months in a cycle. Ten cycles in a decade. Ten decades in a century.

Ravenholme – Now synonymous with The Covenant, Ravenholme is a rogue guild created by Malthus Tetherow that split from The Covenant (original). Originally The Covenant was created in opposition to The Oathsworn. Members of Ravenholme believe that the darkly and supernatural should be revealed to the public, not kept hidden.

Shufa – A powerful drug that can be smoked or consumed with food.

Star maidens, The – The angelic beings followed within the Omedran faith. They are also known as the Amendeiya. Within the order of the cloth maidens are Lirae (a house mother), Rin (a handmaid to a Ve'Lir), and Ve'Lir (a cloth maiden in study).

Wretchrot – A deadly poison that eats away at the insides of any poor bastard unfortunate enough to ingest it, resulting in the discharge of a strange bright pink substance.

RACES

Ashaeydir, The – A race of militaristic creatures with the ability to change their skin. Midarans often confuse the ashaeydir's abilities with that of the vishura shiroe (changeling).

Chandii, The – An ancient race highly attuned to the gift. They are also known as flamekin, summerblood, and summerkin of the Summer Isles due to their distinctive bright, fiery orange and red hair. They were once believed to be beast whisperers, familiars of the dracari, and, thusly, dragonriders.

Dracari, The – The race of dragons. Dracthonir is the name of the dracari language.

Dwarves, The – The race of short and absurdly strong creatures that primarily live within mountains and caves in the central part of Midara, rarely will you find one of the dwarvenfolk above ground.

Midarans, The – The race of humans that primarily populate the continent of Midara.

Vharyn'ashi, The – An ancient race of demonic creatures with the ability to possess other sentient beings.

Vishura shiroe, The – The name of the changeling race. Though it is widely believed these creatures are merely myth and fairytale fodder used to frighten children into behaving properly.

Wngar, The – The race of giantfolk that live to the far north beyond The Scar.

Y'deman, The – The race of fae folk (elves) locked in a longstanding war with the ashaeydir.

THE KNOWN UNIVERSE (the sister moons)

Ashira – The crimson moon. It is now wasting away and nearly uninhabitable.

Dalynisa – The big blue planet thought to be completely ocean.

Lumos – The smallest of the sister moons. She is known for her pale white appearance.

Vaelsyntheria – The golden moon.

Y'dema – The giant green moon. It was said to be razed by the ashaeydir after the fall of Ashira.

MAGIC TERMS

Bloodbind, The – It is a pocket dimension, a place out of time and space, much like The Spellbind. Unlike The Spellbind, however, it cannot be breached by any giftborn, rather it appears to be a curse tied to a haxanblade and specific group of giftborn (Lita Drufellyn, Marsea Lanier, Morgandrel Tully, and Stella Critchlow).

Blood candles – They are the stored mold of a giftborn's blood. It allows the user to enhance their inherited abilities, sometimes by considerable margins. They are known to be heavily addictive and can be deadly. The use of varying types of blood can alter and sometimes poison the blood system. Though not entirely banned by the Ministry, the use of blood candles is generally frowned upon through The Midaran Commonwealth especially at the universities of magic.

Blood merchants (warlocks) – Those who hunt fellow giftborn to drain them of their blood for wholesale.

Codices and Grimoires – Tomes and grimoires contain spoken word magic, including spells, recipes, sigils, wards, and bestiaries. This type of magic existed in previous ages, but has become more archaic in the Age of The Giftborn. It is largely considered an inferior form of magic by comparison to gift conjuring.

Eldn fire – A form of magic conjured and controlled by the dracari. It is the most powerful form of known magic and is one of the few defenses left against the nether. It manifests when called forth as azure and white flame.

Giftborn – A person with magical abilities. They can inherently perform great magical feats. The quality varies and is typically bloodline-based. To conjure magic the person must sacrifice something in return. They are less commonly referred to as warders and spellslingers.

Godsblood, Of the – Also referred to as the maker's ichor. It is the term the dracari use to describe giftborn descended of the older bloodlines with a deep connection to magic.

Gravedancer – A giftborn with the ability to resurrect the dead.

Haxanblade – A possessed weapon. This unfortunate soulmeld occurs through a curse or a mishandled enchantment.

Kindleblade – An iron-forged weapon, typically a ritual dagger or a sword, that is enchanted and soulmelded to a master.

Night writing – Raised code substituting for words. It is often times used with codices.

Soul magic (black magic) – Magic that feeds off of the soul rather than the physical body. This form of magic is very powerful, but also that much more risky and dangerous. Too much use can twist and deform the conjurer's appearance. It can whiten the hair, pale the skin, and rapidly age the conjurer.

Spellbind, The – A sliver of The Pale that was long ago cut away. It is a pocket dimension. A place out of time and space. One must be greatly gifted or use a blood candle, sacrificing something of their own health to enter. A studied giftborn can transfer their consciousness to The Spellbind. It can be a place of great healing or great destruction.

Totems – Enchanted trinkets, typically made of whittled wood or carved stone.

Varg – The ability of a giftborn to enter the mind of a soulbound familiar and take command of their actions. This ability leaves the conjurer in a vulnerable, almost corpse-like state during its casting.

Wands – Enchanted weapons created by giftborn to channel magic. They form a bond with a master through a soulmeld and will only react to that user's gift.

Wards – There are two primary forms of magic. Elemental-based magic and Soul and body-based magic. Elemental magic consists of Fire (Pyromancy), Water (Hydromancy), Earth (Terramancy), and Wind (Aeromancy). These forms of magic were common during the Age of Dragons. Soul and body-based magic consists of Shadows (Necromancy), Spirit (Psychomancy), Blood (Hemomancy), and Flesh and bone (Carnomancy). These forms of magic are common in the Age of The Giftborn. Powerful giftborn can merge two and three mantia at once.

MILITARY TERMS

Crownswatch, The – Liveried in crimson, they are also known as bloodcoats and redcoats. These soldiers man the northern highlands from The Straights to The Scar.

Emperorswatch, The – Liveried in gold, they are also known as goldcoats (and derogatorily as pisscoats). These soldiers man the Vinteyama swamplands and the flatlands between the highlands and southlands. They are noted for not allowing women to enlist in their guard.

Kingswatch, The – Liveried in blue, they are also known as bluecoats. These soldiers man Lancastle and her surrounding hamlets. They also man The King's Wall, a massive construct that separates the highlands from the lands now occupied by the ashaeydir.

Lordswatch, The – Liveried in gray, they are also known as graycoats. These soldiers man the lands east of the Morrigar Mountains, from the north to the southland provinces just outside Six Ports.

Royalguard, The – The overarching term referencing any coat of arms inside the midaran military.

WEAPONRY

Helanderan sword – A one-handed sword of varying lengths, edged on both sides, and generally paired with the use of a shield.

Ka'rym chii – A set of ashaeydir weapons primarily indicating a mae'chii and sy'chii.

Mae'chii – A long, slender, single-edged blade.

Sy'chii – A shorter single-edged blade.

Trezsu implant – An implant surgically embedded in ashaeydir soldiers that allows them to alter aspects of their appearance.

ACKNOWLEDGMENTS

Once again, I'd like to thank my friends at Falstaff Books; in particular, John G. Hartness, and my editors Erin Penn, Tuppence Van de Vaarst, Kristen Gould, and Joe Crowe for reading and continuing to support my crazy ass nightmare world shenanigans.

Also, a million thank-yous to my family, who keep me sane (mostly). One of these days one of you are actually going to read the Acknowledgments section in one of my books and feel good about yourself. My vote is on Atia.

And finally, to the readers of the first three (maybe four?) volumes: Thank you. Truly. I will always write for me, but I must admit, it feels pretty damn awesome to write for others too. Nothing quite makes the day like a reader who loves your words and/or characters and can't wait for more of your demented little head stories. I promise there are tales aplenty stewing about the old think box both in and outside the world of The Giftborn Chronicles and I can't wait to share them with the world.

As before, as always, may you count some measure of hope and inspiration from some place within.

ABOUT THE AUTHOR

Drew Bailey is an emerging author of horror and fantasy. Though he attended college to expand his knowledge of Literature and History, it still took him the better part of a decade to actually mold it into something worth chasing after. Better late than never, as they say. The Royal Nothings is his first novel. In his spare time, Drew is a chronic coffee drinker, avid movie watcher, and follows Liverpool F.C. and the Green Bay Packers. He currently resides in Charleston, South Carolina.

ALSO BY DREW BAILEY

STAY IN TOUCH!

If you enjoyed this book, please leave a review on Amazon, Goodreads, or wherever you like.

If you'd like to hear more about or from the author, please join our mailing list at https://www.subscribepage.com/g8d0a9.

You can get some free short stories just for signing up, and whenever a book gets 50 reviews, the author gets a unicorn. I need another unicorn. The ones I have are getting lonely. So please leave a review and get me another unicorn!

FRIENDS OF FALSTAFF

Thank You to All our Falstaff Books Patrons, who get extra digital content each month! To be featured here and see what other great rewards we offer, go to www.patreon.com/falstaffbooks.

PATRONS

Dino Hicks
John Hooks
John Kilgallon
Larissa Lichty
Travis & Casey Schilling
Staci-Leigh Santore
Sheryl R. Hayes
Scott Norris
Samuel Montgomery-Blinn
Junkle

Thank You for Supporting Independent Publishing!

We believe that you should be able
to read your books, your way.
That's why this Falstaff Books
print edition includes a digital copy
at no additional cost!

Just scan the QR code with your device,
follow the directions on Prolific Works,
and enjoy!
You can also join our newsletter when prompted,
and never miss an awesome Falstaff Release!

FALSTAFF
BOOKS
WWW.FALSTAFFBOOKS.COM